THE VERY BEST OF CHARLES DE LINT

Praise for Charles de Lint

"There is no better writer now than Charles de Lint at bringing out the magic in everyday life." —Orson Scott Card

"One of the most original fantasy writers currently working." —*Booklist*

"Charles de Lint is the modern master of urban fantasy. Folktale, myth, fairy tale, dreams, urban legend—all of it adds up to pure magic in de Lint's vivid, original world. No one does it better."—Alice Hoffman

"De Lint creates an entirely organic mythology that seems as real as the folklore from which it draws." —*Publishers Weekly*, starred review

"Charles de Lint is an impossibly, ridiculously talented sort of man—and I've been reading him for so long that he pretty much crafted my own ideas of what a fairy tale ought to be." —Cherie Priest

"Charles de Lint is a folksinger as well as a writer and it is this voice we hear... both old and new, lyric, longing, touched by magic." —Jane Yolen

"He shows that, far from being escapism, contemporary fantasy can be the deep mythic literature of our time." —*Fantasy & Science Fiction*

"A master storyteller, he blends Celtic, Native American, and other cultures into a seamless mythology that resonates with magic and truth."
—*Library Journal*

"One of the most gifted storytellers writing fantasy today." —*Locus*

"You open a de Lint story, and like the interior of a very genial Pandora's box, the atmosphere is suddenly full of deep woods and quaint city streets and a magic that's nowhere near so far removed as Middle Earth."
—James P. Blaylock

"De Lint is a romantic; he believes in the great things, faith, hope, and charity (especially if love is included in that last), but he also believes in the power of magic—or at least the magic of fiction—to open our eyes to a larger world."
—*Edmonton Journal*

"It's hard not to feel encouraged to be a better person after reading a book by Ottawa's Charles de Lint." —*Halifax Chronicle Herald*

"De Lint's greatest skill is his human focus—the mythic elements never overshadow his intimate study of character. To read de Lint is to fall under the spell of a master storyteller, to be reminded of the greatness of life, of the beauty and majesty lurking in shadows and empty doorways."
—*Quill & Quire*

"Part of the beauty of Newford is the sense that it has always been there, that de Lint is a reporter who occasionally files stories from a reality stranger and more beautiful than ours. De Lint also manages to keep each new Newford story fresh and captivating because he is so generous and loving in his depiction of the characters. Yes, there is group of core characters whose stories recur most often, but a city like Newford has so many intriguing people in it, so many diverse stories to tell, so much pain and triumph to chronicle."
—*Challenging Destiny*

"De Lint can feel the beauty of the ancient lore he is evoking. He can well imagine what it would be like to conjure the Other World among ancient standing stones. His characters have a certain fallibility that makes them multidimensional and human, and his settings are gritty. This is no Disneylike Never-Never Land. Life and death in de Lint's world are more than a matter of a few words or a magic crystal." —Darrell Schweitzer

"Mr. de Lint's handling of ancient folklore to weave an entirely new pattern has never, to my knowledge, been equaled." —Andre Norton

this one's for my readers
with a deep appreciation
for all your support
over the years

with a special thanks to those of you
on Facebook and MySpace
who helped choose the stories

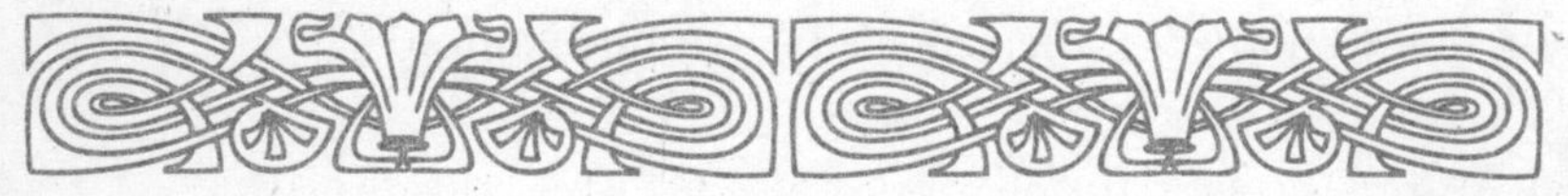

THE VERY BEST OF

CHARLES DE LINT

TACHYON

The Very Best of Charles de Lint

Cover illustration by Charles Vess
Copyright © 2004 by Charles Vess
Interior and cover design by
John Coulthart

Tachyon Publications
1459 18th Street #139
San Francisco, CA 94107
(415) 285-5615
www.tachyonpublications.com
tachyon@tachyonpublications.com

Series Editor: Jacob Weisman
Editor: Jill Roberts
ISBN 13: 978-1-892391-96-4
ISBN 10: 1-892391-96-1

Printed in the United States
of America by Worzalla
First Edition: 2010
9 8 7 6 5 4 3 2 1

Copyrights & Acknowledgements

"In Which We Meet Jilly Coppercorn" first appeared as part of "Uncle Dobbin's Parrot Fair" in *Isaac Asimov's Science Fiction Magazine*, November 1987. Copyright (c) 1987 by Davis Publications.

"Coyote Stories" first appeared as a limited edition chapbook published by Triskell Press, 1993. Copyright (c) 1993 by Charles de Lint. Grateful acknowledgements are made to Kiya Heartwood for the use of a verse from "Wishing Well" from her album *True Frontiers*. Copyright (c) 1993 by Kiya Heartwood; lyrics reprinted by permission. For more information about Kiya's music, go to www.terrakin.com

"Laughter in the Leaves" first appeared as a limited edition chapbook published by Triskell Press, 1984. Copyright (c) 1984 by Charles de Lint.

"The Badger in the Bag" first appeared as a limited edition chapbook published by Triskell Press, 1985. Copyright (c) 1985 by Charles de Lint.

"And the Rafters Were Ringing" first appeared as a limited edition chapbook published by Triskell Press, 1986. Copyright (c) 1986 by Charles de Lint.

"Merlin Dreams in the Mondream Wood" first appeared in *Pulphouse*, Issue Seven, edited by Kristine Kathryn Rusch; Pulphouse Publishing, 1990. Copyright (c) 1990 by Charles de Lint.

"The Stone Drum" first appeared as a limited edition chapbook published by Triskell Press, 1989. Copyright (c) 1989 by Charles de Lint.

"Timeskip" first appeared in *Post Mortem*, edited by Paul F. Olson and David B. Silva; St. Martin's Press, 1989. Copyright (c) 1989 by Charles de Lint.

"Freewheeling" first appeared in *Pulphouse, the Hardback Magazine #6*; Pulphouse Publishing, 1990. Copyright (c) 1990 by Charles de Lint.

"A Wish Named Arnold" first appeared in *Spaceships & Spells*, edited by Jane Yolen, Martin H. Greenberg, and Charles Waugh; Harper & Row, 1987. Copyright (c) 1987 by Charles de Lint.

"Into the Green" first appeared in *Sword and Sorceress V*, edited by Marion Zimmer Bradley; DAW Books, 1988. Copyright (c) 1988 by Charles de Lint.

"The Graceless Child" first appeared in *Halflings, Hobbits, Warrows & Wee Folk*, edited by Baird Searles and Brian Thomsen; Warner, 1991. Copyright (c) 1991 by Charles de Lint.

"Winter Was Hard" first appeared in *Pulphouse* #10, Winter 1991, edited by Kristine Kathryn Rusch. Copyright (c) 1991 by Charles de Lint.

"The Conjure Man" first appeared in *After the King*, edited by Martin H. Greenberg;, Tor Books, 1991. Copyright (c) 1991 by Charles de Lint.

"We Are Dead Together" first appeared in *Under the Fang*, edited by Robert R. McCammon; Borderlands Press, 1991. Copyright (c) 1991 by Charles de Lint.

"Mr. Truepenny's Book Emporium and Gallery" first appeared in a limited edition chapbook published by Cheap Street, 1992. Copyright (c) 1992 by Charles de Lint.

"In the House of My Enemy" first appeared in the collection *Dreams Underfoot*; Tor Books, 1993. Copyright (c) 1993 by Charles de Lint.

"The Moon Is Drowning While I Sleep" first appeared in *Snow White, Blood Red*, edited by Ellen Datlow and Terri Windling; AvoNova, 1993. Copyright (c) 1993 by Charles de Lint.

"Crow Girls" first appeared as a limited edition chapbook published by Triskell Press, 1995. Copyright (c) 1995 by Charles de Lint.

"Birds" first appeared in *The Shimmering Door*, edited by Katharine Kerr; HarperPrism, 1996. Copyright (c) 1996 by Charles de Lint.

"Held Safe by Moonlight and Vines" first appeared in *Castle Fantastic*, edited by John DeChancie and Martin H. Greenberg; DAW Books, 1996. Copyright (c) 1996 by Charles de Lint.

"In the Pines" first appeared in *Destination Unknown*, edited by Peter Crowther; White Wolf Publishing, 1997. Copyright (c) 1997 by Charles de Lint.

"Pixel Pixies" first appeared as a limited edition chapbook published by Triskell Press, 1999. Copyright (c) 1999 by Charles de Lint.

"Many Worlds Are Born Tonight" first appeared in Lisa Snelling's *Strange Attractions*, edited by Edward E. Kramer: ShadowLands Press, 2000. Copyright (c) 2000 by Charles de Lint.

"Sisters" first appeared in *Waifs & Strays*; Viking, 2002. Copyright (c) 2002 by Charles de Lint.

"Pal o' Mine" first appeared in *Christmas Forever*, edited by David G. Hartwell; Tor Books, 1993. Copyright (c) 1993 by Charles de Lint.

"That Was Radio Clash" first appeared in *Taverns of the Dead*, edited by Kealan Patrick Burke; Cemetery Dance, 2005. Copyright (c) 2005 by Charles de Lint.

"Old Man Crow" first appeared as a limited edition chapbook published by Triskell Press, 2006. Copyright (c) 2006 by Charles de Lint.

"The Fields Beyond the Fields" first appeared as a limited edition chapbook published by Triskell Press, 1997. Copyright (c) 1997 by Charles de Lint.

C O N T

E N T S

INTRODUCTION

Over the years I've put together a number of collections of my own work. It's a fairly painless process, since I usually have some specific theme in mind as I begin to gather the stories. A collection might be centered around Newford (as in *Dreams Underfoot*, through to the fifth and most recent one, *Muse & Reverie*), early stories (*A Handful of Coppers* and its two sequels), stories with teenagers as the protagonists (*Waifs & Strays*), stories for children (*What the Mouse Found*), or even a chronological collection of the chapbooks I used to write at the end of the year and send out as Christmas cards (the two *Triskell Tales* collections).

There's still work to do on such books: going over each story to make sure there are no typos or mistakes in the text, tracking down the copyright acknowledgements, writing introductions for either the collection as a whole or the individual stories—sometimes both. But *choosing* stories hasn't been so hard.

That wasn't the case for this book.

My editor here at Tachyon was set on using the title *The Very Best of Charles de Lint* and I had no idea how to choose what would be included. Selecting my *favourite* stories would have been hard (because they're all like my kids and how do you choose which of your kids is your favourite?), but with a lot of back-and-forthing, it would probably be doable. But my *best* stories?

I really didn't know where to begin. I have my own ideas as to which are the best, but my judgement is coloured by circumstances and events that have less to do with the actual stories themselves and more to do with what was going on in my life while I was writing them, or what I was trying to accomplish.

The *actual* best stories? How could I ever be objective enough to put such a collection together?

I suppose I could have asked some of the editors and reviewers I know to help me out, but then I realized that if I was going to turn to outside help, I should ask the people who really know. Those who have put their hard-earned money down, year after year, and bought the books and magazines where these stories first appeared. The ones that buy my books and give me the gift of being able to do this thing I love as a living.

In other words, my readers.

So I went on a few of the social networking sites and asked my readers to name their favourite stories. They responded enthusiastically and what we have collected here are the stories that got the most votes. Mostly. I added a few to make this collection more representative of all the styles in which I've written, but ninety percent of what is to be found in these pages was chosen by my readers.

Here's hoping you agree with them.

If any of you are on the Internet, come visit my home page at www.charlesdelint.com. I'm also at MySpace, Facebook, and Twitter, so you can drop in and say hello to me there as well.

Charles de Lint
Ottawa, Autumn 2009

In Which We Meet Jilly Coppercorn

Bramley Dapple was the wizard in "A Week of Saturdays," the third story in Christy Riddell's *How to Make the Wind Blow.* He was a small wizened old man, spry as a kitten, thin as a reed, with features lined and brown as a dried fig. He wore a pair of wire-rimmed spectacles without prescription lenses that he polished incessantly and he loved to talk.

"It doesn't matter what they believe," he was saying to his guest, "so much as what *you* believe."

He paused as the brown-skinned goblin who looked after his house came in with a tray of biscuits and tea. His name was Goon, a tallish creature at three-foot-four who wore the garb of an organ grinder's monkey: striped black and yellow trousers, a red jacket with yellow trim, small black slippers, and a little green and yellow cap that pushed down an unruly mop of thin dark curly hair. Gangly limbs with a protruding tummy, puffed cheeks, a wide nose, and tiny black eyes added to his monkey-like appearance.

The wizard's guest observed Goon's entrance with a startled look which pleased Bramley to no end.

"There," he said. "Goon proves my point."

"I beg your pardon?"

"We live in a consensual reality where things exist because we want them to exist. I believe in Goon, Goon believes in Goon, and you, presented with his undeniable presence, tea tray in hand, believe in Goon as well. Yet, if you were to listen to the world at large, Goon is nothing more than a figment of some fevered writer's imagination—a literary construct, an artistic representation of something that can't possibly exist in the world as we know it."

Goon gave Bramley a sour look, but the wizard's guest leaned forward, hand outstretched, and brushed the goblin's shoulder with a feather-light touch. Slowly she leaned back into the big armchair, cushions so comfortable they seemed to embrace her as she settled against them.

"So...*anything* we can imagine can exist?" she asked finally.

Goon turned his sour look on her now.

She was a student at the university where the wizard taught; third year, majoring in fine arts, and she had the look of an artist about her. There were old paint stains on her jeans and under her fingernails. Her hair was a thick tangle of brown hair, more unruly than Goon's curls. She had a smudge of a nose and thin puckering lips, workman's boots that stood by the door with a history of scuffs and stains written into their leather, thick woolen socks with a hole in the left heel, and one shirttail that had escaped the waist of her jeans. But her eyes were a pale, pale blue, clear and alert, for all the casualness of her attire.

Her name was Jilly Coppercorn.

Bramley shook his head. "It's not imagining. It's *knowing* that it exists—without one smidgen of doubt."

"Yes, but someone had to think him up for him to...." She hesitated as Goon's scowl deepened. "That is...."

Bramley continued to shake his head. "There *is* some semblance of order to things," he admitted, "for if the world was simply everyone's different conceptual universe mixed up together, we'd have nothing but chaos. It all relies on will, you see—to observe the changes, at any rate. Or the differences. The anomalies. Like Goon—oh, do stop scowling," he added to the goblin.

"The world as we have it," he went on to Jilly, "is here mostly because of habit. We've all agreed that certain things exist—we're taught as impressionable infants that this is a table and this is what it looks like, that's a tree out the window there, a dog looks and sounds just so. At the same time we're informed that Goon and his like don't exist, so we don't—or can't—see them."

"They're not made up?" Jilly asked.

This was too much for Goon. He set the tray down and gave her leg a pinch. Jilly jumped away from him, trying to back deeper into the chair as the goblin grinned, revealing two rows of decidedly nasty-looking teeth.

"Rather impolite," Bramley said, "but I suppose you do get the point?"

Jilly nodded quickly. Still grinning, Goon set about pouring their teas.

"So," Jilly asked, "how can someone...how can *I* see things as they really are?"

"Well, it's not that simple," the wizard told her. "First you have to know what it is that you're looking for—before you can find it, you see."

Coyote Stories

Four directions blow the sacred winds
We are standing at the center
Every morning wakes another chance
To make our lives a little better
—Kiya Heartwood, from "Wishing Well"

This day Coyote is feeling pretty thirsty, so he goes into Joey's Bar, you know, on the corner of Palm and Grasso, across from the Men's Mission, and he lays a nugget of gold down on the counter, but Joey he won't serve him.

"So you don't serve skins no more?" Coyote he asks him.

"Last time you gave me gold, it turned to shit on me," is what Joey says. He points to the Rolex on Coyote's wrist. "But I'll take that. Give you change and everything."

Coyote scratches his muzzle and pretends he has to think about it. "Cost me twenty-five dollars," he says. "It looks better than the real thing."

"I'll give you fifteen, cash, and a beer."

"How about a bottle of whiskey?"

So Coyote comes out of Joey's Bar and he's missing his Rolex now, but he's got a bottle of Jack in his hand and that's when he sees Albert, just around the corner, sitting on the ground with his back against the brick wall and his legs stuck out across the sidewalk so you have to step over them, you want to get by.

"Hey, Albert," Coyote says. "What's your problem?"

"Joey won't serve me no more."

"That because you're indigenous?"

"Naw. I got no money."

So Coyote offers him some of his whiskey. "Have yourself a swallow," he says, feeling generous, because he only paid two dollars for the Rolex and it never worked anyway.

"Thanks, but I don't think so," is what Albert tells him. "Seems to me I've been given a sign. Got no money means I should stop drinking."

Coyote shakes his head and takes a sip of his Jack. "You are one crazy skin," he says.

That Coyote he likes his whiskey. It goes down smooth and puts a gleam in his eye. Maybe, he drinks enough, he'll remember some good time and smile, maybe he'll get mean and pick himself a fight with a lamppost like he's done before. But one thing he knows, whether he's got money or not's got nothing to do with omens. Not for him, anyway.

But a lack of money isn't really an omen for Albert either; it's a way of life. Albert, he's like the rest of us skins. Left the reserve, and we don't know why. Come to the city, and we don't know why. Still alive, and we don't know why. But Albert, he remembers it being different. He used to listen to his grandmother's stories, soaked them up like the dirt will rain, thirsty after a long drought. And he tells stories himself, too, or pieces of stories, talk to you all night long if you want to listen to him.

It's always Coyote in Albert's stories, doesn't matter if he's making them up or just passing along gossip. Sometimes Coyote's himself, sometimes he's Albert, sometimes he's somebody else. Like it wasn't Coyote sold his Rolex and ran into him outside Joey's Bar that day, it was Billy Yazhie. Maybe ten years ago now, Billy he's standing under a turquoise sky beside Spider Rock one day, looking up, looking up for a long time, before he turns away and walks to the nearest highway, sticks out his thumb and he doesn't look back till it's too late. Wakes up one morning and everything he knew is gone and he can't find his way back.

Oh that Billy he's a dark skin, he's like leather. You shake his hand and it's like you took hold of a cowboy boot. He knows some of the old songs and he's got himself a good voice, strong, ask anyone. He used to drum for the dancers back home, but his hands shake too much now, he says. He doesn't sing much anymore, either. He's got to be like the rest of us, hanging out in Fitzhenry Park, walking the streets, sleeping in an alleyway because the Men's Mission it's out of beds. We've got the stoic faces down real good, but you look in our eyes, maybe catch us off guard, you'll see we don't forget anything. It's just most times we don't want to remember.

This Coyote he's not too smart sometimes. One day he gets into a fight with a biker, says he going to count coup like his Plains brothers, knock that biker all over the street, only the biker's got himself a big hickory-handled hunting knife and he cuts Coyote's head right off. Puts a quick end to that fight, I'll tell you. Coyote he spends the rest of the afternoon running around, trying to find somebody to sew his head back on again.

"That Coyote," Jimmy Coldwater says, "he's always losing his head over one thing or another."

I tell you we laughed.

But Albert he takes that omen seriously. You see him drinking still, but he's drinking coffee now, black as a raven's wing, or some kind of tea he brews for himself in a tin can, makes it from weeds he picks in the empty lots and dries in the sun. He's living in an abandoned factory these days, and he's got this one wall, he's gluing feathers and bones to it, nothing fancy, no eagles' wings, no bear's jaw, wolf skull, just what he can find lying around, pigeon feathers and crows', rat bones, bird bones, a necklace of mouse skulls strung on a wire. Twigs and bundles of weeds, rattles he makes from tin cans and bottles and jars. He paints figures on the wall, in between all the junk. Thunderbird. Bear. Turtle. Raven.

Everybody's starting to agree, that Albert he's one crazy skin.

Now when he's got money, he buys food with it and shares it out. Sometimes he walks over to Palm Street where the skin girls are working the trade and he gives them money, asks them to take a night off. Sometimes they take the money and just laugh, getting into the next car that pulls up. But sometimes they take the money and they sit in a coffee shop, sit there by the window, drinking their coffee and look out at where they don't have to be for one night.

And he never stops telling stories.

"That's what we are," he tells me one time. Albert he's smiling, his lips are smiling, his eyes are smiling, but I know he's not joking when he tells me that. "Just stories. You and me, everybody, we're a set of stories, and what those stories are is what makes us what we are. Same thing for whites as skins. Same thing for a tribe and a city and a nation and the world. It's all these stories and how they braid together that tells us who and what and where we are.

"We got to stop forgetting and get back to remembering. We got to stop asking for things, stop waiting for people to give us the things we think we need. All we really need is the stories. We have the stories and they'll give us the one thing nobody else can, the thing we can only take for ourselves, because there's nobody can give you back your pride. You've got to take it back yourself.

"You lose your pride and you lose everything. We don't want to know the stories, because we don't want to remember. But we've got to take the good with the bad and make ourselves whole again, be proud again. A proud people can never be defeated. They lose battles, but they'll never lose the war, because for them to lose the war you've got to go out and kill each and every one of them, everybody with even a drop of the blood. And even then, the stories will go on. There just won't be any skins left to hear them."

This Coyote he's always getting in trouble. One day he's sitting at a park bench, reading a newspaper, and this cop starts to talk big to one of the skin girls, starts talking mean, starts pushing her around. Coyote's feeling chivalrous that day, like he's in a white man's movie, and he gets into a fight with the cop. He gets beat up bad and then more cops come and they take him away, put him in jail.

The judge he turns Coyote into a mouse for a year so that there's Coyote, got that same lopsided grin, got that sharp muzzle and those long ears and the big bushy tail, but he's so small now you can hold him in the palm of your hand.

"Doesn't matter how small you make me," Coyote he says to the judge. "I'm still Coyote."

Albert he's so serious now. He gets out of jail and he goes back to living in the factory. Kids've torn down that wall of his, so he gets back to fixing it right, gets back to sharing food and brewing tea and helping the skin girls out when he can, gets back to telling stories. Some people they start thinking of him as a shaman and call him by an old Kickaha name.

Dan Whiteduck he translates the name for Billy Yazhie, but Billy he's not quite sure what he's heard. Know-more-truth, or No-more-truth?

"You spell that with a 'k' or what?" Billy he asks Albert.

"You take your pick how you want to spell it," Albert he says.

Billy he learns how to pronounce that old name and that's what he uses when he's talking about Albert. Lots of people do. But most of us we just keep on calling him Albert.

One day this Coyote decides he wants to have a powwow, so he clears the trash from this empty lot, makes the circle, makes the fire. The people come but no one knows the songs anymore, no one knows the drumming that the dancers need, no one knows the steps. Everybody they're just standing around, looking at each other, feeling sort of stupid, until Coyote he starts singing, *ya-ha-hey, ya-ha-hey,* and he's stomping around the circle, kicking up dirt and dust.

People they start to laugh, then, seeing Coyote playing the fool.

"You are one crazy skin!" Angie Crow calls to him and people laugh some more, nodding in agreement, pointing at Coyote as he dances round and round the circle.

But Jimmy Coldwater he picks up a stick and he walks over to the drum Coyote made. It's this big metal tub, salvaged from a junkyard, that Coyote's covered with a skin and who knows where he got that skin, nobody's asking. Jimmy he hits the skin of the drum and everybody they stop laughing and look at him, so Jimmy he hits the skin again. Pretty soon he's got the rhythm to Coyote's dance and then Dan Whiteduck he picks up a stick, too, and joins Jimmy at the drum.

Billy Yazhie he starts up to singing then, takes Coyote's song and turns it around so that he's singing about Spider Rock and turquoise skies, except everybody hears it their own way, hears the stories they want to hear in it. There's more people drumming and there's people dancing and before anyone knows it, the night's over and there's the dawn poking over the roof of an abandoned factory, thinking, these are some crazy skins. People they're lying around and sitting around, eating the flatbread and drinking the tea that Coyote provided, and they're all tired, but there's something in their hearts that feels very full.

"This was one fine powwow," Coyote he says.

Angie she nods her head. She's sitting beside Coyote all sweaty and hot and she's never looked quite so good before.

"Yeah," she says. "We got to do it again."

We start having regular powwows after that night, once, sometimes twice a month. Some of the skins they start to making dancing outfits, going back up to the reserve for visits and asking about steps and songs from the old folks. Gets to be we feel like a community, a small skin nation living here in exile with the ruins of broken-down tenements and abandoned buildings all around us. Gets to be we start remembering some of our stories and sharing them with each other instead of sharing bottles. Gets to be we have something to feel proud about.

Some of us we find jobs. Some of us we try to climb up the side of the wagon but we keep falling off. Some of us we go back to homes we can hardly remember. Some of us we come from homes where we can't live, can't even breathe, and drift here and there until we join this tribe that Albert he helped us find.

And even if Albert he's not here anymore, the stories go on. They have to go on, I know that much. I tell them every chance I get.

See, this Coyote he got in trouble again, this Coyote he's always getting in trouble, you know that by now, same as me. And when he's in jail this time he sees that it's all tribes inside, the same as it is outside. White tribes, black tribes, yellow tribes, skin tribes. He finally understands, finally realizes that maybe there can't ever be just one tribe, but that doesn't mean we should stop trying.

But even in jail this Coyote he can't stay out of trouble and one day he gets into another fight and he gets cut again, but this time he thinks maybe he's going to die.

"Albert," Coyote he says, "I am one crazy skin. I am never going to learn, am I?"

"Maybe not this time," Albert says, and he's holding Coyote's head and he's wiping the dribble of blood that comes out of the side of Coyote's mouth and is trickling down his chin. "But that's why you're Coyote. The wheel goes round and you'll get another chance."

Coyote he's trying to be brave, but he's feeling weaker and it hurts, it hurts, this wound in his chest that cuts to the bone, that cuts the thread that binds him to this story.

"There's a thing I have to remember," Coyote he says, "but I can't find it. I can't find its story...."

"Doesn't matter how small they try to make you," Albert he reminds Coyote. "You're still Coyote."

"*Ya-ha-hey*," Coyote he says. "Now I remember."

Then Coyote he grins and he lets the pain take him away into another story.

LAUGHTER IN THE LEAVES

...but the wind was always
laughter in the leaves to me.
—Wendelessen,
from "An Fear Glas"

"Listen," Meran said.

By the hearth, her husband laid his hand across the strings of his harp to still them and cocked his head. "I don't hear a thing," he said. "Only the wind."

"That's just it," Meran replied. "It's on the wind. Laughter. Giggles. I tell you, he's out there again."

Cerin laid his instrument aside. "I'll go see," he said.

Outside, the long grey skies of autumn were draining into night. The wind that came down from the heaths was gusting through the forest, rattling the leaves, gathering them up in eddying whirls and rushing them between the trees in a swirling dance. The moon was just starting to tip the eastern horizon, but there was no one out there. Only Old Badger, lying in his special spot between the cottage and the rose bushes, who lifted his striped head and made a questioning sort of noise at the harper standing in the doorway.

"Did you see him?" Cerin asked.

The badger regarded him for a few moments, then laid his head back down on his crossed forepaws.

"I've only seen him once myself," Meran said, joining Cerin at the door.

"But I know he's out there. He knows you're going tomorrow and is letting me know that he means to pull a trick or two while you're gone."

"Then I won't go."

"Don't be silly. You have to go. You promised."

"Then you must come. You were invited."

"I think I'd prefer to put up with our bodach's tricks to listening to the dry talk of harpers for two whole nights and the day in between too, I'll wager."

Cerin sighed. "It won't be all talk..."

"Oh, no," Meran replied with a smile. "There'll be fifteen versions of the same tune, all played in a row, and then a discussion as to which of twenty titles is the oldest for this particular tune. Wonderfully interesting stuff, I don't doubt, but it's not for me. And besides," she added, after stooping down to give Old Badger a quick pat and then closing the door, "I mean to have a trick or two ready for our little bodach myself this time."

Cerin sighed again. He believed there was a bodach, even though neither he nor anyone but Meran had ever seen it—and even then only in passing from the corner of her eye. But sometimes he had to wonder if every bit of mischief that took place around the cottage could all be blamed on it. Whether it was a broken mug or a misplaced needle, it was always the bodach this and the bodach that.

"I don't know if it's such a wise idea to go playing tricks on a bodach," he said as he made his way back to the hearth. "They're quick to anger and—"

"So am I!" Meran interrupted. "No, Cerin. You go to your Harper's Meet and don't worry about me. One way or another, we'll have come to an agreement while you're gone. Now play me a tune before we go to bed. He's gone now—I can tell. Do you hear the wind?"

Cerin nodded. But it sounded no different to him now than it had before.

"The smile's gone from it," Meran explained. "That's how you can tell that he's gone."

"I don't know why you don't just let me catch him with a harpspell."

Meran shook her head. "Oh, no. I'll best this little fellow with my wits, or not at all. I made that bargain with myself the first time he tripped me in the woods. Now come. Where's that tune you promised me?"

Cerin brought Telynros up onto his lap and soon the cottage rang with the music that spilled from the roseharp's strings. Outside, Old Badger listened and the wind continued to make a dance of the leaves between the trees and only Meran could have said if the smile returned to its voice or not, but she would speak no more of bodachs that night.

The morning Cerin left, Meran's favourite mug fell from the shelf where it was perched and shattered on the stone floor, her hair when she woke was a tangle of elfknots that she didn't even bother to comb out, and the porridge boiled over for all that she stood over it and stirred and watched and took the best of care. She stamped her foot, but neither she nor Cerin made any comment. She saw him to the road with a smile, gave him a kiss and a jaunty wave along his way, and watched him go. Not until he was lost from sight, up the track and over the hill, with the sun in his eyes and the wind at his back, did she turn and face the woods, arms akimbo, to give the trees a long considering look.

"Now we'll see," she said.

She returned to the cottage, Old Badger at her heels.

The morning passed with her pretending to ignore the presence she knew was watching her from the forest. She combed out her hair, unravelling each knot that the little gnarled fingers of an elfman had tied in it last night. She picked up the shards of her mug, cleaned the burnt porridge from the stove, then straightened the kindling pile that had toppled over with a clatter and spill while she was busy inside the cottage. The smile on her lips was a little thin, but it never faltered.

She hummed to herself and it seemed that the wind in the trees put words to the tune:

Catch me, snatch me,
Catch me if you can!
You'll never put the fetters
On a little kowrie man!

"That's as may be," Meran said as she got the last of the kindling stacked once more. She tied it in place with knots that only an oakmaid would know, for she was the daughter of the Oak King of Ogwen Wood and knew a spell or two of her own. "But still we'll see."

When she went back inside, she could hear the kindling sticks rattle about a bit, but her knots held firm. And so it went through the day. She rearranged everything in the cottage, laying tiny holding spells here, there and everywhere. She hung fetishes over each window—tiny bundles made up of dried oak leaves and acorns to represent herself, wren's feathers for Cerin, a lock of bristly badger hair for Old Badger, and rowan sprigs for their magic to seal the spell. Only the door she left untouched. By then twilight was at hand, stealing softfooted across the wood, so she pulled up a chair to face the door and sat down to wait.

And the night went by.

The wind made its teasing sounds around the cottage, Old Badger slept under her chair. She stayed awake, watching the door, firmly resolved to stay up the whole night if that was what it took. But as the hours crept by after midnight, she began to nod, blinked awake, nodded again, and finally slept. When she woke in the morning, the door stood ajar, her hair was a crow's nest of tangles, and there was a small mocking stick figure drawn with charcoal on the floor at her feet, one arm lifted and a wide grin almost making two halves of the head.

The wind gusted in through the door as soon as she was awake, sending a great spill of leaves that rattled like laughter across the floor. Stiff from an uncomfortable night spent in a chair, Meran made herself some tea and went outside to sit on the stoop. She refused to show even a tad of the frustration she felt. Instead she calmly drank her tea, pulled loose the new night's worth of tangles, then went inside to sweep the leaves and other debris from the cottage. The stick figure she left where it had been drawn to remind her of last night's failure.

"Well," she said to Old Badger as she went to set down a bowl of food for him. "And what did you see?"

The striped head lifted, eyes mournful, until the bowl was on the floor. And then he was too busy to reply—even if he'd had a voice with which to do so.

Meran knew she should get some rest for the next night, but she was too busy trying to think up a new way to stay awake to be able to sleep. It was self-contradictory, and she knew it, but it couldn't be helped. A half year of the bodach's tricks was too long. Five minutes worth would be too long. As it drew near the supper hour, she finally gave up trying to rest and went to the well for water. A footfall on the road startled her as she was drawing the bucket up. She turned, losing her grip on the well's rope. The bucket went rattling down the well until it hit the bottom with a heavy splash. But she didn't hear it. Her attention was on the figure that stood on the track.

It was an old man that was standing there, an old travelling man in a tattered blue coat and yellow breeches, with his tinker's pack on his back and his face brown as a nut and lined with age. He regarded her with a smile, blue eyes twinkling.

"Evening, ma'am," he said. "It's been an awfully dry road I've been wending, no doubt about that. Could you see yourself clear to sparing me a drink from that well of yours?"

It's the bodach, Meran thought. Oh, you mischief-maker, I have you now.

"Of course," she replied, smiling sweetly. "And you'll stay for supper, won't you?"

"Oh, no, ma'am. I wouldn't want to put you to any trouble."

"It's no trouble at all."

"That's kind of you."

Meran drew the bucket up once more. "Come along to the house and we'll brew up some tea—it'll do more for your thirst than just water."

"Oh, it does that," the old man agreed as he followed her back to the cottage.

Meran watched him with many a sidelong glance as they entered the cottage. He gave the chair facing the door an odd look, and the charcoal drawing an even odder one, but said nothing. Playing the part of an old tinker man, she supposed the bodach meant to stay in character. A tinker would know better than to make remarks about whatever oddities his hostess might have in her house. He laid his pack by the door and Meran put the kettle on.

"Have you been travelling far?" she asked.

"Oh, far enough for these old bones. I'm bound for Matchtem—by the sea, you know. My son has a wagon there and we winter a little further down the coast near Applewater."

Meran nodded. "Do have a seat," she said.

The old man looked around. She was busy at the table where the other chair was, so he sat down gingerly in the one facing the door. No sooner was he sitting, than Meran slipped up behind him and tossed a chain with tiny iron links over him, tying it quickly to the chair. Oh, the links were small and a boy could have easily broken free of them, but anything with iron in it bound a bodach or one of the kowrie folk. Everyone knew that. Meran danced around in front of the chair.

"Now I have you!" she cried. "Oh, you wicked bodach! I'll teach you to play your tricks on me."

"I *am* an old man," the tinker said, eyeing her carefully, "but I've played no tricks on you, ma'am—or at least none that I know of. My name's Yocky John, and I'm just a plain travelling man."

Meran smiled at the name, for she knew a word or two in the old tinker language. Clever John, the bodach might call himself, but he wasn't clever enough for her.

"Oh?" she asked. "You didn't tangle my hair, nor break my crockery, nor play a hundred other little mischiefs and tricks on me? And who was it then?"

"Is it trouble with the little folk you're having?" Yocky John asked.

"Just one. You. And I have you now."

"But you don't. All you've caught is an old tinker, too tired to even get up out of this chair now that he's sitting. But I can help you with your bodach, I surely can. Yocky John's got a trick or two for them."

Outside the wind made the leaves laugh as they rushed in a rattling spray against the walls of the cottage. Meran listened, then looked uncertainly at the tinker. Had she made a mistake, or was this just another of the bodach's mischiefs?

"What sort of tricks?" she asked.

"Well, first I must know how you've gained the little fellow's ill will."

"I don't know. There's no reason for it—save his nature."

"Oh, no," Yocky John said. "They always have a reason." He looked slowly around the room. "It's a snug place you have here—but it's not so old, is it?"

Meran shook her head. It was just a year now since she'd lost her tree—the tree that a wooderl needs to survive. It was only through Cerin and the spells of his roseharp that she was able to live without it and in this cottage that they'd built where her tree had once stood.

"A very snug place," the old man said. "Magicked, too, I'd say."

"My husband's a harper."

"Ah. That explains it. Harp magic's heady stuff. A bodach can't live in a harper's home—not without an invitation."

"Still he comes and goes as he pleases," Meran said. "He breaks things and disrupts things and generally causes no end of mischief. Who'd *want* to have a bodach living with them?"

"Well, it's cold in the winter," Yocky John said. "Out in the woods, with no shelter but a cloak of leaves, maybe, or a rickety lean-to that the wind howls through. The winds of winter aren't a bodach's friends—not like the winds of summer are. And I know cold, too. Why do you think I winter with my son? Only a fool tries to sleep in the snow."

Meran sighed. She pictured a little kowrie man, huddled in a bare-limbed winter tree, shivering in the cold, denied the warmth of a cottage because of a harper's magics.

"Well, if he felt that way," she said, "why didn't he come to us? Surely he'd have seen that we never turn a guest away. Are we ogres?"

"Well, you know bodachs," Yocky John said. "He'd be too proud and too shy. They like to creep into a place, all secret like, and hide out in the rafters or wherever, paying for their way with the odd good turn or two. It's the winter that's hard on them—even magical kowrie folk like they are. The summer's not so bad—for then even an old man like myself can sleep out-of-doors. But in the winter...."

Meran sighed again. "I never thought of it like that," she said. She studied the tinker, a smile twinkling in her eyes. "Well, Yocky John the bodach. You're welcome to stay in our rafters through the winter—but mind you leave my husband and I some privacy. Do you hear? And no more tricks. Or this time I'll let his roseharp play a spell."

"I'm not a bodach," Yocky John said. "At least not as you mean it."

"Yes, I know. A bodach's an old man too—or it was in the old days."

"Do I look like a kowrie man to you?"

Meran grinned. "Who knows what a kowrie man would look like? It all depends on the shape he chooses to wear when you see him, don't you think? And I see you're still sitting there with that wee bit of iron chain wrapped around you."

"That's only because I'm too tired to get up."

"Have it your way."

She removed the chain then and went back to making supper. When she called him to the table, Yocky John rose very slowly to his feet and made his way over to the table. Meran laughed, thinking, oh, yes, play the part to the hilt, you old trickster, and went and fetched his chair for him. They ate and talked awhile, then Meran went to bed, leaving the old man to sleep on the mound of blankets that she'd readied for him in front of the hearth. When she woke in the morning, he was gone. And so was the charcoal drawing on the floor.

"So," Cerin said when he came home that night. "How went the great war between the fierce mistress of the oak wood and the equally fierce bodach that challenged her?"

Meran looked up towards the rafters where a small round face peered down at her for a moment, then quickly popped out of sight. It didn't looked at all like the old tinker man she'd guested last night, but who could know what was what or who was who when it came to mischief-makers like a bodach? And was a tinker all that different really? They were as much tricksters themselves. So whether Yocky John and the bodach were one and the same, or merely similar, she supposed she'd never know.

"Oh, we made our peace," she said.

THE BADGER IN THE BAG

This is what happens:
there is a magic made.
—Wendelessen,
from "The Old Tunes"

THEY TRAVELLED IN a tinker wagon that year, up hill and down. By the time they rolled into summer they were a long way from Abercorn and the Vale of the Oak King, roaming through Whistlederry now, and into the downs of Dunmadden.

The wagon belonged to Jen Kelledy who was a niece of Old Tess, Cerin's foster-mother, making her a cousin of sorts. She was a thin reed woman with a thatch of nutbrown hair as tangled as Meran's, but without the strands of oakmaid green that streaked Meran's brown curls. Among the tinkerfolk she was known as Tulo Jen—Fat Jen—because she was so thin.

The road had called to them that spring—to Meran who was no longer bound to her tree, and to her husband the harper—so they packed the cottage up tight when Tulo Jen's wagon pulled into their yard one fine morning and, before the first tulip bloomed, they were away, looking like the three tinkers that one of them was, following the road to wherever it led. They left Old Badger behind, for he was never one to travel, but they carried a badger all the same.

Tulo Jen had a fiddle with a boar's striped head carved into the scroll. She called it her badger and kept it in a bag that hung from the cluttered wall inside the wagon, just above the spot where Cerin's harp was tied in place. There wasn't a tune that, once heard, Tulo Jen couldn't play on her fiddle.

"There's a trick to it," she explained to Meran, who played the flute. Meran could pick up a tune quicker than most, but she still felt like a plodding turtle compared to the tinker.

"There's a trick to anything," Cerin said.

Tulo Jen gave him a mock frown. "Aye—just like there's a trick to listening when someone else is talking and not adding your own two pennies every few words like some kind of bodach."

"Oh, don't talk about bodachs," Meran said. "I've had my fill of them this winter."

Having let one stay in their rafters over the winter, she and Cerin had found themselves with the dubious honour of guesting up to a half-dozen of the little pranksters some nights.

"Part of the trick," Tulo Jen went on as though she hadn't been interrupted, "is to give your instrument the right sort of a name. Now a badger knows his tricks and, what's more, he never lets go, so when Whizzy Fettle explained this thing about names to me, I knew straight-off what to call my fiddle."

Meran looked down at her flute. "I don't know," she said. "This looks more like a snake to me. I don't much like snakes—at least I can't imagine putting one up to my mouth."

"And besides," Cerin added. "You already had the scroll carved into a badger's head. How could you *not* call it that?"

"What did I say about listening? Broom and heather, it's like I'm talking to the wind. First off—" Tulo Jen, bristling, made a show of counting on her fingers, "—the badger's head came after, but that's another story. Secondly, it has to be the right sort of a name and you'll *know* when it comes to you and not before. And thirdly, the second thing I was going to say was that one should listen, *really* listen—"

"Thirdly, the second thing?" Cerin asked.

"I'm getting confused," Meran added. "Does the name come first or…"

Tulo Jen looked straight ahead and stiffly concentrated on keeping the horses on the road—make-work, really, for they were too well-trained to stray. She said nothing, letting the clatter of the wooden wheels on the road fill the place left by her lack of words.

"I was only teasing," Cerin said after a few moments of her silence.

"Oh, aye."

"It was a joke."

"And a grand one, too."

"I really do want to learn the trick," Meran added.

"Oh, hear me laugh."

"That's the trouble with Kelledys," Cerin said to his wife. "They don't like to get bogged down with all sorts of silly things like facts and the like when they're telling a story. So when you ask them to explain something, well...." He shrugged, smiling before giving Tulo Jen a quick glance.

The tinker tried to keep a straight face, but it was no use. "You're a hundred times worse than Uncle Finan," she said at last, "and Ballan knows, *he* could drive a soul to the whiskey sack without even trying."

"You were talking about Whizzy Fettle's advice," Cerin reminded her. "Something about tricking a name out of an instrument."

"You're the one to talk—with that roseharp of yours sitting in the back. Do you mean to tell me that *its* name means nothing?"

"Well, no...."

Telynros was a gift from the Tuathan, an enchanted harp that bore the touch of the Old Gods in its workmanship. Silver-stringed, with deeply resonating wood, it bore a living rose in the joint where the forepillar met the curving neck. A rose the colour of twilight skies.

"Well then, listen to what I have to say, or at least let me tell Meran without all your interruptions—would that be possible?"

There was an obvious glint of humour in her fierce gaze and Cerin nodded solemnly in acquiescence. Tulo Jen cleared her throat.

"As I was saying," she said, looking at Meran, "the name comes first. But that alone would never be enough. So...."

The road wound on and Cerin closed his eyes, listening to the rise and fall of the tinker's voice. The summer air was thick with the scent of hedgerow flowers and weeds. He was soon nodding. The sound of the wheels and the horses' hooves, the buzz of Tulo Jen's voice, all faded and he fell asleep with his head on Meran's shoulder. The two women exchanged smiles and continued their talk.

That night they camped in a field, close by a stream. They had a fire for their supper, but let the coals die down after they made a last pot of tea, for the night was warm. When they finally went to their beds, they rolled out their blankets on the grass and slept under the stars. All except for Meran.

She couldn't sleep, so she lay staring up at the night sky, tracing the constellations and remembering the tales her mother had told her of how they came to be. After awhile, she got up and dressed, then went to sit on the flat stones by the stream. The horses snorted at her as she went by and she gave them both a quick pat.

By the stream the night seemed quieter still. The water moved too slowly to make a sound, the wind had died away. She took her flute from its bag at her belt and turned it over in her hands.

A name, she thought.

Her husband had carved the flute for her, carved it from the wood of her own lifetree when it came down in a storm. With three charms carved from its wood, he'd drawn her back from the realm of the dead—a hair comb, an oak leaf-shaped pendant, and the flute. Three charms and his love had set her free from the need of an oakmaid's lifetree.

The flute was very plain, but it had a lovely tone for all that it was carved from an oak. Something of a harpspell from Telynros gave its music its rich flavour.

Shall I call you roseflute? she thought with a grin, imagining Cerin's face when she told him. How he'd frown. Oakrose, maybe? Roseoak? The flute was so slender, perhaps she should call it Tulo Fluto.

She stifled a giggle and looked back at the camp, then froze. Something moved close to the ground, creeping towards the sleeping figures of Tulo Jen and her husband. She was about to call out a warning to them when she recognized the shape for what it was by its striped head.

It was a badger—like Old Badger, whom they'd left back in Abercorn. Meran knew the look of a badger by night. She'd seen it often enough, traipsing through the woods with Old Badger. But this badger looked small. A babe separated from a sow, Meran guessed.

She rose quietly so as not to startle it and padded softly back to the wagon. When she reached the camp she was just in time to see the little badger crawl into Tulo Jen's fiddle bag.

Oh, no, you mustn't, Meran thought.

She hurried over and knelt by the bag, but when she touched its side, all she could feel was the shape of the fiddle and the bow inside. Slowly she drew the instrument out and studied it under the starlight. It looked the same as it had when Tulo Jen had been playing it this evening. The wood had a hue somewhere between chestnut and amber and the carved badger's head on the scroll regarded her with a half-smile in its eyes. Meran admired the workmanship of the carving for a moment, then set the fiddle aside. She reached into the bag again, took out the bow and shook the bag, half-expecting a baby badger to tumble out, for all that the weight was wrong.

There was nothing inside.

She was letting the night fill her head with an impossibility, Meran thought. Too many tinker's stories and harper's tall tales—that was the trouble. She replaced the fiddle and bow in their bag and laid down on her own blankets beside Cerin. She'd say nothing about this in the morning, she decided, but tomorrow night, oh, she'd be watching. Never have a doubt about that.

She watched the next night, and the night after that, and the third night as well, but all there was in Tulo Jen's bag was a fiddle and a bow. She gave up after the fourth night and put it down to her imagination and perhaps missing Old Badger. But she had to wonder. If she called her flute a snake, would it slither out of its bag one night and go adventuring? If she called it an oakrose, would the scent of acorns and roses spill out of the bag?

She meant to talk to the others about it the next day, but by the time she woke, she'd forgotten, and when she did remember, she was a little embarrassed about the whole affair. The teasing she'd get from that pair—tinkers were bad enough and Cerin was always twice as bad in their company. So she kept it to herself, but did wonder about a name for her flute. She'd finger it through its bag during the day, listen to its tone when she played tunes with the others around the fire in the evening, and late at night, she'd sit up sometimes, looking at its wooden gleam in the moonlight and under the stars.

Two weeks later they were camping in a hollow, with hills on one side, rolling off into gorse-thick downs, and dunes on the other, shifting to the sea. They all stayed up late that night, drinking a little too much of Tulo Jen's heather whiskey. Eventually, Cerin and the tinker fell asleep, but the strong drink just made Meran feel too awake. She got up and wandered down by the water to see if she could make out what the tide was saying to the shore.

There was something hypnotic about the lap of the waves as they came to land. If she didn't love her father's wood so much, she could easily live by the sea, forever and a day. She came upon an outfall not far from the camp, a brook that ran down to the water from the gorse-backed hills. Seabirds stood by it, settled down for the night. A black and white oyster-catcher, as big as a duck, took to flight when she came too near, its wings beating rapidly as it flew off along the shore, sounding its high piping alarm call. But the gulls stayed put and watched her.

She backed away, not wanting to disturb them as well, and made a slow circuit back towards the camp. Standing on the highest dune, the one that overlooked the camp, she held her breath as a small greyish shape with a striped head crept away from where Tulo Jen and Cerin lay sleeping. Meran slipped out of sight behind the dune and then followed the little shape, her heart beating fast in her breast. She gave herself a pinch at one point, just to make absolutely sure that she wasn't dreaming, then realized that she could just as easily be drunk.

The little badger led her a good distance away from the camp before it finally paused and crouched down amongst driftwood and drying seaweed to gaze out to sea. It began to sing then, a low mournful song that sounded for all the world like a fiddle's strings when the bow pulled a slow air from them.

Oh, this can't be, Meran thought, who'd seen marvels in her time, but nothing like this. Not ever anything like this.

But the little badger stayed there by the edge of the sea and sang, sometimes jaunty tunes and sometimes sad airs. The jigs and reels made Meran want to get up and dance in the wet sand, to feel it press up between her toes as she stomped about to the music. The slower tunes made her want to weep. Then her fingers crept to the bag that held her flute and she caressed the wood through the cloth, wanting to play along with the badger, but not daring to break the spell.

There were more sad tunes than happy ones. And after awhile, there were no more happy ones. What could make it feel such hurt? Meran wondered. When the little badger finally fell quiet, Meran's eyes were brimmed with tears as salty as the briny water that lapped against the sand.

"Don't go!" she called softly as the little beast began to leave.

The badger froze and met her gaze with eyes that seemed to hold their own inner light.

"Who are you?" Meran asked. "What makes you so sad? Why were you singing?"

Her head was filled with a hundred questions and they all came out in a jumble when all she really wanted to ask was, how can I ease your hurt?

I sing the music that was never played on me, the little badger replied. His voice was like fiddle notes resounding in her head, staccato notes played on the high strings. Not unpleasant, just strange sounding. *The music that never had a chance to live. If I leave it unsounded, it builds up in me until I can no longer bear it. It becomes a pain that...hurts.*

"Are you sad?" she asked, coming nearer.

The badger held its ground, watching her. *No. Not sad. Just....* Its grey shoulders lifted and fell and a long note came from it, filling her head. It wasn't a word, just a bittersweet sound.

"Do...do all instruments feel that way?"

It was perhaps the whiskey that made her take this all so seriously, a part of her decided.

No, the badger replied. *Just those with names.*

Meran thought about that. She imagined Cerin's harp taking a walk to play some music for itself, then realized that there were times when she woke, late at night, and thought she heard it playing, thought it was just a dream....

Instruments with names. She touched her flute.

"Would you rather not have been named?" she asked.

Without a name, how could I live? And besides, what instrument sounds so sweet as one that has been loved and given a name?

"But..." Meran began, yet between one blink and the next, the badger had scurried away.

By the time she returned to the camp, she was still feeling woozy from the drinks and the walk, but tired enough to sleep. Before she lay down, she took the time to touch Tulo Jen's bag. There was a fiddle inside, and a bow—wood and gut strings and horsehair. No live badger. Meran went to sleep, holding her flute, and dreamed of an orchestra of instruments that changed into animals as they sounded, leapt from their player's hands and capered about, still making music. She smiled in her sleep.

It was a week after that, as they were travelling through the wooded vales of Osterwen, the tag-end of the summer in the air now, that Tulo Jen asked Meran if she'd thought of a name for her flute yet.

"Well, I'm not sure," Meran replied. "I don't know if it wants a name."

"Everything wants a name," Tulo Jen said, and then she echoed the little badger's words. "How else can it live?"

Meran had been thinking about that, wondering if an instrument did want to live in such a way, but she hadn't been able to come up with an answer that satisfied her. So she told Tulo Jen about what she'd seen happen to the tinker's own fiddle.

"Broom and heather," Tulo Jen said when Meran was done. "Now there's a marvel!" She never doubted the tale for a moment and for that, Meran was relieved.

"I've heard that tale before," Cerin said, "only it was a set of bagpipes and they set up such a wail every night at the stroke of midnight that—"

"Oh, do be still!" Tulo Jen told him.

Cerin bit back the joking retort that was on the tip of his tongue when he saw that the pair of them were serious.

"Did you know about it?" Meran asked the tinker. "About the little badger and all?"

"No. But Ballan knows, it makes sense in a lovely sort of a way, don't you think?"

"I suppose. But now you can see why I'm not sure what I should do. What if the flute doesn't want a name? What if I give it the wrong one?"

"You couldn't do that," Cerin said, all jokes aside.

"But how's one supposed to know?"

Tulo Jen and the harper exchanged glances. It was Cerin who answered. "Because when the name comes to you, it will come from the instrument. It's the same as Old Badger. We don't call him Duffer or Stripes or anything but Old Badger, because that's who he is. You'll just *know*."

"Oh, it's easy for you to say. You're a harper."

"I didn't name Old Badger."

"Well, he's always been Old Badger," Meran said. "Ever since I can remember."

But as she spoke, she could remember the first time the name had come to her. She was tousling with the old fellow, back in a time before she'd met Cerin, when she'd still been tied to her tree. She could remember the exact instant that the name had formed in her mind and then sounded in the air for the first time. She'd called him many things before that moment, but when that name came, she'd just *known* it was the right one.

"I see," she said slowly.

"So will you name your flute?" Tulo Jen asked. "Because that's the first part of the trick, you know. And then it's just listening."

Meran thought of badgers in bags that were fiddles sometimes and other times were not. She touched her flute, then drew it from its bag and studied it in the sunlight. The wood gleamed, its grain rich with spiraling curlicues.

Badgers were tricksters, she remembered Tulo Jen telling her, and she could see that, considering the mischief Old Badger could get into. And there was a trick to learning tunes quickly. But like it or not, the image of the little brown man who lived in their rafters came to mind and, looking at her flute and thinking of him, she knew she had no choice.

Oh, but it was just making trouble for Cerin and herself, for now they'd have a pair of them in their rafters every night, not just the odd night when their gnarled little bodach had his friends over.

"I'll have to call it Bodach," she said, "because that's its name."

Cerin looked at her with raised eyebrows, but Tulo Jen nodded her head.

"That's a good name," she said.

Meran thought she heard a laugh in the wind that blew through the branches of the trees overhead and wondered if she'd been tricked into the whole thing. She sighed and pushed the flute back into its bag. As she put it away, she thought it moved in her hands, but perhaps it was just the way it had rolled between her fingers.

"Just you remember," she told it. "Your tricks are supposed to *help* me."

This time she was sure she heard a laugh on the wind.

∷AND THE RAFTERS WERE RINGING∷

"SHE'LL HAVE TO be young," Yocky John said. "Otherwise she won't believe."

Wee Jack, skinny as a stick figure, nodded his narrow little head. "And pretty, too."

"Pretty's not so important," Yocky John said with a frown. "What good's pretty? But weight's important. Furey's already carrying Peadin and you and me—he'll want her to be thin."

Wee Jack hugged his knobby knees and rocked back and forth. He almost fell from the rafter, but Yocky John caught hold of his jacket and pulled him back into place.

"Hsst!" he said with a sharp breath. "Keep it down."

Wee Jack stared from their perch on the rafter to the bed below. The couple lying there appeared to be asleep. Then he caught the gleam of an eye and knew that Meran at least was awake and watching. He ducked quickly back out of sight.

They were bodachs these two, a pair of tricksters hiding up in the rafters of a harper's stone cottage. Yocky John was the older of the pair, a grizzled gnome of a bodach who took his name from an old tinker man he'd once befriended and whose shape he could wear if the fancy took him. But usually he looked like the bodach he was—bearded and brown with thick brows like tufts of grass over a pair of glittering eyes, slight of figure, though not so skinny as his companion.

Wee Jack had a pair of shapes, too. There was the one he wore now, and the one he wore when Meran put her lips to her flute. For then he *was* her flute, given life after she named him Bodach. Yocky John didn't much care to call him Bodach. To his mind, that was like the pair below calling each other Man and Woman, instead of by their given names. So he called the younger bodach Wee Jack. Soon enough all the kowrie folk, from Furey who lived in the river to the ravens who nested in the Oak King's Wood, were doing the same.

"The Mistress spied me," Wee Jack told Yocky John.

"I'm not surprised," the older bodach replied, "what with the way you carry on. I swear, if there's something to trip on, you will."

"Maybe so," Wee Jack said. "But all the same, I know someone's who's young and thin and pretty, too."

"You don't."

"I do. Hather the shepherd's youngest daughter Liane."

A wide grin beamed across Yocky John's face. "I never thought of her." He leaned closer to his companion. "We'll snatch her at moonrise and won't that be a night for her! She'll remember it until she's wizened and old, and still she won't forget."

"Maybe I should be called Yocky Jack," Wee Jack said, puffing up his chest, "because I've gone all clever." Yocky was a tinker word that meant just that. "And you can be Wee John, because your brain's gone all small on you."

Yocky John aimed a cuff at the younger bodach, who backed quickly away and lost his balance again. Yocky John snatched him out of the air by his collar before he could fall.

"Whose brain is wee?" he asked.

"Not yours," Wee Jack said quickly.

Down below, Meran stared up at what she could see of the pair in the rafters. "They're up to no good," she whispered to her husband.

Cerin turned onto his back and looked up. "You're always saying that. How can you tell this time?"

"I can feel it. Besides, they're bodachs and bodachs are always up to no good."

"It wasn't I who invited the one to live here and named the other," Cerin said.

Meran gave him a poke in the ribs with her elbow.

"Still," Cerin amended. "It wouldn't hurt to keep an eye on them, now would it?"

"Just what I was thinking," Meran said.

Cerin rolled over again and went back to sleep, but his wife stayed awake a long time, staring up into the rafters and straining to hear what the two little pranksters were talking about.

The next morning, while Cerin was transcribing some tunes that he'd recently picked up from one of his tinker cousins, Meran kept a sharp eye out for Yocky

John. When he slipped away from the cottage at midmorning, she followed, keeping well back as he made his way through the oak wood, which was the holding of the Oak King Ogwen, Meran's father. Old Badger tramped at Meran's heels, his broad striped head almost directly underfoot. As the hour drew closer to noon, Yocky John emerged from the forest and clambered up a short hill. A reed-thin figure was waiting for him there by a rough cairn of old grey stones.

Meran recognized the figure easily enough. It was Peadin the hillhob. His skin was as dark as the earth of his hills, his hair a dull red thatch. Eyes like small saucers predominated his features. With his brown jacket and trousers, and skin darker still, he could be almost invisible, even when standing just a few feet away. Meran had spied him from time to time on her midnight rambles with Old Badger, so she knew him by sight and by the rumours of his prankish nature, but not to talk to.

Leaving Old Badger at the foot of the hill, she crept up the slope, bent low in the gorse, but close as she got, she only made out a few words.

Spree...snatch...Liane....

That was enough. Before she could be spotted, she hurried back to where Old Badger was waiting and the pair of them disappeared into her father's wood. The badger regarded her quizzically.

"I knew it," she told him. "I knew he was up to no good. Cerin can tease me all he wants, but I know what I know."

And what she knew at this moment was that the tricksters meant to kidnap Hather's daughter for who knew what purpose. She turned her steps now towards that part of the moors where the shepherd's cot looked out over the Dolking Downs. Old Badger followed dutifully on her heels.

Liane was at home in her father's cot, carding wool. She was a slender red-haired girl, the red a bright flame rather that the dull burn of Peadin's unruly locks. Seeing that hair, Meran understood why the bodachs had chosen her. Red was the colour of poets and bards and the colour kowrie folk liked best in their humans. Liane rose from her work with a smile when she saw Meran approaching.

"It's not often the Oak King's daughter herself comes to visit," she said as she set about readying tea for them both.

Liane lived alone with her father. Her mother had died and her two older sisters were married now and lived in other parts of Abercorn.

"I've come with a warning," Meran said. She sat down on a chair by the hearth, Old Badger stretched out by her feet.

"A warning?" Liane's eyebrows rose questioningly.

Meran told her of what she'd overheard and explained her suspicions.

Liane smiled. "Oh, the hobs would never hurt me," she said. "They tease a bit, but we put out their bowl of cream every night and sometimes they even leave behind a fairy cake in exchange." At the look that came into Meran's eyes at that, Liane's smile widened and she added, "Oh, we take care not to thank them for it. We might live a simple life, but we're not simple people."

The kettle began to whistle over the fire and Liane busied herself with steeping them each a strong cup of tea. She served oatmeal cookies when the tea was ready, and talked readily about whatever came to hand, but she took no more notice of Meran's warnings at the end of the visit than she had when Meran had first arrived. Finally Meran gave up and returned home across the downs.

She found Cerin by the river where he was still worrying over the transcriptions of his harp tunes. She talked to him there, rather than at home where Yocky John might be able to listen in on their conversation if the bodach had already returned.

"She just wouldn't listen," Meran said, obviously frustrated. "It's hard when even a fourteen-year-old human won't take you seriously."

An oakmaid such as Meran lived a long life—as long as her tree. She had green blood running in her veins and green tints in her curly nut-brown hair. She no longer had a lifetree, but her husband's harp magics had drawn her back from the veil that separates the world of the living from that of the dead.

"Maybe *you're* taking it too seriously," Cerin tried, keeping the tone of his voice as diplomatic as possible.

"Oh, really!" Meran replied, tapping her foot with a dangerous gleam in her eyes. "And when her father wakes tomorrow morning and finds she's been snatched by a rowdy band of tricksters? Will you still think I'm taking it all too seriously?"

"The bodachs never hurt anyone," Cerin protested. "They have a bit of fun, I'll admit, and they can be wearying at times, but they're not going to hurt anyone."

Meran sighed. "I wish they'd snatch you," she muttered and returned to their cottage to leave him sitting there, the roseharp on his knee, his gaze following the stiff set of her back.

He didn't like seeing her so upset, but when it came to bodachs she had a stubborn streak three field-lengths wide and there was simply no shifting her once she had her mind set that they were up to mischief. He considered finishing up his work early, but when he heard the clank and rattle of pots and pans being knocked about, he thought better of it. Glancing down at the music he'd just written out, he ran through the passage that was giving him difficulty again.

That night, as soon as Yocky John was sure that Meran and Cerin were asleep, he gave a low whistle. In its bag, Meran's flute changed into a little bodach and Wee Jack crawled out from the cloth folds, rubbing his hands together and dancing on the spot, hardly able to keep quiet for excitement. Before he could wake the sleeping pair, Yocky John swung down from the rafters and, grabbing Wee Jack by his jacket collar, steered him outside.

"Oh, won't this be fun," Wee Jack said. "Won't it *just*."

Yocky John looked up into the night skies, deep with stars, and nodded. "Oh, it's a grand night for a spree," he said. "Now come along and do be quiet."

He set off for the riverbank where a black horse shape rose from the water and pranced onto land. The kelpie shook his coat and water sprayed all about, glinting in the starlight.

"Ho there, Furey!" Yocky John called softly. "Are you still in the mood for a night of drink and dance?"

The kelpie shimmered in the darkness until he stood there in a bulky man-like shape. Water and weeds dripped from his clothes. His black hair lay flat against his head. Dark eyes gleamed with good humour.

"What do you think?" a new voice asked and then Peadin was stepping out from between the trees.

"Time to ride," Furey said in a deep voice. His shape shimmered again and the black horse was back. The hillhob and bodachs clambered up onto his tall back and with a shout from Wee Jack, they were off.

Meran rose as soon as the bodachs left the house. She didn't follow them to the riverbank, but made straightway for Hather's cot on the downs. But by the time she arrived it was only to see Peadin and Yocky John carrying the shepherd's daughter out of the cot. Peadin leapt nimbly onto Furey's back, then he and Wee Jack reached down to take the weight of the girl from Yocky John. The older bodach took his place behind Liane as soon as she was hoisted from his arms. Before Meran could call out, they were off again with the girl seated between Yocky John and the hillhob and Wee Jack at the fore clinging to Furey's mane.

Meran followed at a run—the quick distance-eating gait that only kowrie folk can maintain, all night if need be. But quick though she was, the kelpie was quicker, burdened down and all. Across the downs he galloped, the gorse and heather disappearing underhoof with a blur. Meran could only follow as best she could, trying to keep them in sight. When they reached the stone formation known as the Five Auld Maids, she was still a hill and a half away.

She could see Furey encircle the stones. Once. Oh, there's a spell brewing, she thought, and put on more speed. Furey circled the stones a second time, hooves drumming hollowly on the sod. An amber glow sprang up around the hill. Meran's heart was fit to burst and a pain stitched her side. Furey completed the third circuit, then leapt into the center of the standing stones with a high belling cry. Meran covered the remaining distance at a desperate gait and threw herself in amongst them as well, just as the kelpie's spell took hold, and then they were all spirited away.

A moment later, the hilltop stood empty, except for five old stones.

Cerin stirred restlessly in his sleep. He threw out an arm across the bed, but there was no oakmaid there to snuggle close to. His hand hung over the edge of the bed. He woke when Old Badger gave it a lick with his rough tongue.

Sitting up, Cerin stared around the darkened cottage. "Meran?" he called.

When there was no answer, he looked up to the rafters. There was no one there either.

"Why don't I listen to her?" he asked Old Badger as he hurriedly threw on his clothes. Slinging his roseharp across his shoulder, he set off for Hather's cot at a quick walk.

The room was smoky, especially up in the rafters where Meran found herself precariously balanced and about to fall until she clutched a support beam. She wrapped both arms around it, took a few quick breaths to steady herself, then looked around.

Further along the rafter, she spied the kowrie folk with Liane's bright red-haired head lifting above the other four. They didn't seem to be aware of Meran's presence. Below them was the commonroom of an inn. Music was playing—two fiddlers and a piper, with an old man sitting off to one side rattling a pair of bones in time to the tune. Meran recognized it as a reel that Cerin played sometimes called "The Pinch of Snuff." There were a half a dozen other mortals in the crowd—a pair dancing, three by the hearth, and the landlord on a chair by the kitchen door, tapping a foot to the music.

It was one of those rambling houses, Meran realized. A place where the local folk gathered for music and stories and songs, with the tunes and the drink and the dance going on until late in the night. No one ever knew how a certain place came to be known as the local rambling house. It was never planned. It might be a cobbler's kitchen or a farmer's barn, as soon as an inn. The best of such places simply happened. Meran had been in any number of them, for Cerin and his tinker cousins seemed to sniff them out no matter where they happened to be.

It was not a place for a girl of fourteen, Meran thought. She wondered why on earth the kowrie folk needed Liane here. She turned her attention back to them.

"Now do you remember the words we taught you?" Yocky John was asking Liane in a low voice that Meran could only just make out.

The shepherd girl nodded. Her face was flushed and there was a sparkle of excitement in her eyes. She cleared her throat and leaned over the rafter.

"Liane, don't!" Meran called to her, pitching her voice as low as Yocky John's.

Five heads turned as one towards her.

"Oh-oh," Wee Jack said nervously.

"Have you lost your senses?" Meran demanded. "What are you doing to the poor girl?"

"No harm, that's for sure," Yocky John retorted. "Broom and heather, Mistress, what do you take us for?"

"Incorrigible mischief-makers. Kidnappers. Troublemakers. That child you've stolen—she's just fourteen."

"We needed her young," Yocky John said. "We needed a human to speak the charm that will let us join the spree below without the folk knowing we've come, and we needed her young because it's the young humans that still believe enough to make a kowrie spell work from their lips."

Meran left her perch and edged carefully along the rafter towards them. "Well, she's coming straight home with me and you can speak your own spells."

"Oh, please," Wee Jack said. He stood up and came towards her. "Don't spoil the fun. I've never been to a spree."

"You move aside, or I'll—"

Meran never finished her threat. Wee Jack, swaying on the rafter, lost his balance and fell.

Yocky John grabbed for his collar and missed.

Meran grabbed as well, but her fingers closed only on air.

Horrified, they watched Wee Jack fall, wailing and cartwheeling his limbs. But when he hit the floor, it was a flute that struck the hardwood boards and broke in two with a snap.

Utter silence fell like a leaden weight across the commonroom. Ten humans looked from the broken instrument lying on the floor, up to the rafters where they all clung, staring down.

"Oh, no." Meran was sure her heart had stopped. Tears welled in her eyes.

"You've killed him," Yocky John said flatly.

"Hey!" the inn's landlord called up in an angry voice. "What are you doing up there?"

"Take us away," Peadin said to Furey.

"Can't," the kelpie replied. "Wee Jack was a part of the coming spell, so he's got to be a part of the going back one as well."

The landlord got a big axe from behind his kitchen door and waved it in their direction. A couple of the other men ranked themselves beside him, stout canes in hand.

"Get down here!" the landlord cried. "I'll have your skins for sneaking about in my rafters."

"It's looking ugly," Furey said softly to Yocky John. "Best we get down there and I'll give them a taste of a kelpie's hooves. We'll see how well they can shout while they're choking on their own teeth."

Meran barely heard what any of them were saying. She stared down at the broken flute through a blur of tears. She couldn't believe that the little bodach was dead. And that was not all.... The flute was one of the three charms that Cerin had made from her lifetree to call her back from the realm of the dead. A comb and a pendant were the other two. She had them still, but it needed all three for the harper's spell to work. Already she could feel the dead lands calling to her.

"Mistress?" Yocky John called softly to her. She looked so pale and wan.

"I did kill him," she said hoarsely. "And now I'm dying, too."

Below them, the bones player and one of the fiddlers had fetched a ladder and leaned it up against the rafters.

"If you don't come down, then," the landlord cried, "I'll come up and throw you all down."

"That man has too many unpleasant words stored away in him," Furey said. "He needs to be thrashed."

"Don't make it worse than it is," Peadin said. "We'll have to pay for our trespass."

Yocky John nodded glumly. "Though we've already paid too dear a price," he said, looking down at what was left of his friend. And Meran.... She appeared to be losing her substance now as the grip of the dead lands grew stronger on her.

"Take ahold of your anger!" Peadin called to the men below. "We're coming down."

One by one they descended the ladder. Last to come was Meran who ignored the men and went to the broken flute. Sitting on the floor, she took the broken pieces onto her lap and held them tightly.

"I didn't mean to hurt you," she whispered. "I've cheated death once, so every day I've had since then has been a gift. But you—I made you. You were meant to live a long and merry life...."

"They're kowries," the landlord said, staring at them. Here and there, some of the men made the Sign of Horns to ward themselves against evil. "Look at the green in that one's hair and the strange faces of the others."

"She's no kowrie," the piper said, pointing to Liane.

The landlord nodded. "Come here, girl. We'll rescue you."

"I don't want to be rescued," Liane told them.

"They'll have gold hidden somewhere," one of the landlord's customers said greedily. "Make them give us their gold, or we'll take it out of their skins."

The landlord didn't seem so certain anymore. Now that the little bedraggled company was standing in front of him, his anger ran from him. It was wonder he felt at this moment, that he should see such magical folk.

"I have an old flute some traveller left behind," he said to Meran. "Would you like that to replace the one that broke?"

"You don't give kowries gifts," the other man protested. "You take their gold, Oarn." He hefted his cane. "Or you lather their backs with a few sharp blows—just to keep them in line."

He took a step forward with upraised cane, but at that moment the front door of the inn was flung open and a tall figure stood outlined in the doorway.

He had long braided hair, and a long beard, and there was a fey light glimmering in his eyes. A harp was slung over his shoulder.

"Whose back do you mean to lather?" he asked in a grim voice.

"Mind your own business," the man said.

"This is my business," the harper replied. "That's my wife you mean to beat. My neighbour's child. My friends."

"Then perhaps you should pay their coin," the man said, taking a step towards the harper with his upraised cane.

"No!" the landlord cried. "No fighting!"

But he need not have spoken. Cerin brought his harp around in front of him and drew a sharp angry chord from its strings. The harp was named Telynros, a gift from the Tuathan, the Bright Gods, and it played spells as well as music. That first chord shattered the man's cane. The second loosed all the stitches in his clothing so that shirt, tunic and trousers fell away from him and he stood bare-assed naked in front of them all. The third woke a wind and propelled the man out the door. Cerin stood aside as he went by and gave him a kick on his backside to help him on his way.

"Good Master," the landlord began as Cerin turned back to face him. "We never meant—"

"They trespassed," Cerin said, "so you had reason to be angry."

"Yes, but—"

"Please," the harper said. "I have a more pressing concern."

He crossed the room to where not much more than a ghost of his wife sat, holding the two broken halves of her flute on her lap.

"Oh, Cerin," she said, looking up at him. "I've made such a botch of things." Her voice was like a whisper now, as though she spoke from a great distance away.

"You meant well."

"But I did wrong all the same, and now I have to pay the price."

Cerin shook his head. "What was broken can be mended," he said.

He sat on the floor beside her and took Telynros upon his lap. Music spilled from the roseharp's strings, a soft, healing music. Meran grew more solid and colour returned to her cheeks. The two halves of the flute joined and the wood knitted until, by the time the tune was finished, there was no sign that there had ever been a break. As Cerin took his hands from the roseharp's strings, the flute shimmered and Wee Jack lay there in Meran's lap.

"I...I think I fell," he said.

"You did," Meran told him with a smile that was warm with relief.

"I was in such a cold place. Did you catch me?"

Meran shook her head. "Cerin did."

Wee Jack looked around at the circle of faces peering down at them. Yocky John had a broad grin that almost split his face in two.

"Did I miss the spree?" Wee Jack asked.

"Is that why you came?" the landlord asked. "Because you wanted a bit of craic? Well, you're welcome to stay the night—you and all your friends."

So Cerin joined the other musicians and Meran joined him, playing the flute that the landlord had offered her earlier so that Wee Jack could caper and dance with the others. The jigs and reels sprang from their instruments until the rafters were ringing. Liane drank cider and giggled a great deal. The bodachs and Peadin stamped about the wooden floors with human partners. Furey sat in a corner with the landlord, drinking ale, swapping tales and playing endless games of sticks-a-penny. When they finally left, dawn was cracking in the eastern skies.

"You're welcome back, whenever you're by," the landlord told them, and he spoke the words from the pleasure he'd had with their company, rather than out of fear because they were kowrie folk.

"Watch what you promise bodachs," Cerin said before he spelled the roseharp and took them all home the way he'd come—on the strains of his music.

Meran held a sleepy Wee Jack in her arms. "Oh, they mean well," she said.

Behind her, Yocky John and the others laughed to hear her change her tune.

MERLIN DREAMS IN THE MONDREAM WOOD

mondream — an Anglo-Saxon word
which means the dream of life
among men

I am Merlin
Who follow the Gleam
—Tennyson, from "Merlin and the Gleam"

In the heart of the house lay a garden.

In the heart of the garden stood a tree.

In the heart of the tree lived an old man who wore the shape of a red-haired boy with crackernut eyes that seemed as bright as salmon tails glinting up the water.

His was a riddling wisdom, older by far than the ancient oak that housed his body. The green sap was his blood and leaves grew in his hair. In the winter, he slept. In the spring, the moon harped a windsong against his antler tines as the oak's boughs stretched its green buds awake. In the summer, the air was thick with the droning of bees and the scent of the wildflowers that grew in stormy profusion where the fat brown bole became root.

And in the autumn, when the tree loosed its bounty to the ground below, there were hazelnuts lying in among the acorns.

The secrets of a Green Man.

"When I was a kid, I thought it was a forest," Sara said.

She was sitting on the end of her bed, looking out the window over the garden, her guitar on her lap, the quilt bunched up under her knees. Up by the headboard, Julie Simms leaned forward from its carved wood to look over Sara's shoulder at what could be seen of the garden from their vantage point.

"It sure looks big enough," she said.

Sara nodded. Her eyes had taken on a dreamy look.

It was 1969 and they had decided to form a folk band—Sara on guitar, Julie playing recorder, both of them singing. They wanted to change the world with music because that was what was happening. In San Francisco. In London. In Vancouver. So why not in Ottawa?

With their faded bell bottom jeans and tie-dyed shirts, they looked just like any of the other seventeen-year-olds who hung around the War Memorial downtown, or could be found crowded into coffeehouses like Le Hibou and Le Monde on the weekends. Their hair was long—Sara's a cascade of brown ringlets, Julie's a waterfall spill the colour of a raven's wing; they wore beads and feather earrings and both eschewed makeup.

"I used to think it spoke to me," Sara said.

"What? The garden?"

"Um-hmm."

"What did it say?"

The dreaminess in Sara's eyes became wistful and she gave Julie a rueful smile.

"I can't remember," she said.

It was three years after her parents had died—when she was nine years old—that Sara Kendell came to live with her Uncle Jamie in his strange rambling house. To an adult perspective, Tamson House was huge: an enormous, sprawling affair of corridors and rooms and towers that took up the whole of a city block; to a child of nine, it simply went on forever.

She could wander down corridor after corridor, poking about in the clutter of rooms that spread like a maze from the northwest tower near Bank Street—where her bedroom was located—all the way over to her uncle's study overlooking O'Conner Street on the far side of the house, but mostly she spent her time in the library and in the garden. She liked the library because it was like a museum. There were walls of books, rising two floors high up to a domed ceiling, but there were also dozens of glass display cases scattered about the main floor area, each of which held any number of fascinating objects.

There were insects pinned to velvet and stone artifacts; animal skulls and clay flutes in the shapes of birds; old manuscripts and hand-drawn maps, the parchment yellowing, the ink a faded sepia; kabuki masks and a miniature Shinto shrine made of ivory and ebony; corn-husk dolls, Japanese *netsuke* and porcelain miniatures; antique jewelry and African beadwork; kachina dolls and a brass fiddle, half the size of a normal instrument....

The cases were so cluttered with interesting things that she could spend a whole day just going through one case and still have something to look at when she went back to it the next day. What interested her most, however, was that her uncle had a story to go with each and every item in the cases. No matter what she brought up to his study—a tiny ivory *netsuke* carved in the shape of a badger crawling out of a teapot, a flat stone with curious scratches on it that looked like Ogham script—he could spin out a tale of its origin that might take them right through the afternoon to suppertime.

That he dreamed up half the stories, only made it more entertaining, for then she could try to trip him up in his rambling explanations, or even just try to top his tall tales.

But if she was intellectually precocious, emotionally she still carried scars from her parents' death and the time she'd spent living with her other uncle—her father's brother. For three years Sara had been left in the care of a nanny during the day—amusing herself while the woman smoked cigarettes and watched the soaps—while at night she was put to bed promptly after dinner. It wasn't a normal family life; she could only find that vicariously in the books she devoured with a voracious appetite.

Coming to live with her Uncle Jamie, then, was like constantly being on holiday. He doted on her and on those few occasions when he *was* too busy, she could always find one of the many houseguests to spend some time with her.

All that marred her new life in Tamson House were her night fears.

She wasn't frightened of the house itself. Nor of bogies or monsters living in her closet. She knew that shadows were shadows, creaks and groans were only the house settling when the temperature changed. What haunted her nights was waking up from a deep sleep, shuddering uncontrollably, her pajamas stuck to her like a second skin, her heartbeat thundering at twice its normal tempo.

There was no logical explanation for the terror that gripped her—once, sometimes twice a week. It just came, an awful, indescribable panic that left her shivering and unable to sleep for the rest of the night.

It was on the days following such nights that she went into the garden. The greenery and flowerbeds and statuary all combined to soothe her. Invariably, she found herself in the very center of the garden where an ancient oak tree stood on a knoll and overhung a fountain. Lying on the grass sheltered by its boughs, with the soft lullaby of the fountain's water murmuring close at hand, she would find what the night fears had stolen from her the night before.

She would sleep.

And she would dream the most curious dreams.

"The garden has a name, too," she told her uncle when she came in from sleeping under the oak one day.

The house was so big that many of the rooms had been given names just so that they could all be kept straight in their minds.

"It's called the Mondream Wood," she told him.

She took his look of surprise to mean that he didn't know or understand the word.

"It means that the trees in it dream that they're people," she explained.

Her uncle nodded. "'The dream of life among men.' It's a good name. Did you think it up yourself?"

"No. Merlin told me."

"*The* Merlin?" her uncle asked with a smile.

Now it was her turn to look surprised.

"What do you mean *the* Merlin?" she asked.

Her uncle started to explain, astonished that in all her reading she hadn't come across a reference to Britain's most famous wizard, but then just gave her a copy of Malory's *La Morte d'Arthure* and, after a moment's consideration, T. H. White's *The Sword in the Stone* as well.

"Did you ever have an imaginary friend when you were a kid?" Sara asked as she finally turned away from the window.

Julie shrugged. "My mom says I did, but I can't remember. Apparently he was a hedgehog the size of a toddler named Whatzit."

"I never did. But I can remember that for a long time I used to wake up in the middle of the night just terrified and then I wouldn't be able to sleep again for the rest of the night. I used to go into the middle of the garden the next day and sleep under that big oak that grows by the fountain."

"How pastoral," Julie said.

Sara grinned. "But the thing is, I used to dream that there was a boy living in that tree and his name was Merlin."

"Go on," Julie scoffed.

"No, really. I mean, I really had these dreams. The boy would just step out of the tree and we'd sit there and talk away the afternoon."

"What did you talk about?"

"I don't remember," Sara said. "Not the details—just the feeling. It was all very magical and…healing, I suppose. Jamie said that my having those night fears was just my unconscious mind's way of dealing with the trauma of losing my parents and then having to live with my dad's brother who only wanted my inheritance, not me. I was too young then to know anything about that kind of thing; all I knew was that when I talked to Merlin, I felt better. The night fears started coming less and less often and then finally they went away altogether.

"I think Merlin took them away for me."

"What happened to him?"

"Who?"

"The boy in the tree," Julie said. "Your Merlin. When did you stop dreaming about him?"

"I don't really know. I guess when I stopped waking up terrified, I just stopped sleeping under the tree so I didn't see him anymore. And then I just forgot that he'd ever been there…."

Julie shook her head. "You know, you can be a bit of flake sometimes."

"Thanks a lot. At least I didn't hang around with a giant hedgehog named Whatzit when I was a kid."

"No. You hung out with tree-boy."

Julie started to giggle and then they both broke up. It was a few moments before either of them could catch their breath.

"So what made you think of your tree-boy?" Julie asked.

Another giggle welled up in Julie's throat, but Sara's gaze had drifted back out the window and become all dreamy again.

"I don't know," she said. "I was just looking out at the garden and I suddenly found myself remembering. I wonder whatever happened to him?"

"Jamie gave me some books about a man with the same name as you," she told the red-haired boy the next time she saw him. "And after I read them, I went into the library and found some more. He was quite famous, you know."

"So I'm told," the boy said with a smile.

"But it's all so confusing," Sara went on. "There's all these different stories, supposedly about the same man.... How are you supposed to know which of them is true?"

"That's what happens when legend and myth meet," the boy said. "Everything gets tangled."

"Was there even a *real* Merlin, do you think? I mean, besides you."

"A great magician who was eventually trapped in a tree?"

Sara nodded.

"I don't think so," the boy said.

"Oh."

Sara didn't even try to hide her disappointment.

"But that's not to say there was never a man named Merlin," the boy added. "He might have been a bard, or a follower of old wisdoms. His enchantments might have been more subtle than the great acts of wizardry ascribed to him in the stories."

"And did he end up in a tree?" Sara asked eagerly. "That would make him like you. I've also read that he got trapped in a cave, but I think a tree's much more interesting, don't you?"

Because her Merlin lived in a tree.

"Perhaps it was in the idea of a tree," the boy said.

Sara blinked in confusion. "What do you mean?"

"The stories seem to be saying that one shouldn't teach, or else the student becomes too knowledgeable and then turns on the teacher. I don't believe that. It's not the passing on of knowledge that would root someone like Merlin."

"Well, then what would?"

"Getting too tangled up in his own quest for understanding. Delving so deeply into the calendaring trees that he lost track of where he left his body, until one day he looked around to find that he'd become what he was studying."

"I don't understand."

The red-haired boy smiled. "I know. But I can't speak any more clearly."

"Why not?" Sara asked, her mind still bubbling with the tales of quests and wizards and knights that she'd been reading. "Were you enchanted? Are you trapped in that oak tree?"

She was full of curiosity and determined to find out all she could, but in that practiced way that the boy had, he artfully turned the conversation onto a different track and she never did get an answer to her questions.

It rained that night, but the next night the skies were clear. The moon hung above the Mondream Wood like a fat ball of golden honey; the stars were so bright and close Sara felt she could just reach up and pluck one as though it was an apple, hanging in a tree. She had crept from her bedroom in the northwest tower and gone out into the garden, stepping secretly as a thought through the long darkened corridors of the house until she was finally outside.

She was looking for magic.

Dreams were one thing. She knew the difference between what you found in a dream and when you were awake; between a fey red-haired boy who lived in a tree and real boys; between the dream-like enchantments of the books she'd been reading—enchantments that lay thick as acorns under an oak tree—and the real world where magic was a card trick, or a stage magician pulling a rabbit out of a hat on the *Ed Sullivan Show*.

But the books also said that magic came awake in the night. It crept from its secret hidden places—called out by starlight and the moon—and lived until the dawn pinked the eastern skies. She always dreamed of the red-haired boy when she slept under his oak in the middle of the garden. But what if he was more than a dream? What if at night he stepped out of his tree—really and truly, flesh and blood and bone real?

There was only one way to find out.

Sara felt restless after Julie went home. She put away her guitar and then distractedly set about straightening up her room. But for every minute she spent on the task, she spent three just looking out the window at the garden.

I never dream, she thought.

Which couldn't be true. Everything she'd read about sleep research and dreaming said that she had to dream. People just needed to. Dreams were supposed to be the way your subconscious cleared up the day's clutter. So, *ipso facto*, everybody dreamed. She just didn't remember hers.

But I did when I was a kid, she thought. Why did I stop? How could I have forgotten the red-haired boy in the tree?

Merlin.

Dusk fell outside her window to find her sitting on the floor, arms folded on the windowsill, chin resting on her arms as she looked out over the garden. As the twilight deepened, she finally stirred. She gave up the pretense of cleaning up her room. Putting on a jacket, she went downstairs and out into the garden.

Into the Mondream Wood.

Eschewing the paths that patterned the garden, she walked across the dew-wet grass, fingering the damp leaves of the bushes and the low-hanging branches of the trees. The dew made her remember Gregor Penev—an old Bulgarian artist who'd been staying in the house when she was a lot younger. He'd been full of odd little stories and explanations for natural occurrences much like Jamie was, which was probably why Gregor and her uncle had gotten along so well.

"*Zaplakala e gorata*," he'd replied when she'd asked him where dew came from and what it was for. "The forest is crying. It remembers the old heroes who lived under its branches—the heroes and the magicians, all lost and gone now. Robin Hood. Indje Voivode. Myrddin."

Myrddin. That was another name for Merlin. She remembered reading somewhere that Robin Hood was actually a Christianized Merlin, the Anglo version of his name being a variant of his Saxon name of Rof Breocht Woden—the Bright Strength of Wodan. But if you went back far enough, all the names and stories got tangled up in one story. The tales of the historical Robin Hood, like those of the historical Merlin of the Borders, had acquired older mythic elements common to the world as a whole by the time they were written down. The story that their legends were really telling was that of the seasonal hero-king, the May Bride's consort, who, with his cloak of leaves and his horns, and all his varying forms, was the secret truth that lay in the heart of every forest.

"But those are European heroes," she remembered telling Gregor. "Why would the trees in our forest be crying for them?"

"All forests are one," Gregor had told her, his features serious for a change. "They are all echoes of the first forest that gave birth to Mystery when the world began."

She hadn't really understood him then, but she was starting to understand him now as she made her way to the fountain at the center of the garden where the old oak tree stood guarding its secrets in the heart of the Mondream Wood. There were two forests for every one you entered. There was the one you walked in, the physical echo, and then there was the one that was connected to all the other forests, with no consideration of distance, or time.

The forest primeval. Remembered through the collective memory of every tree in the same way that people remembered myth—through the collective subconscious that Jung mapped, the shared mythic resonance that lay buried in every human mind. Legend and myth, all tangled in an alphabet of trees, remembered, not always with understanding, but with wonder. With awe.

Which was why the druids' Ogham was also a calendar of trees.

Why Merlin was often considered to be a druid.

Why Robin was the name taken by the leaders of witch covens.

Why the Green Man had antlers—because a stag's tines are like the branches of a tree.

Why so many of the early avatars were hung from a tree. Osiris. Balder. Dionysus. Christ.

Sara stood in the heart of the Mondream Wood and looked up at the old oak tree. The moon lay behind its branches, mysteriously close. The air was filled with an electric charge, as though a storm was approaching, but there wasn't a cloud in the sky.

"Now I remember what happened that night," Sara said softly.

Sara grew to be a small woman, but at nine years old she was just a tiny waif—no bigger than a minute, as Jamie liked to say. With her diminutive size she could slip soundlessly through thickets that would allow no egress for an adult. And that was how she went.

She was a curly-haired gamine, ghosting through the hawthorn hedge that bordered the main path. Whispering across the small glade guarded by the statue of a little horned man that Jamie said was Favonius, but she privately thought of as Peter Pan, though he bore no resemblance to the pictures in her Barrie book. Tiptoeing through the wildflower garden, a regular gallimaufry of flowering plants, both common and exotic. And then she was near the fountain. She could see Merlin's oak, looming up above the rest of the garden like the lordly tree it was.

And she could hear voices.

She crept nearer, a small shadow hidden in deeper patches cast by the fat yellow moon.

"—never a matter of choice," a man's voice was saying. "The lines of our lives are laid out straight as a dodman's leys, from event to event. You chose your road."

She couldn't see the speaker, but the timbre of his voice was low and resonating, like a deep bell. She couldn't recognize it, but she did recognize Merlin's when he replied to the stranger.

"When I chose my road, there was no road. There was only the trackless wood; the hills, lying crest to crest like low-backed waves; the glens where the harps were first imagined and later strung. Ca'canny, she told me when I came into the Wood. I thought go gentle meant go easy, not go fey; that the oak guarded the Borders, marked its boundaries. I never guessed it was a door."

"All knowledge is a door," the stranger replied. "You knew that."

"In theory," Merlin replied.

"You meddled."

"I was born to meddle. That was the part I had to play."

"But when your part was done," the stranger said, "you continued to meddle."

"It's in my nature, father. Why else was I chosen?"

There was a long silence then. Sara had an itch on her nose but she didn't dare move a hand to scratch it. She mulled over what she'd overheard, trying to understand.

It was all so confusing. From what they were saying it seemed that her Merlin *was* the Merlin in the stories. But if that was true, then why did he look like a boy her own age? How could he even still be alive? Living in a tree in Jamie's garden and talking to his father....

"I'm tired," Merlin said. "And this is an old argument, father. The winters are too short. I barely step into a dream and then it's spring again. I need a longer rest. I've earned a longer rest. The Summer Stars call to me."

"Love bound you," the stranger said.

"An oak bound me. I never knew she was a tree."

"You knew. But you preferred to ignore what you knew because you had to riddle it all. The salmon wisdom of the hazel wasn't enough. You had to partake of the fruit of every tree."

"I've learned from my error," Merlin said. "Now set me free, father."

"I can't. Only love can unbind you."

"I can't be found, I can't be seen," Merlin said. "What they remember of me is so tangled up in Romance, that no one can find the man behind the tales. Who is there to love me?"

Sara pushed her way out of the thicket where she'd been hiding and stepped into the moonlight.

"There's me," she began, but then her voice died in her throat.

There was no red-haired boy standing by the tree. Instead, she found an old man with the red-haired boy's eyes. And a stag. The stag turned its antlered head towards her and regarded her with a gaze that sent shivers scurrying up and down her spine. For a long moment its gaze held hers, then it turned, its flank flashing red in the moonlight, and the darkness swallowed it.

Sara shivered. She wrapped her arms around herself, but she couldn't escape the chill.

The stag....

That was impossible. The garden had always been strange, seeming so much larger than its acreage would allow, but there couldn't possibly be a deer living in it without her having seen it before. Except.... What about a boy becoming an old man overnight? A boy who really and truly did live in a tree?

"Sara," the old man said.

It was Merlin's voice. Merlin's eyes. Her Merlin grown into an old man.

"You...you're old," she said.

"Older than you could imagine."

"But—"

"I came to you as you'd be most likely to welcome me."

"Oh."

"Did you mean what you said?" he asked.

Memories flooded Sara. She remembered a hundred afternoons of warm companionship. All those hours of quiet conversation and games. The peace that came from her night fears. If she said yes, then he'd go away. She'd lose her friend. And the night fears.... Who'd be there to make the terrors go away? Only he had been able to help her. Not Jamie nor anyone else who lived in the house, though they'd all tried.

"You'll go away...won't you?" she said.

He nodded. An old man's nod. But the eyes were still young. Young and old, wise and silly, all at the same time. Her red-haired boy's eyes.

"I'll go away," he replied. "And you won't remember me."

"I won't forget," Sara said. "I would never forget."

"You won't have a choice," Merlin said. "Your memories of me would come with me when I go."

"They'd be...gone forever...?"

That was worse than losing a friend. That was like the friend never having been there in the first place.

"Forever," Merlin said. "Unless...."

His voice trailed off, his gaze turned inward.

"Unless what?" Sara asked finally.

"I could try to send them back to you when I reach the other side of the river."

Sara blinked with confusion. "What do you mean? The other side of what river?"

"The Region of the Summer Stars lies across the water that marks the boundary between what is and what has been. It's a long journey to that place. Sometimes it takes many lifetimes."

They were both quiet then. Sara studied the man that her friend had become. The gaze he returned her was mild. There were no demands in it. There was only regret. The sorrow of parting. A fondness that asked for nothing in return.

Sara stepped closer to him, hesitated a moment longer, then hugged him.

"I do love you, Merlin," she said. "I can't say I don't when I do."

She felt his arms around her, the dry touch of his lips on her brow.

"Go gentle," he said. "But beware the calendaring of the trees."

And then he was gone.

One moment they were embracing and the next her arms only held air. She let them fall limply to her sides. The weight of an awful sorrow bowed her head. Her throat grew thick, her chest tight. She swayed where she stood, tears streaming from her eyes.

The pain felt like it would never go away.

But the next thing she knew she was waking in her bed in the northwest tower and it was the following morning. She woke from a dreamless sleep, clear-eyed and smiling. She didn't know it, but her memories of Merlin were gone.

But so were her night fears.

The older Sara, still not a woman, but old enough to understand more of the story now, fingered a damp leaf and looked up into the spreading canopy of the oak above her.

Could any of that really have happened? she wondered.

The electric charge she'd felt in the air when she'd approached the old oak was gone. That pregnant sense of something about to happen had faded. She was left with the moon, hanging lower now, the stars still bright, the garden quiet. It was all magical, to be sure, but natural magic—not supernatural.

She sighed and kicked at the autumn debris that lay thick about the base of the old tree. Browned leaves, broad and brittle. And acorns. Hundreds of acorns. Fred the gardener would be collecting them soon for his compost—at least those that the black squirrels didn't hoard away against the winter. She went down on one knee and picked up a handful of them, letting them spill out of her hand.

Something different about one of them caught her eye as it fell and she plucked it up from the ground. It was a small brown ovoid shape, an incongruity in the crowded midst of all the capped acorns. She held it up to her eye. Even in the moonlight she could see what it was.

A hazelnut.

Salmon wisdom locked in a seed.

Had she regained memories, memories returned to her now from a place where the Summer Stars always shone, or had she just had a dream in the Mondream Wood where as a child she'd thought that the trees dreamed they were people?

Smiling, she pocketed the nut, then slowly made her way back into the house.

THE STONE DRUM

There is no question that there
is an unseen world. The problem
is how far is it from midtown and
how late is it open?
—attributed to Woody Allen

It was Jilly Coppercorn who found the stone drum, late one afternoon.

She brought it around to Professor Dapple's rambling Tudor-styled house in the old quarter of Lower Crowsea that same evening, wrapped up in folds of brown paper and tied with twine. She rapped sharply on the Professor's door with the little brass lion's head knocker that always seemed to stare too intently at her, then stepped back as Olaf Goonasekara, Dapple's odd little housekeeper, flung the door open and glowered out at where she stood on the rickety porch.

"You," he grumbled.

"Me," she agreed, amicably. "Is Bramley in?"

"I'll see," he replied and shut the door.

Jilly sighed and sat down on one of the two worn rattan chairs that stood to the left of the door, her package bundled on her knee. A black and orange cat regarded her incuriously from the seat of the other chair, then turned to watch the progress of a woman walking her dachshund down the street.

Professor Dapple still taught a few classes at Butler U., but he wasn't nearly as involved with the curriculum as he had been when Jilly attended the university. There'd been some kind of a scandal—something about a Bishop, some old coins and the daughter of a Tarot reader—but Jilly had never quite got the story straight. The Professor was a jolly fellow—wizened like an old apple, but more active than many who were only half his apparent sixty years of age. He could talk and joke all night, incessantly polishing his wire-rimmed spectacles for which he didn't even have a prescription.

What he was doing with someone like Olaf Goonasekara as a housekeeper Jilly didn't know. It was true that Goon looked comical enough, what with his protruding stomach and puffed cheeks, the halo of unruly hair and his thin little arms and legs, reminding her of nothing so much as a pumpkin with twig limbs, or a monkey. His usual striped trousers, organ grinder's jacket and the little green and yellow cap he liked to wear, didn't help. Nor did the fact that he was barely four feet tall and that the Professor claimed he was a goblin and just called him Goon.

It didn't seem to allow Goon much dignity and Jilly would have understood his grumpiness, if she didn't know that he himself insisted on being called Goon and his wardrobe was entirely of his own choosing. Bramley hated Goon's sense of fashion—or rather, his lack thereof.

The door was flung open again and Jilly stood up to find Goon glowering at her once more.

"He's in," he said.

Jilly smiled. As if he'd actually had to go in and check.

They both stood there, Jilly on the porch and he in the doorway, until Jilly finally asked, "Can he see me?"

Giving an exaggerated sigh, Goon stepped aside to let her in.

"I suppose you'll want something to drink?" he asked as he followed her to the door of the Professor's study.

"Tea would be lovely."

"Hrumph."

Jilly watched him stalk off, then tapped a knuckle on the study's door and stepped into the room. Bramley lifted his gaze from a desk littered with tottering stacks of books and papers and grinned at her from between a gap in the towers of paper.

"I've been doing some research since you called," he said. He poked a finger at a book that Jilly couldn't see, then began to clean his glasses. "Fascinating stuff."

"And hello to you, too," Jilly said.

"Yes, of course. Did you know that the Kickaha had legends of a little people long before the Europeans ever settled this area?"

Jilly could never quite get used to Bramley's habit of starting conversations in the middle. She removed some magazines from a club chair and perched on the edge of its seat, her package clutched to her chest.

"What's that got to do with anything?" she asked.

Bramley looked surprised. "Why everything. We *are* still looking into the origins of this artifact of yours, aren't we?"

Jilly nodded. From her new position of vantage she could make out the book he'd been reading. *Underhill and Deeper Still*, a short story collection by Christy Riddell. Riddell made a living of retelling the odd stories that lie just under the skin of any large city. This particular one was a collection of urban legends of Old City and other subterranean fancies—not exactly the factual reference source she'd been hoping for.

Old City was real enough; that was where she'd found the drum this afternoon. But as for the rest of it—albino crocodile subway conductors, schools of dog-sized intelligent goldfish in the sewers, mutant rat debating societies and the like....

Old City was the original heart of Newford. It lay deep underneath the subway tunnels—dropped there in the late eighteen hundreds during the Great Quake. The present city, including its sewers and underground transportation tunnels, had been built above the ruins of the old one. There'd been talk in the early seventies of renovating the ruins as a tourist attraction—as had been done in Seattle—but Old City lay too far underground for easy access. After numerous studies on the project, the city council had decided that it simply wouldn't be cost efficient.

With that decision Old City had rapidly gone from a potential tourist attraction to a home for skells—winos, bagladies and the other homeless. Not to mention, if one was to believe Bramley and Riddell, bands of ill-mannered goblin-like creatures that Riddell called skookin—a word he'd stolen from old Scots which meant, variously, ugly, furtive and sullen.

Which, Jilly realized once when she thought about it, made it entirely appropriate that Bramley should claim Goon was related to them.

"You're not going to tell me it's a skookin artifact are you?" she asked Bramley now.

"Too soon to say," he replied. He nodded at her parcel. "Can I see it?"

Jilly got up and brought it over to the desk where Bramley made a great show of cutting the twine and unwrapping the paper. Jilly couldn't decide if he was pretending it was the unveiling of a new piece at the museum or his birthday. But then the drum was sitting on the desk, the mica and quartz veins in its stone catching the light from Bramley's desk lamp in a magical glitter, and she was swallowed up in the wonder of it again.

It was tube-shaped, standing about a foot high, with a seven-inch diameter at the top and five inches at the bottom. The top was smooth as the skin head of a drum. On the sides were what appeared to be the remnants of a bewildering flurry of designs. But what was most marvelous about it was that the stone was hollow. It weighed about the same as a fat hardcover book.

"Listen," Jilly said and gave the top of the drum a rap-a-tap-tap.

The stone responded with a quiet rhythm that resonated eerily in the study. Unfortunately, Goon chose that moment to arrive in the doorway with a tray laden with tea mugs, teapot and a platter of his homemade biscuits. At the sound of the drum, the tray fell from his hands. It hit the floor with a crash, spraying tea, milk, sugar, biscuits and bits of crockery every which way.

Jilly turned, her heartbeat double-timing in her chest, just in time to see an indescribable look cross over Goon's features. It might have been surprise, it might have been laughter, but it was gone too quickly for her to properly note. He merely stood in the doorway now, his usual glowering look on his face, and all Jilly was left with was a feeling of unaccountable guilt.

"I didn't mean…." Jilly began, but her voice trailed off.

"Bit of a mess," Bramley said.

"I'll get right to it," Goon said.

His small dark eyes centered their gaze on Jilly for too long a moment, then he turned away to fetch a broom and dustpan. When Jilly turned back to the desk, she found Bramley rubbing his hands together, face pressed close to the stone drum. He looked up at her over his glasses, grinning.

"Did you see?" he said. "Goon recognized it for what it is, straight off. It has to be a skookin artifact. Didn't like you meddling around with it either."

That was hardly the conclusion that Jilly would have come to on her own. It was the sudden and unexpected sound that had more than likely startled Goon—as it might have startled anyone who wasn't expecting it. That was the reasonable explanation, but she knew well enough that reasonable didn't necessarily always mean right. When she thought of that look that had passed over Goon's features, like a trough of surprise or mocking humour between two cresting glowers, she didn't know what to think, so she let herself get taken away by the Professor's enthusiasm, because…well, just what if…?

Judging by all of Christy Riddell's accounts, there wasn't a better candidate for skookin-dom than Bramley's housekeeper.

"What does it mean?" she asked.

Bramley shrugged and began to polish his glasses. Jilly was about to nudge him into making at least the pretense of a theory, but then she realized that the Professor had simply fallen silent because Goon was back to clean up the mess. She waited until Goon had made his retreat with the promise of putting on another pot of tea, before she leaned over Bramley's desk.

"Well?" she asked.

"Found it in Old City, did you?" he replied.

Jilly nodded.

"You know what they say about skookin treasure…?"

They meaning he and Riddell, Jilly thought, but she obliging tried to remember that particular story from *Underhill and Deeper Still.* She had it after a moment. It was the one called "The Man With the Monkey" and had something to do with a stolen apple that was withered and moldy in Old City but became solid gold when it was brought above ground. At the end of the story, the man who'd stolen it from the skookin was found in little pieces scattered all over Fitzhenry Park….

Jilly shivered.

"Now I remember why I don't always like to read Christy's stuff," she said. "He can be so sweet on one page, and then on the next he's taking you on a tour through an abattoir."

"Just like life," Bramley said.

"Wonderful. So what are you saying?"

"They'll be wanting it back," Bramley said.

Jilly woke some time after midnight with the Professor's words ringing in her ears.

They'll be wanting it back.

She glanced at the stone drum where it sat on a crate by the window of her Yoors Street loft in Foxville. From where she lay on her Murphy bed, the streetlights coming in the window woke a haloing effect around the stone artifact.

The drum glimmered with magic—or at least with a potential for magic. And there was something else in the air. A humming sound, like barely audible strains of music. The notes seemed disconnected, drifting randomly through the melody like dust motes dancing in a beam of sunlight, but there was still a melody present.

She sat up slowly. Pushing the quilt aside, she padded barefoot across the room. When she reached the drum, the change in perspective made the street-light halo slide away; the drum's magic fled. It was just an odd stone artifact once more. She ran her finger along the smoothed indentations that covered the sides of the artifact, but didn't touch the top. It was still marvelous enough—a hollow stone, a mystery, a puzzle. But....

She remembered the odd almost-but-not-quite music she'd heard when she first woke and cocked her ear, listening for it.

Nothing.

Outside, a light drizzle had wet the pavement, making Yoors Street glisten and sparkle with its sheen. She knelt down by the windowsill and leaned forward, looking out, feeling lonely. It'd be nice if Geordie were here, even if his brother did write those books that had the Professor so enamoured, but Geordie was out of town this week. Maybe she should get a cat or a dog—just something to keep her company when she got into one of these odd funks—but the problem with pets was that they tied you down. No more gallivanting about whenever and wherever you pleased. Not when the cat needed to be fed. Or the dog had to be walked.

Sighing, she started to turn from the window, then paused. A flicker of uneasiness stole up her spine as she looked more closely at what had caught her attention—there, across the street. Time dissolved into a pattern as random as that faint music she'd heard when she woke earlier. Minutes and seconds marched sideways; the hands of the old Coors clock on her wall stood still.

A figure leaned against the wall, there, just to one side of the display window of the Chinese grocer across the street, a figure as much a patchwork as the disarray in the shop's window. Pumpkin head under a wide-brimmed hat. A larger pumpkin for the body with what looked like straw spilling out from between the buttons of its too-small jacket. Arms and legs as thin as broom handles. A wide slit for a mouth; eyes like the sharp yellow slits of a Jack o' Lantern with a candle burning inside.

A Halloween creature. And not alone.

There was another, there, in the mouth of that alleyway. A third clinging to the wall of the brownstone beside the grocer. Four more on the rooftop directly across the street—pumpkinheads lined up along the parapet, all in a row.

Skookin, Jilly thought and she shivered with fear, remembering Christy's story.

Damn Christy for tracking that story down, and damn the Professor for reminding her of it. And damn the job that had sent her down into Old City in the first place to take photos for the background of the painting she was currently working on.

Because there shouldn't be any such thing as skookin. Because....

She blinked, then rubbed her eyes. Her gaze darted left and right, up and down, raking the street and the faces of buildings across the way.

Nothing.

No pumpkin goblins watching her loft.

The sound of her clock ticking the seconds away was suddenly loud in her ears. A taxi went by on the street below, spraying a fine sheet of water from its wheels. She waited for it to pass, then studied the street again.

There were no skookin.

Of course there wouldn't be, she told herself, trying to laugh at how she'd let her imagination run away with itself, but she couldn't muster up even the first hint of a smile. She looked at the drum, reached a hand towards it, then let her hand fall to her lap, the drum untouched. She turned her attention back to the street, watching it for long moments before she finally had to accept that there was nothing out there, that she had only peopled it with her own night fears.

Pushing herself up from the sill, she returned to bed and lay down again. The palm of her right hand itched a little, right where she'd managed to poke herself on a small nail or wood sliver while she was down in Old City. She scratched her hand and stared up at the ceiling, trying to go to sleep, but not expecting to have much luck. Surprisingly, she drifted off in moments.

And dreamed.

Of Bramley's study. Except the Professor wasn't ensconced behind his desk as usual. Instead, he was setting out a serving of tea for her and Goon, who had taken the Professor's place behind the tottering stacks of papers and books on the desk.

"Skookin," Goon said, when the Professor had finished serving them their tea and left the room. "They've never existed, of course."

Jilly nodded in agreement.

"Though in some ways," Goon went on, "they've always existed. In here—" He tapped his temple with a gnarly, very skookin-like finger. "In our imaginations."

"But—" Jilly began, wanting to tell him how she'd *seen* skookin, right out there on her very own street tonight, but Goon wasn't finished.

"And that's what makes them real," he said.

His head suddenly looked very much like a pumpkin. He leaned forward, eyes glittering as though a candle was burning there inside his head, flickering in the wind.

"And if they're real," he said.

His voice wound down alarmingly, as though it came from the spiraling groove of a spoken word album that someone had slowed by dragging their finger along on the vinyl.

"Then. You're. In. A. Lot. Of—"

Jilly awoke with a start to find herself backed up against the frame of the head of her bed, her hands worrying and tangling her quilt into knots.

Just a dream. Cast-off thoughts, tossed up by her subconscious. Nothing to worry about. Except....

She could finish the dream-Goon's statement.

If they were real....

Never mind being in trouble. If they were real, then she was doomed.

She didn't get any more sleep that night, and first thing the next morning, she went looking for help.

"Skookin," Meran said, trying hard not to laugh.

"Oh, I know what it sounds like," Jilly said, "but what can you do? Christy's books are Bramley's pet blind spot and if you listen to him long enough, he'll have you believing anything."

"But skookin," Meran repeated and this time she did giggle.

Jilly couldn't help but laugh with her.

Everything felt very different in the morning light—especially when she had someone to talk it over with whose head wasn't filled with Christy's stories.

They were sitting in Kathryn's Café—an hour or so after Jilly had found Meran Kelledy down by the Lake, sitting on the Pier and watching the early morning joggers run across the sand—yuppies from downtown, health-conscious gentry from the Beaches.

It was a short walk up Battersfield Road to where Kathryn's was nestled in the heart of Lower Crowsea. Like the area itself, with its narrow streets and old stone buildings, the café had an old world feel about it—from the dark wood paneling and hand-carved chair backs to the small round tables, with checkered tablecloths, fat glass condiment containers and straw-wrapped wine bottles used as candleholders. The music piped in over the house sound system was mostly along the lines of Telemann and Vivaldi, Kitaro and old Bob James albums. The waitresses wore cream-coloured pinafores over flowerprint dresses.

But if the atmosphere was old world, the clientele were definitely contemporary. Situated so close to Butler U., Kathryn's had been a favourite haunt of the university's students since it first opened its doors in the mid-sixties as a coffeehouse. Though much had changed from those early days, there was still music played on its small stage on Friday and Saturday nights, as well as poetry recitations on Wednesdays, and Sunday morning storytelling sessions.

Jilly and Meran sat by a window, coffee and homemade banana muffins set out on the table in front of them.

"Whatever were you *doing* down there anyway?" Meran asked. "It's not exactly the safest place to be wandering about."

Jilly nodded. The skells in Old City weren't all thin and wasted. Some were big and mean-looking, capable of anything—not really the sort of people Jilly should be around, because if something went wrong. . .well, she was the kind of woman for whom the word petite had been coined. She was small and slender—her tiny size only accentuated by the oversized clothing she tended to wear. Her brown hair was a thick tangle, her eyes the electric blue of sapphires.

She was too pretty and too small to be wandering about in places like Old City on her own.

"You know the band, No Nuns Here?" Jilly asked.

Meran nodded.

"I'm doing the cover painting for their first album," Jilly explained. "They wanted something moody for the background—sort of like the Tombs, but darker and grimmer—and I thought Old City would be the perfect place to get some reference shots."

"But to go there on your own. . . ."

Jilly just shrugged. She was known to wander anywhere and everywhere, at any time of the night or day, camera or sketchbook in hand, often both.

Meran shook her head. Like most of Jilly's friends, she'd long since given up trying to point out the dangers of carrying on the way Jilly did.

"So you found this drum," she said.

Jilly nodded. She looked down at the little scab on the palm of her hand. It itched like crazy, but she was determined not to open it again by scratching it.

"And now you want to…?"

Jilly looked up. "Take it back. Only I'm scared to go there on my own. I thought maybe Cerin would come with me—for moral support, you know?"

"He's out of town," Meran said.

Meran and her husband made up the two halves of the Kelledys, a local traditional music duo that played coffeehouses, festivals and colleges from one coast to the other. For years now, however, Newford had been their home base.

"He's teaching another of those harp workshops," Meran added.

Jilly did her best to hide her disappointment.

What she'd told Meran about "moral support" was only partly the reason she'd wanted their help because, more so than either Christy's stories, or Bramley's askewed theories, the Kelledys were the closest thing to real magic that she could think of in Newford. There was an otherwordly air about the two of them that went beyond the glamour that seemed to always gather around people who became successful in their creative endeavours.

It wasn't something Jilly could put her finger on. It wasn't as though they went on and on about this sort of thing at the drop of a hat the way that Bramley did. Nor that they were responsible for anything more mysterious than the enchantment they awoke on stage when they were playing their instruments. It was just there. Something that gave the impression that they were aware of what lay beyond the here and now. That they could see things others couldn't; knew things that remained secret to anyone else.

Nobody even knew where they had come from; they'd just arrived in Newford a few years ago, speaking with accents that had rapidly vanished, and here they'd pretty well stayed ever since. Jilly had always privately supposed that if there was a place called Faerie, then that was from where they'd come, so when she woke up this morning, deciding she needed magical help, she'd gone looking for one or the other and found Meran. But now….

"Oh," she said.

Meran smiled.

"But that doesn't mean I can't try to help," she said.

Jilly sighed. Help with what? she had to ask herself. The more she thought about it, the sillier it all seemed. Skookin. Right. Maybe they held debating contests with Christy's mutant rats.

"I think maybe I'm nuts," she said finally. "I mean, goblins living under the city...?"

"I believe in the little people," Meran said. "We called them bodachs where I come from."

Jilly just looked at her.

"But you laughed when I talked about them," she said finally.

"I know—and I shouldn't have. It's just that whenever I hear that name that Christy's given them, I can't help myself. It's so silly."

"What I saw last night didn't feel silly," Jilly said.

If she'd actually seen anything. By this point—even with Meran's apparent belief—she wasn't sure what to think anymore.

"No," Meran said. "I suppose not. But—you're taking the drum back, so why are you so nervous?"

"The man in Christy's story returned the apple he stole," Jilly said, "and you know what happened to him...."

"That's true," Meran said, frowning.

"I thought maybe Cerin could...." Jilly's voice trailed off.

A small smile touched Meran's lips. "Could do what?"

"Well, this is going to sound even sillier," Jilly admitted, "but I've always pictured him as sort of a wizard type."

Meran laughed. "He'd love to hear that. And what about me? Have I acquired wizardly status as well?"

"Not exactly. You always struck me as being an earth spirit—like you stepped out of an oak tree or something." Jilly blushed, feeling as though she was making even more of a fool of herself than ever, but now that she'd started, she felt she had to finish. "It's sort of like he learned magic, while you just are magic."

She glanced at her companion, looking for laughter, but Meran was regarding her gravely. And she did look like a dryad, Jilly thought, what with the green streaks in the long, nut-brown ringlets of her hair and her fey sort of Pre-Raphaelite beauty. Her eyes seemed to provide their own light, rather than take it in.

"Maybe I did step out of a tree one day," Meran said.

Jilly could feel her mouth forming a surprised "O," but then Meran laughed again.

"But probably I didn't," she said. Before Jilly could ask her about that "probably," Meran went on. "We'll need some sort of protection against them."

Jilly made her mind shift gears, from Meran's origins to the problem at hand.

"Like holy water or a cross?" she asked.

Her head filled with the plots of a hundred bad horror films, each of them clamoring for attention.

"No," Meran said. "Religious artifacts and trappings require faith—a belief in their potency that the skookin undoubtedly don't have. The only thing I know for certain that they can't abide is the truth."

"The truth?"

Meran nodded. "Tell them the truth—even it's only historical facts and trivia—and they'll shun you as though you were carrying a plague."

"But what about after?" Jilly said. "After we've delivered the drum and they come looking for me? Do I have to walk around carrying a cassette machine spouting dates and facts for the rest of my life?"

"I hope not."

"But. . . ."

"Patience," Meran replied. "Let me think about it for awhile."

Jilly sighed. She regarded her companion curiously as Meran took a sip of her coffee.

"You really believe in this stuff, don't you?" she said finally.

"Don't you?"

Jilly had to think about that for a moment.

"Last night I was scared," she said, "and I'm returning the drum because I'd rather be safe than sorry, but I'm still not sure."

Meran nodded understandingly, but, "Your coffee's getting cold," was all she had to say.

Meran let Jilly stay with her that night in the rambling old house where she and Cerin lived. Straddling the border between Lower Crowsea and Chinatown, it was a tall, gabled building surrounded by giant oak trees. There was a rounded tower in the front, to the right of a long screen-enclosed porch, stables around the back and a garden along the west side of the house that seemed to have been plucked straight from a postcard of the English countryside.

Jilly loved this area. The Kelledys' house was the easternmost of the stately estates that stood, row on row, along McKennit Street, between Lee and Yoors.

Whenever Jilly walked along this part of McKennit, late at night when the streetcars were tucked away in their downtown station and there was next to no other traffic, she found it easy to imagine that the years had wound back to a bygone age when time moved at a different pace, when Newford's streets were cobblestoned and the vehicles that traversed them were horse-drawn, rather than horse-powered.

"You'll wear a hole in the glass if you keep staring through it so intently."

Jilly started. She turned long enough to acknowledge her hostess's presence, then her gaze was dragged back to the window, to the shadows cast by the oaks as twilight stretched them across the lawn, to the long low wall that bordered the lawn, to the street beyond.

Still no skookin. Did that mean they didn't exist, or that they hadn't come out yet? Or maybe they just hadn't tracked her here to the Kelledys' house.

She started again as Meran laid a hand on her shoulder and gently turned her from the window.

"Who knows what you'll call to us, staring so," Meran said.

Her voice held the same light tone as it had when she'd made her earlier comment, but this time a certain sense of caution lay behind the words.

"If they come, I want to see them," Jilly said.

Meran nodded. "I understand. But remember this: the night's a magical time. The moon rules her hours, not the sun."

"What does that mean?"

"The moon likes secrets," Meran said. "And secret things. She lets mysteries bleed into her shadows and leaves us to ask whether they originated from otherworlds, or from our own imaginations."

"You're beginning to sound like Bramley," Jilly said. "Or Christy."

"Remember your Shakespeare," Meran said. "'This fellow's wise enough to play the fool.' Did you ever think that perhaps their studied eccentricity protects them from sharper ridicule?"

"You mean all those things Christy writes about are true?"

"I didn't say that."

Jilly shook her head. "No. But you're talking in riddles just like a wizard out of some fairy tale. I never understood why they couldn't talk plainly."

"That's because some things can only be approached from the side. Secretively. Peripherally."

Whatever Jilly was about to say next, died stillborn. She pointed out the window to where the lawn was almost swallowed by shadows.

"Do...." She swallowed thickly, then tried again. "Do you see them?"

They were out there, flitting between the wall that bordered the Kelledys' property and those tall oaks that stood closer to the house. Shadow shapes. Fat, pumpkin-bodied and twig-limbed. There were more of them than there'd been last night. And they were bolder. Creeping right up towards the house. Threats burning in their candle-flicker eyes. Wide mouths open in Jack o' Lantern grins, revealing rows of pointed teeth.

One came sidling right up the window, its face monstrous at such close proximity. Jilly couldn't move, couldn't even breathe. She remembered what Meran had said earlier—

they can't abide the truth

—but she couldn't frame a sentence, never mind a word, and her mind was filled with only a wild unreasoning panic. The creature reached out a hand towards the glass, clawed fingers extended. Jilly could feel a scream building up, deep inside her. In a moment that hand would come crashing through the window, shattering glass, clawing at her throat. And she couldn't move. All she could do was stare, stare as the claws reached for the glass, stare as it drew back to—

Something fell between the creature and the house—a swooping, shapeless thing. The creature danced back, saw that it was only the bough of one of the oak trees and was about to begin its approach once more, but the cries of its companions distracted it. Not until it turned its horrible gaze from her, did Jilly feel able to lift her own head.

She stared at the oaks. A sudden wind had sprung up, lashing the boughs about so that the tall trees appeared to be giants, flailing about their many-limbed arms like monstrous, agitated octopi. The creatures in the yard scattered and in moments they were gone—each and every one of them. The wind died down; the animated giants became just oak trees once more.

Jilly turned slowly from the window to find Meran pressed close beside her.

"Ugly, furtive and sullen," Meran said. "Perhaps Christy wasn't so far off in naming them."

"They...they're real, aren't they?" Jilly asked in a small voice.

Meran nodded. "And not at all like the bodachs of my homeland. Bodachs are mischievous and prone to trouble, but not like this. Those creatures were weaned on malevolence."

Jilly leaned weakly against the windowsill.

"What are we going to do?" she asked.

She scratched at her palm—the itch was worse than ever. Meran caught her hand, pulled it away. There was an unhappy look in her eyes when she lifted her gaze from the mark on Jilly's palm.

"Where did you get that?" she asked.

Jilly looked down at her palm. The scab was gone, but the skin was all dark around the puncture wound now—an ugly black discolouration that was twice the size of the original scab.

"I scratched myself," she said. "Down in Old City."

Meran shook her head. "No," she said. "They've marked you."

Jilly suddenly felt weak. Skookin were real. Mysterious winds rose to animate trees. And now she was marked?

She wasn't even sure what that meant, but she didn't like the sound of it. Not for a moment.

Her gaze went to the stone drum where it stood on Meran's mantel. She didn't think she'd ever hated an inanimate object so much before.

"Marked...me...?" she asked.

"I've heard of this before," Meran said, her voice apologetic. She touched the mark on Jilly's palm. "This is like a...bounty."

"They really want to kill me, don't they?"

Jilly was surprised that her voice sounded as calm as it did. Inside she felt as though she was crumbling to little bits all over the place.

"Skookin are real," she went on, "and they're going to tear me up into little pieces—just like they did to the man in Christy's stupid story."

Meran gave her a sympathetic look.

"We have to go now," she said. "We have to go and confront them now, before...."

"Before what?"

Jilly's control over her voice was slipping. Her last word went shrieking up in pitch.

"Before they send something worse," Meran said.

Oh great, Jilly thought, as she waited for Meran to change into clothing more suitable for the underground trek to Old City. Not only were skookin real, but there were worse things than those pumpkinhead creatures living down there under the city.

She slouched in one of the chairs by the mantelpiece, her back to the stone drum, and pretended that her nerves weren't all scraped raw, that she was just over visiting a friend for the evening and everything was just peachy, thank you. Surprisingly, by the time Meran returned, wearing jeans, sturdy walking shoes and a thick woolen shirt under a denim jacket, she did feel better.

"The bit with the trees," she asked as she rose from her chair. "Did you do that?"

Meran shook her head.

"But the wind likes me," she said. "Maybe it's because I play the flute."

And maybe it's because you're a dryad, Jilly thought, and the wind's got a thing about oak trees, but she let the thought go unspoken.

Meran fetched the long, narrow bag that held her flute and slung it over her shoulder.

"Ready?" she asked.

"No," Jilly said.

But she went and took the drum from the mantelpiece and joined Meran by the front door. Meran stuck a flashlight in the pocket of her jacket and handed another to Jilly, who thrust it into the pocket of the coat Meran was lending her. It was at least two sizes too big for her, which suited Jilly just fine.

Naturally, just to make the night complete, it started to rain before they got halfway down the walk to McKennit Street.

For safety's sake, city work crews had sealed up all the entrances to Old City in the mid-seventies—all the entrances of which the city was aware, at any rate. The street people of Newford's back lanes and alleys knew of anywhere from a half-dozen to twenty others that could still be used, the number depending only on who was doing the bragging. The entrance to which Jilly led Meran was the most commonly known and used—a steel maintenance door situated two hundred yards or so down the east tracks of the Grasso Street subway station.

The door led into the city's sewer maintenance tunnels, but had long since been abandoned. Skells had broken the locking mechanism and the door stood continually ajar. Inside, time and weathering had worn down a connecting wall between the maintenance tunnels and what had once been the top floor of one of Old City's proud skyscrapers—an office complex that had towered some four stories above the city's streets before the quake dropped it into its present subterranean setting.

It was a good fifteen-minute walk from the Kelledys' house to the Grasso Street station and Jilly plodded miserably through the rain at Meran's side for every block of it. Her sneakers were soaked and her hair plastered against her scalp. She carried the stone drum tucked under one arm and was very tempted to simply pitch it in front of a bus.

"This is crazy," Jilly said. "We're just giving ourselves up to them."

Meran shook her head. "No. We're confronting them of our own free will—there's a difference."

"That's just semantics. There won't be a difference in the results."

"That's where you're wrong."

They both turned at the sound of a new voice to find Goon standing in the doorway of a closed antique shop. His eyes glittered oddly in the poor light, reminding Jilly all too much of the skookin, and he didn't seem to be the least bit wet.

"What are you doing here?" Jilly demanded.

"You must always confront your fears," Goon said as though she hadn't spoken. "Then skulking monsters become merely unfamiliar shadows, thrown by a tree bough. Whispering voices are just the wind. The wild flare of panic is merely a burst of emotion, not a terror spell cast by some evil witch."

Meran nodded. "That's what Cerin would say. And that's what I mean to do. Confront them with a truth so bright that they won't dare come near us again."

Jilly held up her hand. The discolouration was spreading. It had grown from its pinprick inception, first to the size of a dime, now to that of a silver dollar.

"What about this?" she asked.

"There's always a price for meddling," Goon agreed. "Sometimes it's the simple curse of knowledge."

"There's always a price," Meran agreed.

Everybody always seemed to know more than she did these days, Jilly thought unhappily.

"You still haven't told me what you're doing here," she told Goon. "Skulking about and following us."

Goon smiled. "It seems to me, that you came upon me."

"You know what I mean."

"I have my own business in Old City tonight," he said. "And since we all have the same destination in mind, I thought perhaps you would appreciate the company."

Everything was wrong about this, Jilly thought. Goon was never nice to her. Goon was never nice to anyone.

"Yeah, well, you can just—" she began.

Meran laid a hand on Jilly's arm. "It's bad luck to turn away help when it's freely offered."

"But you don't know what he's like," Jilly said.

"Olaf and I have met before," Meran said.

Jilly caught the grimace on Goon's face at the use of his given name. It made him seem more himself, which, while not exactly comforting, was at least familiar. Then she looked at Meran. She thought of the wind outside the musician's house driving away the skookin, the mystery that cloaked her, which ran even deeper, perhaps, than that which Goon wore so easily....

"Sometimes you just have to trust in people," Meran said, as though reading Jilly's mind.

Jilly sighed. She rubbed her itchy palm against her thigh, shifted the drum into a more comfortable position.

"Okay," she said. "So what're we waiting for?"

The few times Jilly had come down to Old City, she'd been cautious, perhaps even a little nervous, but never frightened. Tonight was different. It was always dark in Old City, but the darkness had never seemed so...so watchful before. There were always odd little sounds, but they had never seemed so furtive. Even with her companions—maybe because of them, she thought, thinking mostly of Goon—she felt very much alone in the eerie darkness.

Goon didn't appear to need the wobbly light of their flashlights to see his way and though he seemed content enough to simply follow them, Jilly couldn't shake the feeling that he was actually leading the way. They were soon in a part of the subterranean city that she'd never seen before.

There was less dust and dirt here. No litter, nor the remains of the skells' fires. No broken bottles, nor the piles of newspapers and ratty blanketing that served the skells as bedding. The buildings seemed in better repair. The air had a clean, dry smell to it, rather than the close, musty reek of refuse and human waste that it carried closer to the entrance.

And there were no people.

From when they'd first stepped through the steel door in Grasso Street station's east tunnel, she hadn't seen a baglady or wino or any kind of skell, and that in itself was odd because they were always down here. But there was something sharing the darkness with them. Something watched them, marked their progress, followed with a barely discernible pad of sly footsteps in their wake and on either side.

The drum seemed warm against the skin of her hand. The blemish on her other palm prickled with itchiness. Her shoulder muscles were stiff with tension.

"Not far now," Goon said softly and Jilly suddenly understood what it meant to jump out of one's skin.

The beam of her flashlight made a wild arc across the faces of the buildings on either side of her as she started. Her heartbeat jumped into second gear.

"What do you see?" Meran asked, her voice calm.

The beam of her flashlight turned towards Goon and he pointed ahead.

"Turn off your flashlights," he said.

Oh sure, Jilly thought. Easy for you to say.

But she did so a moment after Meran had. The sudden darkness was so abrupt that Jilly thought she'd gone blind. But then she realized that it wasn't as black as it should be. Looking ahead to where Goon had pointed, she could see a faint glow seeping onto the street ahead of them. It was a little less than a half block away, the source of the light hidden behind the squatting bulk of a half-tumbled down building.

"What could it...?" Jilly started to say, but then the sounds began, and the rest of her words dried up in her throat.

It was supposed to be music, she realized after a few moments, but there was no discernible rhythm and while the sounds were blown or rasped or plucked from instruments, they searched in vain for a melody.

"It begins," Goon said.

He took the lead, hurrying them up to the corner of the street.

"What does?" Jilly wanted to know.

"The king appears—as he must once a moon. It's that or lose his throne."

Jilly wanted to know what he was talking about—better yet, *how* he knew what he was talking about—but she didn't have a chance. The discordant not-music scraped and squealed to a kind of crescendo. Suddenly they were surrounded by the capering forms of dozens of skookin that bumped them, thin long fingers tugging at their clothing. Jilly shrieked at the first touch. One of them tried to snatch the drum from her grip. She regained control of her nerves at the same time as she pulled the artifact free from the grasping fingers.

"1789," she said. "That's when the Bastille was stormed and the French Revolution began. Uh, 1807, slave trade was abolished in the British Empire. 1776, the Declaration of Independence was signed."

The skookin backed away from her, as did the others, hissing and spitting. The not-music continued, but its tones were softened.

"Let me see," Jilly went on. "Uh, 1981, the Argentines invade—I can't keep this up, Meran—the Falklands. 1715...that was the year of the first Jacobite uprising."

She'd always been good with historical trivia—having a head for dates—but the more she concentrated on them right now, the further they seemed to slip away. The skookin were regarding her with malevolence, just waiting for her to falter.

"1978," she said. "Sandy Denny died, falling down some stairs...."

She'd got that one from Geordie. The skookin took another step back and she stepped towards them, into the light, her eyes widening with shock. There was a small park there, vegetation dead, trees leafless and skeletal, shadows dancing from the light cast by a fire at either end of the open space. And it was teeming with skookin.

There seemed to be hundreds of the creatures. She could see some of the musicians who were making that awful din—holding their instruments as though they'd never played them before. They were gathered in a semi-circle around a dais made from slabs of pavement and building rubble. Standing on it was the weirdest looking skookin she'd seen yet. He was kind of withered and stood stiffly. His eyes flashed with a dead, cold light. He had the grimmest look about him that she'd seen on any of them.

There was no way her little bits of history were going to be enough to keep back this crew. She turned to look at her companions. She couldn't see Goon, but Meran was tugging her flute free from its carrying bag.

What good was that going to do? Jilly wondered.

"It's another kind of truth," Meran said as she brought the instrument up to her lips.

The flute's clear tones echoed breathily along the street, cutting through the jangle of not-music like a glass knife through muddy water. Jilly held her breath. The music was so beautiful. The skookin cowered where they stood. Their cacophonic noisemaking faltered, then fell silent.

No one moved.

For long moments, there was just the clear sound of Meran's flute, breathing a slow plaintive air that echoed and sang down the street, winding from one end of the park to the other.

Another kind of truth, Jilly remembered Meran saying just before she began to play. That's exactly what this music was, she realized. A kind of truth.

The flute playing finally came to an achingly sweet finale and a hush fell in Old City. And then there was movement. Goon stepped from behind Jilly and walked through the still crowd of skookin to the dais where their king stood. He clambered up over the rubble until he was beside the king. He pulled a large clasp knife from the pocket of his coat. As he opened the blade, the skookin king made a jerky motion to get away, but Goon's knife hand moved too quickly.

He slashed and cut.

Now he's bloody done it, Jilly thought as the skookin king tumbled to the stones. But then she realized that Goon hadn't cut the king. He'd cut the air above the king. He'd cut the...the realization only confused her more...strings holding him?

"What...?" she said.

"Come," Meran said.

She tucked her flute under her arm and led Jilly towards the dais.

"This is your king," Goon was saying.

He reached down and pulled the limp form up by the fine-webbed strings that were attached to the king's arms and shoulders. The king dangled loosely under his strong grip—a broken marionette. A murmur rose from the crowd of skookin—part ugly, part wondering.

"The king is dead," Goon said. "He's been dead for moons. I wondered why Old City was closed to me this past half year, and now I know."

There was movement at the far end of the park—a fleeing figure. It had been the king's councilor, Goon told Jilly and Meran later. Some of the skookin made to chase him, but Goon called them back.

"Let him go," he said. "He won't return. We have other business at hand."

Meran had drawn Jilly right up to the foot of the dais and was gently pushing her forward.

"Go on," she said.

"Is he the king now?" Jilly asked.

Meran smiled and gave her another gentle push.

Jilly looked up. Goon seemed just like he always did when she saw him at

Bramley's—grumpy and out of sorts. Maybe it's just his face, she told herself, trying to give herself courage. There's people who look grumpy no matter how happy they are. But the thought didn't help contain her shaking much as she slowly made her way up to where Goon stood.

"You have something of ours," Goon said.

His voice was grim. Christy's story lay all too clearly in Jilly's head. She swallowed dryly.

"Uh, I never meant...." she began, then simply handed over the drum.

Goon took it reverently, then snatched her other hand before she could draw away. Her palm flared with sharp pain—all the skin, from the base of her hand to the ends of her fingers, was black.

The curse, she thought. It's going to make my hand fall right off. I'm never going to paint again....

Goon spat on her palm and the pain died as though it had never been. With wondering eyes, Jilly watched the blackness dry up and begin to flake away. Goon gave her hand a shake and the blemish scattered to fall to the ground. Her hand was completely unmarked.

"But...the curse," she said. "The bounty on my head. What about Christy's story...?"

"Your curse is knowledge," Goon said.

"But...?"

He turned away to face the crowd, drum in hand. As Jilly made her careful descent back to where Meran was waiting for her, Goon tapped his fingers against the head of the drum. An eerie rhythm started up—a real rhythm. When the skookin musicians began to play, they held their instruments properly and called up a sweet stately music to march across the back of the rhythm. It was a rich tapestry of sound, as different from Meran's solo flute as sunlight is from twilight, but it held its own power. Its own magic.

Goon led the playing with the rhythm he called up from the stone drum, led the music as though he'd always led it.

"He's really the king, isn't he?" Jilly whispered to her companion.

Meran nodded.

"So then what was he doing working for Bramley?"

"I don't know," Meran replied. "I suppose a king—or a king's son—can do pretty well what he wants just so long as he comes back here once a moon to fulfill his obligation as ruler."

"Do you think he'll go back to work for Bramley?"

"I know he will," Meran replied.

Jilly looked out at the crowd of skookin. They didn't seem at all threatening anymore. They just looked like little men—comical, with their tubby bodies and round heads and their little broomstick limbs—but men all the same. She listened to the music, felt its trueness and had to ask Meran why it didn't hurt them.

"Because it's their truth," Meran replied.

"But truth's just truth," Jilly protested. "Something's either true or it's not."

Meran just put her arm around Jilly's shoulder. A touch of a smile came to the corners of her mouth.

"It's time we went home," she said.

"I got off pretty lightly, didn't I?" Jilly said as they started back the way they'd come. "I mean, with the curse and all."

"Knowledge can be a terrible burden," Meran replied. "It's what some believe cast Adam and Eve from Eden."

"But that was a good thing, wasn't it?"

Meran nodded. "I think so. But it brought pain with it—pain we still feel to this day."

"I suppose."

"Come on," Meran said, as Jilly lagged a little to look back at the park.

Jilly quickened her step, but she carried the scene away with her. Goon and the stone drum. The crowd of skookin. The flickering light of their fires as it cast shadows over the Old City buildings.

And the music played on.

Professor Dapple had listened patiently to the story he'd been told, managing to keep from interrupting through at least half of the telling. Leaning back in his chair when it was done, he took off his glasses and began to needlessly polish them.

"It's going to be very good," he said finally.

Christy Riddell grinned from the club chair where he was sitting.

"But Jilly's not going to like it," Bramley went on. "You know how she feels about your stories."

"But she's the one who told me this one," Christy said.

Bramley rearranged his features to give the impression that he'd known this all along.

"Doesn't seem like much of a curse," he said, changing tack.

Christy raised his eyebrows. "What? To know that it's all real? To have to seriously consider every time she hears about some seemingly preposterous thing, that it might very well be true? To have to keep on guard with what she says so that people won't think she's gone off the deep end?"

"Is that how people look at us?" Bramley asked.

"What do you think?" Christy replied with a laugh.

Bramley harrumphed. He fidgeted with the papers on his desk, making more of a mess of them, rather than less.

"But Goon," he said, finally coming to the heart of what bothered him with what he'd been told. "It's like some retelling of 'The King of the Cats,' isn't it? Are you really going to put that bit in?"

Christy nodded. "It's part of the story."

"I can't see Goon as a king of anything," Bramley said. "And if he *is* a king, then what's he doing still working for me?"

"Which do you think would be better," Christy asked. "To be a king below, or a man above?"

Bramley didn't have an answer for that.

TIMESKIP

Every time it rains a ghost comes walking.

He goes up by the stately old houses that line Stanton Street, down Henratty Lane to where it leads into the narrow streets and crowded back alleys of Crowsea, and then back up Stanton again in an unvarying routine.

He wears a worn tweed suit—mostly browns and greys with a faint rosy touch of heather. A shapeless cap presses down his brown curls. His features give no true indication of his age, while his eyes are both innocent and wise. His face gleams in the rain, slick and wet as that of a living person. When he reaches the streetlamp in front of the old Hamill estate, he wipes his eyes with a brown hand. Then he fades away.

Samantha Rey knew it was true because she'd seen him.

More than once.

She saw him every time it rained.

"So, have you asked her out yet?" Jilly wanted to know.

We were sitting on a park bench, feeding pigeons the leftover crusts from our lunches. Jilly had worked with me at the post office, that Christmas they hired outside staff instead of letting the regular employees work the overtime, and we'd been friends ever since. These days she worked three nights a week as a waitress, while I made what I could busking on the Market with my father's old Czech fiddle.

Jilly was slender, with a thick tangle of brown hair and pale blue eyes, electric as sapphires. She had a penchant for loose clothing and fingerless gloves when she wasn't waitressing. There were times, when I met her on the streets in the evening, that I mistook her for a baglady: skulking in an alleyway, gaze alternating between the sketchbook held in one hand and the faces of the people on the streets as they walked by. She had more sketches of me playing my fiddle than had any right to exist.

"She's never going to know how you feel until you talk to her about it," Jilly went on when I didn't answer.

"I know."

I'll make no bones about it: I was putting the make on Sam Rey and had been ever since she'd started to work at Gypsy Records half a year ago. I never much went in for the blonde California beach-girl type, but Sam had a look all her own. She had some indefinable quality that went beyond her basic cheerleader appearance. Right. I can hear you already. Rationalizations of the North American libido. But it was true. I didn't just want Sam in my bed; I wanted to know we were going to have a future together. I wanted to grow old with her. I wanted to build up a lifetime of shared memories.

About the most Sam knew about all this was that I hung around and talked to her a lot at the record store.

"Look," Jilly said. "Just because she's pretty, doesn't mean she's having a perfect life or anything. Most guys look at someone like her and they won't even approach her because they're sure she's got men coming out of her ears. Well, it doesn't always work that way. For instance—" she touched her breastbone with a narrow hand and smiled, "—consider yours truly."

I looked at her long fingers. Paint had dried under her nails.

"You've started a new canvas," I said.

"And you're changing the subject," she replied. "Come on, Geordie. What's the big deal? The most she can say is no."

"Well, yeah. But...."

"She intimidates you, doesn't she?"

I shook my head. "I talk to her all the time."

"Right. And that's why I've got to listen to your constant mooning over her." She gave me a sudden considering look, then grinned. "I'll tell you what, Geordie, me lad. Here's the bottom line: I'll give you twenty-four hours to ask her out. If you haven't got it together by then, I'll talk to her myself."

"Don't even joke about it."

"Twenty-four hours," Jilly said firmly. She looked at the chocolate chip cookie in my hand. "Are you eating that?" she added in that certain tone of voice of hers that plainly said, all previous topics of conversation have been dealt with and completed. We are now changing topics.

So we did. But all the while we talked, I thought about going into the record store and asking Sam out, because if I didn't, Jilly would do it for me.

Whatever else she might be, Jilly wasn't shy. Having her go in to plead my case would be as bad as having my mother do it for me. I'd never be able to show my face in there again.

Gypsy Records is on Williamson Street, one of the city's main arteries. The street begins as Highway 14 outside the city, lined with a sprawl of fast food outlets, malls and warehouses. On its way downtown, it begins to replace the commercial properties with ever-increasing handfuls of residential blocks until it reaches the downtown core where shops and low-rise apartments mingle in gossiping crowds.

The store gets its name from John Butler, a short round-bellied man without a smidgen of Romany blood, who began his business out of the back of a hand-drawn cart that gypsied its way through the city's streets for years, always keeping just one step ahead of the municipal licensing board's agents. While it carries the usual bestsellers, the lifeblood of its sales are more obscure titles—imports and albums published by independent record labels. Albums, singles and compact discs of punk, traditional folk, jazz, heavy metal and alternative music line its shelves. Barring Sam, most of those who work there would look just as at home in the fashion pages of the most current British alternative fashion magazines.

Sam was wearing a blue cotton dress today, embroidered with silver threads. Her blonde hair was cut in a short shag on the top, hanging down past her shoulders at the back and sides. She was dealing with a defect when I came in. I don't know if the record in question worked or not, but the man returning it was definitely defective.

"It sounds like there's a radio broadcast right in the middle of the song," he was saying as he tapped the cover of the Pink Floyd album on the counter between them.

"It's supposed to be there," Sam explained. "It's *part* of the song." The tone of her voice told me that this conversation was going into its twelfth round or so.

"Well, I don't like it," the man told her. "When I buy an album of music, I expect to get just music on it."

"You still can't return it."

I worked in a record shop one Christmas—two years before the post office job. The best defect I got was from someone returning an in concert album by Marcel Marceau. Each side had thirty minutes of silence, with applause at the end—I kid you not.

I browsed through the Celtic records while I waited for Sam to finish with her customer. I couldn't afford any of them, but I liked to see what was new. Blasting out of the store's speakers was the new Beastie Boys album. It sounded like a cross between heavy metal and bad rap and was about as appealing as being hit by a car. You couldn't deny its energy, though.

By the time Sam was free I'd located five records I would have bought in more flush times. Leaving them in the bin, I drifted over to the front cash just as the Beastie Boys' last cut ended. Sam replaced them with a tape of New Age piano music.

"What's the new Oyster Band like?" I asked.

Sam smiled. "It's terrific. My favourite cut's 'The Old Dance.' It's sort of an allegory based on Adam and Eve and the serpent that's got a great hook in the chorus. Telfer's fiddling just sort of skips ahead, pulling the rest of the song along."

That's what I like about alternative record stores like Gypsy's—the people working in them actually know something about what they're selling.

"Have you got an open copy?" I asked.

She nodded and turned to the bin of opened records behind her to find it. With her back to me, I couldn't get lost in those deep blue eyes of hers. I seized my opportunity and plunged ahead.

"Areyouworkingtonight, wouldyouliketogooutwithmesomewhere?"

I'd meant to be cool about it, except the words all blurred together as they left my throat. I could feel the flush start up the back of my neck as she turned and looked back at me with those baby blues.

"Say what?" she asked.

Before my throat closed up on me completely, I tried again, keeping it short. "Do you want to go out with me tonight?"

Standing there with the Oyster Band album in her hand, I thought she'd never looked better. Especially when she said, "I thought you'd never ask."

I put in a couple of hours of busking that afternoon, down in Crowsea's Market, the fiddle humming under my chin to the jingling rhythm of the coins that passersby threw into the case lying open in front of me. I came away with twenty-six dollars and change—not the best of days, but enough to buy a halfway decent dinner and a few beers.

I picked up Sam after she finished work and we ate at The Monkey Woman's Nest, a Mexican restaurant on Williamson just a couple of blocks down from

Gypsy's. I still don't know how the place got its name. Ernestina Verdad, the Mexican woman who owns the place, looks like a showgirl and not one of her waitresses is even vaguely simian in appearance.

It started to rain as we were finishing our second beer, turning Williamson Street slick with neon reflections. Sam got a funny look on her face as she watched the rain through the window. Then she turned to me.

"Do you believe in ghosts?" she asked.

The serious look in her eyes stopped the half-assed joke that two beers brewed in the carbonated swirl of my mind. I never could hold my alcohol. I wasn't drunk, but I had a buzz on.

"I don't think so," I said carefully. "At least I've never seriously stopped to think about it."

"Come on," she said, getting up from the table. "I want to show you something."

I let her lead me out into the rain, though I didn't let her pay anything towards the meal. Tonight was my treat. Next time I'd be happy to let her do the honours.

"Every time it rains," she said, "a ghost comes walking down my street...."

She told me the story as we walked down into Crowsea. The rain was light and I was enjoying it, swinging my fiddle case in my right hand, Sam hanging onto my left as though she'd always walked there. I felt like I was on top of the world, listening to her talk, feeling the pressure of her arm, the bump of her hip against mine.

She had an apartment on the third floor of an old brick and frame building on Stanton Street. It had a front porch that ran the length of the house, dormer windows—two in the front and back, one on each side—and a sloped mansard roof. We stood on the porch, out of the rain which was coming down harder now. An orange and white tom was sleeping on the cushion of a white wicker chair by the door. He twitched a torn ear as we shared his shelter, but didn't bother to open his eyes. I could smell the mint that was growing up alongside the porch steps, sharp in the wet air.

Sam pointed down the street to where the yellow glare of a streetlamp glistened on the rain-slicked cobblestone walk that led to the Hamill estate. The Hamill house itself was separated from the street by a low wall and a dark expanse of lawn, bordered by the spreading boughs of huge oak trees.

"Watch the street," she said. "Just under the streetlight."

I looked, but I didn't see anything. The wind gusted suddenly, driving the rain in hard sheets along Stanton Street, and for a moment we lost all visibility. When it cleared, he was standing there, Sam's ghost, just like she'd told me. As he started down the street, Sam gave my arm a tug. I stowed my fiddle case under the tom's wicker chair, and we followed the ghost down Henratty Lane.

By the time he returned to the streetlight in front of the Hamill estate, I was ready to argue that Sam was mistaken. There was nothing in the least bit ghostly about the man we were following. When he returned up Henratty Lane, we had to duck into a doorway to let him pass. He never looked at us, but I could see the rain hitting him. I could hear the sound of his shoes on the pavement. He had to have come out of the walk that led up to the estate's house, at the same time as that sudden gust of wind-driven rain. It had been a simple coincidence, nothing more. But when he returned to the streetlight, he lifted a hand to wipe his face, and then he was gone. He just winked out of existence. There was no wind. No gust of rain. No place he could have gone. A ghost.

"Jesus," I said softly as I walked over to the pool of light cast by the streetlamp. There was nothing to see. But there had been a man there. I was sure of that much.

"We're soaked," Sam said. "Come on up to my place and I'll make us some coffee."

The coffee was great and the company was better. Sam had a small clothes drier in her kitchen. I sat in the living room in an oversized housecoat while my clothes tumbled and turned, the machine creating a vibration in the floorboards that I'm sure Sam's downstairs neighbours must have just loved. Sam had changed into a dark blue sweatsuit—she looked best in blue, I decided—and dried her hair while she was making the coffee. I'd prowled around her living room while she did, admiring her books, her huge record collection, her sound system, and the mantel above a working fireplace that was crammed with knickknacks.

All her furniture was the kind made for comfort—they crouched like sleeping animals about the room. Fat sofa in front of the fireplace, an old pair of matching easy chairs by the window. The bookcases, record cabinet, side tables and trim were all natural wood, polished to a shine with furniture oil.

We talked about a lot of things, sitting on the sofa, drinking our coffees, but mostly we talked about the ghost.

"Have you ever approached him?" I asked at one point.

Sam shook her head. "No. I just watch him walk. I've never even talked about him to anybody else." That made me feel good. "You know, I can't help but feel that he's waiting for something, or someone. Isn't that the way it usually works in ghost stories?"

"This isn't a ghost story," I said.

"But we didn't imagine it, did we? Not both of us at the same time?"

"I don't know."

But I knew someone who probably did. Jilly. She was into every sort of strange happening, taking all kinds of odd things seriously. I could remember her telling me that Bramley Dapple—one of her professors at Butler U. and a friend of my brother's—was really a wizard who had a brown-skinned goblin for a valet, but the best thing I remembered about her was her talking about that scene in Disney's *101 Dalmatians*, where the dogs are all howling to send a message across town, one dog sending it out, another picking it up and passing it along, all the way across town and out into the country.

"That's how they do it," she'd said. "Just like that."

And if you walked with her at night and a dog started to howl, if no other dog picked it up, then she'd pass it on. She could mimic any dog's bark or howl so perfectly it was uncanny. It could also be embarrassing, because she didn't care who was around or what kinds of looks she got. It was the message that had to be passed on that was important.

When I told Sam about Jilly, she smiled, but there wasn't any mockery in her smile. Emboldened, I related the ultimatum that Jilly had given me this afternoon.

Sam laughed aloud. "Jilly sounds like my kind of person," she said. "I'd like to meet her."

When it started to get late, I collected my clothes and changed in the bathroom. I didn't want to start anything, not yet, not this soon, and I knew that Sam felt the same way, though neither of us had spoken of it. She kissed me at the door, a long warm kiss that had me buzzing again.

"Come see me tomorrow?" she asked. "At the store?"

"Just try and keep me away," I replied.

I gave the old tom on the porch a pat and whistled all the way home to my own place on the other side of Crowsea.

Jilly's studio was its usual organized mess. It was an open loft-like affair that occupied half of the second floor of a four-story brown brick building on Yoors

Street where Foxville's low rentals mingle with Crowsea's shops and older houses. One half of the studio was taken up with a Murphy bed that was never folded back into the wall, a pair of battered sofas, a small kitchenette, storage cabinets and a tiny box-like bathroom obviously designed with dwarves in mind.

Her easel stood in the other half of the studio, by the window where it could catch the morning sun. All around it were stacks of sketchbooks, newspapers, unused canvases and art books. Finished canvases leaned face front, five to ten deep, against the back wall. Tubes of paint covered the tops of old wooden orange crates—the new ones lying in neat piles like logs by a fireplace, the used ones in a haphazard scatter, closer to hand. Brushes sat waiting to be used in mason jars. Others were in liquid waiting to be cleaned. Still more, their brushes stiff with dried paint, lay here and there on the floor like discarded pick-up-sticks.

The room smelled of oil paint and turpentine. In the corner furthest from the window was a life-sized fabric maché sculpture of an artist at work that bore an uncanny likeness to Jilly herself, complete with Walkman, one paintbrush in hand, another sticking out of its mouth. When I got there that morning, Jilly was at her new canvas, face scrunched up as she concentrated. There was already paint in her hair. On the windowsill behind her a small ghetto blaster was playing a Bach fugue, the piano notes spilling across the room like a light rain. Jilly looked up as I came in, a frown changing liquidly into a smile as she took in the foolish look on my face.

"I should have thought of this weeks ago," she said. "You look like the cat who finally caught the mouse. Did you have a good time?"

"The best."

Leaving my fiddle by the door, I moved around behind her so that I could see what she was working on. Sketched out on the white canvas was a Crowsea street scene. I recognized the corner—McKennitt and Lee. I'd played there from time to time, mostly in the spring. Lately a rockabilly band called the Broken Hearts had taken over the spot.

"Well?" Jilly prompted.

"Well what?"

"Aren't you going to give me all the lovely sordid details?"

I nodded at the painting. She'd already started to work in the background with oils.

"Are you putting in the Hearts?" I asked.

Jilly jabbed at me with her paintbrush, leaving a smudge the colour of a Crowsea red brick tenement on my jean jacket.

"I'll thump you if you don't spill it all, Geordie, me lad. Just watch if I don't."

She was liable to do just that, so I sat down on the ledge behind her and talked while she painted. We shared a pot of her cowboy coffee which was what Jilly called the foul brew she made from used coffee grounds. I took two spoons of sugar to my usual one, just to cut back on the bitter taste it left in my throat. Still beggars couldn't be choosers. That morning I didn't even have used coffee grounds at my own place.

"I like ghost stories," she said when I was finished telling her about my evening. She'd finished roughing out the buildings by now and bent closer to the canvas to start working on some of the finer details before she lost the last of the morning light.

"Was it real?" I asked.

"That depends. Bramley says—"

"I know, I know," I said breaking in.

If it wasn't Jilly telling me some weird story about him, it was my brother. What Jilly liked best about him was his theory of consensual reality, the idea that things exist *because* we agree that they exist.

"But think about it," Jilly went on. "Sam sees a ghost—maybe because she expects to see one—and you see the same ghost because you care about her, so you're willing to agree that there's one there where she says it will be."

"Say it's not that, then what could it be?"

"Any number of things. A timeslip—a bit of the past slipping into the present. It could be a restless spirit with unfinished business. From what you say Sam's told you, though, I'd guess that it's a case of a timeskip."

She turned to grin at me which let me know that the word was one of her own coining. I gave her a dutifully admiring look, then asked, "A what?"

"A timeskip. It's like a broken record, you know? It just keeps playing the same bit over and over again, only unlike the record it needs something specific to cue it in."

"Like rain."

"Exactly." She gave me a sudden sharp look. "This isn't for one of your brother's stories, is it?"

My brother Christy collects odd tales just like Jilly does, only he writes them down. I've heard some grand arguments between the two of them comparing the superior qualities of the oral versus written traditions.

"I haven't seen Christy in weeks," I said.

"All right, then."

"So how do you go about handling this sort of thing?" I asked. "Sam thinks he's waiting for something."

Jilly nodded. "For someone to lift the tone arm of time." At the pained look on my face, she added, "Well, have you got a better analogy?"

I admitted that I didn't. "But how do you do that? Do you just go over and talk to him, or grab him, or what?"

"Any and all might work. But you have to be careful about that kind of thing."

"How so?"

"Well," Jilly said, turning from the canvas to give me a serious look, "sometimes a ghost like that can drag you back to whenever it is that he's from and you'll be trapped in his time. Or you might end up taking his place in the timeskip."

"Lovely."

"Isn't it?" She went back to the painting. "What colour's that sign Duffy has over his shop on McKennitt?" she asked.

I closed my eyes, trying to picture it, but all I could see was the face of last night's ghost, wet with rain.

It didn't rain again for a couple of weeks. They were good weeks. Sam and I spent the evenings and weekends together. We went out a few times, twice with Jilly, once with a couple of Sam's friends. Jilly and Sam got along just as well as I'd thought they would—and why shouldn't they? They were both special people. I should know.

The morning it did rain was Sam's day off from Gypsy's. The previous night was the first I'd stayed over all night. The first we made love. Waking up in the morning with her warm beside me was everything I thought it would be. She was sleepy-eyed and smiling, more than willing to nestle deep under the comforter while I saw about getting some coffee together.

When the rain started, we took our mugs into the living room and watched the street in front of the Hamill estate. A woman came by walking one of those fat white bull terriers that look like they're more pig than dog. The terrier didn't seem to mind the rain but the woman at the other end of the leash was less than pleased. She alternated between frowning at the clouds and tugging him along. About five minutes after the pair had rounded the corner, our ghost showed up, just winking into existence out of nowhere. Or out of a slip in time. One of Jilly's timeskips.

We watched him go through his routine. When he reached the streetlight and vanished again, Sam leaned her head against my shoulder. We were cozied up together in one of the big comfy chairs, feet on the windowsill.

"We should do something for him," she said.

"Remember what Jilly said," I reminded her.

Sam nodded. "But I don't think he's out to hurt anybody. It's not like he's calling out to us or anything. He's just there, going through the same moves, time after time. The next time it rains...."

"What're we going to do?"

Sam shrugged. "Talk to him, maybe?"

I didn't see how that could cause any harm. Truth to tell, I was feeling sorry for the poor bugger myself.

"Why not?" I said.

About then Sam's hands got busy and I quickly lost interest in the ghost. I started to get up, but Sam held me down in the chair.

"Where you going?" she asked.

"Well, I thought the bed would be...."

"We've never done it in a chair before."

"There's a lot of places we haven't done it yet," I said.

Those deep blue eyes of hers, about five inches from my own, just about swallowed me.

"We've got all the time in the world," she said.

It's funny how you remember things like that later.

The next time it rained, Jilly was with us. The three of us were walking home from Your Second Home, a sleazy bar on the other side of Foxville where the band of a friend of Sam's was playing. None of us looked quite right for the bar when we walked in. Sam was still the perennial California beach girl, all blonde and curves in a pair of tight jeans and a white T-shirt, with a faded jean jacket overtop. Jilly and I looked like the scruffs we were.

The bar was a place for serious drinking during the day serving mostly unemployed blue-collar workers spending their welfare cheques on a few hours of forgetfulness. By the time the band started around nine, though, the clientele underwent a drastic transformation. Scattered here and there through the crowd was the odd individual who still dressed for volume—all the colours turned up loud—but mostly we were outnumbered thirty-to-one by spike-haired punks in their black leathers and blue jeans. It was like being on the inside of a bruise.

The band was called the Wang Boys and ended up being pretty good—especially on their original numbers—if a bit loud. My ears were ringing when we finally left the place sometime after midnight. We were having a good time on the walk home. Jilly was in rare form, half-dancing on the street around us, singing the band's closing number, making up the words, turning the piece into a punk gospel number. She kept bouncing around in front of us, skipping backwards as she tried to get us to sing along.

The rain started as a thin drizzle as we were making our way through Crowsea's narrow streets. Sam's fingers tightened on my arm and Jilly stopped fooling around as we stepped into Henratty Lane, the rain coming down in earnest now. The ghost was just turning in the far end of the lane.

"Geordie," Sam said, her fingers tightening more.

I nodded. We brushed by Jilly and stepped up our pace, aiming to connect with the ghost before he made his turn and started back towards Stanton Street.

"This is not a good idea," Jilly warned us, hurrying to catch up. But by then it was too late.

We were right in front of the ghost. I could tell he didn't see Sam or me and I wanted to get out of his way before he walked right through us—I didn't relish the thought of having a ghost or a timeskip or whatever he was going through me. But Sam wouldn't move. She put out her hand, and as her fingers brushed the wet tweed of his jacket, everything changed.

The sense of vertigo was strong. Henratty Lane blurred. I had the feeling of time flipping by like the pages of a calendar in an old movie, except each page was a year, not a day. The sounds of the city around us—sounds we weren't normally aware of—were noticeable by their sudden absence. The ghost jumped at Sam's touch. There was a bewildered look in his eyes and he backed away. That sensation of vertigo and blurring returned until Sam caught him by the arm and everything settled down again. Quiet, except for the rain and a far-off voice that seemed to be calling my name.

"Don't be frightened," Sam said keeping her grip on the ghost's arm. "We want to help you."

"You should not be here," he replied. His voice was stiff and a little formal. "You were only a dream—nothing more. Dreams are to be savoured and remembered, not walking the streets."

Underlying their voices I could still hear the faint sound of my own name being called. I tried to ignore it, concentrating on the ghost and our surroundings. The lane was cleaner than I remembered it—no trash littered against the walls, no graffiti scrawled across the bricks. It seemed darker, too. It was almost possible to believe that we'd been pulled back into the past by the touch of the ghost.

I started to get nervous then, remembering what Jilly had told us. Into the past. What if we *were* in the past and we couldn't get out again? What if we got trapped in the same timeskip as the ghost and were doomed to follow his routine each time it rained?

Sam and the ghost were still talking but I could hardly hear what they were saying. I was thinking of Jilly. We'd brushed by her to reach the ghost, but she'd been right behind us. Yet when I looked back, there was no one there. I remembered that sound of my name, calling faint across some great distance. I listened now, but heard only a vague unrecognizable sound. It took me long moments to realize that it was a dog barking.

I turned to Sam, tried to concentrate on what she was saying to the ghost. She was starting to pull away from him, but now it was his hand that held her arm. As I reached forward to pull her loose, the barking suddenly grew in volume—not one dog's voice, but those of hundreds, echoing across the years that separated us from our own time. Each year caught and sent on its own dog's voice, the sound building into a cacophonous chorus of yelps and barks and howls.

The ghost gave Sam's arm a sharp tug and I lost my grip on her, stumbling as the vertigo hit me again. I fell through the sound of all those barking dogs, through the blurring years, until I dropped to my knees on the wet cobblestones, my hands reaching for Sam. But Sam wasn't there.

"Geordie?"

It was Jilly, kneeling by my side, hand on my shoulder. She took my chin and turned my face to hers, but I pulled free.

"Sam!" I cried.

A gust of wind drove rain into my face, blinding me, but not before I saw that the lane was truly empty except for Jilly and me. Jilly, who'd mimicked the barking of dogs to draw us back through time. But only I'd returned. Sam and the ghost were both gone.

"Oh, Geordie," Jilly murmured as she held me close. "I'm so sorry."

I don't know if the ghost was ever seen again, but I saw Sam one more time after that night. I was with Jilly in Moore's Antiques in Lower Crowsea, flipping through a stack of old sepia-toned photographs, when a group shot of a family on their front porch stopped me cold. There, amongst the somber faces, was Sam. She looked different. Her hair was drawn back in a tight bun and she wore a plain unbecoming dark dress, but it was Sam all right. I turned the photograph over and read the photographer's date on the back. 1912.

Something of what I was feeling must have shown on my face, for Jilly came over from a basket of old earrings that she was looking through.

"What's the matter, Geordie, me lad?" she asked.

Then she saw the photograph in my hand. She had no trouble recognizing Sam either. I didn't have any money that day, but Jilly bought the picture and gave it to me. I keep it in my fiddle case.

I grow older each year, building up a lifetime of memories, only I've no Sam to share them with. But often when it rains, I go down to Stanton Street and stand under the streetlight in front of the old Hamill estate. One day I know she'll be waiting there for me.

FREEWHEELING

There is apparently nothing that cannot happen.
—attributed to Mark Twain

There are three kinds of people: those who make things happen, those who watch things happen, and those who wonder, 'What happened?'
—message found inside a Christmas cracker

I

He stood on the rain-slick street, a pale fire burning behind his eyes. Nerve ends tingling, he watched them go—a slow parade of riderless bicycles.

Ten-speeds and mountain bikes. Domesticated, urban. So inbred that all they were was spoked wheels and emaciated frames, mere skeletons of what their genetic ancestors had been. They had never known freedom, never known joy; only the weight of serious riders in slick, leather-seated shorts, pedaling determinedly with their cycling shoes strapped to the pedals, heads encased in crash helmets, fingerless gloves on the hands gripping the handles tightly.

He smiled and watched them go. Down the wet street, wheels throwing up arcs of fine spray, metal frames glistening in the streetlights, reflector lights winking red.

The rain had plastered his hair slick against his head, his clothes were sodden, but he paid no attention to personal discomfort. He thought instead of that fat-wheeled aboriginal one-speed that led them now. The maverick who'd come from who-knows-where to pilot his domesticated brothers and sisters away.

For a night's freedom. Perhaps for always.

The last of them were rounding the corner now. He lifted his right hand to wave goodbye. His left hand hung down by his leg, still holding the heavy-duty wire cutters by one handle, the black rubber grip making a ribbed pattern on the palm of his hand. By fences and on porches, up and down the street, locks had been cut, chains lay discarded, bicycles ran free.

He heard a siren approaching. Lifting his head, he licked the raindrops from his lips. Water got in his eyes, gathering in their corners. He squinted, enamoured by the kaleidoscoping spray of lights this caused to appear behind his eyelids. There were omens in lights, he knew. And in the night sky, with its scattershot sweep of stars. So many lights.... There were secrets waiting to unfold there, mysteries that required a voice to be freed.

Like the bicycles were freed by their maverick brother.

He could be that voice, if he only knew what to sing.

He was still watching the sky for signs when the police finally arrived.

"Let me go, boys, let me go...."

The new Pogues album *If I Should Fall From Grace With God* was on the turntable. The title cut leaked from the sound system's speakers, one of which sat on a crate crowded with half-used paint tubes and tins of turpentine, the other perched on the windowsill, commanding a view of rainswept Yoors Street one floor below. The song was jauntier than one might expect from its subject matter, while Shane MacGowan's voice was as rough as ever, chewing the words and spitting them out, rather than singing them.

It was an angry voice, Jilly decided as she hummed softly along with the chorus. Even when it sang a tender song. But what could you expect from a group that had originally named itself Pogue Mahone—Irish Gaelic for "Kiss my ass"?

Angry and brash and vulgar. The band was all of that. But they were honest, too—painfully so, at times—and that was what brought Jilly back to their music, time and again. Because sometimes things just had to be said.

"I don't get this stuff," Sue remarked.

She'd been frowning over the lyrics that were printed on the album's inner sleeve. Leaning her head against the patched backrest of one of Jilly's two old sofas, she set the sleeve aside.

"I mean, music's supposed to make you feel good, isn't it?" she went on.

Jilly shook her head. "It's supposed to make you feel something—happy, sad, angry, whatever—just so long as it doesn't leave you brain-dead the way most Top 40 does. For me, music needs meaning to be worth my time—preferably something more than 'I want your body, babe,' if you know what I mean."

"You're beginning to develop a snooty attitude, Jilly."

"Me? To laugh, dahling."

Susan Ashworth was Jilly's uptown friend. As a pair, the two women made a perfect study in contrasts.

Sue's blonde hair was straight, hanging to just below her shoulders, where Jilly's was a riot of brown curls, made manageable tonight only by a clip that drew it all up to the top of her head before letting it fall free in the shape of something that resembled nothing so much as a disenchanted Mohawk. They were both in their twenties, slender and blue-eyed—the latter expected in a blonde; the electric blue of Jilly's eyes gave her, with her darker skin, a look of continual startlement. Where Sue wore just the right amount of makeup, Jilly could usually be counted on having a smudge of charcoal somewhere on her face and dried oil paint under her nails.

Sue worked for the city as an architect; she lived uptown and her parents were from the Beaches where it seemed you needed a permit just to be out on the sidewalks after eight in the evening—or at least that was the impression that the police patrols left when they stopped strangers to check their ID. She always had that upscale look of one who was just about to step out to a restaurant for cocktails and dinner.

Jilly's first love was art of a freer style than designing municipal necessities, but she usually paid her rent by waitressing and other odd jobs. She tended to wear baggy clothes—like the oversized white T-shirt and blue poplin lace-front pants she had on tonight—and always had a sketchbook close at hand.

Tonight it was on her lap as she sat propped up on her Murphy bed, toes in their ballet slippers tapping against one another in time to the music. The Pogues were playing an instrumental now—"Metropolis"—which sounded like a cross between a Celtic fiddle tune and the old *Dragnet* theme.

"They're really not for me," Sue went on. "I mean if the guy could sing, maybe, but—"

"It's the feeling that he puts into his voice that's important," Jilly said. "But this is an instrumental. He's not even—"

"Supposed to be singing. I know. Only—"

"If you'd just—"

The jangling of the phone sliced through their discussion. Because she was closer—and knew that Jilly would claim some old war wound or any excuse not to get up, now that she was lying down—Sue answered it. She listened for a long moment, an odd expression on her face, then slowly cradled the receiver.

"Wrong number?"

Sue shook her head. "No. It was someone named...uh, Zinc? He said that he's been captured by two Elvis Presleys disguised as police officers and would you please come and explain to them that he wasn't stealing bikes, he was just setting them free. Then he just hung up."

"Oh, shit!" Jilly stuffed her sketchbook into her shoulderbag and got up.

"This makes sense to you?"

"He's one of the street kids."

Sue rolled her eyes, but she got up as well. "Want me to bring my chequebook?"

"What for?

"Bail. It's what you have to put up to spring somebody from jail. Don't you ever watch TV?"

Jilly shook her head. "What? And let the aliens monitor my brainwaves?"

"What scares me," Sue muttered as they left the loft and started down the stairs, "is that sometimes I don't think you're kidding."

"Maybe I'm not," Jilly said.

Sue shook her head. "I'm going to pretend I didn't hear that."

Jilly knew people from all over the city, in all walks of life. Socialites and bagladies. Street kids and university profs. Nobody was too poor, or, conversely, too rich for her to strike up a conversation with, no matter where they happened to meet, or under what circumstances. Detective Lou Fucceri, of the Crowsea Precinct's General Investigations squad, she met when he was still a patrolman, walking the Stanton Street Combat Zone beat. Jilly was there, taking reference photos for a painting she was planning. When she had asked Lou to pose for a couple of shots, he tried to run her in on a soliciting charge.

"Is it true?" Sue wanted to know as soon as the desk sergeant showed them into Lou's office. "The way you guys met?"

"You mean UFO-spotting in Butler U. Park?" he replied.

Sue sighed. "I should've known. I must be the only person who's maintained her sanity after meeting Jilly."

She sat down on one of the two wooden chairs that faced Lou's desk in the small cubicle that passed for his office. There was room for a bookcase behind him, crowded with law books and file folders, and a brass coat rack from which hung a lightweight sportsjacket. Lou sat at the desk, white shirt sleeves rolled halfway up to his elbows, collar open, black tie hanging loose.

His Italian heritage was very much present in the Mediterranean cast to his complexion, his dark brooding eyes and darker hair. As Jilly sat down in the chair Sue had left for her, he shook a cigarette free from a crumpled pack that he dug out from under the litter of files on his desk. He offered them around, tossing the pack back down on the desk and lighting his own when there were no takers.

Jilly pulled her chair closer to the desk. "What did he do, Lou? Sue took the call, but I don't know if she got the message right."

"I *can* take a message," Sue began, but Jilly waved a hand in her direction. She wasn't in the mood for banter just now.

Lou blew a stream of blue-grey smoke towards the ceiling. "We've been having a lot of trouble with a bicycle theft ring operating in the city," he said. "They've hit the Beaches, which was bad enough, though with all the Mercedes and BMWs out there, I doubt they're going to miss their bikes a lot. But rich people like to complain, and now the gang's moved their operations into Crowsea."

Jilly nodded. "Where for a lot of people, a bicycle's the only way they *can* get around."

"You got it."

"So what does that have to do with Zinc?"

"The patrol car that picked him up found him standing in the middle of the street with a pair of heavy-duty wire cutters in his hand. The street'd been cleaned right out, Jilly. There wasn't a bike left on the block—just the cut locks and chains left behind."

"So where are the bikes?"

Lou shrugged. "Who knows. Probably in a Foxville chopshop having their serial numbers changed. Jilly, you've got to get Zinc to tell us who he was working with. Christ, they took off, leaving him to hold the bag. He doesn't owe them a thing now."

Jilly shook her head slowly. "This doesn't make any sense. Zinc's not the criminal kind."

"I'll tell you what doesn't make any sense," Lou said. "The kid himself. He's heading straight for the loonie bin with all his talk about Elvis clones and

Venusian thought machines and feral-fuc—" He glanced at Sue and covered up the profanity with a cough. "Feral bicycles leading the domesticated ones away."

"He said that?"

Lou nodded. "That's why he was clipping the locks—to set the bikes free so that they could follow their, and I quote, 'spiritual leader, home to the place of mystery.'"

"That's a new one," Jilly said.

"You're having me on—right?" Lou said. "That's all you can say? It's a new one? The Elvis clones are old hat now? Christ on a comet. Would you give me a break? Just get the kid to roll over and I'll make sure things go easy for him."

"Christ on a comet?" Sue repeated softly.

"C'mon, Lou," Jilly said. "How can I make Zinc tell you something he doesn't know? Maybe he found those wire cutters on the street—just before the patrol car came. For all we know he could—"

"He *said* he cut the locks."

The air went out of Jilly. "Right," she said. She slouched in her chair. "I forgot you'd said that."

"Maybe the bikes really did just go off on their own," Sue said.

Lou gave her a weary look, but Jilly sat up straighter. "I wonder," she began.

"Oh, for God's sake," Sue said. "I was only joking."

"I know you were," Jilly said. "But I've seen enough odd things in this world that I won't say anything's impossible anymore."

"The police department doesn't see things quite the same way," Lou told Jilly. The dryness of his tone wasn't lost on her.

"I know."

"I want these bike thieves, Jilly."

"Are you arresting Zinc?"

Lou shook his head. "I've got nothing to hold him on except for circumstantial evidence."

"I thought you said he admitted to cutting the locks," Sue said.

Jilly shot her a quick fierce look that plainly said, don't make waves when he's giving us what we came for.

Lou nodded. "Yeah. He admitted to that. He also admitted to knowing a hobo who was really a spy from Pluto. Asked why the patrolmen had traded in their white Vegas suits for uniforms and wanted to hear them sing 'Heartbreak Hotel'. For next of kin he put down Bigfoot."

"*Gigantopithecus blacki,*" Jilly said.

Lou looked at her. "What?"

"Some guy at Washington State University's given Bigfoot a Latin name now. *Giganto—*"

Lou cut her off. "That's what I thought you said." He turned back to Sue. "So you see, his admitting to cutting the locks isn't really going to amount to much. Not when a lawyer with half a brain can get him off without even having to work up a sweat."

"Does that mean he's free to go then?" Jilly asked.

Lou nodded. "Yeah. He can go. But keep him out of trouble, Jilly. He's in here again, and I'm sending him straight to the Zeb for psychiatric testing. And try to convince him to come clean on this—okay? It's not just for me, it's for him too. We break this case and find out he's involved, nobody's going to go easy on him. We don't give out rainchecks."

"Not even for dinner?" Jilly asked brightly, happy now that she knew Zinc was getting out.

"What do you mean?"

Jilly grabbed a pencil and paper from his desk and scrawled "Jilly Coppercorn owes Hotshot Lou one dinner, restaurant of her choice," and passed it over to him.

"I think they call this a bribe," he said.

"I call it keeping in touch with your friends," Jilly replied and gave him a big grin.

Lou glanced at Sue and rolled his eyes.

"Don't look at me like that," she said. "I'm the sane one here."

"You wish," Jilly told her.

Lou heaved himself to his feet with exaggerated weariness. "C'mon, let's get your friend out of here before he decides to sue us because we don't have our coffee flown in from the Twilight Zone," he said as he led the way down to the holding cells.

Zinc had the look of a street kid about two days away from a good meal. His jeans, T-shirt, and cotton jacket were ragged, but clean; his hair had the look of a badly-mown lawn, with tufts standing up here and there like exclamation points. The pupils of his dark brown eyes seemed too large for someone who never did drugs. He was seventeen, but acted half his age.

The only home he had was a squat in Upper Foxville that he shared with a couple of performance artists, so that was where Jilly and Sue took him in Sue's Mazda. The living space he shared with the artists was on the upper story of a deserted tenement where someone had put together a makeshift loft by the simple method of removing all the walls, leaving a large empty area cluttered only by support pillars and the squatters' belongings.

Lucia and Ursula were there when they arrived, practicing one of their pieces to the accompaniment of a ghetto blaster pumping out a mixture of electronic music and the sound of breaking glass at a barely-audible volume. Lucia was wrapped in plastic and lying on the floor, her black hair spread out in an arc around her head. Every few moments one of her limbs would twitch, the plastic wrap stretching tight against her skin with the movement. Ursula crouched beside the blaster, chanting a poem that consisted only of the line, "There are no patterns." She'd shaved her head since the last time Jilly had seen her.

"What am I doing here?" Sue asked softly. She made no effort to keep the look of astonishment from her features.

"Seeing how the other half lives," Jilly said as she led the way across the loft to where Zinc's junkyard of belongings took up a good third of the available space.

"But just look at this stuff," Sue said. "And how did he get that in here?"

She pointed to a Volkswagen bug that was sitting up on blocks, missing only its wheels and front hood. Scattered all around it was a hodgepodge of metal scraps, old furniture, boxes filled with wiring and God only knew what.

"Piece by piece," Jilly told her.

"And then he assembled it here?"

Jilly nodded.

"Okay. I'll bite. Why?"

"Why don't you ask him?"

Jilly grinned as Sue quickly shook her head. The entire trip from the precinct station, Zinc had carefully explained his theory of the world to her, how the planet earth was actually an asylum for insane aliens, and that was why nothing made sense.

Zinc followed the pair of them across the room, stopping only long enough to greet his squat-mates. "Hi, Luce. Hi, Urse."

Lucia never looked at him.

"There are no patterns," Ursula said.

Zinc nodded thoughtfully.

"Maybe there's a pattern in that," Sue offered.

"Don't start," Jilly said. She turned to Zinc. "Are you going to be all right?"

"You should've seen them go, Jill," Zinc said. "All shiny and wet, just whizzing down the street, heading for the hills."

"I'm sure it was really something, but you've got to promise me to stay off the streets for awhile. Will you do that, Zinc? At least until they catch this gang of bike thieves?"

"But there weren't any thieves. It's like I told Elvis Two, they left on their own."

Sue gave him an odd look. "Elvis too?"

"Don't ask," Jilly said. She touched Zinc's arm. "Just stay in for awhile—okay? Let the bikes take off on their own."

"But I like to watch them go."

"Do it as a favour to me, would you?"

"I'll try."

Jilly gave him a quick smile. "Thanks. Is there anything you need? Do you need money for some food?"

Zinc shook his head. Jilly gave him a quick kiss on the cheek and tousled the exclamation point hair tufts sticking up from his head.

"I'll drop by to see you tomorrow, then—okay?" At his nod, Jilly started back across the room. "C'mon, Sue," she said when her companion paused beside the tape machine where Ursula was still chanting.

"So what about this stock market stuff?" she asked the poet.

"There are no patterns," Ursula said.

"That's what I thought," Sue said, but then Jilly was tugging her arm.

"Couldn't resist, could you?" Jilly said.

Sue just grinned.

"Why do you humour him?" Sue asked when she pulled up in front of Jilly's loft.

"What makes you think I am?"

"I'm being serious, Jilly."

"So am I. He believes in what he's talking about. That's good enough for me."

"But all this stuff he goes on about...Elvis clones and insane aliens—"

"Don't forget animated bicycles."

Sue gave Jilly a pained look. "I'm not. That's just what I mean—it's all so crazy."

"What if it's not?"

Sue shook her head. "I can't buy it."

"It's not hurting anybody." Jilly leaned over and gave Sue a quick kiss on the cheek. "Gotta run. Thanks for everything."

"Maybe it's hurting him," Sue said as Jilly opened the door to get out. "Maybe it's closing the door on any chance he has of living a normal life. You know—opportunity comes knocking, but there's nobody home? He's not just eccentric, Jilly. He's crazy."

Jilly sighed. "His mother was a hooker, Sue. The reason he's a little flaky is her pimp threw him down two flights of stairs when he was six years old—not because Zinc did anything, or because his mother didn't trick enough johns that night, but just because the creep felt like doing it. That's what normal was for Zinc. He's happy now—a lot happier than when Social Services tried to put him in a foster home where they only wanted him for the support cheque they got once a month for taking him in. And a lot happier than he'd be in the Zeb, all doped up or sitting around in a padded cell whenever he tried to tell people about the things he sees.

"He's got his own life now. It's not much—not by your standards, maybe not even by mine, but it's his and I don't want anybody to take it away from him."

"But—"

"I know you mean well," Jilly said, "but things don't always work out the way we'd like them to. Nobody's got time for a kid like Zinc in Social Services. There he's just a statistic that they shuffle around with all the rest of their files and red tape. Out here on the street, we've got a system that works. We take care of our own. It's that simple. Doesn't matter if it's the Cat Lady, sleeping in an alleyway with a half-dozen mangy toms, or Rude Ruthie, haranguing the commuters on the subway, we take care of each other."

"Utopia," Sue said.

A corner of Jilly's mouth twitched with the shadow of a humourless smile. "Yeah. I know. We've got a high asshole quotient, but what can you do? You try to get by—that's all. You just try to get by."

"I wish I could understand it better," Sue said.

"Don't worry about it. You're good people, but this just isn't your world. You can visit, but you wouldn't want to live in it, Sue."

"I guess."

Jilly started to add something more, but then just smiled encouragingly and got out of the car.

"See you Friday?" she asked, leaning in the door.

Sue nodded.

Jilly stood on the pavement and watched the Mazda until it turned the corner and its rear lights were lost from view, then she went upstairs to her apartment. The big room seemed too quiet and she felt too wound up to sleep, so she put a cassette in the tape player—Lynn Harrell playing a Schumann concerto—and started to prepare a new canvas to work on in the morning when the light would be better.

2

It was raining again, a soft drizzle that put a glistening sheen on the streets and lampposts, on porch handrails and street signs. Zinc stood in the shadows that had gathered in the mouth of an alleyway, his new pair of wire cutters a comfortable weight in his hand. His eyes sparked with reflected lights. His hair was damp against his scalp. He licked his lips, tasting mountain heights and distant forests within the drizzle's slightly metallic tang.

Jilly knew a lot about things that were, he thought, and things that might be, and she always meant well, but there was one thing she just couldn't get right. You didn't make art by capturing an image on paper, or canvas, or in stone. You didn't make it by writing down stories and poems. Music and dance came closest to what real art was—but only so long as you didn't try to record or film it. Musical notation was only so much dead ink on paper. Choreography was planning, not art.

You could only make art by setting it free. Anything else was just a memory, no matter how you stored it. On film or paper, sculpted or recorded.

Everything that existed, existed in a captured state. Animate or inanimate, everything wanted to be free.

That's what the lights said; that was their secret. Wild lights in the night skies, and domesticated lights, right here on the street, they all told the same tale. It was so plain to see when you knew *how* to look. Didn't neon and streetlights yearn to be starlight?

To be free.

He bent down and picked up a stone, smiling at the satisfying crack it made when it broke the glass protection of the streetlight, his grin widening as the light inside flickered, then died.

It was part of the secret now, part of the voices that spoke in the night sky.

Free.

Still smiling, he set out across the street to where a bicycle was chained to the railing of a porch.

"Let me tell you about art," he said to it as he mounted the stairs.

Psycho Puppies were playing at the YoMan on Gracie Street near the corner of Landis Avenue that Friday night. They weren't anywhere near as punkish as their name implied. If they had been, Jilly would never have been able to get Sue out to see them.

"I don't care if they damage themselves," she'd told Jilly the one and only time she'd gone out to one of the punk clubs further west on Gracie, "but I refuse to pay good money just to have someone spit at me and do their best to rupture my eardrums."

The Puppies were positively tame compared to how that punk band had been. Their music was loud, but melodic, and while there was an undercurrent of social conscience to their lyrics, you could dance to them as well. Jilly couldn't help but smile to see Sue stepping it up to a chorus of, "You can take my job, but you can't take me, ain't nobody gonna steal my dignity."

The crowd was an even mix of slumming uptowners, Crowsea artists and the neighbourhood kids from surrounding Foxville. Jilly and Sue danced with each other, not from lack of offers, but because they didn't want to feel obligated to any guy that night. Too many men felt that one dance entitled them to ownership—for the night, at least, if not forever—and neither of them felt like going through the ritual repartee that the whole business required.

Sue was on the right side of a bad relationship at the moment, while Jilly was simply eschewing relationships on general principle these days. Relationships required changes, and she wasn't ready for changes in her life just now. And besides, all the men she'd ever cared for were already taken and she didn't think it likely that she'd run into her own particular Prince Charming in a Foxville nightclub.

"I like this band," Sue confided to her when they took a break to finish the beers they'd ordered at the beginning of the set.

Jilly nodded, but she didn't have anything to say. A glance across the room caught a glimpse of a head with hair enough like Zinc's badly-mown lawn scalp to remind her that he hadn't been home when she'd dropped by his place on the way to the club tonight.

Don't be out setting bicycles free, Zinc, she thought.

"Hey, Tomas. Check this out."

There were two of them, one Anglo, one Hispanic, neither of them much more than a year or so older than Zinc. They both wore leather jackets and jeans, dark hair greased back in ducktails. The drizzle put a sheen on their jackets and hair. The Hispanic moved closer to see what his companion was pointing out.

Zinc had melted into the shadows at their approach. The streetlights that he had yet to free whispered, *careful, careful*, as they wrapped him in darkness, their electric light illuminating the pair on the street.

"Well, shit," the Hispanic said. "Somebody's doing our work for us."

As he picked up the lock that Zinc had just snipped, the chain holding the bike to the railing fell to the pavement with a clatter. Both teenagers froze, one checking out one end of the street, his companion the other.

"'Scool," the Anglo said. "Nobody here but you, me and your cooties."

"Chew on a big one."

"I don't do myself, puto."

"That's 'cos it's too small to find."

The pair of them laughed—a quick nervous sound that belied their bravado—then the Anglo wheeled the bike away from the railing.

"Hey, Bobby-o," the Hispanic said. "Got another one over here."

"Well, what're you waiting for, man? Wheel her down to the van."

They were setting bicycles free, Zinc realized—just like he was. He'd gotten almost all the way down the block, painstakingly snipping the shackle of each lock, before the pair had arrived.

Careful, careful, the streetlights were still whispering, but Zinc was already moving out of the shadows.

"Hi, guys," he said.

The teenagers froze, then the Anglo's gaze took in the wire cutters in Zinc's hand.

"Well, well," he said. "What've we got here? What're you doing on the night side of the street, kid?"

Before Zinc could reply, the sound of a siren cut the air. A lone siren, approaching fast.

The Chinese waitress looked great in her leather miniskirt and fishnet stockings. She wore a blood-red camisole tucked into the waist of the skirt, which made her pale skin seem ever paler. Her hair was the black of polished jet, pulled up in a loose bun that spilled stray strands across her neck and shoulders. Blue-black eye shadow made her dark eyes darker. Her lips were the same red as her camisole.

"How come she looks so good," Sue wanted to know, "when I'd just look like a tart if I dressed like that?"

"She's inscrutable," Jilly replied. "You're just obvious."

"How sweet of you to point that out," Sue said with a grin. She stood up from their table. "C'mon. Let's dance."

Jilly shook her head. "You go ahead. I'll sit this one out."

"Uh-uh. I'm not going out there alone."

"There's LaDonna," Jilly said, pointing out a girl they both knew. "Dance with her."

"Are you feeling all right, Jilly?"

"I'm fine—just a little pooped. Give me a chance to catch my breath."

But she wasn't all right, she thought as Sue crossed over to where LaDonna da Costa and her brother Pipo were sitting. Not when she had Zinc to worry about. If he was out there, cutting off the locks of more bicycles....

You're not his mother, she told herself. Except—

Out here on the streets we take care of our own.

That's what she'd told Sue. And maybe it wasn't true for a lot of people who hit the skids—the winos and the losers and the bag people who were just too screwed up to take care of themselves, not to be mentioned look after anyone else—but it was true for her.

Someone like Zinc—he was an in-betweener. Most days he could take care of himself just fine, but there was a fey streak in him so that sometimes he carried a touch of the magic that ran wild in the streets, the magic that was loose late at night when the straights were in bed and the city belonged to the night people. That magic took up lodgings in people like Zinc. For a week. A day. An hour. Didn't matter if it was real or not, if it couldn't be measured or catalogued, it was real to them. It existed all the same.

Did that make it true?

Jilly shook her head. It wasn't her kind of question and it didn't matter anyway. Real or not, it could still be driving Zinc into breaking corporeal laws—the kind that'd have Lou breathing down his neck, real fast. The kind that'd put him in jail with a whole different kind of loser.

The kid wouldn't last out a week inside.

Jilly got up from the table and headed across the dance floor to where Sue and LaDonna were jitterbugging to a tune that sounded as though Buddy Holly could have penned the melody, if not the words.

"Fuck this, man!" the Anglo said.

He threw down the bike and took off at a run, his companion right on his heels, scattering puddles with the impact of their boots. Zinc watched them go. There was a buzzing in the back of his head. The streetlights were telling him to run too, but he saw the bike lying there on the pavement like a wounded animal, one wheel spinning forlornly, and he couldn't just take off.

Bikes were like turtles. Turn 'em on their backs—or a bike on its side—and they couldn't get up on their own again.

He tossed down the wire cutters and ran to the bike. Just as he was leaning it up against the railing from which the Anglo had taken it, a police cruiser came around the corner, skidding on the wet pavement, cherry light gyrating—screaming, *Run, run*! in its urgent high-pitched voice—headlights pinning Zinc where he stood.

Almost before the cruiser came to a halt, the passenger door popped open and a uniformed officer had stepped out. He drew his gun. Using the cruiser as a shield, he aimed across its roof at where Zinc was standing.

"Hold it right there, kid!" he shouted. "Don't even blink."

Zinc was privy to secrets. He could hear voices in lights. He knew that there was more to be seen in the world if you watched it from the corner of your eye, than head on. It was a simple truth that every policeman he ever saw looked just like Elvis. But he hadn't survived all his years on the streets without protection.

He had a lucky charm. A little tin monkey pendant that had originally lived in a box of Crackerjacks—back when Crackerjacks had real prizes in them. Lucia had given it to him. He'd forgotten to bring it out with him the other night when the Elvises had taken him in. But he wasn't stupid. He'd remembered it tonight.

He reached into his pocket to get it out and wake its magic.

"You're just being silly," Sue said as they collected their jackets from their chairs.

"So humour me," Jilly asked.

"I'm coming, aren't I?"

Jilly nodded. She could hear the voice of Zinc's roommate Ursula in the back of her head—

There are no patterns.

—but she could feel one right now, growing tight as a drawn bowstring, humming with its urgency to be loosed.

"C'mon," she said, almost running from the club.

Police officer Mario Hidalgo was still a rookie—tonight was only the beginning of his third month of active duty—and while he'd drawn his sidearm before, he had yet to fire it in the line of duty. He had the makings of a good cop. He was steady; he was conscientious. The street hadn't had a chance to harden him yet, though it had already thrown him more than a couple of serious uglies in his first eight weeks of active duty.

But steady though he'd proved himself to be so far, when he saw the kid reaching into his the pocket of his baggy jacket, Hidalgo had a single moment of unreasoning panic.

The kid's got a gun, that panic told him. The kid's going for a weapon.

One moment was all it took.

His finger was already tightening on the trigger of his regulation .38 as the kid's hand came out of his pocket. Hidalgo wanted to stop the pressure he was putting on the gun's trigger, but it was like there was a broken circuit between his brain and his hand.

The gun went off with a deafening roar.

Got it, Zinc thought as his fingers closed on the little tin monkey charm. Got my luck.

He started to take it out of his pocket, but then something hit him straight in the chest. It lifted him off his feet and threw him against the wall behind him with enough force to knock all the wind out of his lungs. There was a raw pain firing every one of his nerve ends. His hands opened and closed spastically, the charm falling out of his grip to hit the ground moments before his body slid down the wall to join it on the wet pavement.

Goodbye, goodbye, sweet friend, the streetlights cried.

He could sense the spin of the stars as they wheeled high above the city streets, their voices joining the electric voices of the streetlights.

My turn to go free, he thought as a white tunnel opened in his mind. He could feel it draw him in, and then he was falling, falling, falling....

"Goodbye...." he said, thought he said, but no words came forth from between his lips.

Just a trickle of blood that mingled with the rain that now began to fall in earnest, as though it too was saying its own farewell.

All Jilly had to see was the red spinning cherries of the police cruisers to know where the pattern she'd felt in the club was taking her. There were a lot of cars here—cruisers and unmarked vehicles, an ambulance—all on official business, their presence coinciding with her business. She didn't see Lou approach until he laid his hand on her shoulder.

"You don't want to see," he told her.

Jilly never even looked at him. One moment he was holding her shoulder, the next she'd shrugged herself free of his grip and just kept on walking.

"Is it...is it Zinc?" Sue asked the detective.

Jilly didn't have to ask. She knew. Without being told. Without having to see the body.

An officer stepped in front of her to stop her, but Lou waved him aside. In her peripheral vision she saw another officer sitting inside a cruiser, weeping, but it didn't really register.

"I thought he had a gun," the policeman was saying as she went by. "Oh, Jesus. I thought the kid was going for a gun...."

And then she was standing over Zinc's body, looking down at his slender frame, limbs flung awkwardly like those of a ragdoll that had been tossed into a corner and forgotten. She knelt down at Zinc's side. Something glinted on the wet pavement. A small tin monkey charm. She picked it up, closed it tightly in her fist.

"C'mon, Jilly," Lou said as he came up behind her. He helped her to her feet.

It didn't seem possible that anyone as vibrant—as *alive*—as Zinc had been could have any relation whatsoever with that empty shell of a body that lay there on the pavement.

As Lou led her away from the body, Jilly's tears finally came, welling up from her eyes to salt the rain on her cheek.

"He…he wasn't…stealing bikes, Lou.…" she said.

"It doesn't look good," Lou said.

Often when she'd been with Zinc, Jilly had had a sense of that magic that touched him. A feeling that even if she couldn't see the marvels he told her about, they still existed just beyond the reach of her sight.

That feeling should be gone now, she thought.

"He was just…setting them free," she said.

The magic should have died, when he died. But she felt, if she just looked hard enough, that she'd see him, riding a maverick bike at the head of a pack of riderless bicycles—metal frames glistening, reflector lights glinting red, wheels throwing up arcs of fine spray, as they went off down the wet street.

Around the corner and out of sight.

"Nice friends the kid had," a plainclothes detective who was standing near them said to the uniformed officer beside him. "Took off with just about every bike on the street and left him holding the bag."

Jilly didn't think so. Not this time.

This time they'd gone free.

A WISH NAMED ARNOLD

MARGUERITE KEPT A wish in a brass egg and its name was Arnold.

The egg screwed apart in the middle. Inside, wrapped in a small piece of faded velvet, was the wish. It was a small wish, about the length of a man's thumb, and was made of black clay in the rough shape of a bird. Marguerite decided straight away that it was a crow, even if it did have a splash of white on its head. That made it just more special for her because she'd dyed a forelock of her own dark hair a peroxide white just before the summer started—much to her parents' dismay.

She'd found the egg under a pile of junk in Miller's while tagging along with her mother and aunt on their usual weekend tour of the local antique shops. Miller's was near their cottage on Otty Lake, just down the road from Rideau Ferry, and considered to be the best antique shop in the area.

The egg and its dubious contents were only two dollars, and maybe the egg was dinged-up a little and didn't screw together quite right, and maybe the carving didn't look so much like a crow as it did a lump of black clay with what could be a beak on it, but she'd bought it all the same.

It wasn't until Arnold talked to her that she found out he was a wish.

"What do you mean you're a wish?" she'd asked, keeping her voice low so that her parents wouldn't think she'd taken to talking in her sleep. "Like a genie in a lamp?"

Something like that.

It was all quite confusing. Arnold lay in her hand, an unmoving lump that was definitely not alive even if he did like look a bird, sort of. That was a plain fact, as her father liked to say. On the other hand, someone was definitely speaking to her in a low buzzing voice that tickled pleasantly inside her head.

I wonder if I'm dreaming, she thought.

She gave her white forelock a tug, then brushed it away from her brow and bent down to give the clay bird a closer look.

"What sort of a wish can you give me?" she asked finally.

Think of something—any one thing that you want—and I'll give it to you.

"Anything?"

Within reasonable limits.

Marguerite nodded sagely. She was all too familiar with *that* expression. "Reasonable limits" was why she only had one forelock dyed instead of a whole swath of rainbow colours like her friend Tina, or a Mohawk like Sheila. If she just washed her hair and let it dry, *and* you ignored the dyed forelock, she had a most reasonable short haircut. But all it took was a little gel that she kept hidden in her purse and by the time she joined her friends down at the mall, her hair was sticking out around her head in a bristle of spikes. It was just such a pain wearing a hat when she came home and having to wash out the gel right away.

Maybe that should be her wish. That she could go around looking just however she pleased and nobody could tell her any different. Except that seemed like a waste of a wish. She should probably ask for great heaps of money and jewels. Or maybe for a hundred more wishes.

"How come I only get one wish?" she asked.

Because that's all I am, Arnold replied. *One small wish.*

"Genies and magic fish give three. In fact *everybody* in *all* the stories usually gets three. Isn't it a tradition or something?"

Not where I come from.

"Where *do* you come from?"

There was a moment's pause, then Arnold said softly, *I'm not really sure.*

Marguerite felt a little uncomfortable at that. The voice tickling her mind sounded too sad and she started to feel ashamed of being so greedy.

"Listen," she said. "I didn't really mean to...you know...."

That's all right, Arnold replied. *Just let me know when you've decided what your wish is.*

Marguerite got a feeling in her head then as though something had just slipped away, like a lost memory or a half-remembered thought, then she realized that Arnold had just gone back to wherever it was that he'd been before she'd opened the egg. Thoughtfully, she wrapped him up in the faded velvet, then shut him away in the egg. She put the egg under her pillow and went to sleep.

All the next day she kept thinking about the brass egg and the clay crow inside it, about her one wish and all the wonderful things that there were to wish for.

She meant to take out the egg right away, first thing in the morning, but she never quite found the time. She went fishing with her father after breakfast, and then she went into Perth to shop with her mother, and then she went swimming with Steve who lived two cottages down and liked punk music as much as she did, though maybe for different reasons. She didn't get back to her egg until bedtime that night.

"What happens to you after I've made my wish?" she asked after she'd taken Arnold out of his egg.

I go away.

Marguerite asked, "Where to?" before she really thought about what she was saying, but this time Arnold didn't get upset.

To be somebody else's wish, he said.

"And after that?"

Well, after they've made their *wish, I'll go on to the next and the next....*

"It sounds kind of boring."

Oh, no. I get to meet all sorts of interesting people.

Marguerite scratched her nose. She'd gotten a mosquito bite right on the end of it and felt very much like Pinocchio though she hadn't been telling any lies.

"Have you always been a wish?" she asked, not thinking again.

Arnold's voice grew so quiet that it was just a feathery touch in her mind. *I remember being something else...a long time ago....*

Marguerite leaned closer, as though that would help her hear him better. But there was a sudden feeling in her as though Arnold had shaken himself out of his reverie.

Do you know what you're going to wish for yet? he asked briskly.

"Not exactly."

Well, just let me know when you're ready, he said and then he was gone again.

Marguerite sighed and put him away. This didn't seem to be at all the way this whole wishing business should go. Instead of feeling all excited about being able to ask for any one thing—*anything!*—she felt guilty because she kept making Arnold feel bad. Mind you, she thought. He did seem to be a gloomy sort of a genie when you came right down to it.

She fell asleep wondering if he looked the same wherever he went to when he left her as he did when she held him in her hand. Somehow his ticklish raspy voice didn't quite go with the lumpy clay figure that lay inside the brass egg. She supposed she'd never know.

As the summer progressed they became quite good friends, in an odd sort of way. Marguerite took to carrying the egg around with her in a small quilted cotton bag that she slung over her shoulder. At opportune moments, she'd take Arnold out and they'd talk about all sorts of things.

Arnold, Marguerite discovered, knew a lot that she hadn't supposed a genie would know. He was current with all the latest bands, seemed to have seen all the best movies, knew stories that could make her giggle uncontrollably or shiver with chills under her blankets late at night. If she didn't press him for information about his past, he proved to be the best friend a person could want and she found herself telling him things that she'd never think of telling anyone else.

It got to the point where Marguerite forgot he was a wish. Which was fine until the day that she left her quilted cotton bag behind in a restaurant in Smith Falls on a day's outing with her mother. She became totally panic-stricken until her mother took her back to the restaurant, but by then her bag was gone, and so was the egg, and with it Arnold.

Marguerite was inconsolable. She moped around for days and nothing that anyone could do could cheer her up. She missed Arnold passionately. Missed their long talks when she was supposed to be sleeping. Missed the weight of his egg in her shoulderbag and the companionable presence of just knowing he was there. And also, she realized, she'd missed her chance of using her wish.

She could have had anything she wanted. She could have asked for piles of money. For fame and fortune. To be a lead singer in a band like 10,000 Maniacs. To be another Molly Ringwald and star in all kinds of movies. She could have wished that Arnold would stay with her forever. Instead, jerk that she was, she'd never used the wish and now she had nothing. How could she be so stupid?

"Oh," she muttered one night in her bed. "I wish I...I wish...."

She paused then, feeling a familiar tickle in her head.

Did you finally decide on your wish? Arnold asked.

Marguerite sat up so suddenly that she knocked over her water glass on the night table. Luckily it was empty.

"Arnold?" she asked, looking around. "Are you here?"

Well, not exactly here, as it were, but I can hear you.

"Where have you *been*?"

Waiting for you to make your wish.

"I've really missed you," Marguerite said. She patted her comforter with eager hands, trying to find Arnold's egg. "How did you get back here?"

I'm not exactly here, Arnold said.

"How come you never talked to me when I've been missing you all this time?"

I can't really initiate these things, Arnold explained. *It gets rather complicated, but even though my egg's with someone else, I can't really be their wish until I've finished being yours.*

"So we can still talk and be friends even though I've lost the egg?"

Not exactly. I can fulfill your wish, but since I'm not with *you, as it were, I can't really stay unless you're ready to make your wish.*

"You can't?" Marguerite wailed.

Afraid not. I don't make the rules, you know.

"I've got it," Marguerite said. And she did have it too. If she wanted to keep Arnold with her, all she had to do was wish for him to always be her friend. Then no one could take him away from her. They'd always be together.

"I wish...." she began.

But that didn't seem quite right, she realized. She gave her dyed forelock a nervous tug. It wasn't right to *make* someone be your friend. But if she didn't do that, if she wished something else, then Arnold would just go off and be somebody else's wish. Oh, if only things didn't have to be complicated. Maybe she should just wish herself to the moon and be done with all her problems. She could lie there and stare at the world from a nice long distance away while she slowly asphyxiated. That would solve everything.

She felt that telltale feeling in her mind that let her know that Arnold was leaving again.

"Wait," she said. "I haven't made my wish yet."

The feeling stopped. *Then you've decided?* Arnold asked.

She hadn't, but as soon as he asked, she realized that there was only one fair wish she could make.

"I wish you were free," she said.

The feeling that was Arnold moved blurrily inside her.

You what? he asked.

"I wish you were free. I *can* wish that, can't I?"

Yes, but.... Wouldn't you rather have something...well, something for yourself?

"This *is* for myself," Marguerite said. "Your being free would be the best thing I could wish for because you're my friend and I don't want you to be trapped anymore." She paused for a moment, brow wrinkling. "Or is there a rule against that?"

No rule, Arnold said softly. His ticklish voice bubbled with excitement. *No rule at all against it.*

"Then that's my wish," Marguerite said.

Inside her mind, she felt a sensation like a tiny whirlwind spinning around and around. It was like Arnold's voice and an autumn leaves smell and a kaleidoscope of dervishing lights, all wrapped up in one whirling sensation.

Free! Arnold called from the center of that whirlygig.

A sudden weight was in Marguerite's hand and she saw that the brass egg had appeared there. It lay open on her palm, the faded velvet spilled out of it. It seemed so very small to hold so much happiness, but fluttering on tiny wings was the clay crow, rising up in a spin that twinned Arnold's presence in Marguerite's mind.

Her fingers closed around the brass egg as Arnold doubled, then tripled his size in an explosion of black feathers. His voice was like a chorus of bells, ringing and ringing between Marguerite's ears. Then with an exuberant caw, he stroked the air with his wings, flew out the cottage window and was gone.

Marguerite sat quietly, staring out the window and holding the brass egg. A big grin stretched her lips. There was something so *right* about what she'd just done that she felt an overwhelming sense of happiness herself, as though she'd been the one trapped in a treadmill of wishes in a brass egg, and Arnold had been the one to free *her.*

At last she reached out and picked up from the comforter a small glossy black feather that Arnold had left behind. Wrapping it in the old velvet, she put it into the brass egg and screwed the egg shut once more.

That September a new family moved in next door with a boy her age named Arnold. Marguerite was delighted and, though her parents were surprised, she and the new boy became best friends almost immediately. She showed him the egg one day that winter and wasn't at all surprised that the feather she still kept in it was the exact same shade of black as her new friend's hair.

Arnold stroked the feather with one finger when she let him see it. He smiled at her and said, "I had a wish once...."

INTO THE GREEN

STONE WALLS CONFINE a tinker; cold iron binds a witch; but a musician's music can never be fettered, for it lives first in her heart and mind.

The harp was named Garrow—born out of an old sorrow to make weary hearts glad. It was a small lap harp, easy to carry, with a resonance that let its music carry to the far ends of a crowded commonroom. The long fingers of the red-haired woman could pull dance tunes from its strings, lilting jigs or reels that set feet tapping until the floorboards shook and the rafters rang. But some nights the memory of old sorrows returned. Lying in wait like marsh mists, they clouded her eyes with their arrival. On those nights, the music she pulled from Garrow's metal-strung strings was more bitter than sweet, slow airs that made the heart regret and brought unbidden memories to haunt the minds of those who listened.

"Enough of that," the innkeeper said.

The tune faltered and Angharad looked up into his angry face. She lay her hands across the strings, stilling the harp's plaintive singing.

"I said you could make music," the innkeeper told her, "not drive my customers away."

It took Angharad a few moments to return from that place in her memory that the music had brought her to this inn where her body sat, drawing the music from the strings of her harp. The commonroom was half-empty and oddly subdued, where earlier every table had been filled and men stood shoulder-to-shoulder at the bar, joking and telling each other ever more embroidered tales. The few who spoke did so in hushed voices; fewer still would meet her gaze.

"You'll have to go," the innkeeper said, his voice not so harsh now. She saw in his eyes that he too was remembering a forgotten sorrow.

"I...."

How to tell him that on nights such as these, the sorrow came, whether she willed it or not? That if she had her choice she would rather forget as well. But the harp was a gift from Jacky Lantern's kin, as was the music she pulled from its strings. She used it in her journeys through the Kingdoms of the Green Isles, to wake the Summerblood where it lay sleeping in folk who never knew they were witches. That was how the Middle Kingdom survived—by being remembered, by its small magics being served, by the interchange of wisdom and gossip between man and those with whom he shared the world.

But sometimes the memories the music woke were not so gay and charming. They hurt. Yet such memories served a purpose, too, as the music knew well. They helped to break the circles of history so that mistakes weren't repeated. But how was she to explain such things to this tall, grim-faced innkeeper who'd been looking only for an evening's entertainment for his customers? How to put into words what only music could tell?

"I…I'm sorry," she said.

He nodded, almost sympathetically. Then his eyes grew hard. "Just go."

She made no protest. She knew what she was—tinker, witch and harper. This far south of Kellmidden, only the latter allowed her much acceptance with those who travelled a road just to get from here to there, rather than for the sake of the travelling itself. For the sake of the road that led into the green, where poetry and harping met to sing of the Middle Kingdom.

Standing, she swung the harp up on one shoulder, a small journeypack on the other. Her red hair was drawn back in two long braids. She wore a tinker's plaited skirt and white blouse with a huntsman's leather jerkin overtop. At the door she collected her staff of white rowan wood. Witches' wood. Not until the door swung closed behind her did the usual level of conversation and laughter return to the commonroom.

But they would remember. Her. The music. There was one man who watched her from a corner, face dark with brooding. She meant to leave before they remembered other things. Before one or another wondered aloud if it was true that witch's skin burned at the touch of cold iron—as did that of the kowrie folk.

As she stepped away from the door, a huge shadowed shape arose from where it had been crouching by a window. The quick tattoo of her pulse only sharpened when she saw that it was a man—a misshapen man. His chest was massive, his arms and legs like small trees. But a hump rose from his back, and his head jutted almost from his chest at an awkward angle. His legs were bowed as though his weight was almost too much for them. He shuffled, rather than walked, as he closed the short space between them.

Light from the window spilled across his features. One eye was set higher in that broad face than the other. The nose had been broken—more than once. His hair was a knotted thicket, his beard a bird's nest of matted tangles.

Angharad began to bring her staff between them. The white rowan wood could call up a witchfire that was good for little more than calling up a flame in a damp camp fire, but it could startle. That might be enough for her to make her escape.

The monstrous man reached a hand towards her. "Puh-pretty," he said.

Before Angharad could react, there came a quick movement from around the side of the inn.

"Go on!" the newcomer cried. It was the barmaid from the inn, a slender blue-eyed girl whose blonde hair hung in one thick braid across her breast. The innkeeper had called her Jessa. "Get away from her, you big oaf." She made a shooing motion with her hand.

Angharad saw something flicker briefly in the man's eyes as he turned. A moment of shining light. A flash of regret. She realized then that he'd been speaking of her music, not her. He'd been reaching to touch the harp, not her. She wanted to call him back, but the barmaid was thrusting a package wrapped in unbleached cotton at her. The man had shambled away, vanishing into the darkness in the time it took Angharad to look from the package to where he'd been standing.

"Something for the road," Jessa said. "It's not much—some cheese and bread."

"Thank you," Angharad replied. "That man…?"

"Oh, don't mind him. That's only Pog—the village half-wit. Fael lets him sleep in the barn in return for what work he can do around the inn." She smiled suddenly. "He's seen the kowrie folk, he has. To hear him tell it—and you'd need the patience of one of Dath's priests to let him get the tale out—they dance all round the Stones on a night such as this."

"What sort of a night is this?"

"Full moon."

Jessa pointed eastward. Rising above the trees there, Angharad saw the moon rising, swollen and round above the trees. She remembered a circle of old longstones that she'd passed on the road that took her to the inn. They stood far off from the road on a hill overlooking the Grey Sea, a league or so west of the village. Old stones, like silent sentinels, watching the distant waves. A place where kowries would dance, she thought, if they were so inclined.

"You should go," Jessa said.

Angharad gave her a questioning look.

The barmaid nodded towards the inn. "They're talking about witches in there, and spells laid with music. They're not bad men, but any man who drinks. . . ."

Angharad nodded. A hard day's work, then drinking all night. To some it was enough to excuse any deed. They were honest folk, after all. Not tinkers. Not witches.

She touched Jessa's arm. "Thank you."

"We're both women," the barmaid said with a smile. "We have to stick together, now don't we?" Her features, half-hidden in the gloom, grew more serious as she added, "Stay off the road if you can. Depending on how things go. . . . Well, there's some's as have horses."

Angharad thought of a misshapen man and a place of standing stones, of moonlight and dancing kowries.

"I will," she said.

Jessa gave her another quick smile, then slipped once more around the corner of the inn. Angharad listened to her quiet footfalls as she ran back to the kitchen. Giving the inn a considering look, she stuffed the barmaid's gift of food into her journeypack and set off down the road, staff in hand.

There were many tales told of the menhir and stone circles that dotted the Kingdoms of the Green Isles. Wizardfolk named them holy places, sacred to the Summerlord; reservoirs where the old powers of hill and moon could be gathered by the rites of dhruides and the like. The priests of Dath named them evil and warned all to shun their influence. The commonfolk were merely wary of them—viewing them as neither good nor evil, but rather places where mysteries lay too deep for ordinary folk.

And there *was* mystery in them, Angharad thought.

From where she stood, she could see their tall fingers silhouetted against the sky. Mists lay thick about their hill—drawn up from the sea that murmured a stone's throw or two beyond. The moon was higher now; the night as still as an inheld breath. Expectant. Angharad left the road to approach the stone circle where Pog claimed the kowrie danced on nights of the full moon. Nights when her harp played older musics than she knew, drawing the airs more from the wind, it seemed, than the flesh and bone that held the instrument and plucked its strings.

The gorse was damp underfoot. In no time at all, her bare legs were wet. She circled around two stone outcrops, her route eventually bringing her up the hill from the side facing the sea. The murmur of its waves was very clear now. The sharp tang of its salt was in the mist. Angharad couldn't see below her waist for that mist, but the hilltop was clear. And the Stones.

They rose high above her, four times her height, grey and weathered. Before she entered their circle, she dropped her journeypack and staff to the ground. From its sheath on the inside of her jerkin, she took out a small knife and left that as well. If this was a place to which the kowrie came, she knew they would have no welcome for one bearing cold iron. Lastly, she unbuttoned her shoes and set them beside her pack. Only then did she enter the circle, barefoot, with only her harp in hand.

She wasn't surprised to find the hunchback from the village inside the circle. He was perched on the kingstone, short legs dangling.

"Hello, Pog," she said.

She had no fear of him as she crossed the circle to where he sat. There was more kinship between them than either might claim outside this circle. Their Summerblood bound them.

"Huh-huh-huh...." Frustration tightened every line of his body as he struggled to shape the word. "Huh-low...."

Angharad stepped close and laid her hand against his cheek. She wondered, what songs were held prisoner by that stumbling tongue? For she could see a poetry in his eyes, denied its voice. A longing, given no release.

"Will you sing for me, Pog?" she asked. "Will you help me call the stones to dance?"

The eagerness in his nod almost made her weep. But it was not for pity that she was here tonight. It was to commune with a kindred spirit. He caught her hand with his and she gave it a squeeze before gently freeing her fingers. She sat at the foot of the stone and brought her harp around to her lap. Pog was awkward as he scrambled down from his perch to sit where he could watch her.

Fingers to strings. Once, softly, one after the other, to test the tuning. And then she began to play.

It was the same music that the instrument had offered at the inn, but in this place it soared so freely that there could be no true comparison. There was nothing to deaden the ringing of the strings here. No stone walls and wooden roof. No metal furnishings and trappings. No hearts that had to be tricked into listening.

The moon was directly overhead now and the music resounded between it and the sacred hill of the stone circle. It woke echoes like the skirling of pipes, like the thunder of hooves on sod. It woke lights in the old grey stones—flickering glimmers that sparked from one tall menhir to the other. It woke a song so bright in Angharad's heart that her chest hurt. It woke a dance in her companion so that he rose to his feet and shuffled between the stones.

Pog sang as he moved, a tuneless singing that made strange harmonies with Angharad's harping. Against the moonlight of her harp notes, it was the sound of earth shifting, stones grinding. When it took on the bass timbre of a stag's belling call, Angharad thought she saw antlers rising from his brow, the tines pointing skyward to the moon like the menhir. His back was straighter as he danced, the hump gone.

It's Hafarl, Angharad thought, awestruck. The Summerlord's possessed him.

Their music grew more fierce, a wild exultant sound that rang between the stones. The sparking flickers of light moved so quickly they were like streaming ribbons, bright as moonlight. The mist scurried in between the stones, swirling in its own dance, so that more often than not Angharad could only catch glimpses of the antlered dancing figure. His movements were liquid, echoing each rise and fall of the music. Angharad's heart reached out to him. He was—

Something struck her across the head. The music faltered, stumbled, then died as her harp was knocked from her grip. A hand grabbed one of her braids and hauled her to her feet.

"Do you see? Did you hear?" a harsh voice demanded.

Angharad could see them now—men from the inn. Their voices were loud in the sudden silence. Their shapes exaggerated, large and threatening in the mist.

"We see, Macal."

It was the one named Macal who had struck her. Who had watched her so intently in the commonroom of the inn. Who held her by her braid. Who hit her again. He stank of sweat and strong drink. And fear.

"Calling down a curse on us, she was," Macal cried. "And what better place than these damned Stones?"

Other men gripped her now. They shackled her wrists with cold iron and pulled her from the circle by a chain attached to those shackles. She fell to her knees and looked back. There was no sign of Pog, no sign of anything but her harp, lying on its side near the kingstone. The men dragged her to her feet.

"Leave me alo—" she began, finally finding her voice.

Macal hit her a third time. "You'll not speak again, witch. Not till the priest questions you. Understand?"

They tore cloth strips from her skirt then to gag her. They tore open her blouse and fondled and pinched her as they dragged her back to town. They threw her into the small storage room of the village's mill. Four stone walls. A door barred on the outside by a wooden beam, slotted in place. Two drunk men for guards outside, laughing and singing.

It took a long time for Angharad to lift her bruised body up from the stone floor and work free the gag. She closed her blouse somewhat by tying together the shirt tails. She hammered at the door with her shackled fists. There was no answer. Finally she sank to her knees and laid her head against the wall. She closed her eyes, trying to recapture the moment before this horror began, but all she could recall was the journey from the stone circle to this prison. The cruel men and the joy they took from her pain.

Then she thought of Pog.... Had they captured him as well? When she tried to bring his features to mind, all that came was an image of a stag on a hilltop, bellowing at the moon. She could see....

The stag. Pog. Changed into an image of Hafarl by the music. Left as a stag in the stone circle by the intrusion of the men from the inn who'd come, cursing and drunk, to find themselves a witch. The men hadn't seen him. But as Angharad's assailants dragged her from the stone circle, grey-clad shapes stepped from the stones, where time held them bound except for nights such as this when the moon was full.

They were kowrie, thin and wiry, with narrow dark-skinned faces and feral eyes. Their dark hair was braided with shells and feathers; their jerkins, trousers, boots and cloaks were the grey of the Stones. One by one, they stepped out into the circle until there were as many of them as there were Stones. Thirteen kowrie. The stag bellowed at the moon, a trumpeting sound. The kowrie touched Angharad's harp with fingers thin as rowan twigs.

"Gone now," one said, her voice a husky whisper.

Another drew a plaintive note from Angharad's harp. "Music stolen, moonlight spoiled," he said.

A third laid her narrow hands on the stag's trembling flanks. "Lead us to her, Summerborn," she said.

Other kowrie approached the beast.

"The cold iron bars us from their dwellings," one said.

Another nodded. "But not you."

"Lead us to her."

"Open their dwellings to us."

"We were but waking."

"We missed our dance."

"A hundred moons without music."

"We would hear her harp."

"We would follow our kin."

"Into the green."

The green, where poetry and harping met and opened a door to the Middle Kingdom. The stag pawed at the ground, hearing the need in their voices. It lifted its antlered head, snorting at the sky. The men. Where had they taken her? The stag remembered a place where men dwelt in houses set close to each other. There was pain in that place....

Angharad opened her eyes. What had she seen? A dream? Pog, with that poetry in his eyes, become a stag, surrounded by feral-eyed kowrie.... She pushed herself away from the wall and sat on her haunches, shackled wrists held on her lap before her. The stone walls of her prison bound her. The cold chains weighed her down. Still, her heart beat, her thoughts were her own. Her voice had not been taken from her.

She began to sing.

It was the music of hill and moon, a calling-down music, keening and wild. There was a stag's lowing in it, the murmur of sea against shore. There was moonlight in it and the slow grind of earth against stone. There was harping in it, and the sound of the wind as it sped across the gorse-backed hills.

On a night such as this, she thought, there was no stilling such music. It was not bound by walls or shackles. It ran free, out from her prison, out of the village; into the night, into the hills. It was heard there, by kowrie and stag. It was heard closer as well.

From the faraway place that the music took her, Angharad heard the alarm raised outside her prison. The wooden beam scraping as it was drawn from the door. The door was pushed open and the small chamber where her body sat singing grew bright from the glare of torches. But she was hardly even there anymore. She was out on the hills, running with the stag and the kowrie, leading them to her with her song, one more ghostly shape in the mist that was rolling down into the village.

"St-stop that you," one of the guards said. His unease was plain in voice and stance. Like his companion, he was suddenly sober.

Angharad heard him, but only from a great distance. Her music never faltered.

The two guards kept to the doorway, staring at her, unsure of what to do. Then Macal was there, with his hatred of witches, and they followed his lead. He struck her until she fell silent, but the music carried on, from her heart into the night, inaudible to these men, but growing louder when they dragged her out. The earth underfoot resounded like a drumskin with her silent song. The moonlit sky above trembled.

"Bring wood," Macal called as he pulled her along the ground by her chains. "We'll burn her now."

"But the priest...." one of the men protested.

Macal glared at the man. "If we wait for him, she'll have us all enspelled. We'll do it now."

No one moved. Other villagers were waking now—Fael the innkeeper and the barmaid Jessa; the miller, roused first by Angharad's singing, now coming to see to what use Macal had put his mill; fishermen, grumpy, for it was still hours before dawn when they'd rise to set their nets out past the shoals; the village goodwives. They looked at the red-haired woman, lying on the ground at Macal's feet, her hands shackled, the chains in Macal's hands. His earlier supporters backed away from him.

"Have you gone mad?" the miller demanded of him.

Macal pointed at Angharad. "Dath damn you, are you blind? She's a witch. She's casting a spell on us all. Can't you smell the stink of it in the air?"

"Let her go," the innkeeper said quietly.

Macal shook his head and drew his sword. "Fire's best—it burns the magic from them—but a sword can do the job as well."

The mist was entering the village now, roiling down the streets, filled with ghostly running shapes. Lifting her head from the ground, Angharad saw the kowrie, saw the stag. She looked at her captor and suddenly understood what drove him to his hate of witches. He had the Summerblood in his veins too.

"There...there's no need for this," she said. "We are kin...."

But Macal didn't hear her. He was staring into the mist. He saw the flickering shapes of the kowrie. And towering over them all he saw the stag, its tined antlers gleaming in the moonlight, the poetry in its eyes that burned like a fire. He dropped the chains and ran towards the beast, swinging his sword two-handedly. Villagers ran to intercept him, but they were too late. Macal's sword bit deep into the stag's throat.

The beast stumbled to its knees, spraying blood. Macal lifted his blade for a second stroke, but strong hands wrestled the sword from him. When he tried to rise, the villagers struck him with their fists.

"Murderer!" the miller cried.

"He never did you harm!"

"It was a beast!" Macal cried. "A demon beast—summoned by the witch!"

They let him rise then to see what he'd slain. Pog lay there, gasping his last breath, the poetry dying in his eyes. Only Macal and Angharad with their Summerblood had seen a stag. To the villagers, Macal had struck down their village half-wit who'd never done a hurtful thing.

"I...." Macal began taking a step forward, but the villagers pushed him away.

The mists swirled thick around him. Only he and Angharad could see the flickering grey shapes that moved in it, feral eyes gleaming, slender fingers pinching and nipping at his skin. He fled, running headlong between the houses. The mist clotted around him as he reached the outskirts of the village. A great wind rushed down from the hills. Hafarl's breath, Angharad thought, watching.

The wind tore away the mists. She saw the kowrie flee with it, thirteen slender shapes running into the hills. Where Macal had fallen, only a squat stone lay that looked for all the world like a crouching man, arms and legs drawn in close to his body. It had not been there before.

The villagers shaped the Sign of Horns to ward themselves. Angharad held out her shackled arms to the innkeeper. Silently he fetched the key from one of Macal's companions. Just as silently Angharad pointed to the men who had attacked her in the stone circle. She met their shamed gazes, one by one, then pointed to where Pog lay.

She waited while they fetched a plank and rolled Pog's body onto it. When they were ready, she led the way out of the village to the stone circle, the men following. Not until they had delivered their burden to the hilltop Stones did she speak.

"Go now."

They left at a run. Angharad stood firm until they were out of sight, then slowly she sank to her knees beside the body. Laying her head on its barrelled chest, she wept.

It was the kowrie who hollowed the ground under the kingstone and laid Pog there. And it was the kowrie who pressed the small harp into Angharad's hands and bade her play. She could feel no joy in this music that her fingers pulled from the strings. The magic was gone. But she played all the same, head bent over her instrument while the kowrie moved amongst the stones in a slow dance to honour the dead.

Mists grew thick again. Then a hoofbeat brought Angharad's head up. Her music faltered. The stag stood there watching her, the poetry alive in its eyes.

"Are you truly there?" she asked the beast. "Or are you but a phantom I've called up to ease my heart?"

The stag stepped forward and pressed a wet nose against her cheek. She stroked its neck. The hairs were coarse. There was no doubt that this was flesh and muscle under her hand. When the stag stepped away, she began to play once more. The music grew of its own accord under her fingers, that wild exultant music that was bitter and sweet, all at once.

Between her music and the poetry in the stag's eyes, Angharad sensed the membrane that separated this world from the Middle Kingdoms of the kowrie growing thin. So thin. Like mist. One by one the dancing kowrie passed through, thirteen grey-cloaked figures with teeth gleaming white in their dark faces as they smiled and stepped from this world to the one beyond. Last to go was the stag, he gave her one final look, the poetry shining in his eyes, then stepped away. The music stilled in Angharad's fingers. The harp fell silent. They were gone now, Pog and his kowrie. Gone from this hill, from this world.

Stepped away.

Into the green.

Hugging her harp to her chest, Angharad waited for the rising sun to wash over the old stone circle and tried not to feel so alone.

THE GRACELESS CHILD

I am not a little girl anymore.
And I am grateful and lighter
for my lessened load.
I have shouldered it.
—Ally Sheedy, from "A Man's World"

Tetchie met the tattooed man the night the wild dogs came down from the hills. She was waiting in among the roots of a tall old gnarlwood tree, waiting and watching as she did for an hour or two every night, nested down on the mossy ground with her pack under her head and her mottled cloak wrapped around her for warmth. The leaves of the gnarlwood had yet to turn, but winter seemed to be in the air that night.

She could see the tattooed man's breath cloud about him, white as pipe smoke in the moonlight. He stood just beyond the spread of the gnarlwood's twisted boughs, in the shadow of the lone standing stone that shared the hilltop with Tetchie's tree. He had a forbidding presence, tall and pale, with long fine hair the colour of bone tied back from his high brow. Above his leather trousers he was bare-chested, the swirl of his tattoos crawling across his blanched skin like pictographic insects. Tetchie couldn't read, but she knew enough to recognize that the dark blue markings were runes.

She wondered if he'd come here to talk to her father.

Tetchie burrowed a little deeper into her moss and cloak nest at the base of the gnarlwood. She knew better than to call attention to herself. When people saw her it was always the same. At best she was mocked, at worst beaten. So she'd learned to hide. She became part of the night, turned to the darkness, away from the sun. The sun made her skin itch and her eyes tear. It seemed to steal the strength from her body until she could only move at a tortoise crawl.

The night was kinder and protected her as once her mother had. Between the teachings of the two, she'd long since learned a mastery over how to remain unseen, but her skills failed her tonight.

The tattooed man turned slowly until his gaze was fixed on her hiding place.

"I know you're there," he said. His voice was deep and resonant; it sounded to Tetchie like stones grinding against each other, deep underhill, the way she imagined her father's voice would sound when he finally spoke to her. "Come out where I can see you, trow."

Shivering, Tetchie obeyed. She pushed aside the thin protection of her cloak and shuffled out into the moonlight on stubby legs. The tattooed man towered over her, but then so did most folk. She stood three-and-a-half feet high, her feet bare, the soles callused to a rocky hardness. Her skin had a greyish hue, her features were broad and square, as though chiseled from rough stone. The crudely-fashioned tunic she wore as a dress hung like a sack from her stocky body.

"I'm not a trow," she said, trying to sound brave.

Trows were tall, trollish creatures, not like her at all. She didn't have the height.

The tattooed man regarded her for so long that she began to fidget under his scrutiny. In the distance, from two hills over and beyond the town, she heard a plaintive howl that was soon answered by more of the same.

"You're just a child," the tattooed man finally said.

Tetchie shook her head. "I'm almost sixteen winters."

Most girls her age already had a babe or two hanging onto their legs as they went about their work.

"I meant in trow terms," the tattooed man replied.

"But I'm not—"

"A trow. I know. I heard you. But you've trow blood all the same. Who was your dame, your sire?"

What business is it of yours? Tetchie wanted to say, but something in the tattooed man's manner froze the words in her throat. Instead she pointed to the longstone that reared out of the dark earth of the hilltop behind him.

"The sun snared him," she said.

"And your mother?"

"Dead."

"At childbirth?"

Tetchie shook her head. "No, she...she lived long enough...."

To spare Tetchie from the worst when she was still a child.

Hanna Lief protected her daughter from the townsfolk and lived long enough to tell her, one winter's night when the ice winds stormed through the town and rattled the loose plank walls of the shed behind The Cotts Inn where they lived,

"Whatever they tell you, Tetchie, whatever lies you hear, remember this: I went to him willingly."

Tetchie rubbed at her eye with the thick knuckles of her hand.

"I was twelve when she died," she said.

"And you've lived—" The tattooed man waved a hand lazily to encompass the tree, the stone, the hills, "—here ever since?"

Tetchie nodded slowly, wondering where the tattooed man intended their conversation to lead.

"What do you eat?"

What she could gather in the hills and the woods below, what she could steal from the farms surrounding the town, what she could plunder from the midden behind the market square those rare nights that she dared to creep into the town.

But she said none of this, merely shrugged.

"I see," the tattooed man said.

She could still hear the wild dogs howl. They were closer now.

Earlier that evening, a sour expression rode the face of the man who called himself Gaedrian as he watched three men approach his table in The Cotts Inn. By the time they had completed their passage through the inn's commonroom and reached him, he had schooled his features into a bland mask. They were merchants, he decided, and was half right. They were also, he learned when they introduced themselves, citizens of very high standing in the town of Burndale.

He studied them carelessly from under hooded eyes as they eased their respective bulks into seats at his table. Each was more overweight than the next. The largest was Burndale's mayor; not quite so corpulent was the elected head of the town guilds; the smallest was the town's sheriff and he carried Gaedrian's weight and half again on a much shorter frame. Silk vests, stretched taut over obesity, were perfectly matched to flounced shirts and pleated trousers. Their boots were leather, tooled with intricate designs and buffed to a high polish. Jowls hung over stiff collars; a diamond stud gleamed in the sheriff's left earlobe.

"Something lives in the hills," the mayor said.

Gaedrian had forgotten the mayor's name as soon as it was spoken. He was fascinated by the smallness of the man's eyes and how closely set they were to each other. Pigs had eyes that were much the same, though the comparison, he chided himself, was insulting to the latter.

"Something dangerous," the mayor added.

The other two nodded, the sheriff adding, "A monster."

Gaedrian sighed. There was always something living in the hills; there were always monsters. Gaedrian knew better than most how to recognize them, but he rarely found them in the hills.

"And you want me to get rid of it?" he asked.

The town council looked hopeful. Gaedrian regarded them steadily for a long time without speaking.

He knew their kind too well. They liked to pretend that the world followed their rules, that the wilderness beyond the confines of their villages and towns could be tamed, laid out in as tidy an order as the shelves of goods in their shops, of the books in their libraries. But they also knew that under the facade of their order, the wilderness came stealing on paws that echoed with the click of claw on cobblestone. It crept into their streets and their dreams and would take up lodging in their souls if they didn't eradicate it in time.

So they came to men such as himself, men who walked the border that lay between the world they knew and so desperately needed to maintain, and the world as it truly was beyond the cluster of their stone buildings, a world that cast long shadows of fear across their streets whenever the moon went behind a bank of clouds and their streetlamps momentarily faltered.

They always recognized him, no matter how he appeared among them. These three surreptitiously studied the backs of his hands and what they could see of the skin at the hollow of his throat where the collar of his shirt lay open. They were looking for confirmation of what their need had already told them he was.

"You have gold, of course?" he asked.

The pouch appeared as if from magic from the inside pocket of the mayor's vest. It made a satisfying clink against the wooden tabletop. Gaedrian lifted a hand to the table, but it was only to grip the handle of his ale flagon and lift it to his lips. He took a long swallow, then set the empty flagon down beside the pouch.

"I will consider your kind offer," he said.

He rose from his seat and left them at the table, the pouch still untouched. When the landlord met him at the door, he jerked a thumb back to where the three men sat, turned in their seats to watch him leave.

"I believe our good lord mayor was buying this round," he told the landlord, then stepped out into the night.

He paused when he stood outside on the street, head cocked, listening. From far off, eastward, over more than one hill, he heard the baying of wild dogs, a distant, feral sound.

He nodded to himself and his lips shaped what might pass for a smile, though there was no humour in the expression. The townsfolk he passed gave him uneasy glances as he walked out of the town, into the hills that rose and fell like the tidal swells of a heathered ocean, stretching as far to the west as a man could ride in three days.

"What...what are you going to do to me?" Tetchie finally asked when the tattooed man's silence grew too long for her.

His pale gaze seemed to mock her, but he spoke very respectfully, "I'm going to save your wretched soul."

Tetchie blinked in confusion. "But I...I don't—"

"Want it saved?"

"Understand," Tetchie said.

"Can you hear them?" the tattooed man asked, only confusing her more. "The hounds," he added.

She nodded uncertainly.

"You've but to say the word and I'll give them the strength to tear down the doors and shutters in the town below. Their teeth and claws will wreak the vengeance you crave."

Tetchie took a nervous step away from him.

"But I don't want anybody to be hurt," she said.

"After all they've done to you?"

"Mama said they don't know any better."

The tattooed man's eyes grew grim. "And so you should just...forgive them?"

Too much thinking made Tetchie's head hurt.

"I don't know," she said, panic edging into her voice.

The tattooed man's anger vanished as though it had never lain there, burning in his eyes.

"Then what *do* you want?" he asked.

Tetchie regarded him nervously. There was something in how he asked that told her he already knew, that this was what he'd been wanting from her all along.

Her hesitation grew into a long silence. She could hear the dogs, closer than ever now, feral voices raised high and keening, almost like children, crying in pain. The tattooed man's gaze bore down on her, forcing her to reply. Her hand shook as she lifted her arm to point at the longstone.

"Ah," the tattooed man said.

He smiled, but Tetchie drew no comfort from that.

"That will cost," he said.

"I...I have no money."

"Have I asked for money? Did I say one word about money?"

"You...you said it would cost...."

The tattooed man nodded. "Cost, yes, but the coin is a dearer mint than gold or silver."

What could be dearer? Tetchie wondered.

"I speak of blood," the tattooed man said before she could ask. "Your blood."

His hand shot out and grasped her before she could flee.

Blood, Tetchie thought. She cursed the blood that made her move so slow.

"Don't be frightened," the tattooed man said. "I mean you no harm. It needs but a pinprick—one drop, perhaps three, and not for me. For the stone. To call him back."

His fingers loosened on her arm and she quickly moved away from him. Her gaze shifted from the stone to him, back and forth, until she felt dizzy.

"Mortal blood is the most precious blood of all," the tattooed man told her.

Tetchie nodded. Didn't she know? Without her trow blood, she'd be just like anyone else. No one would want to hurt her just because of who she was, of how she looked, of what she represented. They saw only midnight fears; all she wanted was to be liked.

"I can teach you tricks," the tattooed man went on. "I can show you how to be anything you want."

As he spoke, his features shifted until it seemed that there was a feral dog's head set upon that tattooed torso. Its fur was the same pale hue as the man's hair had been, and it still had his eyes, but it was undeniably a beast. The man was gone, leaving this strange hybrid creature in his place.

Tetchie's eyes went wide in awe. Her short, fat legs trembled until she didn't think they could hold her upright anymore.

"Anything at all," the tattooed man said, as the dog's head was replaced by his own features once more.

For a long moment, Tetchie could only stare at him. Her blood seemed to sing as it ran through her veins. To be anything at all. To be normal...but then the exhilaration that filled her trickled away. It was too good to be true, so it couldn't be true.

"Why?" she asked. "Why do you want to help me?"

"I take pleasure in helping others," he replied.

He smiled. His eyes smiled. There was such a kindly air about him that Tetchie almost forgot what he'd said about the wild dogs, about sending them down into Burndale to hunt down her tormentors. But she did remember and the memory made her uneasy.

The tattooed man seemed too much the chameleon for her to trust. He could teach her how to be anything she wanted to be. Was that why he could appear to be anything she wanted *him* to be?

"You hesitate," he said. "Why?"

Tetchie could only shrug.

"It's your chance to right the wrong played on you at your birth."

Tetchie's attention focused on the howling of the wild dogs as he spoke. To right the wrong...

Their teeth and claws will wreak the vengeance you crave.

But it didn't have to be that way. She meant no one ill. She just wanted to fit in, not hurt anyone. So, if the choice was hers, she could simply choose not to hurt people, couldn't she? The tattooed man couldn't *make* her hurt people.

"What...what do I have to do?" she asked.

The tattooed man pulled a long silver needle from where it had been stuck in the front of his trousers.

"Give me your thumb," he said.

Gaedrian scented trow as soon as he left Burndale behind him. It wasn't a strong scent, more a promise than an actuality at first, but the further he got from the town, the more pronounced it grew. He stopped and tested the wind, but it kept shifting, making it difficult for him to pinpoint its source. Finally he stripped his shirt, letting it fall to the ground.

He touched one of the tattoos on his chest and a pale blue light glimmered in his palm when he took his hand away. He freed the glow into the air where it turned slowly, end on shimmering end. When it had given him the source of the scent, he snapped his fingers and the light winked out.

More assured now, he set off again, destination firmly in mind. The townsfolk, he realized, had been accurate for a change. A monster did walk the hills outside Burndale tonight.

Nervously, Tetchie stepped forward. As she got closer to him, the blue markings on his chest seemed to shift and move, rearranging themselves into a new pattern that was as indecipherable to her as the old one had been. Tetchie swallowed thickly and lifted her hand, hoping it wouldn't hurt. She closed her eyes as he brought the tip of the needle to her thumb.

"There," the tattooed man said a moment later. "It's all done."

Tetchie blinked in surprise. She hadn't felt a thing. But now that the tattooed man had let go of her hand, her thumb started to ache. She looked at the three drops of blood that lay in the tattooed man's palm like tiny crimson jewels. Her knees went weak again and this time she did fall to the ground. She felt hot and flushed, as though she were up and abroad at high noon, the sun broiling down on her, stealing her ability to move.

Slowly, slowly, she lifted her head. She wanted to see what happened when the tattooed man put her blood on the stone, but all he did was smile down at her and lick three drops with a tongue that seemed as long as a snake's, with the same kind of a twin fork at its tip.

"Yuh…nuh…."

Tetchie tried to speak—what have you done to me? she wanted to say—but the words turned into a muddle before they left her mouth. It was getting harder to think.

"When your mother was so kindly passing along all her advice to you," he said, "she should have warned you about not trusting strangers. Most folk have little use for your kind, it's true."

Tetchie thought her eyes were playing tricks on her, then realized that the tattooed man must be shifting his shape once more. His hair grew darker as she watched, his complexion deepened. No longer pale and wan, he seemed to bristle with sorcerous energy now.

"But then," the tattooed man went on, "they don't have the knowledge I do. I thank you for your vitality, halfling. There's nothing so potent as mortal blood stirred in a stew of faerie. A pity you won't live long enough to put the knowledge to use."

He gave her a mocking salute, fingers tipped against his brow, then away, before turning his back on her. The night swallowed him.

Tetchie fought to get to her own feet, but she just wore herself out until she could no longer even lift her head from the ground. Tears of frustration welled in her eyes. What had he done to her? She'd seen it for herself, he'd taken no more than three drops of her blood. But then why did she feel as though he'd taken it all?

She stared up at the night sky, the stars blurring in her gaze, spinning, spinning, until finally she just let them take her away.

She wasn't sure what had brought her back, but when she opened her eyes, it was to find that the tattooed man had returned. He crouched over her, concern for her swimming in his dark eyes. His skin had regained its almost colourless complexion, his hair was bone white once more. She mustered what little strength she had to work up a gob of saliva and spat in his face.

The tattooed man didn't move. She watched the saliva dribble down his cheek until it fell from the tip of his chin to the ground beside her.

"Poor child," he said. "What has he done to you?"

The voice was wrong, Tetchie realized. He'd changed his voice now. The low grumble of stones grinding against each other deep underhill had been replaced by a soft melodious tonality that was comforting on the ear.

He touched the fingers of one hand to a tattoo high on his shoulder, waking a blue glow that flickered on his fingertips. She flinched when he touched her brow with the hand, but the contact of blue fingers against her skin brought an immediate easing to the weight of her pain. When he sat back on his haunches, she found she had the strength to lift herself up from the ground. Her gaze spun for a moment, then settled down. The new perspective helped stem the helplessness she'd been feeling.

"I wish I could do more for you," the tattooed man said.

Tetchie merely glared at him, thinking, haven't you done enough?

The tattooed man gave her a mild look, head cocked slightly as though listening to her thoughts.

"He calls himself Nallorn on this side of the Gates," he said finally, "but you would call him Nightmare, did you meet him in the land of his origin, beyond the Gates of Sleep. He thrives on pain and torment. We have been enemies for a very long time."

Tetchie blinked in confusion. "But...you...."

The tattooed man nodded. "I know. We look the same. We are brothers, child. I am the elder. My name is Dream; on this side of the Gates I answer to the name Gaedrian."

"He...your brother...he took something from me."

"He stole your mortal ability to dream," Gaedrian told her. "Tricked you into giving it freely so that it would retain its potency."

Tetchie shook her head. "I don't understand. Why would he come to me? I'm no one. I don't have any powers or magics that anyone could want."

"Not that you can use yourself, perhaps, but the mix of trow and mortal blood creates a potent brew. Each drop of such blood is a talisman in the hands of one who understands its properties."

"Is he stronger than you?" Tetchie asked.

"Not in the land beyond the Gates of Sleep. There I am the elder. The Realms of Dream are mine and all who sleep are under my rule when they come through the Gates." He paused, dark eyes thoughtful, before adding, "In this world, we are more evenly matched."

"Nightmares come from him?" Tetchie asked.

Gaedrian nodded. "It isn't possible for a ruler to see all the parts of his kingdom at once. Nallorn is the father of lies. He creeps into sleeping minds when my attention is distracted elsewhere and makes a horror of healing dreams."

He stood up then, towering over her.

"I must go," he said. "I must stop him before he grows too strong."

Tetchie could see the doubt in his eyes and understood then that though he knew his brother to be stronger than him, he would not admit to it, would not turn from what he saw as his duty. She tried to stand, but her strength still hadn't returned.

"Take me with you," she said. "Let me help you."

"You don't know what you ask."

"But I want to help."

Gaedrian smiled. "Bravely spoken, but this is war and no place for a child."

Tetchie searched for the perfect argument to convince him, but couldn't find it. He said nothing, but she knew as surely as if he'd spoken why he didn't want her to come. She would merely slow him down. She had no skills, only her night sight and the slowness of her limbs. Neither would be of help.

During the lull in their conversation when that understanding came to her, she heard the howling once more.

"The dogs," she said.

"There are no wild dogs," Gaedrian told her. "That is only the sound of the wind as it crosses the empty reaches of his soul." He laid a hand on her head, tousled her hair. "I'm sorry for the hurt that's come to you with this night's work. If the fates are kind to me, I will try to make amends."

Before Tetchie could respond, he strode off, westward. She tried to follow, but could barely crawl after him. By the time she reached the crest of the hill, the longstone rearing above her, she saw Gaedrian's long legs carrying him up the side of the next hill. In the distance, blue lightning played, close to the ground.

Nallorn, she thought.

He was waiting for Gaedrian. Nallorn meant to kill the dreamlord and then he would rule the land beyond the Gates of Sleep. There would be no more dreams, only nightmares. People would fear sleep, for it would no longer be a haven. Nallorn would twist its healing peace into pain and despair.

And it was all her fault. She'd been thinking only of herself. She'd wanted to talk to her father, to be normal. She hadn't known who Nallorn was at the time, but ignorance was no excuse.

"It doesn't matter what others think of you," her mother had told her once, "but what you think of yourself. Be a good person and no matter how other people will talk of you, what they say can only be a lie."

They called her a monster and feared her. She saw now that it wasn't a lie.

She turned to the longstone that had been her father before the sun had snared him and turned him to stone. Why couldn't that have happened to her before all of this began, why couldn't she have been turned to stone the first time the sun touched her? Then Nallorn could never have played on her vanity and her need, would never have tricked her. If she'd been stone…

Her gaze narrowed. She ran a hand along the rough surface of the standing stone and Nallorn's voice spoke in her memory.

I speak of blood.

It needs but a pinprick—one drop, perhaps three, and not for me. For the stone. To call him back.

To call him back.

Nallorn had proved there was magic in her blood. If he hadn't lied, if….

Could she call her father back? And if he did return, would he listen to her? It was night, the time when a trow was strongest. Surely when she explained, her father would use that strength to help Gaedrian?

A babble of townsfolk's voices clamored up through her memory.

A trow'll drink your blood as sure as look at you.

Saw one I did, sitting up by the boneyard, and wasn't he chewing on a thigh-bone he'd dug up?

The creatures have no heart.

No soul.

They'll feed on their own, if there's no other meat to be found.

No, Tetchie told herself. Those were the lies her mother had warned her against. If her mother had loved the trow, then he couldn't have been evil.

Her thumb still ached where Nallorn had pierced it with his long silver pin, but the tiny wound had closed. Tetchie bit at it until the salty taste of blood touched her tongue. Then she squeezed her thumb, smearing the few drops of blood that welled up against the rough surface of the stone.

She had no expectations, only hope. She felt immediately weak, just as she had when Nallorn had taken the three small drops of blood from her. The world began to spin for the second time that night, and she started to fall once more, only this time she fell into the stone. The hard surface seemed to have turned to the consistency of mud and it swallowed her whole.

When consciousness finally returned, Tetchie found herself lying with her face pressed against hard packed dirt. She lifted her head, squinting in the poor light. The longstone was gone, along with the world she knew. For as far as she could see, there was only a desolate wasteland, illuminated by a sickly twilight for which she could discover no source. It was still the landscape she knew, the hills and valleys had the same contours as those that lay west of Burndale, but it was all changed. Nothing seemed to grow here anymore; nothing lived at all in this place, except for her, and she had her doubts about that as well.

If this was a dead land, a lifeless reflection of the world she knew, then might she not have died to reach it?

Oddly enough, the idea didn't upset her. It was as though, having seen so much that was strange already tonight, nothing more could surprise her.

When she turned to where the old gnarlwood had been in her world, a dead tree stump stood. It was no more than three times her height, the area about it littered with dead branches. The main body of the tree had fallen away from where Tetchie knelt, lying down the slope.

She rose carefully to her feet, but the dizziness and weakness she'd felt earlier had both fled. In the dirt at her feet, where the longstone would have stood in her world, there was a black pictograph etched deeply into the soil. It reminded her of the tattoos that she'd seen on the chests of the dreamlord and his brother, as though it had been plucked from the skin of one of them, enlarged and cast down on the ground. Goosebumps traveled up her arms.

She remembered what Gaedrian had told her about the land he ruled, how the men and women of her world could enter it only after passing through the Gates of Sleep. She'd been so weak when she offered her blood to the longstone, her eyelids growing so heavy....

Was this all just a dream, then? And if so, what was its source? Did it come from Gaedrian, or from his brother Nallorn at whose bidding nightmares were born?

She went down on one knee to look more closely at the pictograph. It looked a bit like a man with a tangle of rope around his feet and lines standing out from his head as though his hair stood on end. She reached out with one cautious finger and touched the tangle of lines at the foot of the rough figure. The dirt was damp there. She rubbed her finger against her thumb. The dampness was oily to the touch.

Scarcely aware of what she was doing, she reached down again and traced the symbol, the slick oiliness letting her finger slide easily along the edged grooves in the dirt. When she came to the end, the pictograph began to glow. She stood quickly, backing away.

What had she *done?*

The blue glow rose into the air, holding to the shape that lay in the dirt. A faint rhythmic thrumming rose from all around her, as though the ground was shifting, but she felt no vibration underfoot. There was just the sound, low and ominous.

A branch cracked behind her and she turned to the ruin of the gnarlwood. A tall shape stood outlined against the sky. She started to call out to it, but her throat closed up on her. And then she was aware of the circle of eyes that watched her from all sides of the hilltop, pale eyes that flickered with the reflection of the glowing pictograph that hung in the air where the longstone stood in her world. They were set low to the ground; feral eyes.

She remembered the howling of the wild dogs in her own world.

There are no wild dogs, Gaedrian had told her. *That is only the sound of the wind as it crosses the empty reaches of his soul.*

As the eyes began to draw closer, she could make out the triangular-shaped heads of the creatures they belonged to, the high-backed bodies with which they slunk forward.

Oh, why had she believed Gaedrian? She knew him no better than Nallorn. Who was to say that *either* of them was to be trusted?

One of the dogs rose up to its full height and stalked forward on stiff legs. The low growl that arose in his chest echoed the rumble of sound that her foolishness with the glowing pictograph had called up. She started to back away from the dog, but now another, and a third stepped forward and there was no place to which she could retreat. She turned her gaze to the silent figure that stood in among the fallen branches of the gnarlwood.

"Puh—please," she managed. "I...I meant no harm."

The figure made no response, but the dogs growled at the sound of her voice. The nearest pulled its lips back in a snarl.

This was it, Tetchie thought. If she wasn't dead already in this land of the dead, then she soon would be.

But then the figure by the tree moved forward. It had a slow shuffling step. Branches broke underfoot as it closed the distance between them.

The dogs backed away from Tetchie and began to whine uneasily.

"Be gone," the figure said.

Its voice was low and craggy, stone against stone, like that of the first tattooed man, Nallorn, the dreamlord's brother who turned dreams into nightmares. It was a counterpoint to the deep thrumming that seemed to come from the hill under Tetchie's feet.

The dogs fled at the sound of the man's voice. Tetchie's knees knocked against each other as he moved closer still. She could see the rough chiseled shape of his features now, the shock of tangled hair, stiff as dried gorse, the wide bulk of his shoulders and torso, the corded muscle upon muscle that made up his arms and legs. His eyes were sunk deep under protruding brows. He was like the first rough shaping that a sculptor might create when beginning a new work, face and musculature merely outlined rather than clearly defined as it would be when the sculpture was complete.

Except this sculpture wasn't stone, nor clay, nor marble. It was flesh and blood. And though he was no taller than a normal man, he seemed like a giant to Tetchie, towering over her as though the side of a mountain had pulled loose to walk the hills.

"Why did you call me?" he asked.

"C—call?" Tetchie replied. "But I...I didn't...."

Her voice trailed off. She gazed on him with sudden hope and understanding.

"Father?" she asked in a small voice.

The giant regarded her in a long silence. Then slowly he bent down to one knee so that his head was on level with hers.

"You," he said in a voice grown with wonder. "You are Henna's daughter?"

Tetchie nodded, nervously.

"*My* daughter?"

Tetchie's nervousness fled. She no longer saw a fearsome trow out of legend, but her mother's lover. The gentleness and warmth that had called her mother from Burndale to where he waited for her on the moors, washed over her. He opened his arms and she went to him, sighing as he embraced her.

"My name's Tetchie," she said into his shoulder.

"Tetchie," he repeated, making a low rumbling song of her name. "I never knew I had a daughter."

"I came every night to your stone," she said, "hoping you'd return."

Her father pulled back a little and gave her a serious look.

"I can't ever go back," he said.

"But—"

He shook his head. "Dead is dead, Tetchie. I can't return."

"But this is a horrible place to have to live."

He smiled, craggy features shifting like a mountainside suddenly rearranging its terrain.

"I don't live here," he said. "I live...I can't explain how it is. There are no words to describe the difference."

"Is mama there?"

"Hanna...died?"

Tetchie nodded. "Years ago, but I still miss her."

"I will...look for her," the trow said. "I will give her your love." He rose then, looming over her again. "But I must go now, Tetchie. This is unhallowed land, the perilous border that lies between life and death. Bide here too long—living or dead—and you remain here forever."

Tetchie had wanted to ask him to take her with him to look for her mother, to tell him that living meant only pain and sorrow for her, but then she realized she was only thinking of herself again. She still wasn't sure that she trusted Gaedrian, but if he had been telling her the truth, then she had to try to help him. Her own life was a nightmare; she wouldn't wish for all people to share such a life.

"I need your help," she said and told him then of Gaedrian and Nallorn, the war that was being fought between Dream and Nightmare that Nallorn could not be allowed to win.

Her father shook his head sadly. "I can't help you, Tetchie. It's not physically possible for me to return."

"But if Gaedrian loses...."

"That would be an evil thing," her father agreed.

"There must be something we can do."

He was silent for long moments then.

"What is it?" Tetchie asked. "What don't you want to tell me?"

"I can do nothing," her father said, "but you…."

Again he hesitated.

"What?" Tetchie asked. "What is it that I can do?"

"I can give you of my strength," her father said. "You'll be able to help your dreamlord then. But it will cost you. You will be more trow than ever, and remain so."

More trow? Tetchie thought. She looked at her father, felt the calm that seemed to wash in peaceful waves from his very presence. The townsfolk might think that a curse, but she no longer did.

"I'd be proud to be more like you," she said.

"You will have to give up all pretense of humanity," her father warned her. "When the sun rises, you must be barrowed underhill or she'll make you stone."

"I already only come out at night," she said.

Her father's gaze searched hers and then he sighed.

"Yours has not been an easy life," he said.

Tetchie didn't want to talk about herself anymore.

"Tell me what to do," she said.

"You must take some of my blood," her father told her.

Blood again. Tetchie had seen and heard enough about it to last her a lifetime tonight.

"But how can you do that?" she asked. "You're just a spirit…."

Her father touched her arm. "Given flesh in this half-world by your call. Have you a knife?"

When Tetchie shook her head, he lifted his thumb to his mouth and bit down on it. Dark liquid welled up at the cut as he held his hand out to her.

"It will burn," he said.

Tetchie nodded nervously. Closing her eyes, she opened her mouth. Her father brought his thumb down across her tongue. His blood tasted like fire, burning its way down her throat. She shuddered with the searing pain of it, eyes tearing so that even when she opened them, she was still blind.

She felt her father's hand on her head. He smoothed the tangle of her hair and then kissed her.

"Be well, my child," he said. "We will look for you, your mother and I, when your time to join us has come and you finally cross over."

There were a hundred things Tetchie realized that she wanted to say, but vertigo overtook her and she knew that not only was he gone, but the empty world as well. She could feel grass under her, a soft breeze on her cheek. When she opened her eyes, the longstone reared up on one side of her, the gnarlwood on the other. She turned to look where she'd last seen the blue lightning flare before she'd gone into the stone.

There was no light there now.

She got to her feet, feeling invigorated rather than weak. Her night sight seemed to have sharpened, every sense was more alert. She could almost read the night simply through the pores of her skin.

The townsfolk were blind, she realized. *She* had been blind. They had all missed so much of what the world had to offer. But the townsfolk craved a narrower world, rather than a wider one, and she...she had a task yet to perform.

She set off to where the lightning had been flickering.

The grass was all burned away, the ground itself scorched on the hilltop that was her destination. She saw a figure lying in the dirt and hesitated, unsure as to who it was. Gaedrian or his brother? She moved cautiously forward until finally she knelt by the still figure. His eyes opened and looked upon her with a weak gaze.

"I was not strong enough," Gaedrian said, his voice still sweet and ringing, but much subdued.

"Where did he go?" Tetchie asked.

"To claim his own: the land of Dream."

Tetchie regarded him for a long moment, then lifted her thumb to her mouth. It was time for blood again—but this would be the last time. Gaedrian tried to protest, but she pushed aside his hands and let the drops fall into his mouth: one, two, three. Gaedrian swallowed. His eyes went wide with an almost comical astonishment.

"Where...how...?"

"I found my father," Tetchie said. "This is the heritage he left me."

Senses all more finally attuned, to be sure, but when she lifted an arm to show Gaedrian, the skin was darker, greyer than before and tough as bark. And she would never see the day again.

"You should not have—" Gaedrian began, but Tetchie cut him off.

"Is it enough?" she asked. "Can you stop him now?"

Gaedrian sat up. He rolled his shoulders, flexed his hand and arms, his legs.

"More than enough," he said. "I feel a hundred years younger."

Knowing him for what he was, Tetchie didn't think he was exaggerating. Who knew how old the dreamlord was? He would have been born with the first dream.

He cupped her face with his hands and kissed her on the brow.

"I will try to make amends for what my brother has done to you this night," he said. "The whole world owes you for the rescue of its dreams."

"I don't want any reward," Tetchie said.

"We'll talk of that when I return for you," Gaedrian said.

If you can find me, Tetchie thought, but she merely nodded in reply.

Gaedrian stood. One hand plucked at a tattoo just to one side of his breastbone and tossed the ensuing blue light into the air. It grew into a shimmering portal. Giving her one more grateful look, he stepped through. The portal closed behind him, winking out in a flare of blue sparks, like those cast by a fire when a log's tossed on.

Tetchie looked about the scorched hilltop, then set off back to Burndale. She walked its cobblestoned streets, one lone figure, dwarfed by the buildings, more kin to their walls and foundations than to those sleeping within. She thought of her mother when she reached The Cotts Inn and stood looking at the shed around back by the stables where they had lived for all of those years.

Finally, just as the dawn was pinking the horizon, she made her way back to the hill where she'd first met the tattooed men. She ran her fingers along the bark of the gnarlwood, then stepped closer to the longstone, standing on the east side of it.

It wasn't entirely true that she could never see the day again. She *could* see it, if only once.

Tetchie was still standing there when the sun rose and snared her and then there were two standing stones on the hilltop keeping company to the old gnarlwood tree, one tall and one much smaller. But Tetchie herself was gone to follow her parents, a lithe spirit of a child finally, her gracelessness left behind in stone.

WINTER WAS HARD

I pretty much try to stay in a constant
state of confusion just because of the
expression it leaves on my face.
—Johnny Depp

It was the coldest December since they'd first started keeping records at the turn of the century, though warmer, Jilly thought, than it must have been in the ice ages of the Pleistocene. The veracity of that extraneous bit of trivia gave her small comfort, for it did nothing to lessen the impact of the night's bitter weather. The wind shrieked through the tunnel-like streets created by the abandoned buildings of the Tombs, carrying with it a deep, arctic chill. It spun the granular snow into dervishing whirligigs that made it almost impossible to see at times and packed drifts up against the sides of the buildings and derelict cars.

Jilly felt like a little kid, bundled up in her boots and parka, with longjohns under her jeans, a woolen cap pushing down her unruly curls and a long scarf wrapped about fifty times around her neck and face, cocooning her so completely that only her eyes peered out through a narrow slit. Turtle-like, she hunched her shoulders, trying to make her neck disappear into her parka, and stuffed her mittened hands deep in its pockets.

It didn't help. The wind bit through it all as though unhindered, and she just grew colder with each step she took as she plodded on through the deepening drifts. The work crews were already out with their carnival of flashing blue and amber lights, removing the snow on Gracie Street and Williamson, but here in the Tombs it would just lie where it fell until the spring melt. The only signs of humanity were the odd little trails that the derelicts and other inhabitants of the Tombs made as they went about their business, but even those were being swallowed by the storm.

Only fools or those who had no choice were out tonight. Jilly thought she should be counted among the latter, though Geordie had called her the former when she'd left the loft earlier in the evening.

"This is just craziness, Jilly," he'd said. "Look at the bloody weather."

"I've got to go. It's important."

"To you and the penguins, but nobody else."

Still, she'd had to come. It was the eve of the solstice, one year exactly since the gemmin went away, and she didn't feel as though she had any choice in the matter. She was driven to walk the Tombs tonight, never mind the storm. What sent her out from the warm comfort of her loft was like what Professor Dapple said they used to call a geas in the old days—something you just had to do.

So she left Geordie sitting on her Murphy bed, playing his new Copeland whistle, surrounded by finished and unfinished canvases and the rest of the clutter that her motley collection of possessions had created in the loft, and went out into the storm.

She didn't pause until she reached the mouth of the alley that ran along the south side of the old Clark Building. There, under the suspicious gaze of the building's snow-swept gargoyles, she hunched her back against the storm and pulled her scarf down a little, widening the eye slit so that she could have a clearer look down the length of the alley. She could almost see Babe, leaning casually against the side of the old Buick that was still sitting there, dressed in her raggedy T-shirt, black body stocking and raincoat, Doc Martens dark against the snow that lay underfoot. She could almost hear the high husky voices of the other gemmin, chanting an eerie version of a rap song that had been popular at the time.

She could almost—

But no. She blinked as the wind shifted, blinding her with snow. She saw only snow, heard only the wind. But in her memory....

By night they nested in one of those abandoned cars that could be found on any street or alley of the Tombs—a handful of gangly teenagers burrowed under blankets, burlap sacks and tattered jackets, bodies snugly fit into holes that seemed to have been chewed from the ragged upholstery. This morning they had built a fire in the trunk of the Buick, scavenging fuel from the buildings, and one of them was cooking their breakfast on the heated metal of its hood.

Babe was the oldest. She looked about seventeen—it was something in the way she carried herself—but otherwise had the same thin androgynous body as her companions. The other gemmin all had dark complexions and feminine features, but none of them had Babe's short mauve hair, nor her luminous violet eyes. The hair colouring of the others ran more to various shades of henna red; their eyes were mostly the same electric blue that Jilly's were.

That December had been as unnaturally warm as this one was cold, but Babe's open raincoat with the thin T-shirt and body stocking underneath still made Jilly pause with concern. There was such a thing as carrying fashion too far, she thought—had they never heard of pneumonia?—but then Babe lifted her head, her large violet eyes fixing their gaze as curiously on Jilly as Jilly's did on her. Concern fell by the wayside, shifting into a sense of frustration as Jilly realized that all she had in the pocket of her coat that day was a stub of charcoal and her sketchbook instead of the oils and canvas which were all that could really do justice in capturing the startling picture Babe and her companions made.

For long moments none of them spoke. Babe watched her, a half-smile teasing one corner of her mouth. Behind her, the cook stood motionless, a makeshift spatula held negligently in a delicate hand. Eggs and bacon sizzled on the trunk hood in front of her, filling the air with their unmistakable aroma. The other gemmin peered up over the dash of the Buick, supporting their narrow chins on their folded arms.

All Jilly could do was look back. A kind of vertigo licked at the edges of her mind, making her feel as though she'd just stepped into one of her own paintings—the ones that made up her last show, an urban faerie series: twelve enormous canvases, all in oils, one for each month, each depicting a different kind of mythological being transposed from its traditional folkloric rural surroundings onto a cityscape.

Her vague dizziness wasn't caused by the promise of magic that seemed to decorate the moment with a sparkling sense of impossible possibilities as surely as the bacon filled the air with its come-hither smell. It was rather the unexpectedness of coming across a moment like this—in the Tombs, of all places, where winos and junkies were the norm.

It took her awhile to collect her thoughts.

"Interesting stove you've got there," she said finally.

Babe's brow furrowed for a moment, then cleared as a radiant smile first lifted the corners of her mouth, then put an infectious humour into those amazing eyes of hers.

"Interesting, yes," she said. Her voice had an accent Jilly couldn't place and an odd tonality that was at once both husky and high-pitched. "But we—" she frowned prettily, searching for what she wanted to say, "—make do."

It was obvious to Jilly that English wasn't her first language. It was also obvious, the more Jilly looked, that while the girl and her companions weren't at all properly dressed for the weather, it really didn't seem to bother them. Even with the fire in the trunk of the Buick, and mild winter or not, they should still have been shivering, but she couldn't spot one goosebump.

"And you're not cold?" she asked.

"Cold is...?" Babe began, frowning again, but before Jilly could elaborate, that dazzling smile returned. "No, we have comfort. Cold is no trouble for us. We like the winter; we like any weather."

Jilly couldn't help but laugh.

"I suppose you're all snow elves," she said, "so the cold doesn't bother you?"

"Not elves—but we are good neighbours. Would you like some breakfast?"

A year and three days later, the memory of that first meeting brought a touch of warmth to Jilly where she stood shivering in the mouth of the alleyway. Gemmin. She'd always liked the taste of words and that one had sounded just right for Babe and her companions. It reminded Jilly of gummy bears, thick cotton quilts and the sound that the bass strings of Geordie's fiddle made when he was playing a fast reel. It reminded her of tiny bunches of fresh violets, touched with dew, which still couldn't hope to match the incandescent hue of Babe's eyes.

She had met the gemmin at a perfect time. She was in need of something warm and happy just then, being on the wrong end of a nine-month relationship with a guy who, during those many months of their being together, turned out to have been married all along. He wouldn't leave his wife, and Jilly had no taste to be someone's—anyone's—mistress, all of which had been discussed in increasingly raised voices in The Monkey Woman's Nest the last time she saw him. She'd been mortified when she realized that a whole restaurant full of people had been listening to their breaking up argument, but unrepentant.

She missed Jeff—missed him desperately—but refused to listen to any of the subsequent phone calls or answer any of the letters that had deluged her loft over the next few weeks, explaining how they could "work things out." She wasn't interested in working things out. It wasn't just the fact that he had a wife, but that he'd kept it from her. The thing she kept asking her best friend Sue was: having been with him for all that time, how could she not have *known*?

So she wasn't a happy camper, traipsing aimlessly through the Tombs that day. Her normally high-spirited view of the world was overhung with gloominess and there was a sick feeling in the pit of her stomach that just wouldn't go away.

Until she met Babe and her friends.

Gemmin wasn't a name that they used; they had no name for themselves. It was Frank Hodgers who told Jilly what they were.

Breakfast with the gemmin on that long gone morning was...odd. Jilly sat behind the driver's wheel of the Buick, with the door propped open and her feet dangling outside. Babe sat on a steel drum set a few feet from the car, facing her. Four of the other gemmin were crowded in the backseat; the fifth was beside Jilly in the front, her back against the passenger's door. The eggs were tasty, flavoured with herbs that Jilly couldn't recognize; the tea had a similarly odd tang about it. The bacon was fried to a perfect crisp. The toast was actually muffins, neatly sliced in two and toasted on coat hangers rebent into new shapes for that purpose.

The gemmin acted like they were having a picnic. When Jilly introduced herself, a chorus of odd names echoed back in reply: Nita, Emmie, Callio, Yoon, Purspie. And Babe.

"Babe?" Jilly repeated.

"It was a present—from Johnny Defalco."

Jilly had seen Defalco around and talked to him once or twice. He was a hash dealer who'd had himself a squat in the Clark Building up until the end of the summer when he'd made the mistake of selling to a narc and had to leave the city just one step ahead of a warrant. Somehow, she couldn't see him keeping company with this odd little gaggle of street girls. Defalco's taste seemed to run more to what her bouncer friend Percy called the three B's—bold, blonde and built—or at least it had whenever she'd seen him in the clubs.

"He gave all of you your names? Jilly asked.

Babe shook her head. "He only ever saw me, and whenever he did, he'd say, 'Hey Babe, how're ya doin'?'"

Babe's speech patterns seemed to change the longer they talked, Jilly remembered thinking later. She no longer sounded like a foreigner struggling with the language; instead, the words came easily, sentences peppered with conjunctions and slang.

"We miss him," Purspie—or perhaps it was Nita—said. Except for Babe, Jilly was still having trouble telling them all apart.

"He talked in the dark." That was definitely Emmie—her voice was slightly higher than those of the others.

"He told stories to the walls," Babe explained, "and we'd creep close and listen to him."

"You've lived around here for awhile?" Jilly asked.

Yoon—or was it Callio?—nodded. "All our lives."

Jilly had to smile at the seriousness with which that line was delivered. As though, except for Babe, there was one of them older than thirteen.

She spent the rest of the morning with them, chatting, listening to their odd songs, sketching them whenever she could get them to sit still for longer than five seconds. Thanks goodness, she thought more than once as she bent over her sketchbook, for life drawing classes and Albert Choira, her arts instructor at Butler U., who had instilled in her and every one of his students the ability to capture shape and form in just a few quick strokes of charcoal.

Her depression and the sick feeling in her stomach had gone away, and her heart didn't feel nearly so fragile anymore, but all too soon it was noon and time for her to go. She had Christmas presents to deliver at St. Vincent's Home for the Aged where she did volunteer work twice a week. Some of her favourites were going to stay with family during the holidays and today would be her last chance to see them.

"We'll be going soon, too," Babe told her when Jilly explained she had to leave.

"Going?" Jilly repeated, feeling an odd tightness in her chest. It wasn't the same kind of a feeling that Jeff had left in her, but it was discomforting all the same.

Babe nodded. "When the moon's full, we'll sail away."

"Away, away, away," the others chorused.

There was something both sweet and sad in the way they half-spoke, half-chanted the words. The tightness in Jilly's chest grew more pronounced. She wanted to ask, Away to where?, but found herself only saying, "But you'll be here tomorrow?"

Babe lifted a delicate hand to push back the unruly curls that were forever falling in Jilly's eyes. There was something so maternal in the motion that it made Jilly wish she could just rest her head on Babe's breast, to be protected from all that was fierce and mean and dangerous in the world beyond the enfolding comfort that her motherly embrace would offer.

"We'll be here," Babe said.

Then, giggling like schoolgirls, the little band ran off through the ruins, leaving Jilly to stand alone on the deserted street. She felt giddy and lost, all at once. She wanted to run with them, imagining Babe as a kind of archetypal Peter Pan who could take her away to a place where she could be forever young. Then she shook her head, and headed back downtown to St. Vincent's.

She saved her visit with Frank for last, as she always did. He was sitting in a wheelchair by the small window in his room that overlooked the alley between St. Vincent's and the office building next door. It wasn't much of a view, but Frank never seemed to mind.

"I'd rather stare at a brick wall, anytime, than watch that damn TV in the lounge," he'd told Jilly more than once. "That's when things started to go wrong—with the invention of television. Wasn't till then that we found out there was so much wrong in the world."

Jilly was one of those who'd rather know what was going on and try to do something about it, than those who preferred to pretend it wasn't happening and hoped that, by ignoring what was wrong, it would just go away. Truth was, Jilly had long ago learned that trouble never went away. It just got worse—unless you fixed it. But at eighty-seven, she felt that Frank was entitled to his opinions.

His face lit up when she came in the door. He was all lines and bones, as he liked to say. A skinny man, made almost cadaverous by age. His cheeks were hollowed, eyes sunken, torso collapsed in on itself. His skin was wrinkled and dry, his hair just a few white tufts around his ears. But whatever ruin the years had brought to his body, they hadn't managed to get even a fingerhold on his spirit. He could be cantankerous, but he was never bitter.

She'd first met him last spring. His son had died, and with nowhere else to go, he'd come to live at St. Vincent's. From the first afternoon that she met him in his room, he'd become one of her favourite people.

"You've got that look," he said after she'd kissed his cheek and sat down on the edge of his bed.

"What look?" Jilly asked, pretending ignorance.

She often gave the impression of being in a constant state of confusion—which was what gave her her charm, Sue had told her more than once—but she knew that Frank wasn't referring to that. It was that strange occurrences tended to gather around her; mystery clung to her like burrs on an old sweater.

At one time when she was younger, she just collected folktales and odd stories, magical rumours and mythologies—much like Geordie's brother Christy did, although she never published them. She couldn't have explained why she was drawn to that kind of story; she just liked the idea of what they had to say. But then one day she discovered that there *was* an alternate reality, and her view of the world was forever changed.

It had felt like a curse at first, knowing that magic was real, but that if she spoke of it, people would think her mad. But the wonder it woke in her could never be considered a curse and she merely learned to be careful with whom she spoke. It was in her art that she allowed herself total freedom to express what she saw from the corner of her eye. An endless stream of faerie folk paraded from her easel and sketchbook, making new homes for themselves in back alleys and city parks, on the wharves down by the waterfront or in the twisty lanes of Lower Crowsea.

In that way, she and Frank were much alike. He'd been a writer once, but, "I've told all the tales I have to tell by now," he explained to Jilly when she asked him why he'd stopped. She disagreed, but knew that his arthritis was so bad that he could neither hold a pencil nor work a keyboard for any length of time.

"You've seen something magic," he said to her now.

"I have," she replied with a grin and told him of her morning.

"Show me your sketches," Frank said when she was done.

Jilly dutifully handed them over, apologizing for the rough state they were in until Frank told her to shush. He turned the pages of the sketchbook, studying each quick drawing carefully before going on to the next one.

"They're gemmin," he pronounced finally.

"I've never heard of them."

"Most people haven't. It was my grandmother who told me about them—she saw them one night, dancing in Fitzhenry Park—but I never did."

The wistfulness in his voice made Jilly want to stage a breakout from the old folk's home and carry him off to the Tombs to meet Babe, but she knew she couldn't. She couldn't even bring him home to her own loft for the holidays because he was too dependent on the care that he could only get here. She'd never even be able to carry him up the steep stairs to her loft.

"How do you know that they're gemmin and whatever *are* gemmin?" she asked.

Frank tapped the sketchbook. "I know they're gemmin because they look just like the way my gran described them to me. And didn't you say they had violet eyes?"

"But only Babe's got them."

Frank smiled, enjoying himself. "Do you know what violet's made up of?"

"Sure. Blue and red."

"Which, symbolically, stand for devotion and passion; blended into violet, they're a symbol of memory."

"That still doesn't explain anything."

"Gemmin are the spirits of place, just like hobs are spirits of a house. They're what make a place feel good and safeguard its positive memories. When they leave, that's when a place gets a haunted feeling. And then only the bad feelings are left—or no feelings, which is just about the same difference."

"So what makes them go?" Jilly asked, remembering what Babe had said earlier.

"Nasty things happening. In the old days, it might be a murder or a battle. Nowadays we can add pollution and the like to that list."

"But—"

"They store memories you see," Frank went on. "The one you call Babe is the oldest, so her eyes have turned violet."

"So," Jilly asked with a grin, "Does it make their hair go mauve, too?"

"Don't be impudent."

They talked some more about the gemmin, going back and forth between, "Were they really?" and "What else could they be?" until it was time for Frank's supper and Jilly had to go. But first she made him open his Christmas present. His eyes filmed when he saw the tiny painting of his old house that Jilly had done for him. Sitting on the stoop was a younger version of himself with a small faun standing jauntily behind him, elbow resting on his shoulder.

"Got something in my eye," he muttered as he brought his sleeve up to his eyes.

"I just wanted you to have this today, because I brought everybody else their presents," Jilly said, "but I'm coming back on Christmas—we'll do something fun. I'd come Christmas Eve, but I've got to work at the restaurant that night."

Frank nodded. His tears were gone, but his eyes were still shiny.

"The solstice is coming," he said. "In two days."

Jilly nodded, but didn't say anything.

"That's when they'll be going," Frank explained. "The gemmin. The moon'll be full, just like Babe said. Solstices are like May Eve and Halloween—the borders between this world and others are thinnest then." He gave Jilly a sad smile. "Wouldn't I love to see them before they go."

Jilly thought quickly, but she still couldn't think of any way she could maneuver him into the Tombs in his chair. She couldn't even borrow Sue's car, because the streets there were too choked with rubble and refuse. So she picked up her sketchbook and put it on his lap.

"Keep this," she said.

Then she wheeled him off to the dining room, refusing to listen to his protests that he couldn't.

A sad smile touched Jilly's lips as she stood in the storm, remembering. She walked down the alleyway and ran her mittened hand along the windshield of the Buick, dislodging the snow that had gathered there. She tried the door, but it was rusted shut. A back window was open, so she crawled in through it, then clambered into the front seat which was relatively free of snow.

It was warmer inside—probably because she was out of the wind. She sat looking out the windshield until the snow covered it again. It was like being in a cocoon, she thought. Protected. A person could almost imagine that the gemmin were still around, not yet ready to leave. And when they did, maybe they'd take her with them....

A dreamy feeling stole over her and her eyes fluttered, grew heavy, then closed. Outside the wind continued to howl, driving the snow against the car; inside, Jilly slept, dreaming of the past.

The gemmin were waiting for her the day after she saw Frank, lounging around the abandoned Buick beside the old Clark Building. She wanted to talk to them about what they were and why they were going away and a hundred other things, but somehow she just never got around to any of it. She was too busy laughing at their antics and trying to capture their portraits with the pastels she'd brought that day. Once they all sang a long song that sounded like a cross between a traditional ballad and rap, but was in some foreign language that was both flutelike and gritty. Babe later explained that it was one of their traditional song cycles, a part of their oral tradition that kept alive the histories and genealogies of their people and the places where they lived.

Gemmin, Jilly thought. Storing memories. And then she was clear-headed long enough to ask if they would come with her to visit Frank.

Babe shook her head, honest regret in her luminous eyes.

"It's too far," she said.

"Too far, too far," the other gemmin chorused.

"From home," Babe explained.

"But," Jilly began, except she couldn't find the words for what she wanted to say.

There were people who just made other people feel good. Just being around them, made you feel better, creative, uplifted, happy. Geordie said that she was like that herself, though Jilly wasn't so sure of that. She tried to be, but she was subject to the same bad moods as anybody else, the same impatience with stupidity and ignorance which, parenthetically speaking, were to her mind the prime causes of all the world's ills.

The gemmin didn't seem to have those flaws. Even better, beyond that, there was magic about them. It lay thick in the air, filling your eyes and ears and nose and heart with its wild tang. Jilly desperately wanted Frank to share this with her, but when she tried to explain it to Babe, she just couldn't seem to make herself understood.

And then she realized the time and knew she had to go to work. Art was well and fine to feed the heart and mind, and so was magic, but if she wanted to pay the rent on the loft and have anything to eat next month—never mind the endless drain that art supplies made on her meagre budget—she had to go.

As though sensing her imminent departure, the gemmin bounded around her in an abandoned display of wild monkeyshines, and then vanished like so many will-o'-the-wisps in amongst the snowy rubble of the Tombs, leaving her alone once again.

The next day was much the same, except that tonight was the night they were leaving. Babe never made mention of it, but the knowledge hung ever heavier on Jilly as the hours progressed, colouring her enjoyment of their company.

The gemmin had washed away most of the residue of her bad breakup with Jeff, and for that Jilly was grateful. She could look on it now with that kind of wistful remembering one held for high school romances, long past and distanced. But in its place they had left a sense of abandonment. They were going, would soon be gone, and the world would be that much the emptier for their departure.

Jilly tried to find words to express that, but as had happened yesterday when she'd tried to explain Frank's need, she couldn't get the first one past her tongue.

And then again, it was time to go. The gemmin started acting wilder again, dancing and singing around her like a pack of mad imps, but before they could all vanish once more, Jilly caught Babe's arm. Don't go, don't go, she wanted to say, but all that came out was, "I...I don't...I want...."

Jilly, normally never at a loss for something to say, sighed with frustration.

"We won't be gone forever," Babe said, understanding Jilly's unspoken need. She touched a long delicate finger to her temple. "We'll always be with you in here, in your memories of us, and in here—" she tapped the pocket in Jilly's coat that held her sketchbook, "—in your pictures. If you don't forget us, we'll never be gone."

"It...it won't be the same," Jilly said.

Babe smiled sadly. "Nothing is ever the same. That's why we must go now."

She ruffled Jilly's hair—again the motion was like one made by a mother, rather than someone who appeared to be a girl only half Jilly's age—then stepped back. The other gemmin approached, and touched her as well—featherlight fingers brushing against her arms, tousling her hair like a breeze—and then they all began their mad dancing and pirouetting like so many scruffy ballerinas.

Until they were gone.

Jilly thought she would just stay here, never mind going in to work, but somehow she couldn't face a second parting. Slowly, she headed south, towards Gracie Street and the subway that would take her to work. And oddly enough, though she was sad at their leaving, it wasn't the kind of sadness that hurt. It was the kind that was like a singing in the soul.

Frank died that night, on the winter solstice, but Jilly didn't find out until the next day. He died in his sleep, Jilly's painting propped up on the night table beside him, her sketchbook with her initial rough drawings of the gemmin in it held against his thin chest. On the first blank page after her sketches of the gemmin, in an awkward script that must have taken him hours to write, he'd left her a short note:

"I have to tell you this, Jilly. I never saw any real magic—I just pretended that I did. I only knew it through the stories I got from my gran and from you. But I always believed. That's why I wrote all those stories when I was younger, because I wanted others to believe. I thought if enough of us did, if we learned to care again about the wild places from which we'd driven the magic away, then maybe it would return.

"I didn't think it ever would, but I'm going to open my window tonight and call to them. I'm going to ask them to take me with them when they go. I'm all used up—at least the man I am in this world is—but maybe in another world I'll have something to give. I hope they'll give me the chance.

"The faerie folk used to do that in the old days, you know. That was what a lot of the stories were about—people like us, going away, beyond the fields we know.

"If they take me, don't be sad, Jilly. I'll be waiting for you there."

The script was almost illegible by the time it got near the end, but Jilly managed to decipher it all. At the very end, he'd just signed the note with an "F" with a small flower drawn beside it. It looked an awful lot like a tiny violet, though maybe that was only because that was what Jilly wanted to see.

You saw real magic, she thought when she looked up from the sketchbook. You *were* real magic.

She gazed out the window of his room to where a soft snow was falling in the alley between St. Vincent's and the building next door. She hoped that on their way to wherever they'd gone, the gemmin had been able to include the tired and lonely spirit of one old man in their company.

Take care of him, Babe, she thought.

That Christmas was a quiet period in Jilly's life. She had gone to a church service for the first time since she was a child to attend the memorial service that St. Vincent's held for Frank. She and Geordie and a few of the staff of the home were the only ones in attendance. She missed Frank and found herself putting him in crowd scenes in the paintings she did over the holidays—Frank in the crowds, and the thin ghostly shapes of gemmin peering out from behind cornices and rooflines and the corners of alleyways.

Often when she went out on her night walks—after the restaurant was closed, when the city was half-asleep—she'd hear a singing in the quiet snow-muffled streets; not an audible singing, something she could hear with her ears, but one that only her heart and spirit could feel. Then she'd wonder if it was the voices of Frank and Babe and the others she heard, singing to her from the faraway, or that of other gemmin, not yet gone.

She never thought of Jeff, except with distance.

Life was subdued. A hiatus between storms. Just thinking of that time, usually brought her a sense of peace, if not completion. So why...remembering now...this time...?

There was a ringing in her ears—sharp and loud, like thunderclaps erupting directly above her. She felt as though she was in an earthquake, her body being violently shaken. Everything felt topsy-turvy. There was no up and no down, just a sense of vertigo and endless spinning, a roar and whorl of shouting and shaking until—

She snapped her eyes open to find Geordie's worried features peering out at her from the circle that the fur of his parka hood made around his face. He was in the Buick with her, on the front seat beside her. It was his hands on her shoulders, shaking her; his voice that sounded like thunder in the confines of the Buick.

The Buick.

And then she remembered: walking in the Tombs, the storm, climbing into the car, falling asleep....

"Jesus, Jilly," Geordie was saying. He sat back from her, giving her a bit of space, but the worry hadn't left his features yet. "You really are nuts, aren't you? I mean, falling asleep out here. Didn't you ever hear of hypothermia?"

She could have died, Jilly realized. She could have just slept on here until she froze to death and nobody'd know until the spring thaw, or until some poor homeless bugger crawled in to get out of the wind and found himself sharing space with Jilly, the Amazing Dead Woman.

She shivered, as much from dread as the storm's chill.

"How...how did you find me?" she asked.

Geordie shrugged. "God only knows. I got worried, the longer you were gone, until finally I couldn't stand it and had to come looking for you. It was like there was a nagging in the back of my head—sort of a Lassie kind of a thought, you know?"

Jilly had to smile at the analogy.

"Maybe I'm getting psychic—what do you think?" he asked.

"Finding me the way you did, maybe you are," Jilly said.

She sat up a little straighter, then realized that sometime during her sleep, she had unbuttoned her parka enough to stick a hand in under the coat. She pulled it out and both she and Geordie stared at what she held in her mittened hand.

It was a small violet flower, complete with roots.

"Jilly, where did you…?" Geordie began, but then he shook his head. "Never mind. I don't want to know."

But Jilly knew. Tonight was the anniversary, after all. Babe or Frank, or maybe both of them, had come by as well.

If you don't forget us, we'll never be gone.

She hadn't.

And it looked like they hadn't, either, because who else had left her this flower, and maybe sent Geordie out into the storm to find her? How else could he have lucked upon her the way he had with all those blocks upon blocks of the Tombs that he would have to search?

"Are you going to be okay?" Geordie asked.

Jilly stuck the plant back under her parka and nodded.

"Help me home, would you? I feel a little wobbly."

"You've got it."

"And Geordie?"

He looked at her, eyebrows raised.

"Thanks for coming out to look for me."

It was a long trek back to Jilly's loft, but this time the wind was helpful, rather than hindering. It rose up at their backs and hurried them along so that it seemed to only take them half the time it should have to return. While Jilly changed, Geordie made great steaming mugs of hot chocolate for both of them. They sat together on the old sofa by the window, Geordie in his usual rumpled sweater and old jeans, Jilly bundled up in two pairs of sweatpants, fingerless gloves and what seemed like a half-dozen shirts and socks.

Jilly told him her story of finding out about the gemmin, and how they went away. When she was done, Geordie just said, "Wow. We should tell Christy about them—he'd put them in one of his books."

"Yes, we should," Jilly said. "Maybe if more people knew about them, they wouldn't be so ready to go away."

"What about Mr. Hodgers?" Geordie asked. "Do you really think they took him away with them?"

Jilly looked at the newly-potted flower on her windowsill. It stood jauntily in the dirt and looked an awful lot like a drawing in one of her sketchbooks that she hadn't drawn herself.

"I like to think so," she said. "I like to think that St. Vincent's was on the way to wherever they were going." She gave Geordie a smile, more sweet than bitter. "You couldn't see it to look at him," she added, "but Frank had violet eyes, too; he had all kinds of memories stored away in that old head of his—just like Babe did."

Her own eyes took on a distant look, as though she was looking into the faraway herself, through the gates of dream and beyond the fields we know.

"I like to think they're getting along just fine," she said.

THE CONJURE MAN

I do not think it had any friends, or mourners, except myself and a pair of owls.
—J. R. R. Tolkien, from the introductory note to *Tree and Leaf*

You only see the tree by the light of the lamp. I wonder when you would ever see the lamp by the light of the tree.
—G. K. Chesterton, from *The Man Who Was Thursday*

THE CONJURE MAN rode a red, old-fashioned bicycle with fat tires and only one, fixed gear. A wicker basket in front contained a small mongrel dog that seemed mostly terrier. Behind the seat, tied to the carrier, was a battered brown satchel that hid from prying eyes the sum total of all his worldly possessions.

What he had was not much, but he needed little. He was, after all, the conjure man, and what he didn't have, he could conjure for himself.

He was more stout than slim, with a long grizzled beard and a halo of frizzy grey hair that protruded from under his tall black hat like ivy tangled under an eave. Nesting in the hatband were a posy of dried wildflowers and three feathers: one white, from a swan; one black, from a crow; one brown, from an owl. His jacket was an exhilarating shade of blue, the colour of the sky on a perfect summer's morning. Under it he wore a shirt that was as green as a fresh-cut lawn. His trousers were brown corduroy, patched with leather and plaid squares; his boots were a deep golden yellow, the colour of buttercups past their prime.

His age was a puzzle, somewhere between fifty and seventy. Most people assumed he was one of the homeless—more colourful than most, and certainly more cheerful, but a derelict all the same—so the scent of apples that seemed to follow him was always a surprise, as was the good humour that walked hand in hand with a keen intelligence in his bright blue eyes. When he raised his head, hat brim lifting, and he met one's gaze, the impact of those eyes was a sudden shock, a diamond in the rough.

His name was John Windle, which could mean, if you were one to ascribe meaning to names, "favoured of God" for his given name, while his surname was variously defined as "basket," "the red-winged thrush," or "to lose vigour and strength, to dwindle." They could all be true, for he led a charmed life; his mind was a treasure trove storing equal amounts of experience, rumour and history; he had a high clear singing voice; and though he wasn't tall—he stood five-ten in his boots—he had once been a much larger man.

"I was a giant once," he liked to explain, "when the world was young. But conjuring takes its toll. Now John's just an old man, pretty well all used up. Just like the world," he'd add with a sigh and a nod, bright eyes holding a tired sorrow. "Just like the world."

There were some things even the conjure man couldn't fix.

Living in the city, one grew used to its more outlandish characters, eventually noting them in passing with an almost familial affection: The pigeon lady in her faded Laura Ashley dresses with her shopping cart filled with sacks of birdseed and bread crumbs. Paperjack, the old black man with his Chinese fortune-teller and deft origami sculptures. The German cowboy who dressed like an extra from a spaghetti western and made long declamatory speeches in his native language to which no one listened.

And, of course, the conjure man.

Wendy St. James had seen him dozens of times—she lived and worked downtown, which was the conjure man's principal haunt—but she'd never actually spoken to him until one day in the fall when the trees were just beginning to change into their cheerful autumnal party dresses.

She was sitting on a bench on the Ferryside bank of the Kickaha River, a small, almost waif-like woman in jeans and a white T-shirt, with an unzipped brown leather bomber's jacket and hightops. In lieu of a purse, she had a small, worn knapsack sitting on the bench beside her and she was bent over a hardcover journal which she spent more time staring at than actually writing in. Her hair was thick and blonde, hanging down past her collar in a grown-out pageboy with a half-inch of dark roots showing. She was chewing on the end of her pen, worrying the plastic for inspiration.

It was a poem that had stopped her in mid-stroll and plunked her down on the bench. It had glimmered and shone in her head until she got out her journal and pen. Then it fled, as impossible to catch as a fading dream. The more she tried to recapture the impulse that had set her wanting to put pen to paper, the less it seemed to have ever existed in the first place. The annoying presence of three teenage boys clowning around on the lawn a half-dozen yards from where she sat didn't help at all.

She was giving them a dirty stare when she saw one of the boys pick up a stick and throw it into the wheel of the conjure man's bike as he came riding up on the park path that followed the river. The small dog in the bike's wicker basket jumped free, but the conjure man himself fell in a tangle of limbs and spinning wheels. The boys took off, laughing, the dog chasing them for a few feet, yapping shrilly, before it hurried back to where its master had fallen.

Wendy had already put down her journal and pen and reached the fallen man by the time the dog got back to its master's side.

"Are you okay?" Wendy asked the conjure man as she helped him untangle himself from the bike.

She'd taken a fall herself in the summer. The front wheel of her ten-speed struck a pebble, the bike wobbled dangerously and she'd grabbed at the brakes, but her fingers closed over the front ones first, and too hard. The back of the bike went up, flipping her right over the handlebars and she'd had the worst headache for at least a week afterwards.

The conjure man didn't answer her immediately. His gaze followed the escaping boys.

"As you sow," he muttered.

Following his gaze, Wendy saw the boy who'd thrown the stick trip and go sprawling in the grass. An odd chill danced up her spine. The boy's tumble came so quickly on the heels of the conjure man's words, for a moment it felt to her as though he'd actually caused the boy's fall.

As you sow, so shall you reap.

She looked back at the conjure man, but he was sitting up now, fingering a tear in his corduroys which already had a quiltwork of patches on them. He gave her a quick smile that traveled all the way up to his eyes and she found herself thinking of Santa Claus. The little dog pressed its nose up against the conjure man's hand, pushing it away from the tear. But the tear was gone.

It had just been a fold in the cloth, Wendy realized. That was all.

She helped the conjure man limp to her bench, then went back and got his bike. She righted it and wheeled it over to lean against the back of the bench before sitting down herself. The little dog leaped up onto the conjure man's lap.

"What a cute dog," Wendy said, giving it a pat. "What's her name?"

"Ginger," the conjure man replied as though it was so obvious that he couldn't understand her having to ask.

Wendy looked at the dog. Ginger's fur was as grey and grizzled as her master's beard without a hint of the spice's strong brown hue.

"But she's not at all brown," Wendy found herself saying.

The conjure man shook his head. "It's what she's made of—she's a gingerbread dog. Here." He plucked a hair from Ginger's back which made the dog start and give him a sour look. He offered the hair to Wendy. "Taste it."

Wendy grimaced. "I don't think so."

"Suit yourself," the conjure man said. He shrugged and popped the hair into his own mouth, chewing it with relish.

Oh boy, Wendy thought. She had a live one on her hands.

"Where do you think ginger comes from?" the conjure man asked her.

"What, do you mean your dog?"

"No, the spice."

Wendy shrugged. "I don't know. Some kind of plant, I suppose."

"And that's where you're wrong. They shave gingerbread dogs like our Ginger here and grind up the hair until all that's left is a powder that's ever so fine. Then they leave it out in the hot sun for a day and half—which is where it gets its brownish colour."

Wendy only just stopped herself from rolling her eyes. It was time to extract herself from this encounter, she realized. Well past the time. She'd done her bit to make sure he was all right and since the conjure man didn't seem any worse for the wear from his fall—

"Hey!" she said as he picked up her journal and started to leaf through it. "That's personal."

He fended off her reaching hand with his own and continued to look through it.

"Poetry," he said. "And lovely verses they are, too."

"Please. . . ."

"Ever had any published?"

Wendy let her hand drop and leaned back against the bench with a sigh.

"Two collections," she said, adding, "and a few sales to some of the literary magazines."

Although, she corrected herself, "sales" was perhaps a misnomer since most of the magazines only paid in copies. And while she did have two collections in print, they were published by the East Street Press, a small local publisher, which meant the bookstores of Newford were probably the only places in the world where either of her books could be found.

"Romantic, but with a very optimistic flavour," the conjure man remarked as he continued to look through her journal where all her false starts and incomplete drafts were laid out for him to see. "None of that *Sturm und drang* of the earlier romantic era and more like Yeats's twilight or, what did Chesterton call it? *Mooreeffoc*—that queerness that comes when familiar things are seen from a new angle."

Wendy couldn't believe she was having this conversation. What was he? A renegade English professor living on the street like some hedgerow philosopher of old? It seemed absurd to be sitting here, listening to his discourse.

The conjure man turned to give her a charming smile. "Because that's our hope for the future, isn't it? That the imagination reaches beyond the present to glimpse not so much a sense of meaning in what lies all around us, but to let us simply see it in the first place?"

"I...I don't know what to say," Wendy replied.

Ginger had fallen asleep on his lap. He closed her journal and regarded her for a long moment, eyes impossibly blue and bright under the brim of his odd hat.

"John has something he wants to show you," he said.

Wendy blinked. "John?" she asked, looking around.

The conjure man tapped his chest. "John Windle is what those who know my name call me."

"Oh."

She found it odd how his speech shifted from that of a learned man to a much simpler idiom, even referring to himself in the third person. But then, if she stopped to consider it, everything about him was odd.

"What kind of something?" Wendy asked cautiously.

"It's not far."

Wendy looked at her watch. Her shift started at four, which was still a couple of hours away, so there was plenty of time. But she was fairly certain that interesting though her companion was, he wasn't at all the sort of person with whom she wanted to involve herself any more than she already had. The dichotomy between the nonsense and substance that peppered his conversation made her uncomfortable.

It wasn't so much that she thought him dangerous. She just felt as though she was walking on boggy ground that might at any minute dissolve into quicksand with a wrong turn. Despite hardly knowing him at all, she was already sure that listening to him would be full of the potential for wrong turns.

"I'm sorry," she said, "but I don't have the time."

"It's something that I think only you can, if not understand, then at least appreciate."

"I'm sure it's fascinating, whatever it is, but—"

"Come along, then," he said.

He handed her back her journal and stood up, dislodging Ginger who leapt to the ground with a sharp yap of protest. Scooping the dog up, he returned her to the wicker basket that hung from his handlebars, then wheeled the bike in front of the bench where he stood waiting for Wendy.

Wendy opened her mouth to continue her protest, but then simply shrugged. Well, why not? He really didn't look at all dangerous and she'd just make sure that she stayed in public places.

She stuffed her journal back into her knapsack and then followed as he led the way south along the park path up to where the City Commission's lawns gave way to Butler University's common. She started to ask him how his leg felt, since he'd been limping before, but he walked at a quick, easy pace—that of someone half his apparent age—so she just assumed he hadn't been hurt that badly by his fall after all.

They crossed the common, eschewing the path now to walk straight across the lawn towards the G. Smithers Memorial Library, weaving their way in between islands of students involved in any number of activities, none of which included studying. When they reached the library, they followed its ivy-hung walls to the rear of the building where the conjure man stopped.

"There," he said, waving his arm in a gesture that took in the entire area behind the library. "What do you see?"

The view they had was of an open space of land backed by a number of other buildings. Having attended the university herself, Wendy recognized all three: the Student Centre, the Science Building and one of the dorms, though she couldn't remember which one. The landscape enclosed by their various bulking presences had the look of recently having undergone a complete overhaul. All the lilacs and hawthorns had been cut back, brush and weeds were now just an uneven stubble of ground covering, there were clumps of raw dirt, scattered here and there, where trees had obviously been removed, and right in the middle was an enormous stump.

It had been at least fifteen years since Wendy had had any reason to come here in behind the library. But it was so different now. She found herself looking around with a "what's wrong with this picture?" caption floating in her mind. This had been a little cranny of wild wood when she'd attended Butler, hidden away from all the trimmed lawns and shrubbery that made the rest of the university so picturesque. But she could remember slipping back here, journal in hand, and sitting under that huge....

"It's all changed," she said slowly. "They cleaned out all the brush and cut down the oak tree...."

Someone had once told her that this particular tree was—had been—a rarity. It had belonged to a species not native to North America—the *Quercus robur*, or common oak of Europe—and was supposed to be over four hundred years old which made it older than the university, older than Newford itself.

"How could they just...cut it down...?" she asked.

The conjure man jerked a thumb over his shoulder towards the library.

"Your man with the books had the work done—didn't like the shade it was throwing on his office. Didn't like to look out and see an untamed bit of the wild hidden in here disturbing his sense of order."

"The head librarian?" Wendy asked.

The conjure man just shrugged.

"But—didn't anyone complain? Surely the students...."

In her day there would have been protests. Students would have formed a human chain around the tree, refusing to let anyone near it. They would have camped out, day and night. They....

She looked at the stump and felt a tightness in her chest as though someone had wrapped her in wet leather that was now starting to dry out and shrink.

"That tree was John's friend," the conjure man said. "The last friend I ever had. She was ten thousand years old and they just cut her down."

Wendy gave him an odd look. Ten thousand years old? Were we exaggerating now or what?

"Her death is a symbol," the conjure man went on. "The world has no more time for stories."

"I'm not sure I follow you," Wendy said.

He turned to look at her, eyes glittering with a strange light under the dark brim of his hat.

"She was a Tree of Tales," he said. "There are very few of them left, just as there are very few of me. She held stories, all the stories the wind brought to her that were of any worth, and with each such story she heard, she grew."

"But there's always going to be stories," Wendy said, falling into the spirit of the conversation even if she didn't quite understand its relevance to the situation at hand. "There are more books being published today than there ever have been in the history of the world."

The conjure man gave her a sour frown and hooked his thumb towards the library again. "Now you sound like him."

"But—"

"There's stories and then there's stories," he said, interrupting her. "The ones with any worth change your life forever, perhaps only in a small way, but once you've heard them, they are forever a part of you. You nurture them and pass them on and the giving only makes you feel better.

"The others are just words on a page."

"I know that," Wendy said.

And on some level she did, though it wasn't something she'd ever really stopped to think about. It was more an instinctive sort of knowledge that had always been present inside her, rising up into her awareness now as though called forth by the conjure man's words.

"It's all machines now," the conjure man went on. "It's a—what do they call it?—high tech world. Fascinating, to be sure, but John thinks that it estranges many people, cheapens the human experience. There's no more room for the stories that matter, and that's wrong, for stories are a part of the language of dream—they grow not from one writer, but from a people. They become the voice of a country, or a race. Without them, people lose touch with themselves."

"You're talking about myths," Wendy said.

The conjure man shook his head. "Not specifically—not in the classical sense of the word. Such myths are only a part of the collective story that is harvested in a Tree of Tales. In a world as pessimistic as this has become, that collective story is all that's left to guide people through the encroaching dark. It serves to create a sense of options, the possibility of permanence out of nothing."

Wendy was really beginning to lose the thread of his argument now.

"What exactly is it that you're saying?" she asked.

"A Tree of Tales is an act of magic, of faith. Its existence becomes an affirmation of the power that the human spirit can have over its own destiny. The stories are just stories—they entertain, they make one laugh or cry—but if they have any worth, they carry within them a deeper resonance that remains long after the final page is turned, or the storyteller has come to the end of her tale. Both aspects of the story are necessary for it to have any worth."

He was silent for a long moment, then added, "Otherwise the story goes on without you."

Wendy gave him a questioning look.

"Do you know what 'ever after' means?" he asked.

"I suppose."

"It's one bookend of a tale—the kind that begins with 'once upon a time.' It's the end of the story when everybody goes home. That's what they said at the end of the story John was in, but John wasn't paying attention, so he got left behind."

"I'm not sure I know what you're talking about," Wendy said.

Not sure? she thought. She was positive. It was all so much...well, not exactly nonsense, as queer. And unrelated to any working of the world with which she was familiar. But the oddest thing was that everything he said continued to pull a kind of tickle out from deep in her mind so that while she didn't completely understand him, some part of her did. Some part, hidden behind the person who took care of all the day-to-day business of her life, perhaps the same part of her that pulled a poem onto the empty page where no words had ever existed before. The part of her that was a conjurer.

"John took care of the Tale of Trees," the conjure man went on. "Because John got left behind in his own story, he wanted to make sure that the stories themselves would at least live on. But one day he went wandering too far—just like he did when his story was ending—and when he got back she was gone. When he got back, they'd done *this* to her."

Wendy said nothing. For all that he was a comical figure in his bright clothes and with his Santa Claus air, there was nothing even faintly humourous about the sudden anguish in his voice.

"I'm sorry," she said.

And she was. Not just in sympathy with him, but because in her own way she'd loved that old oak tree as well. And—just like the conjure man, she supposed—she'd wandered away as well.

"Well then," the conjure man said. He rubbed a sleeve up against his nose and looked away from her. "John just wanted you to see."

He got on his bike and reached forward to tousle the fur around Ginger's ears. When he looked back to Wendy, his eyes glittered like tiny blue fires.

"I knew you'd understand," he said.

Before Wendy could respond, he pushed off and pedaled away, bumping across the uneven lawn to leave her standing alone in that once wild place that was now so dispiriting. But then she saw something stir in the middle of the broad stump.

At first it was no more than a small flicker in the air like a heat ripple. Wendy took a step forward, stopping when the flicker resolved into a tiny sapling. As she watched, it took on the slow stately dance of time-lapse photography: budded, unfurled leaves, grew taller, its growth like a rondo, a basic theme that brackets two completely separate tunes. Growth was the theme, while the tunes on either end began with the tiny sapling and ended with a full-grown oak tree as majestic as the behemoth that had originally stood there. When it reached its full height, light seemed to emanate from its trunk, from the roots underground, from each stalkless, broad saw-toothed leaf.

Wendy stared, wide-eyed, then stepped forward with an outstretched hand. As soon as her fingers touched the glowing tree, it came apart, drifting like mist until every trace of it was gone. Once more, all that remained was the stump of the original tree.

The vision, combined with the tightness in her chest and the sadness the conjure man had left her, transformed itself into words that rolled across her mind, but she didn't write them down. All she could do was stand and look at the tree stump for a very long time, before she finally turned and walked away.

Kathryn's Café was on Battersfield Road in Lower Crowsea, not far from the university but across the river and far enough that Wendy had to hurry to make it to work on time. But it was as though a black hole had swallowed the two hours from when she'd met the conjure man to when her shift began. She was late getting to work—not by much, but she could see that Jilly had already taken orders from two tables that were supposed to be her responsibility.

She dashed into the restaurant's washroom and changed from her jeans into a short black skirt. She tucked her T-shirt in, pulled her hair back into a loose bun, then bustled out to stash her knapsack and pick up her order pad from the storage shelf behind the employee's coat rack.

"You're looking peaked," Jilly said as she finally got out into the dining area.

Jilly Coppercorn and Wendy were almost a matched pair. Both women were small, with slender frames and attractive delicate features, though Jilly's hair was a dark curly brown—the same as Wendy's natural hair colour. They both moonlighted as waitresses, saving their true energy for creative pursuits: Jilly for her art, Wendy her poetry.

Neither had known the other until they began to work at the restaurant together, but they'd become fast friends from the very first shift they shared.

"I'm feeling confused," Wendy said in response to Jilly's comment.

"You're confused? Check out table five—he's changed his mind three times since he first ordered. I'm going to stand here and wait five minutes before I give Frank his latest order, just in case he decides he wants to change it again."

Wendy smiled. "And then he'll complain about slow service and won't leave you much of a tip."

"If he leaves one at all."

Wendy laid a hand on Jilly's arm. "Are you busy tonight?"

Jilly shook her head. "What's up?"

"I need to talk to someone."

"I'm yours to command," Jilly said. She made a little curtsy which had Wendy quickly stifle a giggle, then shifted her gaze to table five. "Oh bother, he's signalling me again."

"Give me his order," Wendy said. "I'll take care of him."

It was such a nice night that they just went around back of the restaurant when their shift was over. Walking the length of a short alley, they came out on a small strip of lawn and made their way down to the river. There they sat on a stone wall, dangling their feet above the sluggish water. The night felt still. Through some trick of the air, the traffic on nearby Battersfield Road was no more than a distant murmur, as though there was more of a sound baffle between where they sat and the busy street than just the building that housed their workplace.

"Remember that time we went camping?" Wendy said after they'd been sitting for a while in a companionable silence. "It was just me, you and LaDonna. We sat around the campfire telling ghost stories that first night."

"Sure," Jilly said with a smile in her voice. "You kept telling us ones by Robert Aickman and the like—they were all taken from books."

"While you and LaDonna claimed that the ones you told were real and no matter how much I tried to get either of you to admit they weren't, you wouldn't."

"But they were true," Jilly said.

Wendy thought of LaDonna telling them that she'd seen Bigfoot in the Tombs and Jilly's stories about a kind of earth spirit called a gemmin that she'd met in the same part of the city and of a race of goblin-like creatures living in the subterranean remains of the old city that lay beneath Newford's subway system.

She turned from the river to regard her friend. "Do you really believe those things you told me?"

Jilly nodded. "Of course I do. They're true." She paused a moment, leaning closer to Wendy as though trying to read her features in the gloom. "Why? What's happened, Wendy?"

"I think I just had my own close encounter of the weird kind this afternoon."

When Jilly said nothing, Wendy went on to tell her of her meeting with the conjure man earlier in the day.

"I mean, I know why he's called the conjure man," she finished up. "I've seen him pulling flowers out of peoples' ears and all those other stage tricks he does, but this was different. The whole time I was with him I kept feeling like there really was a kind of magic in the air, a *real* magic just sort of humming around him, and then when I saw the…I guess it was a vision of the tree….

"Well, I don't know what to think."

She'd been looking across the river while she spoke, her gaze fixed on the darkness of the far bank. Now she turned to Jilly.

"Who is he?" she asked. "Or maybe should I be asking *what* is he?"

"I've always thought of him as a kind of anima," Jilly said. "A loose bit of myth that got left behind when all the others went on to wherever it is that myths go when we don't believe in them anymore."

"That's sort of what he said. But what does it mean? What is he really?"

Jilly shrugged. "Maybe what he is isn't so important as *that* he is." At Wendy's puzzled look, she added, "I can't explain it any better. I…look, it's like it's not so important that he is or isn't what he says he is, but *that* he says it. That he believes it."

"Why?"

"Because it's just like he told you," Jilly said. "People are losing touch with themselves and with each other. They need stories because they really are the only thing that brings us together. Gossip, anecdotes, jokes, stories—these are the things that we used to exchange with each other. It kept the lines of communication open, let us touch each other on a regular basis.

"That's what art's all about, too. My paintings and your poems, the books Christy writes, the music Geordie plays—they're all lines of communication. But they're harder to keep open now because it's so much easier for most people to relate to a TV set than it is to another person. They get all this data fed into them, but they don't know what to do with it anymore. When they talk to other people, it's all surface. How ya doing, what about the weather. The only opinions they have are those that they've gotten from people on TV shows. They think they're informed, but all they're doing is repeating the views of talk show hosts and news commentators.

"They don't know how to listen to real people anymore."

"I know all that," Wendy said. "But what does any of it have to do with what the conjure man was showing me this afternoon?"

"I guess what I'm trying to say is that he validates an older kind of value, that's all."

"Okay, but what did he want from me?"

Jilly didn't say anything for a long time. She looked out across the river, her gaze caught by the same darkness as Wendy's had earlier when she was relating her afternoon encounter. Twice Wendy started to ask Jilly what she was thinking, but both times she forbore. Then finally Jilly turned to her.

"Maybe he wants you to plant a new tree," she said.

"But that's silly. I wouldn't know how to begin to go about something like that." Wendy sighed. "I don't even know if I believe in a Tree of Tales."

But then she remembered the feeling that had risen in her when the conjure man spoke to her, that sense of familiarity as though she was being reminded of something she already knew, rather than being told what she didn't. And then there was the vision of the tree….

She sighed again.

"Why me?" she asked.

Her words were directed almost to the night at large, rather than just her companion, but it was Jilly who replied. The night held its own counsel.

"I'm going to ask you something," Jilly said, "and I don't want you to think about the answer. Just tell me the first thing that comes to mind—okay?"

Wendy nodded uncertainly. "I guess."

"If you could be granted one wish—anything at all, no limits—what would you ask for?"

With the state the world was in at the moment, Wendy had no hesitation in answering: "World peace."

"Well, there you go," Jilly told her.

"I don't get it."

"You were asking why the conjure man picked you and there's your reason. Most people would have started out thinking of what they wanted for themselves. You know, tons of money, or to live forever—that kind of thing."

Wendy shook her head. "But he doesn't even know me."

Jilly got up and pulled Wendy to her feet.

"Come on," she said. "Let's go look at the tree."

"It's just a stump."

"Let's go anyway."

Wendy wasn't sure why she felt reluctant, but just as she had this afternoon, she allowed herself to be led back to the campus.

Nothing had changed, except that this time it was dark, which gave the scene, at least to Wendy's way of thinking, an even more desolate feeling.

Jilly was very quiet beside her. She stepped ahead of Wendy and crouched down beside the stump, running her hand along the top of it.

"I'd forgotten all about this place," she said softly.

That's right, Wendy thought. Jilly'd gone to Butler U. just as she had—around the same time, too, though they hadn't known each other then.

She crouched down beside Jilly, starting slightly when Jilly took her hand and laid it on the stump.

"Listen," Jilly said. "You can almost feel the whisper of a story...a last echo...."

Wendy shivered, though the night was mild. Jilly turned to her. At that moment, the starlight flickering in her companion's blue eyes reminded Wendy very much of the conjure man.

"You've got to do it," Jilly said. "You've got to plant a new tree. It wasn't just the conjure man choosing you—the tree chose you, too."

Wendy wasn't sure what was what anymore. It all seemed more than a little mad, yet as she listened to Jilly, she could almost believe in it all. But then that was one of Jilly's gifts: she could make the oddest thing seem normal. Wendy wasn't sure if you could call a thing like that a gift, but whatever it was, Jilly had it.

"Maybe we should get Christy to do it," she said. "After all, he's the story writer."

"Christy is a lovely man," Jilly said, "but sometimes he's far more concerned with how he says a thing, than with the story itself."

"Well, I'm not much better. I've been known to worry for hours over a stanza—or even just a line."

"For the sake of being clever?" Jilly asked.

"No. So that it's right."

Jilly raked her fingers through the short stubble of the weeds that passed for a lawn around the base of the oak stump. She found something and pressed it into Wendy's hand. Wendy didn't have to look at it to know that it was an acorn.

"You have to do it," Jilly said. "Plant a new Tree of Tales and feed it with stories. It's really up to you."

Wendy looked from the glow of her friend's eyes to the stump. She remembered her conversation with the conjure man and her vision of the tree. She closed her fingers around the acorn, feeling the press of the cap's bristles indent her skin.

Maybe it was up to her, she found herself thinking.

The poem that came to her that night after she left Jilly and got back to her little apartment in Ferryside, came all at once, fully-formed and complete. The act of putting it to paper was a mere formality.

She sat by her window for a long time afterward, her journal on her lap, the acorn in her hand. She rolled it slowly back and forth on her palm. Finally, she laid both journal and acorn on the windowsill and went into her tiny kitchen. She rummaged around in the cupboard under the sink until she came up with an old flowerpot which she took into the backyard and filled with dirt—rich loam, as dark and mysterious as that indefinable place inside herself that was the source of the words that filled her poetry and had risen in recognition to the conjure man's words.

When she returned to the window, she put the pot between her knees. Tearing the new poem out of her journal, she wrapped the acorn up in it and buried it in the pot. She watered it until the surface of the dirt was slick with mud, then placed the flowerpot on her windowsill and went to bed.

That night she dreamed of Jilly's gemmin—slender earth spirits that appeared outside the old three-story building that housed her apartment and peered in at the flowerpot on the windowsill. In the morning, she got up and told the buried acorn her dream.

Autumn turned to winter and Wendy's life went pretty much the way it always had. She took turns working at the restaurant and on her poems, she saw her friends, she started a relationship with a fellow she met at a party in Jilly's loft, but it floundered after a month.

Life went on.

The only change was centered around the contents of the pot on her windowsill. As though the tiny green sprig that pushed up through the dark soil was her lover, every day she told it all the things that had happened to her and around her. Sometimes she read it her favourite stories from anthologies and collections, or interesting bits from magazines and newspapers. She badgered her friends for stories, sometimes passing them on, speaking to the tiny plant in a low, but animated voice, other times convincing her friends to come over and tell the stories themselves.

Except for Jilly, Sophie, LaDonna and the two Riddell brothers, Geordie and Christy, most people thought she'd gone just a little daft. Nothing serious, mind you, but strange all the same.

Wendy didn't care.

Somewhere out in the world, there were other Trees of Tales, but they were few—if the conjure man was to be believed. And she believed him now. She had no proof, only faith, but oddly enough, faith seemed enough. But since she believed, she knew it was more important than ever that her charge should flourish.

With the coming of winter, there were less and less of the street people to be found. They were indoors, if they had such an option, or perhaps they migrated to warmer climes like the swallows. But Wendy still spied the more regular ones in their usual haunts. Paperjack had gone, but the pigeon lady still fed her charges every day, the German cowboy continued his bombastic monologues—though mostly on the subway platforms now. She saw the conjure man, too, but he was never near enough for her to get a chance to talk to him.

By the springtime, the sprig of green in the flowerpot had grown into a sapling that stood almost a foot high. On warmer days, Wendy put the pot out on the back porch steps where it could taste the air and catch the growing warmth of the afternoon sun. She still wasn't sure what she was going to do with it once it outgrew its pot.

But she had some ideas. There was a part of Fitzhenry Park called the Silenus Gardens that was dedicated to the poet Joshua Stanhold. She thought it might be appropriate to plant the sapling there.

One day in late April, she was leaning on the handlebars of her ten-speed in front of the public library in Lower Crowsea, admiring the yellow splash the daffodils made against the building's grey stone walls, when she sensed, more than saw, a red bicycle pull up onto the sidewalk behind her. She turned around to find herself looking into the conjure man's merry features.

"It's spring, isn't it just," the conjure man said. "A time to finally forget the cold and bluster and think of summer. John can feel the leaf buds stir, the flowers blossoming. There's a grand smile in the air for all the growing."

Wendy gave Ginger a pat, before letting her gaze meet the blue shock of his eyes.

"What about a Tree of Tales?" she asked. "Can you feel her growing?"

The conjure man gave her a wide smile. "Especially her." He paused to adjust the brim of his hat, then gave her a sly look. "Your man Stanhold," he added. "Now there was a fine poet—and a fine storyteller."

Wendy didn't bother to ask how he knew of her plan. She just returned the conjure man's smile and then asked, "Do you have a story to tell me?"

The conjure man polished one of the buttons of his bright blue jacket.

"I believe I do," he said. He patted the brown satchel that rode on his back carrier. "John has a thermos filled with the very best tea, right here in his bag. Why don't we find ourselves a comfortable place to sit and he'll tell you how he got this bicycle of his over a hot cuppa."

He started to pedal off down the street, without waiting for her response. Wendy stared after him, her gaze catching the little terrier, sitting erect in her basket and looking back at her.

There seemed to be a humming in the air that woke a kind of singing feeling in her chest. The wind rose up and caught her hair, pushing it playfully into her eyes. As she swept it back from her face with her hand, she thought of the sapling sitting in its pot on her back steps, thought of the wind, and knew that stories were already being harvested without the necessity of her having to pass them on.

But she wanted to hear them all the same.

Getting on her ten-speed, she hurried to catch up with the conjure man.

For J.R.R. Tolkien;
may his own branch of the tree live on forever.

▪WE ARE DEAD TOGETHER▪

The ideal condition
Would be, I admit, that men should be right
by instinct;
But since we are all likely to go astray,
The reasonable thing is to learn from those
who can teach.
—Sophocles

LET IT BE recounted in the *swato*—the stories of my people that chronicle our history and keep it alive—that while Kata Petalo was first and foremost a fool, she meant well. I truly believed there was a road I could walk between the world of the Rom and the *shilmullo*.

We have always been an adaptable people. We'd already lived side-by-side with the *Gaje* for ten times a hundred years, a part of their society, and yet apart from it. The undead were just another kind of non-Gypsy; why shouldn't we be able to to coexist with them as well?

I knew now. I had always known. We didn't call them the *shilmullo*—the cold dead—simply for the touch of their pale flesh, cold as marble. Their hearts were cold, too—cold and black as the hoarfrost that rimmed the hedges by which my ancestors had camped in gentler times.

I had always known, but I had chosen to forget. I had let the chance for survival seduce me.

"*Yekka buliasa nashti beshes pe done gratsende*," was what Bebee Yula used to tell us when we were children. With one behind you cannot sit on two horses. It was an old saying, a warning to those Rom who thought they could be both Rom and *Gaje*, but instead were neither.

I had ridden two horses these past few years, but all my cleverness served me ill in the end, for they took Budo from me all the same; took him, stole his life and left me with his cold, pale corpse that would rise from its death tonight to be forever a part of their world and lost to mine.

For see, the *shilmullo* have no art.

The muses that inspire the living can't find lodging in their dead flesh, can't spark the fires of genius in their cold hearts. The *shilmullo* can mimic, but they can't create. There are no Rembrandts counted in their ranks, no Picassos. No Yeats, no Steinbecks. No Mozarts, no Dylans. For artwork, for music, for plays and films and poetry and books, they need the living—Rom or *Gaje*.

I'm not the best musician in this new world that the *shilmullo* tore from the grave of the old, but I have something not one of them can ever possess, except vicariously: I have the talent to compose. I have written hundreds of manuscripts in honour of my patron, Brian Stansford—yes, that Stansford, the President of Stansford Chemicals—in every style of music. There are sonatas bearing his name and various music hall songs; jazz improvisations, three concertos, one symphony and numerous airs in the traditional style of the Rom; rap music, pop songs, heavy metal anthems.

I have accompanied him to dinners and galas and openings where my performances and music have always gained him the envy of his peers.

In return, like any pet, I was given safety—both for myself and my family. Every member of the Petalo clan has the Stansford tattoo on their left brow, an ornate capital "S," decorated with flowered vines with a tiny wolf's paw print enclosed in the lower curve of the letter. Sixteen Petalos could walk freely in the city and countryside with that mark on their brow.

Only Bebee Yula, my aunt, refused the tattoo.

"You do this for us," she told me, "but I will not be an obligation on any member of my clan. What you do is wrong. We must forget the boundaries that lie between ourselves and the *Gaje* and be united against our common enemy. To look out only for yourself, your family, makes you no better than the *shilmullo* themselves."

"There is no other way," I had explained. "Either I do this, or we die."

"There are worse things than death," she told me. "What you mean to do is one of them. You will lose your soul, Kata. You will become as cold in your heart as those you serve."

I tried to explain it better, but she would not argue further with me at that time. She had the final word. She was an old woman—in her eighties, Papa said—but she killed three *shilmullo* before she herself was slain. We all knew she was brave, but not one of us learned the lesson she'd given her life to tell us.

Sixteen Petalos allowed the blood-red Stansford tattoo to be placed on their brows.

But now there are only fifteen of us, for protected though he was, three *shilmullo* stole Budo from me. Stansford himself spoke to me, explaining how it was an unfortunate accident. They were young, Budo's murderers, they hadn't seen the tattoo until it was too late. Perhaps I would now do as he had previously suggested and bring my family to live in one of his protected enclaves.

"We are Rom," I had said.

He gave me a blank look. "I'm a busy man, Kathy," he said, calling me by my *nav gajikano*—my non-Gypsy name. "Would you get to the point?"

It should have explained everything. To be Rom was to live in all places; without freedom of movement, we might as well be dead. I wanted to explain it to him, but the words wouldn't come.

Stansford regarded me, his flesh white in the fluorescent light of his office, small sparks of red fire deep in his pupils. If I had thought he would have any sympathy, I was sorely mistaken.

"Let Taylor know when you've picked a new mate," was all he said, "and we'll have him—or her—tattooed."

Then he bent down to his paperwork as though I was no longer present.

I had been dismissed. I sat for a long moment, ignored, finally learning to hate him, before I left his office and went back downtown to the small apartment in a deserted tenement where Budo and I had been staying this week.

Budo lay stretched out on newspapers before the large window in the living room where Taylor and another of Stansford's men had left him two days ago. I knelt beside the corpse and looked down at what had been my husband. His throat had been savaged, but otherwise he looked as peaceful as though he was sleeping. His eyes were closed. A lock of his dark hair fell across his brow. I pushed it aside, laid a hand on his cold flesh.

He was dead, but not dead. He had been killed at three A.M. Tonight at the same time, three days after his death, his eyes would open and if I was still here, he would not remember me. They never remember anything until that initial thirst is slaked.

His skin was almost translucent. Pale, far too pale. Where was the dark-skinned Budo I had married?

Gone. Dead. All that remained of him was this bitter memory of pale flesh.

"I was wrong," I said.

I spoke neither to myself, nor to the corpse. My voice was for the ghost of my aunt, Bebee Yula, gone to the land of shadows. Budo would never take that journey—not if I let him wake.

I lifted my gaze to look out through the window at the street below. Night lay dark on its pavement. *Shilmullo* don't need streetlights and what humans remain in the city know better than to walk out-of-doors once the sun has gone down. The emptiness I saw below echoed endlessly inside me.

I rose to my feet and crossed the room to where our two canvas backpacks lay against the wall. My fiddlecase lay between them. I opened it and took out the fiddle. When I ran my thumb across the strings, the notes seemed to be swallowed by the room. They had no ring, no echo.

Budo's death had stolen their music.

For a long moment I held the fiddle against my chest, then I took the instrument by its neck and smashed it against the wall. The strings popped free as the body shattered, the end of one of them licking out to sting my cheek. It drew blood.

I took the fiddle neck back to where Budo's corpse lay and knelt beside him again. Raising it high above my head, I brought the jagged end down, plunging it into his chest—

There!

The corpse bucked as though I'd struck it with an electric current. Its eyes flared open, gaze locking on mine. It was a stranger's gaze. The corpse's hands scrabbled weakly against my arms, but my leather jacket kept me safe from its nails. It was too soon for him to have reached the full power of a *shilmullo*. His hands were weak. His eyes could glare, but not bend me to his will.

It took longer for the corpse to die than I had thought it would.

When it finally lay still, I leaned back on my heels, leaving the fiddle's neck sticking up out of the corpse's chest. I tried to summon tears—my sorrow ran deep; I had yet to cry—but the emptiness just gathered more thickly inside me. So I simply stared at my handiwork, sickened by what I saw, but forcing myself to look so that I would have the courage to finish the night's work.

Bebee Yula had been a wealth of old sayings. "Where you see Rom," she had said once, "there is freedom. Where you do not, there is no freedom."

I had traded our freedom for tattoos. Those tattoos did not mean safety, but *prikaza*—misfortune. Bad luck. We were no longer Rom, my family and I, but only Bebee Yula had seen that.

Until now.

I had a recital the following night—at a gala of Stansford's at the Brewer Theatre. There was a seating capacity of five hundred and, knowing Stansford, he would make certain that every seat was filled.

I walked from the tenement with my fiddlecase in hand. A new piece I'd composed for Stansford last week was to be the finale, so I didn't have to be at the theatre until late, but I was going early. I stopped only once along the way, to meet my brother Vedel. I had explained my needs to him the day before.

"It's about time," had been his only response.

I remembered Bebee Yula telling me she would not be an obligation on any member of her clan and wondered if the rest of my family agreed with her the way that Vedel seemed to. I had always told myself I did what I did for them; now I had learned that it had been for myself.

I wanted to live. I could not bear to have my family unprotected.

Many of the legends that tell of the *shilmullo* are false or embroidered, but this was true: there are only three ways to kill them. By beheading. By a stake in the heart. And by fire.

What Vedel brought me was an explosive device he'd gotten from a member of the local *Gaje* freedom fighters. It was small enough to fit in my empty fiddlecase, but with a firepower large enough to bring down the house. Five hundred would burn in the ensuing inferno. It would not be enough, but it was all I could do.

I embraced Vedel, there on the street, death lying in its case at my feet.

"We are Rom," he whispered into my hair. "We were meant to be free."

I nodded. Slowly stepping back from him, I picked up the case and went on alone to the theatre.

I would not return.

Let it be recounted in the *swato* that while Kata Petalo was first and foremost a fool, she meant well.

Even a fool can learn wisdom, but oh, the lesson is hard.

MR. TRUEPENNY'S BOOK EMPORIUM AND GALLERY

The constellations were consulted for advice, but no one understood them. —Elias Canetti

My name's Sophie and my friend Jilly says I have faerie blood. Maybe she's right.

Faerie are supposed to have problems dealing with modern technology and I certainly have trouble with anything technological. The simplest appliances develop horrendous problems when I'm around. I can't wear a watch because they start to run backwards, unless they're digital; then they just flash random numbers as though the watch's inner workings have taken to measuring fractals instead of time. If I take a subway or bus, it's sure to be late. Or it'll have a new driver who takes a wrong turn and we all get lost.

This kind of thing actually happens to me. Once I got on the #3 at the Kelly Street Bridge and somehow, instead of going downtown on Lee, we ended up heading north into Foxville.

I also have strange dreams.

I used to think they were the place that my art came from, that my subconscious was playing around with images, tossing them up in my sleep before I put them down on canvas or paper. But then a few months ago I had this serial dream that ran on for a half-dozen nights in a row, a kind of fairy tale that was either me stepping into Faerie and therefore real within its own perimeters—which is what Jilly would like me to believe—or it was just my subconscious making another attempt to deal with the way my mother abandoned my father and me when I was a kid. I don't really know which I believe anymore, because I still find myself going back to that dream world from time to time and meeting the people I first met there.

I even have a boyfriend in that place, which probably tells you more about my ongoing social status than it does my state of mind.

Rationally, I know it's just a continuation of that serial dream. And I'd let it go at that, except it feels so damn real. Every morning when I wake up from the latest installment, my head's filled with memories of what I've done that seem as real as anything I do during the day—sometimes more so.

But I'm getting off on a tangent. I started off meaning to just introduce myself, and here I am, giving you my life story. What I really wanted to tell you about was Mr. Truepenny.

The thing you have to understand is that I made him up. He was like one of those invisible childhood friends, except I deliberately created him.

We weren't exactly well-off when I was growing up. When my mother left us, I ended up being one of those latchkey kids. We didn't live in the best part of town; Upper Foxville is a rough part of the city and it could be a scary place for a little girl who loved art and books and got teased for that love by the other neighbourhood kids who couldn't even be bothered to learn how to read. When I got home from school, I went straight in and locked the door.

I'd get supper ready for my dad, but there were always a couple of hours to kill in between my arriving home and when he finished work—longer if he had to work late. We didn't have a TV, so I read a lot, but we couldn't afford to buy books. On Saturday mornings, we'd go to the library and I'd take out my limit—five books—which I'd finish by Tuesday, even if I tried to stretch them out.

To fill the rest of the time, I'd draw on shopping bags or the pads of paper that Dad brought me home from work, but that never seemed to occupy enough hours. So one day I made up Mr. Truepenny.

I'd daydream about going to his shop. It was the most perfect place that I could imagine: all dark wood and leaded glass, thick carpets and club chairs with carved wooden-based reading lamps strategically placed throughout. The shelves were filled with leather-bound books and folios, and there was a small art gallery in the back.

The special thing about Mr. Truepenny's shop was that all its contents only existed within its walls. Shakespeare's *The Storm of Winter. The Chapman's Tale* by Chaucer. *The Blissful Stream* by William Morris. Steinbeck's companion collection to *The Long Valley, Salinas. North Country Stoic* by Emily Brontë.

None of these books existed, of course, but being the dreamy sort of kid that I was, not only could I daydream of visiting Mr. Truepenny's shop, but I could actually read these unwritten stories. The gallery in the back of the shop was much the same. There hung works by the masters that saw the light of day only in my imagination. Van Goghs and Monets and Da Vincis. Rossettis and Homers and Cezannes.

Mr. Truepenny himself was a wonderfully eccentric individual who never once chased me out for being unable to make a purchase. He had a Don

Quixote air about him, a sense that he was forever tilting at windmills. He was tall and thin with a thatch of mouse-brown hair and round spectacles, a rumpled tweed suit and a huge briar pipe that he continually fussed with but never actually lit. He always greeted me with genuine affection and seemed disappointed when it was time for me to go.

My imagination was so vivid that my daydream visits to his shop were as real to me as when my dad took me to the library or the Newford Gallery of Fine Art. But it didn't last. I grew up, went to Butler University on student loans and the money from far too many menial jobs—"got a life," as the old saying goes. I made friends, I was so busy, there was no time, no need to visit the shop anymore. Eventually I simply forgot all about it.

Until I met Janice Petrie.

Wendy and I were in the Market after a late night at her place the previous evening. I was on my way home, but we'd decided to shop for groceries together before I left. Trying to make up my mind between green beans and a head of broccoli, my gaze lifted above the vegetable stand and met that of a little girl standing nearby with her parents. Her eyes widened with recognition though I'd never seen her before.

"You're the woman!" she cried. "You're the woman who's evicting Mr. Truepenny. I think it's a horrible thing to do. You're a horrible woman!"

And then she started to cry. Her mother shushed her and apologized to me for the outburst before bustling the little girl away.

"What was all *that* about, Sophie?" Wendy asked me.

"I have no idea," I said.

But of course I did. I was just so astonished by the encounter that I didn't know what to say. I changed the subject and that was the end of it until I got home. I dug out an old cardboard box from the back of my hall closet and rooted about in it until I came up with a folder of drawings I'd done when I still lived with my dad. Near the back I found the ones I was looking for.

They were studies of Mr. Truepenny and his amazing shop.

God, I thought, looking at these awkward drawings, pencil on brown grocery bag paper, ballpoint on foolscap. The things we forget.

I took them out onto my balcony and lay down on the old sofa, studying them, one by one. There was Mr. Truepenny, writing something in his big leather-bound ledger. Here was another of him, holding his cat Dodger, the two of them looking out the leaded glass windows of the shop. There was a view of the main aisle of the shop, leading down to the gallery, the perspective slightly askew, but not half bad considering I was no older when I did them than was the little girl in the Market today.

How could she have known? I found myself thinking. Mr. Truepenny and his shop was something I'd made up. I couldn't remember ever telling anyone else about it—not even Jilly. And what did she mean about my evicting him from the shop?

I could think of no rational response. After awhile, I just set the drawings aside and tried to forget about it. Exhaustion from the late night before soon had me nodding off and I fell asleep only to find myself, not in my boyfriend's faerie dream world, but on the streets of Mabon, the made-up city in which I'd put Mr. Truepenny's Book Emporium and Gallery.

I'm half a block from the shop. The area's changed. The once-neat cobblestones are thick with grime. Refuse lies everywhere. Most of the storefronts are boarded up, their walls festooned with graffiti. When I reach Mr. Truepenny's shop, I see a sign in the window that reads, "Closing soon due to lease expiration."

Half-dreading what I'll find, I open the door and hear the familiar little bell tinkle as I step inside. The shop's dusty and dim, and much smaller than I remember it. The shelves are almost bare. The door leading to the gallery is shut and has a "Closed" sign tacked onto it.

"Ah, Miss Etoile. It's been so very long."

I turn to find Mr. Truepenny at his usual station behind the front counter. He's smaller than I remember as well and looks a little shabby now. Hair thinning, tweed suit threadbare and more shapeless than ever.

"What...what's happened to the shop?" I ask.

I've forgotten that I'm asleep on the sofa out on my balcony. All I know is this awful feeling I have inside as I look at what's become of my old childhood haunt.

"Well, times change," he says. "The world moves on."

"This—is this my doing?"

His eyebrows rise quizzically.

"I met this little girl and she said I was evicting you."

"I don't blame you," Mr. Truepenny says and I can see in his sad eyes that it's true. "You've no more need for me or my wares, so it's only fair that you let us fade."

"But you...that is...well, you're not real."

I feel weird saying this because while I remember now that I'm dreaming, this place is like one of my faerie dreams that feels as real as the waking world.

"That's not strictly true," he tells me. "You did conceive of the city and this shop, but we were drawn to fit the blueprint of your plan from…elsewhere."

"What elsewhere?"

He frowns, brow furrowing as he thinks.

"I'm not really sure myself," he tells me.

"You're saying I didn't make you up, I just drew you here from somewhere else?"

He nods.

"And now you have to go back?"

"So it would seem."

"And this little girl—how can she know about you?"

"Once a reputable establishment is open for business, it really can't deny any customer access, regardless of their age or station in life."

"She's visiting my daydream?" I ask. This is too much to accept, even for a dream.

Mr. Truepenny shakes his head. "You brought this world into being through your single-minded desire, but now it has a life of its own."

"Until I forgot about it."

"You had a very strong will," he says. "You made us so real that we've been able to hang on for decades. But now we really have to go."

There's a very twisty sort of logic involved here, I can see. It doesn't make sense by way of the waking world's logic, but I think there are different rules in a dreamscape. After all, my faerie boyfriend can turn into a crow.

"Do you have more customers than that little girl?" I ask.

"Oh yes. Or at least, we did." He waves a hand to encompass the shop. "Not much stock left, I'm afraid. That was the first to go."

"Why doesn't *their* desire keep things running?"

"Well, they don't have faerie blood, now do they? They can visit, but they haven't the magic to bring us across or keep us here."

It figures. I think. We're back to that faerie blood thing again. Jilly would love this.

I'm about to ask him to explain it all a little more clearly when I get this odd jangling sound in my ears and wake up back on the sofa. My doorbell's ringing. I go inside the apartment to accept what turns out to be a FedEx package.

"Can dreams be real?" I ask the courier. "Can we invent something in a dream and have it turn out to be a real place?"

"Beats me, lady," he replies, never blinking an eye. "Just sign here."

I guess he gets all kinds.

So now I visit Mr. Truepenny's shop on a regular basis again. The area's vastly improved. There's a café nearby where Jeck—that's my boyfriend that I've been telling you about—and I go for tea after we've browsed through Mr. Truepenny's latest wares. Jeck likes this part of Mabon so much that he's now got an apartment on the same street as the shop. I think I might set up a studio nearby.

I've even run into Janice—the little girl who brought me back here in the first place. She's forgiven me, of course, now that she knows it was all a misunderstanding, and lets me buy her an ice cream from the soda fountain sometimes before she goes home.

I'm very accepting of it all—you get that way after awhile. The thing that worries me now is, what happens to Mabon when I die? Will the city get run down again and eventually disappear? And what about its residents? There's all these people here; they've got family, friends, lives. I get the feeling it wouldn't be the same for them if they have to go back to that elsewhere place Mr. Truepenny was so vague about.

So that's the reason I've written all this down and had it printed up into a little folio by one of Mr. Truepenny's friends in the waking world. I'm hoping somebody out there's like me. Someone's got enough faerie blood to not only visit, but keep the place going. Naturally, not just anyone will do. It has to be the right sort of person, a book-lover, a lover of old places and tradition, as well as the new.

If you think you're the person for the position, please send a resumé to me care of Mr. Truepenny's Book Emporium and Gallery, Mabon. I'll get back to you as soon as I can.

IN THE HOUSE OF MY ENEMY

We have not inherited the earth from our fathers,
we are borrowing it from our children.
—Native American saying

1

THE PAST SCAMPERS like an alleycat through the present, leaving the paw prints of memories scattered helter-skelter—here ink is smeared on a page, there lies an old photograph with a chewed corner, elsewhere still, a nest has been made of old newspapers, the headlines running one into the other to make strange declarations. There is no order to what we recall, the wheel of time follows no straight line as it turns in our heads. In the dark attics of our minds, all times mingle, sometimes literally.

I get so confused. I've been so many people; some I didn't like at all. I wonder that anyone could. Victim, hooker, junkie, liar, thief. But without them, I wouldn't be who I am today. I'm no one special, but I like who I am, lost childhood and all.

Did I have to be all those people to become the person I am today? Are they still living inside me, hiding in some dark corner of my mind, waiting for me to slip and stumble and fall and give them life again?

I tell myself not to remember, but that's wrong, too. Not remembering makes them stronger.

2

The morning sun came in through the window of Jilly's loft, playing across the features of her guest. The girl was still asleep on the Murphy bed, sheets all tangled around her skinny limbs, pulled tight and smooth over the rounded swell of her abdomen. Sleep had gentled her features. Her hair clouded the pillow around her head. The soft morning sunlight gave her a Madonna quality, a nimbus of Botticelli purity that the harsher light of the later day would steal away once she woke.

She was fifteen years old. And eight months pregnant.

Jilly sat in the windowseat, feet propped up on the sill, sketchpad on her lap. She caught the scene in charcoal, smudging the lines with the pad of her middle finger to soften them. On the fire escape outside, a stray cat climbed up the last few metal steps until it was level with where she was sitting and gave a plaintive meow.

Jilly had been expecting the black and white tabby. She reached under her knees and picked up a small plastic margarine container filled with dried kibbles which she set down on the fire escape in front of the cat. As the tabby contentedly crunched its breakfast, Jilly returned to her portrait.

"My name's Annie," her guest had told her last night when she stopped Jilly on Yoors Street just a few blocks south of the loft. "Could you spare some change? I really need to get some decent food. It's not so much for me...."

She put her hand on the swell of her stomach as she spoke. Jilly had looked at her, taking in the stringy hair, the ragged clothes, the unhealthy colour of her complexion, the too-thin body that seemed barely capable of sustaining the girl herself, little say nourishing the child she carried.

"Are you all on your own?" Jilly asked.

The girl nodded.

Jilly put her arm around the girl's shoulder and steered her back to the loft. She let her take a shower while she cooked a meal, gave her a clean smock to wear, and tried not to be patronizing while she did it all.

The girl had lost enough dignity as it was and Jilly knew that dignity was almost as hard to recover as innocence. She knew all too well.

3

Stolen Childhood, by Sophie Etoile. Copperplate engraving. Five Coyotes Singing Studio, Newford, 1988.

A child in a ragged dress stands in front of a ramshackle farmhouse. In one hand she holds a doll—a stick with a ball stuck in one end and a skirt on the other. She wears a lost expression, holding the doll as though she doesn't quite know what to do with it.

A shadowed figure stands behind the screen door, watching her.

I guess I was around three years old when my oldest brother started molesting me. That'd make him eleven. He used to touch me down between my legs while my parents were out drinking or sobering up down in the kitchen. I tried to fight him off, but I didn't really know that what he was doing was wrong—

even when he started to put his cock inside me.

I was eight when my mother walked in on one of his rapes and you know what she did? She walked right out again until my brother was finished and we both had our clothes on again. She waited until he'd left the room, then she came back in and started screaming at me.

"You little slut! Why are you doing this to your own brother?"

Like it was my fault. Like I *wanted* him to rape me. Like the three-year-old I was when he started molesting me had any idea about what he was doing.

I think my other brothers knew what was going on all along, but they never said anything about it—they didn't want to break that macho code-of-honour bullshit. My little sister was just born, too young to know anything. When my dad found out about it, he beat the crap out of my brother, but in some ways it just got worse after that.

My brother didn't molest me anymore, but he'd glare at me all the time, like he was going to pay me back for the beating he got soon as he got a chance. My mother and my other brothers, every time I'd come into a room, they'd all just stop talking and look at me like I was some kind of bug.

I think at first my dad wanted to do something to help me, but in the end he really wasn't any better than my mother. I could see it in his eyes: he blamed me for it, too. He kept me at a distance, never came close to me anymore, never let me feel like I was normal.

He's the one who had me see a psychiatrist. I'd have to go and sit in his office all alone, just a little kid in this big leather chair. The psychiatrist would lean across his desk, all smiles and smarmy understanding, and try to get me to talk, but I never told him a thing. I didn't trust him. I'd already learned that I couldn't trust men. Couldn't trust women either, thanks to my mother. Her idea of working things out was to send me to confession, like the same God who let my brother rape me was now going to make everything okay so long as I owned up to seducing him in the first place.

What kind of a way is that for a kid to grow up?

4

"Forgive me, Father, for I have sinned. I let my brother...."

5

Jilly laid her sketchpad aside when her guest began to stir. She swung her legs down so that they dangled from the windowsill, heels banging lightly against the wall, toes almost touching the ground. She pushed an unruly lock of hair from her brow, leaving behind a charcoal smudge on her temple.

Small and slender, with pixie features and a mass of curly dark hair, she looked almost as young as the girl on her bed. Jeans and sneakers, a dark T-shirt and an oversized peach-coloured smock, only added to her air of slightness and youth. But she was halfway through her thirties, her own teenage years long gone; she could have been Annie's mother.

"What were you doing?" Annie asked as she sat up, tugging the sheets up around herself.

"Sketching you while you slept. I hope you don't mind."

"Can I see?"

Jilly passed the sketchpad over and watched Annie study it. On the fire escape behind her, two more cats had joined the black and white tabby at the margarine container. One was an old alleycat, its left ear ragged and torn, ribs showing like so many hills and valleys against the matted landscape of its fur. The other belonged to an upstairs neighbour; it was making its usual morning rounds.

"You made me look a lot better than I really am," Annie said finally.

Jilly shook her head. "I only drew what was there."

"Yeah, right."

Jilly didn't bother to contradict her. The self-worth speech would keep.

"So is this how you make your living?" Annie asked.

"Pretty well. I do a little waitressing on the side."

"Beats being a hooker, I guess."

She gave Jilly a challenging look as she spoke, obviously anticipating a reaction.

Jilly only shrugged. "Tell me about it," she said.

Annie didn't say anything for a long moment. She looked down at the rough portrait with an unreadable expression, then finally met Jilly's gaze again.

"I've heard about you," she said. "On the street. Seems like everybody knows you. They say. . . ."

Her voice trailed off.

Jilly smiled. "What do they say?"

"Oh, all kinds of stuff." She shrugged. "You know. That you used to live on the street, that you're kind of like a one-woman social service, but you don't lecture. And that you're—" she hesitated, looked away for a moment, "—you know, a witch."

Jilly laughed. "A witch?"

That was a new one on her.

Annie waved a hand towards the wall across from the window where Jilly was sitting. Paintings leaned up against each other in untidy stacks. Above them, the wall held more, a careless gallery hung frame to frame to save space. They were part of Jilly's ongoing "Urban Faerie" series, realistic city scenes and characters to which were added the curious little denizens of lands which never were. Hobs and fairies, little elf men and goblins.

"They say you think all that stuff's real," Annie said.

"What do you think?"

When Annie gave her a "give me a break" look, Jilly just smiled again.

"How about some breakfast?" she asked to change the subject.

"Look," Annie said. "I really appreciate your taking me in and feeding me and everything last night, but I don't want to be a freeloader."

"One more meal's not freeloading."

Jilly pretended to pay no attention as Annie's pride fought with her baby's need.

"Well, if you're sure it's okay," Annie said hesitantly.

"I wouldn't have offered if it wasn't," Jilly told her.

She dropped down from the windowsill and went across the loft to the kitchen corner. She normally didn't eat a big breakfast, but twenty minutes later they were both sitting down to fried eggs and bacon, home fries and toast, coffee for Jilly and herb tea for Annie.

"Got any plans for today?" Jilly asked as they were finishing up.

"Why?" Annie replied, immediately suspicious.

"I thought you might want to come visit a friend of mine."

"A social worker, right?"

The tone in her voice was the same as though she was talking about a cockroach or maggot.

Jilly shook her head. "More like a storefront counselor. Her name's Angelina Marceau. She runs that drop-in center on Grasso Street. It's privately funded, no political connections."

"I've heard of her. The Grasso Street Angel."

"You don't have to come," Jilly said, "but I know she'd like to meet you."

"I'm sure."

Jilly shrugged. When she started to clean up, Annie stopped her.

"Please," she said. "Let me do it."

Jilly retrieved her sketchpad from the bed and returned to the windowseat while Annie washed up. She was just adding the finishing touches to the rough portrait she'd started earlier when Annie came to sit on the edge of the Murphy bed.

"That painting on the easel," Annie said. "Is that something new you're working on?"

Jilly nodded.

"It's not like your other stuff at all."

"I'm part of an artists' group that calls itself the Five Coyotes Singing Studio," Jilly explained. "The actual studio's owned by a friend of mine named Sophie Etoile, but we all work in it from time to time. There's five of us, all women, and we're doing a group show with a theme of child abuse at the Green Man Gallery next month."

"And that painting's going to be in it?" Annie asked.

"It's one of three I'm doing for the show."

"What's that one called?"

"'I Don't Know How to Laugh Anymore.'"

Annie put her hands on top of her swollen stomach.

"Me, neither," she said.

6

I Don't Know How to Laugh Anymore, by Jilly Coppercorn. Oils and mixed media. Yoors Street Studio, Newford, 1991.

A life-sized female subject leans against an inner city wall in the classic pose of a prostitute waiting for a customer. She wears high heels, a micro mini-skirt, tube top and short jacket, with a purse slung over one shoulder, hanging against her hip from a narrow strap. Her hands are thrust into the pockets of her jacket. Her features are tired, the lost look of a junkie in her eyes undermining her attempt to appear sultry.

Near her feet, a condom is attached to the painting, stiffened with gesso.

The subject is thirteen years old.

I started running away from home when I was ten. The summer I turned eleven I managed to make it to Newford and lived on its streets for six months.

I ate what I could find in the dumpsters behind the McDonald's and other fast food places on Williamson Street—there was nothing wrong with the food. It was just dried out from having been under the heating lamps for too long.

I spent those six months walking the streets all night. I was afraid to sleep when it was dark because I was just a kid and who knows what could've happened to me. At least being awake I could hide whenever I saw something that made me nervous. In the daytime I slept where I could—in parks, in the backseats of abandoned cars, wherever I didn't think I'd get caught. I tried to keep myself clean, washed up in restaurant bathrooms and at this gas bar on Yoors Street where the guy running the pumps took a liking to me. Paydays he'd spot me for lunch at the grill down the street.

I started drawing again around that time and for awhile I tried to hawk my pictures to the tourists down by the Pier, but the stuff wasn't all that good and I was drawing with pencils on foolscap or pages torn out of old school notebooks—not exactly the kind of art that looks good in a frame, if you know what I mean. I did a lot better panhandling and shoplifting.

I finally got busted trying to boost a tape deck from Kreiger's Stereo—it used to be where Gypsy Records is. Now it's out on the strip past the Tombs. I've always been small for my age, which didn't help when I tried to convince the cops that I was older than I really was. I figured juvie would be better than going back to my parents' place, but it didn't work. My parents had a missing persons out on me, God knows why. It's not like they could've missed me.

After running away and getting brought back a few times, finally they didn't take me home. My mother didn't want me and my dad didn't argue, so I guess he didn't either. I figured that was great until I started making the rounds of foster homes, bouncing back and forth between them and the Home for Wayward Girls. It's just juvie with an old-fashioned name.

I guess there must be some good foster parents, but I never saw any. All mine ever wanted was to collect their cheque and treat me like I was a piece of shit unless my caseworker was coming by for a visit. Then I got moved up from the mattress in the basement to one of their kids' rooms. The first time I tried to tell the worker what was going down, she didn't believe me and then my foster parents beat the crap out of me once she was gone. I didn't make that mistake again.

I was thirteen and in my fourth or fifth foster home when I got molested again. This time I didn't take any crap. I booted the old pervert in the balls and just took off out of there, back to Newford.

I was older and knew better now. Girls I talked to in juvie told me how to get around, who to trust and who was just out to peddle your ass.

See, I never planned on being a hooker. I don't know what I thought I'd do when I got to the city—I wasn't exactly thinking straight. Anyway, I ended up with this guy—Robert Carson. He was fifteen.

I met him in back of the Convention Centre on the beach where all the kids used to all hang out in the summer and we ended up getting a room together on Grasso Street, near the high school. I was still pretty fucked up about getting physical with a guy but we ended up doing so many drugs—acid, MDA, coke, smack, you name it—that half the time I didn't know when he was putting it to me.

We ran out of money one day, rent was due, no food in the place, no dope, both of us too fucked up to panhandle, when Rob gets the big idea of me selling my ass to bring in a little money. Well, I was screwed up, but not that screwed up. But then he got some guy to front him some smack and next thing I know I'm in this car with some guy I never saw before and he's expecting a blow job and I'm crying and all fucked up from the dope and then I'm doing it and standing out on the street corner where he's dumped me some ten minutes later with forty bucks in my hand and Rob's laughing, saying how we got it made, and all I can do is crouch down on the sidewalk and puke, trying to get the taste of that guy's come out of my mouth.

So Rob thinks I'm being, like, so fucking weird—I mean, it's easy money, he tells me. Easy for him maybe. We have this big fight and then he hits me. Tells me if I don't get my ass out on the street and make some more money, he's going to do worse, like cut me.

My luck, I guess. Of all the guys to hang out with, I've got to pick one who suddenly realizes it's his ambition in life to be a pimp. Three years later he's running a string of five girls, but he lets me pay my respect—two grand which I got by skimming what I was paying him—and I'm out of that scene.

Except I'm not, because I'm still a junkie and I'm too fucked up to work, I've got no ID, I've got no skills except I can draw a little when I'm not fucked up on smack which is just about all the time. I start muling for a couple of dealers in Fitzhenry Park, just to get my fixes, and then one night I'm so out of it, I just collapse in a doorway of a pawn shop up on Perry Street.

I haven't eaten in, like, three days. I'm shaking because I need a fix so bad I can't see straight. I haven't washed in Christ knows how long, so I smell and the clothes I'm wearing are worse. I'm at the end of the line and I know it, when I hear footsteps coming down the street and I know it's the local cop on his beat, doing his rounds.

I try to crawl deeper into the shadows but the doorway's only so deep and the cop's coming closer and then he's standing there, blocking what little light the streetlamps were throwing and I know I'm screwed. But there's no way I'm going back into juvie or a foster home. I'm thinking of offering him a blow job to let me go—so far as the cops're concerned, hookers're just scum, but they'll take a freebie all the same—but I see something in this guy's face, when he turns his head and the streetlight touches it, that tells me he's a family man, walking the straight and narrow. A rookie, true blue, probably his first week on the beat and full of wanting to help everybody and I know for sure I'm screwed. With my luck running true, he's going to be the kind of guy who thinks social workers really want to help someone like me instead of playing bureaucratic mind-fuck games with my head.

I don't think I can take anymore.

I find myself wishing I had Rob's switchblade—the one he liked to push up against my face when he didn't think I was bringing in enough. I just want to cut something. The cop. Myself. I don't really give a fuck. I just want out.

He crouches down so he's kind of level with me, lying there scrunched up against the door, and says, "How bad is it?"

I just look at him like he's from another planet. How bad is it? Can it get any worse I wonder?

"I...I'm doing fine," I tell him.

He nods like we're discussing the weather. "What's your name?"

"Jilly," I say.

"Jilly what?"

"Uh...."

I think of my parents, who've turned their backs on me. I think of juvie and foster homes. I look over his shoulder and there's a pair of billboards on the building behind me. One's advertising a suntan lotion—you know the one with the dog pulling the kid's pants down? I'll bet some old pervert thought that one up. The other's got the Jolly Green Giant himself selling vegetables. I pull a word from each ad and give it to the cop.

"Jilly Coppercorn."

"Think you can stand, Jilly?"

I'm thinking, if I could stand, would I be lying here? But I give it a try. He helps me the rest of the way up, supports me when I start to sway.

"So...so am I busted?" I ask him.

"Have you committed a crime?"

I don't know where the laugh comes from, but it falls out of my mouth all the same. There's no humour in it.

"Sure," I tell him. "I was born."

He sees my bag still lying on the ground. He picks it up while I lean against the wall and a bunch of my drawings fall out. He looks at them as he stuffs them back in the bag.

"Did you do those?"

I want to sneer at him, ask him why the fuck should he care, but I've got nothing left in me. It's all I can do to stand. So I tell him, yeah, they're mine.

"They're very good."

Right. I'm actually this fucking brilliant artist, slumming just to get material for my art.

"Do you have a place to stay?" he asks.

Whoops, did I read him wrong? Maybe he's planning to get me home, clean me up, and then put it to me.

"Jilly?" he asks when I don't answer.

Sure, I want to tell him. I've got my pick of the city's alleyways and doorways. I'm welcome wherever I go. World treats me like a fucking princess. But all I do is shake my head.

"I want to take you to see a friend of mine," he says.

I wonder how he can stand to touch me. I can't stand myself. I'm like a walking sewer. And now he wants to bring me to meet a friend?

"Am I busted?" I ask him again.

He shakes his head. I think of where I am, what I got ahead of me, then I just shrug. If I'm not busted, then whatever's he's got planned for me's got to be better than what I've got right now. Who knows, maybe his friend'll front me with a fix to get me through the night.

"Okay," I tell him. "Whatever."

"C'mon," he says.

He puts an arm around my shoulder and steers me off down the street and that's how I met Lou Fucceri and his girlfriend, the Grasso Street Angel.

7

Jilly sat on the stoop of Angel's office on Grasso Street, watching the passersby. She had her sketchpad on her knee, but she hadn't opened it yet. Instead, she was amusing herself with one of her favourite pastimes: making up stories about the people walking by. The young woman with the child in a stroller, she was a princess in exile, disguising herself as a nanny in a far distant land until she could regain her rightful station in some suitably romantic dukedom in Europe. The old black man with the cane was a physicist studying the effects of Chaos theory in the Grasso Street traffic. The Hispanic girl on her skateboard was actually a mermaid, having exchanged the waves of her ocean for flat concrete and true love.

She didn't turn around when she heard the door open behind her. There was a scuffle of sneakers on the stoop, then the sound of the door closing again. After a moment, Annie sat down beside her.

"How're you doing?" Jilly asked.

"It was weird."

"Good weird, or bad?" Jilly asked when Annie didn't go on. "Or just uncomfortable?"

"Good weird, I guess. She played the tape you did for her book. She said you knew, that you'd said it was okay."

Jilly nodded.

"I couldn't believe it was you. I mean, I recognized your voice and everything, but you sounded so different."

"I was just a kid," Jilly said. "A punky street kid."

"But look at you now."

"I'm nothing special," Jilly said, suddenly feeling self-conscious. She ran a hand through her hair. "Did Angel tell you about the sponsorship program?"

Annie nodded. "Sort of. She said you'd tell me more."

"What Angel does is coordinate a relationship between kids that need help and people who want to help. It's different every time, because everybody's different. I didn't meet my sponsor for the longest time; he just put up the money while Angel was my contact. My lifeline, if you want to know the truth. I can't remember how many times I'd show up at her door and spend the night crying on her shoulder."

"How did you get, you know, cleaned up?" Annie asked. Her voice was shy.

"The first thing is I went into detox. When I finally got out, my sponsor paid for my room and board at the Chelsea Arms while I went through an accelerated high school program. I told Angel I wanted to go on to college, so he cosigned my student loan and helped me out with my books and supplies and stuff. I was working by that point. I had part-time jobs at a couple of stores and with the Post Office, and then I started waitressing, but that kind of money doesn't go far—not when you're carrying a full course load."

"When did you find out who your sponsor was?"

"When I graduated. He was at the ceremony."

"Was it weird finally meeting him?"

Jilly laughed. "Yes and no. I'd already known him for years—he was my art history professor. We got along really well and he used to let me use the sunroom at the back of his house for a studio. Angel and Lou had shown him some of that bad art I'd been doing when I was still on the street and that's why he sponsored me—because he thought I had a lot of talent, he told me later. But he didn't want me to know it was him putting up the money because he thought it might affect our relationship at Butler U." She shook her head. "He said he *knew* I'd be going the first time Angel and Lou showed him the stuff I was doing."

"It's sort of like a fairy tale, isn't it?" Annie said.

"I guess it is. I never thought of it that way."

"And it really works, doesn't it?"

"If you want it to," Jilly said. "I'm not saying it's easy. There's ups and downs—lots more downs at the start."

"How many kids make it?"

"This hasn't got anything to do with statistics," Jilly said. "You can only look at it on a person to person basis. But Angel's been doing this for a long, long time. You can trust her to do her best for you. She takes a lot of flak for what she does. Parents get mad at her because she won't tell them where their kids are. Social services says she's undermining their authority. She's been to jail twice on contempt of court charges because she wouldn't tell where some kid was."

"Even with her boyfriend being a cop?"

"That was a long time ago," Jilly said. "And it didn't work out. They're still friends but—Angel went through an awful bad time when she was a kid. That changes a person, no matter how much they learn to take control of their life. Angel's great with people, especially kids, and she's got a million friends, but she's not good at maintaining a personal relationship with a guy. When it comes down to the crunch, she just can't learn to trust them. As friends, sure, but not as lovers."

"She said something along the same lines about you," Annie said. "She said you were full of love, but it wasn't sexual or romantic so much as a general kindness towards everything and everybody."

"Yeah, well...I guess both Angel and I talk too much."

Annie hesitated for a few heartbeats, then said, "She also told me that you want to sponsor me."

Jilly nodded. "I'd like to."

"I don't get it."

"What's to get?"

"Well, I'm not like you or your professor friend. I'm not, you know, all that creative. I couldn't make something beautiful if my life depended on it. I'm not much good at anything."

Jilly shook her head. "That's not what it's about. Beauty isn't what you see on TV or in magazine ads or even necessarily in art galleries. It's a lot deeper and a lot simpler than that. It's realizing the goodness of things, it's leaving the world a little better than it was before you got here. It's appreciating the inspiration of the world around you and trying to inspire others.

"Sculptors, poets, painters, musicians—they're the traditional purveyors of Beauty. But it can as easily be created by a gardener, a farmer, a plumber, a careworker. It's the intent you put into your work, the pride you take in it—whatever it is."

"But still.... I really don't have anything to offer."

Annie's statement was all the more painful for Jilly because it held no self-pity, it was just a laying out of facts as Annie saw them.

"Giving birth is an act of Beauty," Jilly said.

"I don't even know if I want a kid. I...I don't know what I want. I don't know who I am."

She turned to Jilly. There seemed to be years of pain and confusion in her eyes, far more years than she had lived in the world. When had that pain begun? Jilly thought. Who could have done it to her, beautiful child that she must have been? Father, brother, uncle, family friend?

Jilly wanted to just reach out and hold her, but knew too well how the physical contact of comfort could too easily be misconstrued as an invasion of the private space an abused victim sometimes so desperately needed to maintain.

"I need help," Annie said softly. "I know that. But I don't want charity."

"Don't think of this sponsorship program as charity," Jilly said. "What Angel does is simply what we all should be doing all of the time—taking care of each other."

Annie sighed, but fell silent. Jilly didn't push it any further. They sat for awhile longer on the stoop while the world bustled by on Grasso Street.

"What was the hardest part?" Annie asked. "You know, when you first came off the street."

"Thinking of myself as normal."

8

Daddy's Home, by Isabelle Copley. Painted Wood. Adjani Farm, Wren Island, 1990.

The sculpture is three feet high, a flat rectangle of solid wood, standing on end with a child's face, upper torso and hands protruding from one side, as though the wood is gauze against which the subject is pressing.

The child wears a look of terror.

Annie's sleeping again. She needs the rest as much as she needs regular meals and the knowledge that she's got a safe place to stay. I took my Walkman out onto the fire escape and listened to a copy of the tape that Angel played for her today. I don't much recognize that kid either, but I know it's me.

It's funny, me talking about Angel, Angel talking about me, both of us knowing what the other needs, but neither able to help herself. I like to see my friends as couples. I like to see them in love with each other. But it's not the same for me.

Except who am I kidding? I want the same thing, but I just choke when a man gets too close to me. I can't let down that final barrier, I can't even tell them why.

Sophie says I expect them to just instinctively know. That I'm waiting for them to be understanding and caring without ever opening up to them. If I want them to follow the script I've got written out in my head, she says I have to let them in on it.

I know she's right, but I can't do anything about it.

I see a dog slink into the alleyway beside the building. He's skinny as a whippet, but he's just a mongrel that no one's taken care of for awhile. He's got dried blood on his shoulders, so I guess someone's been beating him.

I go down with some cat food in a bowl, but he won't come near me, no matter how soothingly I call to him. I know he can smell the food, but he's more scared of me than he's hungry. Finally I just leave the bowl and go back up the fire escape. He waits until I'm sitting outside my window again before he goes up to the bowl. He wolfs the food down and then he takes off like he's done something wrong.

I guess that's the way I am when I meet a man I like. I'm really happy with him until he's nice to me, until he wants to kiss me and hold me, and then I just run off like I've done something wrong.

9

Annie woke while Jilly was starting dinner. She helped chop up vegetables for the vegetarian stew Jilly was making, then drifted over to the long worktable that ran along the back wall near Jilly's easel. She found a brochure for the Five Coyotes Singing Studio show in amongst the litter of paper, magazines, sketches and old paintbrushes and brought it over to the kitchen table where she leafed through it while Jilly finished up the dinner preparations.

"Do you really think something like this is going to make a difference?" Annie asked after she'd read through the brochure.

"Depends on how big a difference you're talking about," Jilly said. "Sophie's arranged for a series of lectures to run in association with the show and she's also organized a couple of discussion evenings at the gallery where people who come to the show can talk to us—about their reactions to the show, about their feelings, maybe even share their own experiences if that's something that feels right to them at the time."

"Yeah, but what about the kids that this is all about?" Annie asked.

Jilly turned from the stove. Annie didn't look at all like a young expectant mother, glowing with her pregnancy. She just looked like a hurt and confused kid with a distended stomach, a kind of Ralph Steadman aura of frantic anxiety splattered around her.

"The way we see it," Jilly said, "is if only one kid gets spared the kind of hell we all went through, then the show'll be worth it."

"Yeah, but the only kind of people who are going to go to this kind of thing are those who already know about it. You're preaching to the converted."

"Maybe. But there'll be media coverage—in the papers for sure, maybe a spot on the news. That's where—if we're going to reach out and wake someone up—that's where it's going to happen."

"I suppose."

Annie flipped over the brochure and looked at the four photographs on the back.

"How come there isn't a picture of Sophie?" she asked.

"Cameras don't seem to work all that well around her," Jilly said. "It's like—" she smiled, "—an enchantment."

The corner of Annie's mouth twitched in response.

"Tell me about, you know...." She pointed to Jilly's Urban Faerie paintings. "Magic. Enchanted stuff."

Jilly put the stew on low to simmer then fetched a sketchbook that held some of the preliminary pencil drawings for the finished paintings that were leaning up against the wall. The urban settings were barely realized—just rough outlines and shapes—but the faerie were painstakingly detailed.

As they flipped through the sketchbook, Jilly talked about where she'd done the sketches, what she'd seen, or more properly glimpsed, that led her to make the drawings she had.

"You've really seen all these...little magic people?" Annie asked.

Her tone of voice was incredulous, but Jilly could tell that she wanted to believe.

"Not all of them," Jilly said. "Some I've only imagined, but others...like this one." She pointed to a sketch that had been done in the Tombs where a number of fey figures were hanging out around an abandoned car, Pre-Raphaelite features at odds with their raggedy clothing and setting. "They're real."

"But they could just be people. It's not like they're tiny or have wings like some of the others."

Jilly shrugged. "Maybe, but they weren't just people."

"Do you have to be magic yourself to see them?"

Jilly shook her head. "You just have to pay attention. If you don't, you'll miss them, or see something else—something you expected to see rather than what was really there. Fairy voices become just the wind, a bodach, like this little man here—" she flipped to another page and pointed out a small gnomish figure the size of a cat, darting off a sidewalk, "—scurrying across the street becomes just a piece of litter caught in the backwash of a bus."

"Pay attention," Annie repeated dubiously.

Jilly nodded. "Just like we have to pay attention to each other, or we miss the important things that are going on there as well."

Annie turned another page, but she didn't look at the drawing. Instead she studied Jilly's pixie features.

"You really, really believe in magic, don't you?" she said.

"I really, really do," Jilly told her. "But it's not something I just take on faith. For me, art is an act of magic. I pass on the spirits that I see—of people, of places, mysteries."

"So what if you're not an artist? Where's the magic then?"

"Life's an act of magic, too. Claire Hamill sings a line in one of her songs that really sums it up for me: 'If there's no magic, there's no meaning.' Without magic—or call it wonder, mystery, natural wisdom—nothing has any depth. It's all just surface. You know: what you see is what you get. I honestly believe there's more to everything than that, whether it's a Monet hanging in a gallery or some old vagrant sleeping in an alley."

"I don't know," Annie said. "I understand what you're saying, about people and things, but this other stuff—it sounds more like the kinds of things you see when you're tripping."

Jilly shook her head. "I've done drugs and I've seen Faerie. They're not the same."

She got up to stir the stew. When she sat down again, Annie had closed the sketchbook and was sitting with her hands flat against her stomach.

"Can you feel the baby?" Jilly asked.

Annie nodded.

"Have you thought about what you want to do?"

"I guess. I'm just not sure I even want to keep the baby."

"That's your decision," Jilly said. "Whatever you want to do, we'll stand by you. Either way we'll get you a place to stay. If you keep the baby and want to work, we'll see about arranging daycare. If you want to stay home with the baby, we'll work something out for that as well. That's what this sponsorship's all about. It's not us telling you what to do; we just want to help you be the person you were meant to be."

"I don't know if that's such a good person," Annie said.

"Don't think like that. It's not true."

Annie shrugged. "I guess I'm scared I'll do the same thing to my baby that my mother did to me. That's how it happens, doesn't it? My mom used to beat the crap out of me all the time, didn't matter if I did something wrong or not, and I'm just going to end up doing the same thing to my kid."

"You're only hurting yourself with that kind of thinking," Jilly said.

"But it *can* happen, can't it? Jesus, I.... You know I've been gone from her for two years now, but I still feel like she's standing right next to me half the time, or waiting around the corner for me. It's like I'll never escape. When I lived at home, it was like I was living in the house of an enemy. But running away didn't change that. I still feel like that, except now it's like everybody's my enemy."

Jilly reached over and laid a hand on hers.

"Not everybody," she said. "You've got to believe that."

"It's hard not to."

"I know."

10

This Is Where We Dump Them, by Meg Mullally. Tinted photograph. The Tombs, Newford, 1991.

Two children sit on the stoop of one of the abandoned buildings in the Tombs. Their hair is matted, faces smudged, clothing dirty and ill-fitting. They look like turn-of-the-century Irish tinkers. There's litter all around them: torn garbage bags spewing their contents on the sidewalk, broken bottles, a rotting mattress on the street, half-crushed pop cans, soggy newspapers, used condoms.

The children are seven and thirteen, a boy and a girl. They have no home, no family. They only have each other.

The next month went by awfully fast. Annie stayed with me—it was what she wanted. Angel and I did get her a place, a one-bedroom on Landis that she's going to move into after she's had the baby. It's right behind the loft—you can see her back window from mine. But for now she's going to stay here with me.

She's really a great kid. No artistic leanings, but really bright. She could be anything she wants to be if she can just learn to deal with all the baggage her parents dumped on her.

She's kind of shy around Angel and some of my other friends—I guess they're all too old for her or something—but she gets along really well with Sophie and I. Probably because, whenever you put Sophie and I together in the same room for more than two minutes, we just start giggling and acting about half our respective ages, which would make us, mentally at least, just a few years Annie's senior.

"You two could be sisters," Annie told me one day when we got back from Sophie's studio. "Her hair's lighter, and she's a little chestier, and she's *definitely* more organized than you are, but I get a real sense of family when I'm with the two of you. The way families are supposed to be."

"Even though Sophie's got faerie blood?" I asked her.

She thought I was joking.

"If she's got magic in her," Annie said, "then so do you. Maybe that's what makes you seem so much like sisters."

"I just pay attention to things," I told her. "That's all."

"Yeah, right."

The baby came right on schedule—three-thirty, Sunday morning. I probably would've panicked if Annie hadn't been doing enough of that for both of us. Instead I got on the phone, called Angel, and then saw about helping Annie get dressed.

The contractions were really close by the time Angel arrived with the car. But everything worked out fine. Jillian Sophia Mackle was born two hours and forty-five minutes later at the Newford General Hospital. Six pounds and five ounces of red-faced wonder. There were no complications.

Those came later.

II

The last week before the show was simple chaos. There seemed to be a hundred and one things that none of them had thought of, all of which had to be done at the last moment. And to make matters worse, Jilly still had one unfinished canvas haunting her by Friday night.

It stood on her easel, untitled, barely-sketched in images, still in monochrome. The colours eluded her. She knew what she wanted, but every time she stood before her easel, her mind went blank. She seemed to forget everything she'd ever known about art. The inner essence of the canvas rose up inside her like a ghost, so close she could almost touch it, but then fled daily, like a dream lost upon waking. The outside world intruded. A knock on the door. The ringing of the phone.

The show opened in exactly seven days.

Annie's baby was almost two weeks old. She was a happy, satisfied infant, the kind of baby that was forever making contented little gurgling sounds, as though talking to herself; she never cried. Annie herself was a nervous wreck.

"I'm scared," she told Jilly when she came over to the loft that afternoon. "Everything's going too well. I don't deserve it."

They were sitting at the kitchen table, the baby propped up on the Murphy bed between two pillows. Annie kept fidgeting. Finally she picked up a pencil and started drawing stick figures on pieces of paper.

"Don't say that," Jilly said. "Don't even think it."

"But it's true. Look at me. I'm not like you or Sophie. I'm not like Angel. What have I got to offer my baby? What's she going to have to look up to when she looks at me?"

"A kind, caring mother."

Annie shook her head. "I don't feel like that. I feel like everything's sort of fuzzy and it's like pushing through cobwebs to just to make it through the day."

"We'd better make an appointment with you to see a doctor."

"Make it a shrink," Annie said. She continued to doodle, then looked down at what she was doing. "Look at this. It's just crap."

Before Jilly could see, Annie swept the sheaf of papers to the floor.

"Oh, jeez," she said as they went fluttering all over the place. "I'm sorry. I didn't mean to do that."

She got up before Jilly could and tossed the lot of them in the garbage container beside the stove. She stood there for a long moment, taking deep breaths, holding them, slowly letting them out.

"Annie...?"

She turned as Jilly approached her. The glow of motherhood that had seemed to revitalize her in the month before the baby was born had slowly worn away. She was pale again. Wan. She looked so lost that all Jilly could do was put her arms around her and offer a wordless comfort.

"I'm sorry," Annie said against Jilly's hair. "I don't know what's going on. I just...I know I should be really happy, but I just feel scared and confused." She rubbed at her eyes with a knuckle. "God, listen to me. All it seems I can do is complain about my life."

"It's not like you've had a great one," Jilly said.

"Yeah, but when I compare it to what it was like before I met you, it's like I moved up into heaven."

"Why don't you stay here tonight?" Jilly said.

Annie stepped back out of her arms. "Maybe I will—if you really don't mind…?"

"I really don't mind."

"Thanks."

Annie glanced towards the bed, her gaze pausing on the clock on the wall above the stove.

"You're going to be late for work," she said.

"That's all right. I don't think I'll go in tonight."

Annie shook her head. "No, go on. You've told me how busy it gets on a Friday night."

Jilly still worked part-time at Kathryn's Café on Battersfield Road. She could just imagine what Wendy would say if she called in sick. There was no one else in town this weekend to take her shift, so that would leave Wendy working all the tables on her own.

"If you're sure," Jilly said.

"We'll be okay," Annie said. "Honestly."

She went over to the bed and picked up the baby, cradling her gently in her arms.

"Look at her," she said, almost to herself. "It's hard to believe something so beautiful came out of me." She turned to Jilly, adding before Jilly could speak, "That's a kind of magic all by itself, isn't it?"

"Maybe one of the best we can make," Jilly said.

12

How Can You Call This Love? by Claudia Feder. Oils. Old Market Studio, Newford, 1990.

A fat man sits on a bed in a cheap hotel room. He's removing his shirt. Through the ajar door of the bathroom behind him, a thin girl in bra and panties can be seen sitting on the toilet, shooting up.

She appears to be about fourteen.

I just pay attention to things I told her. I guess that's why, when I got off my shift and came back to loft, Annie was gone. Because I pay such good attention. The baby was still on the bed, lying between the pillows, sleeping. There was a note on the kitchen table:

I don't know what's wrong with me. I just keep wanting to hit something. I look at little Jilly and I think about my mother and I get so scared. Take care of her for me. Teach her magic.

Please don't hate me.

I don't know how long I sat and stared at those sad, piteous words, tears streaming from my eyes.

I should never have gone to work. I should never have left her alone. She really thought she was just going to replay her own childhood. She told me, I don't know how many times she told me, but I just wasn't paying attention, was I?

Finally I got on the phone. I called Angel. I called Sophie. I called Lou Fucceri. I called everybody I could think of to go out and look for Annie. Angel was at the loft with me when we finally heard. I was the one who picked up the phone.

I heard what Lou said: "A patrolman brought her into the General not fifteen minutes ago, ODing on Christ knows what. She was just trying to self-destruct, is what he said. I'm sorry, Jilly. But she died before I got here."

I didn't say anything. I just passed the phone to Angel and went to sit on the bed. I held little Jilly in my arms and then I cried some more.

I was never joking about Sophie. She really does have faerie blood. It's something I can't explain, something we don't talk much about, something I just know and she denies. But she did promise me that she'd bless Annie's baby, just the way fairy godmothers would do it in all those old stories.

"I gave her the gift of a happy life," she told me later. "I never dreamed it wouldn't include Annie."

But that's the way it works in fairy tales, too, isn't it? Something always goes wrong, or there wouldn't be a story. You have to be strong, you have to earn your happily ever after.

Annie was strong enough to go away from her baby when she felt like all she could do was just lash out, but she wasn't strong enough to help herself. That was the awful gift her parents gave her.

I never finished that last painting in time for the show, but I found something to take its place. Something that said more to me in just a few rough lines than anything I've ever done.

I was about to throw out my garbage when I saw those crude little drawings that Annie had been doodling on my kitchen table the night she died. They were like the work of a child.

I framed one of them and hung it in the show.

"I guess we're five coyotes and one coyote ghost now," was all Sophie said when she saw what I had done.

13

In the House of My Enemy, by Annie Mackle. Pencils. Yoors Street Studio, Newford, 1991.

The images are crudely rendered. In a house that is merely a square with a triangle on top, are three stick figures, one plain, two with small "skirt" triangles to represent their gender. The two larger figures are beating the smaller one with what might be crooked sticks, or might be belts.

The small figure is cringing away.

14

In the visitor's book set out at the show, someone wrote: "I can never forgive those responsible for what's been done to us. I don't even want to try."

"Neither do I," Jilly said when she read it. "God help me, neither do I."

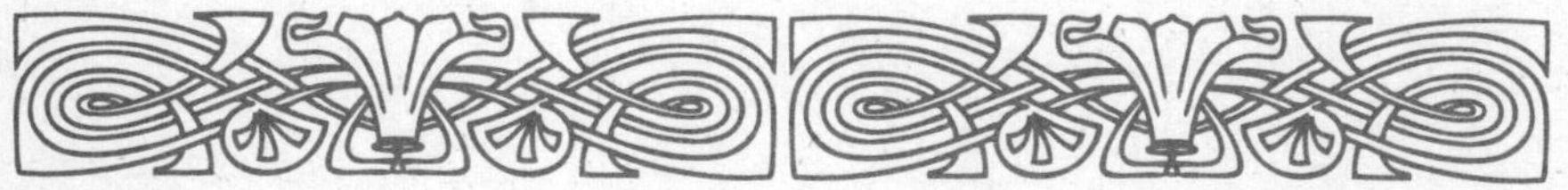

THE MOON IS DROWNING WHILE I SLEEP

If you keep your mind sufficiently open, people will throw a lot of rubbish into it. —William A. Orton

1

ONCE UPON A time there was what there was, and if nothing had happened there would be nothing to tell.

2

It was my father who told me that dreams want to be real. When you start to wake up, he said, they hang on and try to slip out into the waking world when you don't notice. Very strong dreams, he added, can almost do it; they can last for almost half a day, but not much longer.

I asked him if any ever made it. If any of the people our subconscious minds toss up and make real while we're sleeping had ever actually stolen out into this world from the dream world.

He knew of at least one that had, he said.

He had that kind of lost look in his eyes that made me think of my mother. He always looked like that when he talked about her, which wasn't often.

Who was it? I asked, hoping he'd dole out another little tidbit about my mother. Is it someone I know?

Even as I asked, I was wondering how he related my mother to a dream. He'd at least known her. I didn't have any memories, just imaginings. Dreams.

But he only shook his head. Not really, he told me. It happened a long time ago. But I often wondered, he added almost to himself, what did *she* dream of?

That was a long time ago and I don't know if he ever found out. If he did, he never told me. But lately I've been wondering about it. I think maybe they don't dream. I think that if they do, they get pulled back into the dream world.

And if we're not too careful, they can pull us back with them.

3

"I've been having the strangest dreams," Sophie Etoile said, more as an observation than a conversational opener.

She and Jilly Coppercorn had been enjoying a companionable silence while they sat on the stone river wall in the old part of Lower Crowsea's Market. The wall is by a small public courtyard, surrounded on three sides by old three-story brick and stone town houses, peaked with mansard roofs, the dormer windows thrusting out from the walls like hooded eyes with heavy brows. The buildings date back over a hundred years, leaning against each other like old friends too tired to talk, just taking comfort from each other's presence.

The cobblestoned streets that web out from the courtyard are narrow, too tight a fit for a car, even the small imported makes. They twist and turn, winding in and around the buildings more like back alleys than thoroughfares. If you have any sort of familiarity with the area you can maze your way by those lanes to find still smaller courtyards, hidden and private, and deeper still, secret gardens.

There are more cats in Old Market than anywhere else in Newford and the air smells different. Though it sits just a few blocks west of some of the city's principal thoroughfares, you can hardly hear the traffic, and you can't smell it at all. No exhaust, no refuse, no dead air. In Old Market it always seems to smell of fresh bread baking, cabbage soups, frying fish, roses and those tart, sharp-tasting apples that make the best strudels.

Sophie and Jilly were bookended by stairs going down to the Kickaha River on either side of them. Pale yellow light from the streetlamp behind them put a glow on their hair, haloing each with her own nimbus of light—Jilly's darker, all loose tangled curls, Sophie's a soft auburn, hanging in ringlets. They each had a similar slim build, though Sophie was somewhat bustier.

In the half-dark of the streetlamp's murky light, their small figures could almost be taken for each other, but when the light touched their features as they turned to talk to each other, Jilly could be seen to have the quick, clever features of a Rackham pixie, while Sophie's were softer, as though rendered by Rossetti or Burne-Jones.

Though similarly dressed with paint-stained smocks over loose T-shirts and baggy cotton pants, Sophie still managed to look tidy, while Jilly could never seem to help a slight tendency towards scruffiness. She was the only one of the two with paint in her hair.

"What sort of dreams?" she asked.

It was almost four o'clock in the morning. The narrow streets of Old Market lay empty and still about them, except for the odd prowling cat, and cats can be like the hint of a whisper when they want, ghosting and silent, invisible presences. The two women had been working at Sophie's studio on a joint painting, a collaboration that was going to combine Jilly's precise delicate work with Sophie's current penchant for bright flaring colours and loosely-rendered figures.

Neither was sure the experiment would work, but they'd been enjoying themselves immensely with it, so it really didn't matter.

"Well, they're sort of serial," Sophie said. "You know, where you keep dreaming about the same place, the same people, the same events, except each night you're a little further along in the story."

Jilly gave her an envious look. "I've always wanted to have that kind of dream. Christy's had them. I think he told me that it's called lucid dreaming."

"They're anything but lucid," Sophie said. "If you ask me, they're downright strange."

"No, no. It just means that you know you're dreaming, *when* you're dreaming, and have some kind of control over what happens in the dream."

Sophie laughed. "I wish."

4

I'm wearing a long pleated skirt and one of those white cotton peasant blouses that's cut way too low in the bodice. I don't know why. I hate that kind of bodice. I keep feeling like I'm going to fall out whenever I bend over. Definitely designed by a man. Wendy likes to wear that kind of thing from time to time, but it's not for me.

Nor is going barefoot. Especially not here. I'm standing on a path, but it's muddy underfoot, all squishy between my toes. It's sort of nice in some ways, but I keep getting the feeling that something's going to sidle up to me, under the mud, and brush against my foot, so I don't want to move, but I don't want to just stand here either.

Everywhere I look it's all marsh. Low flat fens, with just the odd crack willow or alder trailing raggedy vines the way you see Spanish moss do in pictures of the Everglades, but this definitely isn't Florida. It feels more Englishy, if that makes sense.

I know if I step off the path I'll be in muck up to my knees.

I can see a dim kind of light off in the distance, way off the path. I'm attracted to it, the way any light in the darkness seems to call out, welcoming you, but I don't want to brave the deeper mud or the pools of still water that glimmer in the pale starlight.

It's all mud and reeds, cattails, bulrushes and swamp grass and I just want to be back home in bed, but I can't wake up. There's a funny smell in the air, a mix of things rotting and stagnant water. I feel like there's something horrible in the shadows under those strange overhung trees—especially the willows, the tall sharp leaves of sedge and water plantain growing thick around their trunks. It's like there are eyes watching me from all sides, dark misshapen heads floating frog-like in the water, only the eyes showing, staring. Quicks and bogles and dark things.

I hear something move in the tangle of bulrushes and bur reeds just a few feet away. My heart's in my throat, but I move a little closer to see that it's only a bird caught in some kind of a net.

Hush, I tell it and move closer.

The bird gets frantic when I put my hand on the netting. It starts to peck at my fingers, but I keep talking softly to it until it finally settles down. The net's a mess of knots and tangles and I can't work too quickly because I don't want to hurt the bird.

You should leave him be, a voice says, and I turn to find an old woman standing on the path beside me. I don't know where she came from. Every time I lift one of my feet it makes this creepy sucking sound, but I never even heard her approach.

She looks like the wizened old crone in that painting Jilly did for Geordie when he got onto this kick of learning fiddle tunes with the word "hag" in the title: "The Hag in the Kiln," "Old Hag You Have Killed Me," "The Hag With the Money" and God knows how many more.

Just like in the painting, she's wizened and small and bent over and...dry. Like kindling, like the pages of an old book. Like she's almost all used up. Hair thin, body thinner. But then you look into her eyes and they're so alive it makes you feel a little dizzy.

Helping such as he will only bring you grief, she says.

I tell her that I can't just leave it.

She looks at me for a long moment, then shrugs. So be it, she says.

I wait a moment, but she doesn't seem to have anything else to say, so I go back to freeing the bird. But now, where a moment ago the netting was a hopeless tangle, it just seems to unknot itself as soon as I lay my hand on it. I'm careful when I put my fingers around the bird and pull it free. I get it out of the tangle and then toss it up in the air. It circles above me in the air, once, twice, three times, cawing. Then it flies away.

It's not safe here, the old lady says then.

I'd forgotten all about her. I get back onto the path, my legs smeared with smelly dark mud.

What do you mean? I ask her.

When the Moon still walked the sky, she says, it was safe then. The dark things didn't like her light and fairies fell over themselves to get away when she shone. But they're bold now, tricked and trapped her, they have, and no one's safe. Not you, not me. Best we were away.

Trapped her? I repeat like an echo. The moon?

She nods.

Where?

She points to the light I saw earlier, far out in the fens.

They've drowned her under the Black Snag, she says. I will show you.

She takes my hand before I realize what she's doing and pulls me through the rushes and reeds, the mud squishing awfully under my bare feet, but it doesn't seem to bother her at all. She stops when we're at the edge of some open water.

Watch now, she says.

She takes something from the pocket of her apron and tosses it into the water. It's like a small stone, or a pebble or something, and it enters the water without a sound, without making a ripple. Then the water starts to glow and a picture forms in the dim flickering light.

It's like we have a bird's-eye view of the fens, for a moment, then the focus comes in sharp on the edge of a big still pool, sentried by a huge dead willow. I don't know how I know it, because the light's still poor, but the mud's black around its shore. It almost swallows the pale wan glow coming up from out of the water.

Drowning, the old woman says. The moon is drowning.

I look down at the image that's formed on the surface and I see a woman floating there. Her hair's all spread out from her, drifting in the water like lily roots. There's a great big stone on top of her torso so she's only really visible from the breasts up. Her shoulders are slightly sloped, neck slender, with a swan's curve, but not so long. Her face is in repose, as though she's sleeping, but she's under water, so I know she's dead.

She looks like me.

I turn to the old woman, but before I can say anything, there's movement all around us. Shadows pull away from trees, rise from the stagnant pools, change from vague blotches of darkness, into moving shapes, limbed and headed, pale eyes glowing with menace. The old woman pulls me back onto the path.

Wake quick! she cries.

She pinches my arm—hard, sharp. It really hurts. And then I'm sitting up in my bed.

5

"And did you have a bruise on your arm from where she pinched you?" Jilly asked.

Sophie shook her head and smiled. Trust Jilly. Who else was always looking for the magic in a situation?

"Of course not," she said. "It was just a dream."

"But…"

"Wait," Sophie said. "There's more."

Something suddenly hopped onto the wall between them and they both started, until they realized it was only a cat.

"Silly puss," Sophie said as it walked towards her and began to butt its head against her arm. She gave it a pat.

6

The next night I'm standing by my window, looking out at the street, when I hear movement behind me. I turn and it isn't my apartment anymore. It's like the inside of an old barn, heaped up with straw in a big tidy pile against one wall. There's a lit lantern swinging from a low rafter beam, a dusty but pleasant smell in the air, a cow or maybe a horse making some kind of nickering sound in a stall at the far end.

And there's a guy standing there in the lantern light, a half-dozen feet away from me, not doing anything, just looking at me. He's drop dead gorgeous. Not too thin, not too muscle-bound. A friendly open face with a wide smile and eyes to kill for—long moody lashes, and the eyes are the colour of violets. His hair's thick and dark, long in the back with a cowlick hanging down over his brow that I just want to reach out and brush back.

I'm sorry, he says. I didn't mean to startle you.

That's okay, I tell him.

And it is. I think maybe I'm already getting used to all the to-and-froing.

He smiles. My name's Jeck Crow, he says.

I don't know why, but all of a sudden I'm feeling a little weak in the knees. Ah, who am I kidding? I know why.

What are you doing here? he asks.

I tell him I was standing in my apartment, looking for the moon, but then I remembered that I'd just seen the last quarter a few nights ago and I wouldn't be able to see it tonight.

He nods. She's drowning, he says, and then I remember the old woman from last night.

I look out the window and see the fens are out there. It's dark and creepy and I can't see the distant glow of the woman drowned in the pool from here the way I could last night. I shiver and Jeck comes over all concerned. He's picked up a blanket that was hanging from one of the support beams and he lays it across my shoulders. He leaves his arm there, to keep it in place, and I don't mind. I just sort of lean into him, like we've always been together. It's weird. I'm feeling drowsy and safe and incredibly aroused, all at the same time.

He looks out the window with me, his hip against mine, the press of his arm on my shoulder a comfortable weight, his body radiating heat.

It used to be, he says, that she would walk every night until she grew so weak that her light was almost failing. Then she would leave the world to go to another, into Faerie, it's said, or at least to a place where the darkness doesn't hide quicks and bogles, and there she would rejuvenate herself for her return. We would have three nights of darkness, when evil owned the night, but then we'd see the glow of her lantern approaching and the haunts would flee her light and we could visit with one another again when the day's work was done.

He leans his head against mine, his voice going dreamy.

I remember my mam saying once, how the Moon lived another life in those three days. How time moves differently in Faerie so that what was a day for us, might be a month for her in that place.

He pauses, then adds, I wonder if they miss her in that other world.

I don't know what to say. But then I realize it's not the kind of conversation in which I have to say anything.

He turns to me, head lowering until we're looking straight into each other's eyes. I get lost in the violet and suddenly I'm in his arms and we're kissing. He guides me, step by sweet step, backward towards that heap of straw. We've got the blanket under us and this time I'm glad I'm wearing the long skirt and peasant blouse again, because they come off so easily.

His hands and his mouth are so gentle and they're all over me like moth wings brushing my skin. I don't know how to describe what he's doing to me. It isn't anything that other lovers haven't done to me before, but the way Jeck does it has me glowing, my skin all warm and tingling with this deep slow burn starting up deep between my legs and just firing up along every one of my nerve ends.

I can hear myself making moaning sounds and then he's inside me, his breathing heavy in my ear. All I can feel and smell is him. My hips are grinding against his and we're synched into this perfect rhythm and then I wake up in my own bed and I'm all tangled up in the sheets with my hand between my legs, fingertip right on the spot, moving back and forth and back and forth....

7

Sophie fell silent.

"Steamy," Jilly said after a moment.

Sophie gave a little bit of an embarrassed laugh. "You're telling me. I get a little squirmy just thinking about it. And that night—I was still so fired up when I woke that I couldn't think straight. I just went ahead and finished and then lay there afterwards, completely spent. I couldn't even move."

"You know a guy named Jack Crow, don't you?" Jilly asked.

"Yeah, he's the one who's got that tattoo parlor down on Palm Street. I went out with him a couple of times, but—" Sophie shrugged, "—you know. Things just didn't work out."

"That's right. You told me that all he ever wanted to do was to give you tattoos."

Sophie shook her head, remembering. "In private places so only he and I would know they were there. Boy."

The cat had fallen asleep, body sprawled out on her lap, head pressed tight up against her stomach. A deep resonant purr rose up from him. Sophie just hoped he didn't have fleas.

"But the guy in my dream was nothing like Jack," she said. "And besides, his name was Jeck."

"What kind of a name *is* that?"

"A dream name."

"So did you see him again—the next night?"

Sophie shook her head. "Though not from lack of interest on my part."

8

The third night I find myself in this one-room cottage out of a fairy tale. You know, there's dried herbs hanging everywhere, a big hearth, considering the size of the place, with black iron pots and a kettle sitting on the hearth stones, thick hand-woven rugs underfoot, a small tidy little bed in one corner, a cloak hanging by the door, a rough set of a table and two chairs by a shuttered window.

The old lady is sitting on one of the chairs.

There you are, she says. I looked for you to come last night, but I couldn't find you.

I'm getting so used to this dreaming business by now that I'm not at all weirded out, just kind of accepting it all, but I am a little disappointed to find myself here, instead of in the barn.

I was with Jeck, I say and then she frowns, but she doesn't say anything.

Do you know him? I ask.

Too well.

Is there something wrong with him?

I'm feeling a little flushed, just talking about him. So far as I'm concerned, there's nothing wrong with him at all.

He's not trustworthy, the old lady finally says.

I shake my head. He seems to be just as upset about the drowned lady as you are. He told me all about her—how she used to go into Faerie and that kind of thing.

She never went into Faerie.

Well then, where did she go?

The old lady shakes her head. Crows talk too much, she says and I can't tell if she means the birds, or a whole bunch of Jecks. Thinking about the latter gives me goosebumps. I can barely stay clear-headed around Jeck; a whole crowd of him would probably overload all my circuits and leave me lying on the floor like a little pool of jelly.

I don't tell the old lady any of this. Jeck inspired confidences, as much as sensuality; she does neither.

Will you help us? she says instead.

I sit down at the table with her and ask, Help with what?

The Moon, she says.

I shake my head. I don't understand. You mean the drowned lady in the pool?

Drowned, the old lady says, but not dead. Not yet.

I start to argue the point, but then realize where I am. It's a dream and anything can happen, right?

It needs you to break the bogles' spell, the old lady goes on.

Me? But—

Tomorrow night, go to sleep with a stone in your mouth and a hazel twig in your hands. Now mayhap, you'll find yourself back here, mayhap with your crow, but guard you don't say a word, not one word. Go out into the fen until you find a coffin, and on that coffin a candle, and then look sideways and you'll see that you're in the place I showed you yesternight.

She falls silent.

And then what am I supposed to do? I ask.

What needs to be done.

But—

I'm tired, she says.

She waves her hand at me and I'm back in my own bed again.

9

"And so?" Jilly asked. "Did you do it?"

"Would you have?"

"In a moment," Jilly said. She sidled closer along the wall until she was right beside Sophie and peered into her friend's face. "Oh don't tell me you didn't do it. Don't tell me that's the whole story."

"The whole thing just seemed silly," Sophie said.

"Oh, please!"

"Well, it did. It was all too oblique and riddlish. I know it was just a dream, so that it didn't have to make sense, but there was so much of a coherence to a lot of it that when it did get incomprehensible, it just didn't seem...oh, I don't know. Didn't seem fair, I suppose."

"But you *did* do it?"

Sophie finally relented.

"Yes," she said.

10

I go to sleep with a small smooth stone in my mouth and have the hardest time getting to sleep because I'm sure I'm going to swallow it during the night and choke. And I have the hazel twig as well, though I don't know what help either of them is going to be.

Hazel twig to ward you from quicks and bogles, I hear Jeck say. And the stone to remind you of your own world, of the difference between waking and dream, else you might find yourself sharing the Moon's fate.

We're standing on a sort of grassy knoll, an island of semi-solid ground, but the footing's still spongy. I start to say hello, but he puts his finger to his lips.

She's old, is Granny Weather, he says, and cranky, too, but there's more magic in one of her toenails than most of us will find in a lifetime.

I never really thought about his voice before. It's like velvet, soft and smooth, but not effeminate. It's too resonant for that.

He puts his hands on my shoulders and I feel like melting. I close my eyes, lift my face to his, but he turns me around so that I have my back to him. He cups his hands around my breasts and kisses me on the nape of my neck. I lean back against him, but he lifts his mouth to my ear.

You must go, he says softly, his breath tickling the inside of my ear. Into the fens.

I pull free from his embrace and face him. I start to say, Why me? Why do I have to go alone? But before I can get a word out he has his hand across my mouth.

Trust Granny Weather, he says. And trust me. This is something only you can do. Whether you do it or not, is your choice. But if you mean to try tonight, you mustn't speak. You must go out into the fens and find her. They will tempt you and torment you, but you must ignore them, else they'll have you drowning too, under the Black Snag.

I look at him and I know he can see the need I have for him because in his eyes I can see the same need for me reflected in their violet depths.

I will wait for you, he says. If I can.

I don't like the sound of that. I don't like the sound of any of it, but I tell myself again, it's just a dream, so I finally nod. I start to turn away, but he catches hold of me for a last moment and kisses me. There's a hot rush of tongues touching, arms tight around each other, before he finally steps back.

I love the strength of you, he says.

I don't want to go, I want to change the rules of the dream, but I get this feeling that if I do, if I change one thing, everything'll change, and maybe he won't even exist in whatever comes along to replace it. So I lift my hand and run it along the side of his face, I take a long last drink of those deep violet eyes that just want to swallow me, then I get brave and turn away again.

And this time I go into the fens.

I'm nervous, but I guess that goes without saying. I look back, but I can't see Jeck anymore. I can just feel I'm being watched, and it's not by him. I clutch my little hazel twig tighter, roll the stone around from one side of my mouth to the other, and keep going.

It's not easy. I have to test each step to make sure I'm not just going to sink away forever into the muck. I start thinking of what you hear about dreams, how if you die in a dream, you die for real, that's why you always wake up just in time. Except for those people who die in their sleep, I guess.

I don't know how long I'm slogging through the muck. My arms and legs have dozens of little nicks and cuts—you never think of how sharp the edge of a reed can be until your skin slides across one. It's like a paper cut, sharp and quick, and it stings like hell. I don't suppose all the muck's doing the cuts much good either. The only thing I can be happy about is that there aren't any bugs.

Actually, there doesn't seem to be the sense of anything living at all in the fens, just me, on my own. But I know I'm not alone. It's like a word sitting on the tip of your tongue. I can't see or hear or sense anything, but I'm being watched.

I think of Jeck and Granny Weather, of what they say the darkness hides. Quicks and bogles and haunts.

After awhile I almost forget what I'm doing out here. I'm just stumbling along with a feeling of dread hanging over me that just won't go away. Bogbean and water mint leaves feel like cold wet fingers sliding along my legs. I hear the occasional flutter of wings, and sometimes a deep kind of sighing moan, but I never see anything.

I'm just about played out when suddenly I come upon this tall rock under the biggest crack willow I've seen so far. The tree's dead, drooping leafless branches into the still water around the stone. The stone rises out of the water at a slant, the mud's all really black underfoot, the marsh is, if anything, even quieter here, expectant, almost, and I get the feeling like something—some*things* are closing in all around me.

I start to walk across the dark mud to the other side of the rock until I hit a certain vantage point. I stop when I can see that it's shaped like a big strange coffin and I remember what Granny Weather told me. I look for the candle and I see a tiny light flickering at the very top of the black stone, right where it's pushed up and snagged among the dangling branches of the dead willow. It's no brighter than a firefly's glow, but it burns steady.

I do what Granny Weather told me and look around myself using my peripheral vision. I don't see anything at first, but as I slowly turn towards the water, I catch just a hint of a glow in the water. I stop and then I wonder what to do. Is it still going to be there if I turn to face it?

Eventually, I move sideways towards it, always keeping it in the corner of my eye. The closer I get, the brighter it starts to glow, until I'm standing hip deep in the cold water, the mud sucking at my feet, and it's all around me, this dim eerie glowing. I look down into the water and I see my own face reflected back at me, but then I realize that it's not me I'm seeing, it's the drowned woman, the moon, trapped under the stone.

I stick my hazel twig down the bodice of my blouse and reach into the water. I have to bend down, the dark water licking at my shoulders and chin and smelling something awful, but I finally touch the woman's shoulder. Her skin's warm against my fingers and for some reason that makes me feel braver. I get a grip with one hand on her shoulder, then the other, and give a pull.

Nothing budges.

I try some more, moving a little deeper into the water. Finally I plunge my head under and get a really good hold, but she simply won't move. The rock's got her pressed down tight, and the willow's got the rock snagged, and dream or no dream, I'm not some kind of superwoman. I'm only so strong and I have to breathe.

I come up spluttering and choking on the foul water.

And then I hear the laughter.

I look up and there's these things all around the edge of the pool. Quicks and bogles and small monsters. All eyes and teeth and spindly black limbs and crooked hands with too many joints to the fingers. The tree is full of crows and their cawing adds to the mocking hubbub of sound.

First got one, now got two, a pair of voices chant. Boil her up in a tiddy stew.

I'm starting to shiver—not just because I'm scared, which I am, but because the water's so damn cold. The haunts just keep on laughing and making up these creepy little rhymes that mostly have to do with little stews and barbecues. And then suddenly, they all fall silent and these three figures come swinging down from the willow's boughs.

I don't know where they came from, they're just there all of a sudden. These aren't haunts, nor quicks nor bogles. They're men and they look all too familiar.

Ask for anything, one of them says, and it will be yours.

It's Jeck, I realize. Jeck talking to me, except the voice doesn't sound right. But it looks just like him. All three look like him.

I remember Granny Weather telling me that Jeck was untrustworthy, but then Jeck told me to trust her. And to trust him. Looking at these three Jecks, I don't know what to think anymore. My head starts to hurt and I just wish I could wake up.

You need only tell us what it is you want, one of the Jecks says, and we will give it to you. There should be no enmity between us. The woman is drowned. She is dead. You have come too late. There is nothing you can do for her now. But you can do something for yourself. Let us gift you with your heart's desire.

My heart's desire, I think.

I tell myself, again, it's just a dream, but I can't help the way I start thinking about what I'd ask for if I could really have anything I wanted, anything at all.

I look down into the water at the drowned woman and I think about my dad. He never liked to talk about my mother. It's like she was just a dream, he said once.

And maybe she was, I find myself thinking as my gaze goes down into the water and I study the features of the drowned woman who looks so much like me. Maybe she was the Moon in this world and she came to ours to rejuvenate, but when the time came for her to go back, she didn't want to leave because she loved me and Dad too much. Except she didn't have a choice.

So when she returned, she was weaker, instead of stronger like she was supposed to be, because she was so sad. And that's how the quicks and the bogles trapped her.

I laugh then. What I'm making up, as I stand here waist-deep in smelly dream water, is the classic abandoned child's scenario. They always figure that there was just a mix-up, that one day their real parents are going to show up and take them away to some place where everything's magical and loving and perfect.

I used to feel real guilty about my mother leaving us—that's something else that happens when you're just a kid in that kind of a situation. You just automatically feel guilty when something bad happens, like it's got to be your fault. But I got older. I learned to deal with it. I learned that I was a good person, that it hadn't been my fault, that my dad was a good person, too, and it wasn't his fault either.

I'd still like to know why my mother left us, but I came to understand that whatever the reasons were for her going, they had to do with her, not with us. Just like I know this is only a dream and the drowned woman might look like me, but that's just something I'm projecting onto her. I *want* her to be my mother. I want her having abandoned me and Dad not to have been her fault either. I want to come to her rescue and bring us all back together again.

Except it isn't going to happen. Pretend and real just don't mix.

But it's tempting all the same. It's tempting to let it all play out. I know the haunts just want me to talk so that they can trap me as well, that they wouldn't follow through on any promise they made, but this is *my* dream. I can *make* them keep to their promise. All I have to do is say what I want.

And then I understand that it's all real after all. Not real in the sense that I can be physically harmed in this place, but real in that if I make a selfish choice, even if it's just in a dream, I'll still have to live with the fact of it when I wake up. It doesn't matter that I'm dreaming, I'll *still* have done it.

What the bogles are offering is my heart's desire, if I just leave the Moon to drown. But if I do that, I'm responsible for her death. She might not be real, but it doesn't change anything at all. It'll still mean that I'm willing to let someone die, just so I can have my own way.

I suck on the stone and move it back and forth from one cheek to the other. I reach down into my wet bodice and pluck out the hazel twig from where it got pushed down between my breasts. I lift a hand to my hair and brush it back from my face and then I look at those sham copies of my Jeck Crow and I smile at them.

My dream, I think. What I say goes.

I don't know if it's going to work, but I'm fed up with having everyone else decide what happens in my dream. I turn to the stone and I put my hands upon it, the hazel twig sticking out between the fingers of my right hand, and I give the stone a shove. There's this great big outcry among the quicks and bogles and haunts as the stone starts to topple over. I look down at the drowned woman and I see her eyes open, I see her smile, but then there's too much light and I'm blinded.

When my vision finally clears, I'm alone by the pool. There's a big fat full moon hanging in the sky, making the fens almost as bright as day. They've all fled, the monsters, the quicks and bogles and things. The dead willow's still full of crows, but as soon as I look up, they lift from the tree in an explosion of dark wings, a circling murder, cawing and crying, until they finally go away. The stone's lying on its side, half in the water, half out.

And I'm still dreaming.

I'm standing here, up to my waist in the smelly water, with a hazel twig in my hand and a stone in my mouth, and I stare up at that big full moon until it seems I can feel her light just singing through my veins. For a moment it's like being back in the barn with Jeck. I'm just on fire, but it's a different kind of fire; it burns away the darknesses that have gotten lodged in me over the years, just like they get lodged in everybody, and just for that moment, I'm solid light, innocent and new born, a burning Midsummer fire in the shape of a woman.

And then I wake up, back home again.

I lie there in my bed and look out the window, but it's still the dark of the moon in our world. The streets are quiet outside, there's a hush over the whole city, and I'm lying here with a hazel twig in my hand, a stone in my mouth, pushed up into one cheek, and a warm burning glow deep inside.

I sit up and spit the stone out into my hand. I walk over to the window. I'm not in some magical dream now; I'm in the real world. I know the lighted moon glows with light borrowed from the sun. That she's still out there in the dark of the moon; we just can't see her tonight because the earth is between her and the sun.

Or maybe she's gone into some other world, to replenish her lantern before she begins her nightly trek across the sky once more.

I feel like I've learned something, but I'm not sure what. I'm not sure what any of it means.

11

"How can you say that?" Jilly said. "God, Sophie, it's so obvious. She really was your mother and you really did save her. As for Jeck, he was the bird you rescued in your first dream. Jeck *Crow*—don't you get it? One of the bad guys, only you won him over with an act of kindness. It all makes perfect sense."

Sophie slowly shook her head. "I suppose I'd like to believe that, too," she said, "but what we want and what really is aren't always the same thing."

"But what about Jeck? He'll be waiting for you. And Granny Weather? They both knew you were the Moon's daughter all along. It all means something."

Sophie sighed. She stroked the sleeping cat on her lap, imagining for a moment that it was the soft dark curls of a crow that could be a man, in a land that only existed in her dreams.

"I guess," she said, "it means I need a new boyfriend."

12

Jilly's a real sweetheart, and I love her dearly, but she's naïve in some ways. Or maybe it's just that she wants to play the ingenue. She's always so ready to believe anything that anyone tells her, so long as it's magical.

Well, I believe in magic, too, but it's the magic that can turn a caterpillar into a butterfly, the natural wonder and beauty of the world that's all around me. I can't believe in some dreamland being real. I can't believe what Jilly now insists is true: that I've got faerie blood, because I'm the daughter of the Moon.

Though I have to admit that I'd like to.

I never do get to sleep that night. I prowl around the apartment, drinking coffee to keep me awake. I'm afraid to go to sleep, afraid I'll dream and that it'll all be real.

Or maybe that it won't.

When it starts to get light, I take a long cold shower, because I've been thinking about Jeck again. I guess if my making the wrong decision in a dream would've had ramifications in the waking world, then there's no reason that a rampaging libido shouldn't carry over as well.

I get dressed in some old clothes I haven't worn in years, just to try to recapture a more innocent time. White blouse, faded jeans, and hightops with this smoking jacket overtop that used to belong to my dad. It's made of burgundy velvet with black satin lapels. A black hat, with a flat top and a bit of a curl to its brim, completes the picture.

I look in the mirror and I feel like I'm auditioning to be a stage magician's assistant, but I don't much care.

As soon as the hour gets civilized, I head over to Christy Riddell's house. I'm knocking on his door at nine o'clock, but when he comes to let me in, he's all sleepy-eyed and disheveled and I realize that I should've given him another couple of hours. Too late for that now.

I just come right out with it. I tell him that Jilly said he knew all about lucid dreaming and what I want to know is, is any of it real—the place you dream of, the people you meet there?

He stands there in the doorway, blinking like an owl, but I guess he's used to stranger things, because after a moment he leans against the door jamb and asks me what I know about consensual reality.

It's where everything that we see around us only exists because we all agree it does, I say.

Well, maybe it's the same in a dream, he replies. If everyone in the dream agrees that what's around them is real, then why shouldn't it be?

I want to ask him about what my dad had to say about dreams trying to escape into the waking world, but I decide I've already pushed my luck.

Thanks, I say.

He gives me a funny look. That's it? he asks.

I'll explain it some other time, I tell him.

Please do, he says without a whole lot of enthusiasm, then goes back inside.

When I get home, I go and lie down on the old sofa that's out on my balcony. I close my eyes. I'm still not so sure about any of this, but I figure it can't hurt to see if Jeck and I can't find ourselves one of those happily-ever-afters with which fairy tales usually end.

Who knows? Maybe I really am the daughter of the Moon. If not here, then someplace.

CROW GIRLS

I remember what somebody said about nostalgia. He said
it's okay to look back, as long as you don't stare.
—Tom Paxton, from an interview with Ken Rockburn

PEOPLE HAVE A funny way of remembering where they've been, who they were. Facts fall by the wayside. Depending on their temperament they either remember a golden time when all was better than well, better than it can be again, better than it ever really was: a first love, the endless expanse of a summer vacation, youthful vigor, the sheer novelty of being alive that gets lost when the world starts wearing you down. Or they focus in on the bad, blow little incidents all out of proportion, hold grudges for years, or maybe they really did have some unlucky times, but now they're reliving them forever in their heads instead of moving on.

But the brain plays tricks on us all, doesn't it? We go by what it tells us, have to I suppose, because what else do we have to use as touchstones? Trouble is we don't ask for confirmation on what the brain tells us. Things don't have to be real, we just have to believe they're real, which pretty much explains politics and religion as much as it does what goes on inside our heads.

Don't get me wrong; I'm not pointing any fingers here. My people aren't guiltless either. The only difference is our memories go back a lot further than yours do.

"I don't get computers," Heather said.

Jilly laughed. "What's not to get?"

They were having cappuccinos in the Cyberbean Café, sitting at the long counter with computer terminals spaced along its length the way those little individual jukeboxes used to be in highway diners. Jilly looked as though she'd been using the tips of her dark ringlets as paintbrushes, then cleaned them on the thighs of her jeans—in other words, she'd come straight from the studio without changing first. But however haphazardly messy she might allow herself or her studio to get, Heather knew she'd either cleaned her brushes, or left them soaking in turps before coming down to the café. Jilly might seem terminally easygoing, but some things she didn't blow off. No matter how the work was going—good, bad or indifferent—she treated her tools with respect.

As usual, Jilly's casual scruffiness made Heather feel overdressed. She was only wearing cotton pants and a blouse, nothing fancy. But she always felt a little like that around Jilly, ever since she'd first taken a class from her at the Newford School of Art a couple of winters ago. No matter how hard she tried, she hadn't been able to shake the feeling that she looked so typical: the suburban working mother, the happy wife. The differences since she and Jilly had first met weren't great. Her blonde hair had been long then, while now it was cropped short. She was wearing glasses now instead of her contacts.

And two years ago she hadn't been carrying an empty wasteland around inside her chest.

"Besides," Jilly added. "You use a computer at work, don't you?"

"Sure, but that's work," Heather said. "Not games and computer screen romances and stumbling around the Internet, looking for information you're never going to find a use for outside of Trivial Pursuit."

"I think it's bringing back a sense of community," Jilly said.

"Oh, right."

"No, think about it. All these people who might have been just vegging out in front of a TV are chatting with each other in cyberspace instead—hanging out, so to speak, with kindred spirits that they might never have otherwise met."

Heather sighed. "But it's not real human contact."

"No. But at least it's contact."

"I suppose."

Jilly regarded her over the brim of her glass coffee mug. It was a mild gaze, not in the least probing, but Heather couldn't help but feel as though Jilly was seeing right inside her head, all the way down to where desert winds blew through the empty space where her heart had been.

"So what's the real issue?" Jilly asked.

Heather shrugged. "There's no issue." She took a sip of her own coffee, then tried on a smile. "I'm thinking of moving downtown."

"Really?"

"Well, you know. I already work here. There's a good school for the kids. It just seems to make sense."

"How does Peter feel about it?"

Heather hesitated for a long moment, then sighed again. "Peter's not really got anything to say about it."

"Oh, no. You guys always seemed so…." Jilly's voice trailed off. "Well, I guess you weren't really happy, were you?"

"I don't know what we were anymore. I just know we're not together. There wasn't a big blowup or anything. He wasn't cheating on me and I certainly wasn't cheating on him. We're just…not together."

"It must be so weird."

Heather nodded. "Very weird. It's a real shock, suddenly discovering after all these years, that we really don't have much in common at all."

Jilly's eyes were warm with sympathy. "How are you holding up?"

"Okay, I suppose. But it's so confusing. I don't know what to think, who I am, what I thought I was doing with the last fifteen years of my life. I mean, I don't regret the girls—I'd have had more children if we could have had them—but everything else…."

She didn't know how to begin to explain.

"I married Peter when I was eighteen and I'm forty-one now. I've been a part of a couple for longer than I've been anything else, but except for the girls, I don't know what any of it meant anymore. I don't know who I am. I thought we'd be together forever, that we'd grow old together, you know? But now it's just me. Casey's fifteen and Janice is twelve. I've got another few years of being a mother, but after that, who am I? What am I going to do with myself?"

"You're still young," Jilly said. "And you look gorgeous."

"Right."

"Okay. A little pale today, but still."

Heather shook her head. "I don't know why I'm telling you this. I haven't told anybody."

"Not even your mom or your sister?"

"Nobody. It's…."

She could feel tears welling up, the vision blurring, but she made herself take a deep breath. It seemed to help. Not a lot, but some. Enough to carry on. How to explain why she wanted to keep it a secret? It wasn't as though it was something she could keep hidden forever.

"I think I feel like a failure," she said.

Her voice was so soft she almost couldn't hear herself, but Jilly reached over and took her hand.

"You're not a failure. Things didn't work out, but that doesn't mean it was your fault. It takes two people to make or break a relationship."

"I suppose. But to have put in all those years…."

Jilly smiled. "If nothing else, you've got two beautiful daughters to show for them."

Heather nodded. The girls did a lot to keep the emptiness at bay, but once they were in bed, asleep, and she was by herself, alone in the dark, sitting on the couch by the picture window, staring down the street at all those other houses just like her own, that desolate place inside her seemed to go on forever.

She took another sip of her coffee and looked past Jilly to where two young women were sitting at a corner table, heads bent together, whispering. It was hard to place their ages—anywhere from late teens to early twenties, sisters, perhaps, with their small builds and similar dark looks, their black clothing and short blue-black hair. For no reason she could explain, simply seeing them made her feel a little better.

"Remember what it was like to be so young?" she said.

Jilly turned, following her gaze, then looked back at Heather.

"You never think about stuff like this at that age," Heather went on.

"I don't know," Jilly said. "Maybe not. But you have a thousand other anxieties that probably feel way more catastrophic."

"You think?"

Jilly nodded. "I know. We all like to remember it as a perfect time, but most of us were such bundles of messed-up hormones and nerves I'm surprised we ever managed to reach twenty."

"I suppose. But still, looking at those girls…"

Jilly turned again, leaning her head on her arm. "I know what you mean. They're like a piece of summer on a cold winter's morning."

It was a perfect analogy, Heather thought, especially considering the winter they'd been having. Not even the middle of December and the snowbanks were already higher than her chest, the temperature a seriously cold minus-fifteen.

"I have to remember their faces," Jilly went on. "For when I get back to the studio. The way they're leaning so close to each other—like confidantes, sisters in their hearts, if not by blood. And look at the fine bones in their features… how dark their eyes are."

Heather nodded. "It'd make a great picture."

It would, but the thought of it depressed her. She found herself yearning desperately in that one moment to have had an entirely different life, it almost didn't matter what. Perhaps one that had no responsibility but to draw great art from the world around her the way Jilly did. If she hadn't had to support Peter while he was going through law school, maybe she would have stuck with her art....

Jilly swiveled in her chair, the sparkle in her eyes deepening into concern once more.

"Anything you need, anytime," she said. "Don't be afraid to call me."

Heather tried another smile. "We could chat on the Internet."

"I think I agree with what you said earlier: I like this better."

"Me, too," Heather said. Looking out the window, she added, "It's snowing again."

Maida and Zia are forever friends. Crow girls with spiky blue-black hair and eyes so dark it's easy to lose your way in them. A little raggedy and never quiet, you can't miss this pair: small and wild and easy in their skins, living on Zen time. Sometimes they forget they're crows, left their feathers behind in the long ago, and sometimes they forget they're girls. But they never forget that they're friends.

People stop and stare at them wherever they go, borrowing a taste of them, drawn by they don't know what, they just have to look, try to get close, but keeping their distance, too, because there's something scary/craving about seeing animal spirits so pure walking around on a city street. It's a shock, like plunging into cold water at dawn, waking up from the comfortable familiarity of warm dreams to find, if only for a moment, that everything's changed. And then, just before the way you know the world to be comes rolling back in on you, maybe you hear giddy laughter, or the slow flap of crows' wings. Maybe you see a couple of dark-haired girls sitting together in the corner of a café, heads bent together, pretending you can't see them, or could be they're perched on a tree branch, looking down at you looking up, working hard at putting on serious faces but they can't stop smiling.

It's like that rhyme, "two for mirth." They can't stop smiling and neither can you. But you've got to watch out for crow girls. Sometimes they wake a yearning you'll be hard-pressed to put back to sleep. Sometimes only a glimpse of them can start up a familiar ache deep in your chest, an ache you can't name, but you've felt it before, early mornings, lying alone in your bed, trying to hold onto the fading tatters of a perfect dream. Sometimes they blow bright the coals of a longing that can't ever be eased.

Heather couldn't stop thinking of the two girls she'd seen in the café earlier in the evening. It was as though they'd lodged pieces of themselves inside her, feathery slivers winging dreamily across the wasteland. Long after she'd played a board game with Janice, then watched the end of a Barbara Walters special with Casey, she found herself sitting up by the big picture window in the living room when she should be in bed herself. She regarded the street through a veil of falling snow, but this time she wasn't looking at the houses, so alike, except for the varying heights of their snowbanks, they might as well all be the same one. Instead, she was looking for two small women with spiky black hair, dark shapes against the white snow.

There was no question but that they knew exactly who they were, she thought when she realized what she was doing. Maybe they could tell her who she was. Maybe they could come up with an exotic past for her so that she could reinvent herself, be someone like them, free, sure of herself. Maybe they could at least tell her where she was going.

But there were no thin, dark-haired girls out on the snowy street, and why should there be? It was too cold. Snow was falling thick with another severe winter storm warning in effect tonight. Those girls were safe at home. She knew that. But she kept looking for them all the same because in her chest she could feel the beat of dark wings—not the sudden panic that came out of nowhere when once again the truth of her situation reared without warning in her mind, but a strange, alien feeling. A sense that some otherness was calling to her.

The voice of that otherness scared her almost more than the grey landscape lodged in her chest.

She felt she needed a safety net, to be able to let herself go and not have to worry about where she fell. Somewhere where she didn't have to think, be responsible, to do anything. Not forever. Just for a time.

She knew Jilly was right about nostalgia. The memories she carried forward weren't necessarily the way things had really happened. But she yearned, if only for a moment, to be able to relive some of those simpler times, those years in high school before she'd met Peter, before they were married, before her emotions got so complicated.

And then what?

You couldn't live in the past. At some point you had to come up for air and then the present would be waiting for you, unchanged. The wasteland in her chest would still stretch on forever. She'd still be trying to understand what had happened. Had Peter changed? Had she changed? Had they both changed? And when did it happen? How much of their life together had been a lie?

It was enough to drive her mad.

It was enough to make her want to step into the otherness calling to her from out there in the storm and snow, step out and simply let it swallow her whole.

Jilly couldn't put the girls from the café out of her mind either, but for a different reason. As soon as she'd gotten back to the studio, she'd taken her current work-in-progress down from the easel and replaced it with a fresh canvas. For a long moment she stared at the texture of the pale ground, a mix of gesso and a light burnt ochre acrylic wash, then she took up a stick of charcoal and began to sketch the faces of the two dark-haired girls before the memory of them left her mind.

She was working on their bodies, trying to capture the loose splay of their limbs and the curve of their backs as they'd slouched in towards each other over the café table, when there came a knock at her door.

"It's open," she called over her shoulder, too intent on what she was doing to look away.

"I could've been some mad, psychotic killer," Geordie said as he came in.

He stamped his feet on the mat, brushed the snow from his shoulders and hat. Setting his fiddlecase down by the door, he went over to the kitchen counter to see if Jilly had any coffee on.

"But instead," Jilly said, "it's only a mad, psychotic fiddler, so I'm entirely safe."

"There's no coffee."

"Sure there is. It's just waiting for you to make it."

Geordie put on the kettle, then rummaged around in the fridge, trying to find which tin Jilly was keeping her coffee beans in this week. He found them in one that claimed to hold Scottish shortbreads.

"You want some?" he asked.

Jilly shook her head. "How's Tanya?"

"Heading back to L.A. I just saw her off at the airport. The driving's horrendous. There were cars in the ditch every couple of hundred feet and I thought the bus would never make it back."

"And yet, it did," Jilly said.

Geordie smiled.

"And then," she went on, "because you were feeling bored and lonely, you decided to come visit me at two o'clock in the morning."

"Actually, I was out of coffee and I saw your light was on." He crossed the loft and came around behind the easel so that he could see what she was working on. "Hey, you're doing the crow girls."

"You know them?"

Geordie nodded. "Maida and Zia. You've caught a good likeness of them—especially Zia. I love that crinkly smile of hers."

"You can tell them apart?"

"You can't?"

"I never saw them before tonight. Heather and I were in the Cyberbean and there they were, just asking to be drawn." She added a bit of shading to the underside of a jaw, then turned to look at Geordie. "Why do you call them the crow girls?"

Geordie shrugged. "I don't. Or at least I didn't until I was talking to Jack Daw and that's what he called them when they came sauntering by. The next time I saw them I was busking in front of St. Paul's, so I started to play 'The Blackbird,' just to see what would happen, and sure enough, they came over to talk to me."

"Crow girls," Jilly repeated. The name certainly fit.

"They're some kind of relation to Jack," Geordie explained, "but I didn't quite get it. Cousins, maybe."

Jilly was suddenly struck with the memory of a long conversation she'd had with Jack one afternoon. She was working up sketches of the Crowsea Public Library for a commission when he came and sat beside her on the grass. With his long legs folded under him, black brimmed hat set at a jaunty angle, he'd regaled her with a long, rambling discourse on what he called the continent's real first nations.

"Animal people," she said softly.

Geordie smiled. "I see he fed you that line, too."

But Jilly wasn't really listening—not to Geordie. She was remembering another part of that old conversation, something else Jack had told her.

"The thing we really don't get," he'd said, leaning back in the grass, "is these contracted families you have. The mother, the father, the children, all living alone in some big house. Our families extend as far as our bloodlines and friendship can reach."

"I don't know much about bloodlines," Jilly said. "But I know about friends."

He'd nodded. "That's why I'm talking to you."

Jilly blinked and looked at Geordie. "It made sense what he said."

Geordie smiled. "Of course it did. Immortal animal people."

"That, too. But I was talking about the weird way we think about families and children. Most people don't even like kids—don't want to see, hear, or hear about them. But when you look at other cultures, even close to home...up on the rez, in Chinatown, Little Italy...it's these big rambling extended families, everybody taking care of everybody else."

Geordie cleared his throat. Jilly waited for him to speak but he went instead to unplug the kettle and finish making the coffee. He ground up some beans and the noise of the hand-cranked machine seemed to reach out and fill every corner of the loft. When he stopped, the sudden silence was profound, as though the city outside was holding its breath along with the inheld breath of the room. Jilly was still watching him when he looked over at her.

"We don't come from that kind of family," he said finally.

"I know. That's why we had to make our own."

It's late at night, snow whirling in dervishing gusts, and the crow girls are perched on the top of the wooden fence that's been erected around a work site on Williamson Street. Used to be a parking lot there, now it's a big hole in the ground on its way to being one more office complex that nobody except the contractors wants. The top of the fence is barely an inch wide at the top and slippery with snow, but they have no trouble balancing there.

Zia has a ring with a small spinning disc on it. Painted on the disc is a psychedelic coil that goes spiraling down into infinity. She keeps spinning it and the two of them stare down into the faraway place at the center of the spiral until the disc slows down, almost stops. Then Zia gives it another flick with her fingernail, and the coil goes spiraling down again.

"Where'd you get this anyway?" Maida asks.

Zia shrugs. "Can't remember. Found it somewhere."

"In someone's pocket."

"And you never did?"

Maida grins. "Just wish I'd seen it first, that's all."

They watch the disc some more, content.

"What do you think it's like down there?" Zia says after awhile. "On the other side of the spiral."

Maida has to think about that for a moment. "Same as here," she finally announces, then winks. "Only dizzier."

They giggle, leaning into each other, tottering back and forth on their perch, crow girls, can't be touched, can't hardly be seen, except someone's standing down there on the sidewalk, looking up through the falling snow, his worried expression so comical it sets them off on a new round of giggles.

"Careful now!" he calls up to them. He thinks they're on drugs—they can tell. "You don't want to—"

Before he can finish, they hold hands and let themselves fall backwards, off the fence.

"Oh, Christ!"

He jumps, gets a handhold on the top of the fence and hauls himself up. But when he looks over, over and down, way down, there's nothing to be seen. No girls lying at the bottom of that big hole in the ground, nothing at all. Only the falling snow. It's like they were never there.

His arms start to ache and he lowers himself back down the fence, lets go, bending his knees slightly to absorb the impact of the last couple of feet. He slips, catches his balance. It seems very still for a moment, so still he can hear an odd rhythmical whispering sound. Like wings. He looks up, but there's too much snow coming down to see anything. A cab comes by, skidding on the slick street, and he blinks. The street's full of city sounds again, muffled, but present. He hears the murmuring conversation of a couple approaching him, their shoulders and hair white with snow. A snowplow a few streets over. A distant siren.

He continues along his way, but he's walking slowly now, trudging through the drifts, not thinking so much of two girls sitting on top of a fence as remembering how, when he was a boy, he used to dream that he could fly.

After fiddling a little more with her sketch, Jilly finally put her charcoal down. She made herself a cup of herbal tea with the leftover hot water in the kettle and joined Geordie where he was sitting on the sofa, watching the snow come down. It was warm in the loft, almost cozy compared to the storm on the other side of the windowpanes, or maybe because of the storm. Jilly leaned back on the sofa, enjoying the companionable silence for awhile before she finally spoke.

"How do you feel after seeing the crow girls?" she asked.

Geordie turned to look at her. "What do you mean, how do I feel?"

"You know, good, bad...different...."

Geordie smiled. "Don't you mean 'indifferent'?"

"Maybe." She picked up her tea from the crate where she'd set it and took a sip. "Well?" she asked when he didn't continue.

"Okay. How do I feel? Good, I suppose. They're fun, they make me smile. In fact, just thinking of them now makes me feel good."

Jilly nodded thoughtfully as he spoke. "Me, too. And something else as well."

"The different," Geordie began. He didn't quite sigh. "You believe those stories of Jack's, don't you?"

"Of course. And you don't?"

"I'm not sure," he replied, surprising her.

"Well, I think these crow girls were in the Cyberbean for a purpose," Jilly said. "Like in that rhyme about crows."

Geordie got it right away. "Two for mirth."

Jilly nodded. "Heather needed some serious cheering up. Maybe even something more. You know how when you start feeling low, you can get on this descending spiral of depression...everything goes wrong, things get worse, because you expect them to?"

"Fight it with the power of positive thinking, I always say."

"Easier said than done when you're feeling that low. What you really need at a time like that is something completely unexpected to kick you out of it and remind you that there's more to life than the hopeless, grey expanse you think is stretching in every direction. What Colin Wilson calls absurd good news."

"You've been talking to my brother."

"It doesn't matter where I got it from—it's still true."

Geordie shook his head. "I don't buy the idea that Maida and Zia showed up just to put your friend in a better mood. Even bird people can get a craving for a cup of coffee, can't they?"

"Well, yes," Jilly said. "But that doesn't preclude their being there for Heather as well. Sometimes when a person needs something badly enough, it just comes to them. A personal kind of steam engine time. You might not be able to articulate what it is you need, you might not even know you need something—at least, not at a conscious level—but the need's still there, calling out to whatever's willing to listen."

Geordie smiled. "Like animal spirits."

"Crow girls."

Geordie shook his head. "Drink your tea and go to bed," he told her. "I think you need a good night's sleep."

"But—"

"It was only a coincidence. Things don't always have a meaning. Sometimes they just happen. And besides, how do you even know they had any effect on Heather?"

"I could just tell. And don't change the subject."

"I'm not."

"Okay," Jilly said. "But don't you see? It doesn't matter if it was a coincidence or not. They still showed up when Heather needed them. It's more of that 'small world, spooky world' stuff Professor Dapple goes on about. Everything's connected. It doesn't matter if we can't see how, it's still all connected. You know, chaos theory and all that."

Geordie shook his head, but he was smiling. "Does it ever strike you as weird when something Bramley's talked up for years suddenly becomes an acceptable element of scientific study?"

"Nothing strikes me as truly weird," Jilly told him. "There's only stuff I haven't figured out yet."

Heather barely slept that night. For the longest time she simply couldn't sleep, and then when she finally did, she was awake by dawn. Wide awake, but heavy with an exhaustion that came more from heartache than lack of sleep.

Sitting up against the headboard, she tried to resist the sudden tightness in her chest, but that sad, cold wasteland swelled inside her. The bed seemed depressingly huge. She didn't so much miss Peter's presence as feel adrift in the bed's expanse of blankets and sheets. Adrift in her life. Why was it he seemed to have no trouble carrying on when the simple act of getting up in the morning felt as though it would require far more energy than she could ever hope to muster?

She stared at the snow swirling against her window, not at all relishing the drive into town on a morning like this. If anything, it was coming down harder than it had been last night. All it took was the suggestion of snow and everybody in the city seemed to forget how to drive, never mind common courtesy or traffic laws. A blizzard like this would snarl traffic and back it up as far as the mountains.

She sighed, supposing it was just as well she'd woken so early since it would take her at least an extra hour to get downtown today.

Up, she told herself, and forced herself to swing her feet to the floor and rise. A shower helped. It didn't really ease the heartache, but the hiss of the water made it easier to ignore her thoughts. Coffee, when she was dressed and had brewed a pot, helped more, though she still winced when Janice came bounding into the kitchen.

"It's a snow day!" she cried. "No school. They just announced it on the radio. The school's closed, closed, closed!"

She danced about in her flannel nightie, pirouetting in the small space between the counter and the table.

"Just yours," Heather asked, "or Casey's, too?"

"Mine, too," Casey replied, following her sister into the room.

Unlike Janice, she was maintaining her cool, but Heather could tell she was just as excited. Too old to allow herself to take part in Janice's spontaneous celebration, but young enough to be feeling giddy with the unexpected holiday.

"Good," Heather said. "You can look after your sister."

"*Mom*!" Janice protested. "I'm not a baby."

"I know. It's just good to have someone older in the house when—"

"You can't be thinking of going in to work today," Casey said.

"We could do all kinds of stuff," Janice added. "Finish decorating the house. Baking."

"Yeah," Casey said, "all the things we don't seem to have time for anymore."

Heather sighed. "The trouble is," she explained, "the real world doesn't work like school. We don't get snow days."

Casey shook her head. "That is *so* unfair."

The phone rang before Heather could agree.

"I'll bet it's your boss," Janice said as Heather picked up the phone. "Calling to tell you it's a snow day for you, too."

Don't I wish, Heather thought. But then what would she do at home all day? It was so hard being here, even with the girls and much as she loved them. Everywhere she turned, something reminded her of how the promises of a good life had turned into so much ash. At least work kept her from brooding.

She brought the receiver up to her ear and spoke into the mouthpiece. "Hello?"

"I've been thinking," the voice on the other end of the line said. "About last night."

Heather had to smile. Wasn't that so Jilly, calling up first thing in the morning as though they were still in the middle of last night's conversation.

"What about last night?" she said.

"Well, all sorts of stuff. Like remembering a perfect moment in the past and letting it carry you through a hard time now."

If only, Heather thought. "I don't have a moment that perfect," she said.

"I sort of got that feeling," Jilly told her. "That's why I think they were a message—a kind of perfect moment now that you can use the same way."

"What *are* you talking about?"

"The crow girls. In the café last night."

"The crow...." It took her a moment to realize what Jilly meant. Their complexions had been dark enough so she supposed they could have been Indians. "How do you know what tribe they belonged to?"

"Not crow, Native American," Jilly said, "but crow, bird people."

Heather shook her head as she listened to what Jilly went on to say, for all that only her daughters were here to see the movement. Glum looks had replaced their earlier excitement when they realized the call wasn't from her boss.

"Do you have any idea how improbable all of this sounds?" she asked when Jilly finished. "Life's not like your paintings."

"Says who?"

"How about common sense?"

"Tell me," Jilly said. "Where did common sense ever get you?"

Heather sighed. "Things don't happen just because we want them to," she said.

"Sometimes that's *exactly* why they happen," Jilly replied. "They happen because we need them to."

"I don't live in that kind of a world."

"But you could."

Heather looked across the kitchen at her daughters once more. The girls were watching her, trying to make sense out of the one-sided conversation they were hearing. Heather wished them luck. She was hearing both sides and that didn't seem to help at all. You couldn't simply reinvent your world because you wanted to. Things just were how they were.

"Just think about it," Jilly added. "Will you do that much?"

"I...."

That bleak landscape inside Heather seemed to expand, growing so large there was no way she could contain it. She focused on the faces of her daughters. She remembered the crow girls in the café. There was so much innocence in them all, daughters and crow girls. She'd been just like them once and she knew it wasn't simply nostalgia colouring her memory. She knew there'd been a time when she lived inside each particular day, on its own and by itself, instead of trying to deal with all the days of her life at once, futilely attempting to reconcile the discrepancies and mistakes.

"I'll try," she said into the phone.

They said their goodbyes and Heather slowly cradled the receiver.

"Who was that, Mom?" Casey asked.

Heather looked out the window. The snow was still falling, muffling the world. Covering its complexities with a blanket as innocent as the hope she saw in her daughters' eyes.

"Jilly," she said. She took a deep breath, then smiled at them. "She was calling to tell me that today really is a snow day."

The happiness that flowered on their faces helped ease the tightness in her chest. The grey landscape waiting for her there didn't go away, but for some reason, it felt less profound. She wasn't even worried about what her boss would say when she called to tell him she wouldn't be in today.

Crow girls can move like ghosts. They'll slip into your house when you're not home, sometimes when you're only sleeping, go walking spirit-soft through your rooms and hallways, sit in your favourite chair, help themselves to cookies and beer, borrow a trinket or two which they'll mean to return and usually do. It's not break and enter so much as simple curiosity. They're worse than cats.

Privacy isn't in their nature. They don't seek it and barely understand the concept. Personal property is even more alien. The idea of ownership—that one can lay proprietary claim to a piece of land, an object, another person or creature—doesn't even register.

"Whatcha looking at?" Zia asks.

They don't know whose house they're in. Walking along on the street, trying to catch snowflakes on their tongues, one or the other of them suddenly got the urge to come inside. Upstairs, the family sleeps.

Maida shows her the photo album. "Look," she says. "It's the same people, but they keep changing. See, here's she's a baby, then she's a little girl, then a teenager."

"Everything changes," Zia says. "Even we get old. Look at Crazy Crow."

"But it happens so fast with them."

Zia sits down beside her and they pore over the pictures, munching on apples they found earlier in a cold cellar in the basement.

Upstairs, a father wakes in his bed. He stares at the ceiling, wondering what woke him. Nervous energy crackles inside him like static electricity, a sudden spill of adrenaline, but he doesn't know why. He gets up and checks the children's rooms. They're both asleep. He listens for intruders, but the house is silent.

Stepping back into the hall, he walks to the head of the stairs and looks down. He thinks he sees something in the gloom, two dark-haired girls sitting on the sofa, looking through a photo album. Their gazes lift to meet his and hold it. The next thing he knows, he's on the sofa himself, holding the photo album in his hand. There are no strange girls sitting there with him. The house seems quieter than it's ever been, as though the fridge, the furnace and every clock the family owns are holding their breath along with him.

He sets the album down on the coffee table, walks slowly back up the stairs and returns to his bed. He feels like a stranger, misplaced. He doesn't know this room, doesn't know the woman beside him. All he can think about is the first girl he ever loved and his heart swells with a bittersweet sorrow. An ache pushes against his ribs, makes it almost impossible to breathe.

What if, what if....

He turns on his side and looks at his wife. For one moment her face blurs, becomes a morphing image that encompasses both her features and those of his first true love. For one moment it seems as though anything is possible, that for all these years he could have been married to another woman, to that girl who first held, then unwittingly, broke his heart.

"No," he says.

His wife stirs, her features her own again. She blinks sleepily at him.

"Wha…?" she mumbles.

He holds her close, heartbeat drumming, more in love with her for being who she is than he has ever been before.

Outside, the crow girls are lying on their backs, making snow angels on his lawn, scissoring their arms and legs, shaping skirts and wings. They break their apple cores in two and give their angels eyes, then run off down the street, holding hands. The snow drifts are undisturbed by their weight. It's as though they, too, like the angels they've just made, have wings.

"This is so cool," Casey tells her mother. "It really feels like Christmas. I mean, not like Christmases we've had, but, you know, like really being part of Christmas."

Heather nods. She's glad she brought the girls down to the soup kitchen to help Jilly and her friends serve a Christmas dinner to those less fortunate than themselves. She's been worried about how her daughters would take the break from tradition, but then realized, with Peter gone, tradition is already broken. Better to begin all over again.

The girls had been dubious when she first broached the subject with them—"I don't want to spend Christmas with *losers*," had been Casey's first comment. Heather hadn't argued with her. All she'd said was, "I want you to think about what you just said."

Casey's response had been a sullen look—there were more and more of these lately—but Heather knew her own daughter well enough. Casey had stomped off to her room, but then come back half an hour later and helped her explain to Janice why it might not be the worst idea in the world.

She watches them now, Casey having rejoined her sister where they are playing with the homeless children, and knows a swell of pride. They're such good kids, she thinks as she takes another sip of her cider. After a couple of hours serving coffee, tea and hot cider, she'd really needed to get off her feet for a moment.

"Got something for you," Jilly says, sitting down on the bench beside her.

Heather accepts the small, brightly-wrapped parcel with reluctance. "I thought we said we weren't doing Christmas presents."

"It's not really a Christmas present. It's more an everyday sort of a present that I just happen to be giving you today."

"Right."

"So aren't you going to open it?"

Heather peels back the paper and opens the small box. Inside, nestled in a piece of folded Kleenex, are two small silver earrings cast in the shapes of crows. Heather lifts her gaze.

"They're beautiful."

"Got them at the craft show from a local jeweler. Rory Crowther. See, his name's on the card in the bottom of the box. They're to remind you—"

Heather smiles. "Of crow girls?"

"Partly. But more to remember that this—" Jilly waves a hand that could be taking in the basement of St. Vincent's, could be taking in the whole world. "It's not all we get. There's more. We can't always see it, but it's there."

For a moment, Heather thinks she sees two dark-haired slim figures standing on the far side of the basement, but when she looks more closely they're only a baglady and Geordie's friend Tanya, talking.

For a moment, she thinks she hears the sound of wings, but it's only the murmur of conversation. Probably.

What she knows for sure is that the grey landscape inside her chest is shrinking a little more, every day.

"Thank you," she says.

She isn't sure if she's speaking to Jilly or to crow girls she's only ever seen once, but whose presence keeps echoing through her life. Her new life. It isn't necessarily a better one. Not yet. But at least it's on the way up from wherever she'd been going, not down into a darker despair.

"Here," Jilly says. "Let me help you put them on."

BIRDS

Isn't it wonderful? The world scans.
—Nancy Willard, from "Looking for Mr. Ames"

1

When her head is full of birds, anything is possible. She can understand the slow language of the trees, the song of running water, the whispering gossip of the wind. The conversation of the birds fills her until she doesn't even think to remember what it was like before she could understand them. But sooner or later, the birds go away, one by one, find new nests, new places to fly. It's not that they tire of her; it's simply not in their nature to tarry for too long.

But she misses them. Misses their company, the flutter of wings inside her head and their trilling conversations. Misses the possibilities. The magic.

To call them back she has to approach them as a bride. Dressed in white, with something old and something new, something borrowed and something blue. And a word. A new word, from another's dream. A word that has never been heard before.

2

Katja Faro was out later than she thought safe, at least for this part of town and at this time of night, the minute hand of her old-fashioned wristwatch steadily climbing up the last quarter of her watch face to count the hour. Three A.M. That late.

From early evening until the clubs close, Gracie Street is a jumbled clutter of people, looking for action, looking for gratification, or just out and about, hanging, gossiping with their friends. There's always something happening, from Lee Street all the way across to Williamson, but tag on a few more hours and clubland becomes a frontier. The lights advertising the various cafés, clubs and bars begin to flicker and go out, their patrons and staff have all gone home, and the only people out on the streets are a few stragglers, such as Katja tonight, and the predators.

Purple combat boots scuffing on the pavement, Katja felt adrift on the empty street. It seemed like only moments ago she'd been secure in the middle of good conversation, laughter and espressos; then someone remarked on the time, the café was closing and suddenly she was out here, on the street, by herself, finding her own way home. She held her jean jacket closed at her throat—the buttons had come off, one by one, and she kept forgetting to replace them—and listened to the swish of her long flowered skirt, the sound of her boots on the pavement. Listened as well for other footsteps and prayed for a cab to come by.

She was paying so much attention to what might be lurking behind the shadowed mouths of the alleyways that she almost didn't notice the slight figure curled up in the doorway of the pawn shop on her right. The sight made her pause. She glanced up and down the street before crouching down in the doorway. The figure's features were in shadow, the small body outlined under what looked like a dirty white sheet, or a shawl. By its shape Katja could tell it wasn't a boy.

"Hey, are you okay?" she asked.

When there was no response, she touched the girl's shoulder and repeated her question. Large pale eyes flickered open, their gaze settling on Katja. The girl woke like a cat, immediately aware of everything around her. Her black hair hung about her face in a tangle. Unlike most street people, she had a sweet smell, like a field of clover, or a potpourri of dried rosehips and herbs, gathered in a glass bowl.

"What makes you think I'm not okay?" the girl asked.

Katja pushed the fall of her own dark hair back from her brow and settled back on her heels.

"Well, for one thing," she said, "you're lying here in a doorway, on a bed of what looks like old newspapers. It's not exactly the kind of place people pick to sleep in if they've got a choice."

She glanced up and down the street again as she spoke, still wary of her surroundings and their possible danger, still hoping to see a cab.

"I'm okay," the girl told her.

"Yeah, right."

"No, really."

Katja had to smile. She wasn't so old that she'd forgotten what it felt like to be in her late teens and immortal. Remembering, looking at this slight girl with her dark hair and strangely pale eyes, she got this odd urge to take in a stray the way that Angel and Jilly often did. She wasn't sure why. She liked to think that she had as much sympathy as the next person, but normally it was hard to muster much of it at this time of night. Normally she was thinking too much about what terrors the night might hold for her to consider playing the Good Samaritan. But this girl looked so young....

"What's your name?" she asked.

"Teresa. Teresa Lewis."

Katja offered her hand as she introduced herself.

Teresa laughed. "Welcome to my home," she said and shook Katja's hand.

"This a regular squat?" Katja asked. Nervous as she was at being out so late, she couldn't imagine actually sleeping in a place like this on a regular basis.

"No," Teresa said. "I meant the street."

Katja sighed. Immortal. "Look. I don't have that big a place, but there's room on my couch if you want to crash."

Teresa gave her a considering look.

"Well, I know it's not the Harbour Ritz," Katja began.

"It's not that," Teresa told her. "It's just that you don't know me at all. I could be loco, for all you know. Get to your place and rob you...."

"I've got a big family," Katja told her. "They'd track you down and take it out of your skin."

Teresa laughed again. It was like they were meeting at a party somewhere, Katja thought, drinks in hand, no worries, instead of on Gracie Street at three A.M.

"I'm serious," she said. "I've got the room."

Teresa's laughter trailed off. Her pale gaze settled on Katja's features.

"Do you believe in magic?" she asked.

"Say what?"

"Magic. Do you believe in it?"

Katja blinked. She waited for the punch line, but when it didn't come, she said, "Well, I'm not sure. My friend Jilly sure does—though maybe magic's not quite the right word. It's more like she believes there's more to this world than we can always see or understand. She sees things...."

Katja caught herself. How did we get into this? she thought. She wanted to change the subject, she wanted to get off the street before some homeboys showed up with all the wrong ideas in mind, but the steady weight of Teresa's intense gaze wouldn't let her go.

"Anyway," Katja said, "I guess you could say Jilly does. Believes in magic, I mean. Sees things."

"But what about you? Have you seen things?"

Katja shook her head. "Only 'old, unhappy, far-off things, and battles long ago,'" she said. "Wordsworth," she added, placing the quote when Teresa raised her eyebrows in a question.

"Then I guess you couldn't understand," Teresa told her. "See, the reason I'm out here like this is that I'm looking for a word."

3

I can't sleep. I lie in bed for what feels like hours, staring up at the shadows cast on the ceiling from the streetlight outside my bedroom window. Finally I get up. I pull on a pair of leggings and a T-shirt and pad quietly across the room in my bare feet. I stand in the doorway and look at my guest. She's still sleeping, all curled up again, except her nest is made up of a spare set of my sheets and blankets now instead of old newspapers.

I wish it wasn't so early. I wish I could pick up the phone and talk to Jilly. I want to know if the strays she brings home tell stories as strange as mine told me on the way back to my apartment. I want to know if her strays can recognize the egret which is a deposed king. If they can understand the gossip of bees and what crows talk about when they gather in a murder. If they ever don the old woman wisdom to be found in the rattle-and-cough cry of a lonesome gull and wear it like a cloak of story.

I want to know if Jilly's ever heard of bird-brides, because Teresa says that's what she is, what she usually is, until the birds fly away. To gather them back into her head takes a kind of a wedding ritual that's sealed with a dream-word. That's what she was doing out on Gracie Street when I found her: worn out from trying to get strangers to tell her a word that they'd only ever heard before in one of their dreams.

I don't have to tell you how helpful the people she met were. The ones that didn't ignore her or call her names, just gave her spare change instead of the word she needs. But I can't say as I blame them. If she'd come up to me with her spiel I don't know how I'd have reacted. Not well, probably. Wouldn't have listened. Gets so you can't walk down a block some days without getting hit up for change, five or six times. I don't want to be cold; but when it comes down to it, I've only got so much myself.

I look away from my guest, my gaze resting on the phone for a moment, before I turn around and go back into my room. I don't bother undressing. I just lie there on my bed, looking up at the shadow play that's still being staged on my ceiling. I know what's keeping me awake: I can't decide if I've brought home some poor confused kid, or a piece of magic. It's not the one or the other that's brought on my insomnia. It's that I'm seriously considering the fact that it might be one or the other.

4

"No, I have a place to live," Teresa said the next morning. They were sitting at the narrow table in Katja's kitchen that only barely seated the two of them comfortably, hands warming around mugs of freshly-brewed coffee. "I live in a bachelor in an old house on Stanton Street."

Katja shook her head. "Then why were you sleeping in a doorway last night?"

"I don't know. I think because the people on Gracie Street in the evening seem to dream harder than people anywhere else."

"They're just more desperate to have a good time," Katja said.

"I suppose. Anyway, I was sure I'd find my word there and by the time I realized I wouldn't—at least last night—it was so late and I was just too tired to go home."

"But weren't you scared?"

Teresa regarded her with genuine surprise. "Of what?"

How to explain, Katja wondered. Obviously this girl sitting across from her in a borrowed T-shirt, with sleep still gathered in the corners of her eyes, was fearless, like Jilly. Where did you start enumerating the dangers for them? And why bother? Teresa probably wouldn't listen any more than Jilly ever did. Katja thought sometimes that people like them must have guardian angels watching out for them—and working overtime.

"I feel like I'm always scared," she said.

Teresa nodded. "I guess that's the way I feel, when the birds leave and all I have left in my head are empty nests and a few stray feathers. Kind of lonely, and scared that they'll never come back."

That wasn't the way Katja felt at all. Her fear lay in the headlines of newspapers and the sound bites that helped fill newscasts. There was too much evil running loose—random, petty evil, it was true, but evil all the same. Ever present and all around her so that you didn't know who to trust anymore. Sometimes it seemed as though everyone in the world was so much bigger and more capable than her. Too often, confronted with their confidence, she could only feel helpless.

"Where did you hear about this…this thing with the birds?" she said instead. "The way you can bring them back?"

Teresa shrugged. "I just always knew it."

"But you have all these details…."

Borrowed from bridal folklore, Katja added to herself—all except for the word she had to get from somebody else's dream. The question she'd really wanted to ask was *why* those particular details? What made their borrowed possibilities true? Katja didn't want to sound judgemental. The truth, she had to admit if she was honest with herself, wasn't so much that she believed her houseguest as that she didn't disbelieve her. Hadn't she woken up this morning searching the fading remnants of her dreams, looking for a new word that only existed beyond the gates of her sleeping mind?

Teresa was smiling at her. The wattage behind the expression seemed to light the room, banishing shadows and uncertainties, and Katja basked in its glow.

"I know what you're thinking," Teresa said. "They don't even sound all that original except for the missing word, do they? But I believe any of us can make things happen—even magical, impossible things. It's a matter of having faith in the private rituals we make up for ourselves."

"Rituals you make up…?"

"Uh-huh. The rituals themselves aren't all that important on their own—though once you've decided on them, you have to stick to them, just like the old alchemists did. You have to follow them through."

"But if the rituals aren't that important," Katja asked, "then what's the point of them?"

"How they help you focus your will—your intent. That's what magic is, you know. It's having a strong enough sense of self and what's around you to not only envision it being different but *making* it different."

"You really believe this, don't you?"

"Of course," Teresa said. "Don't you?"

"I don't know. You make it sound so logical."

"That's because it's true. Or maybe—" That smile of Teresa's returned, warming the room again, "—because I'm *willing* it to be true."

"So would your ritual work for me?"

"If you believe in it. But you should probably find your own—a set of circumstances that feels right for you." She paused for a moment, then added, "And you have to know what you're asking for. My birds are what got me through a lot of bad times. Listening to their conversations and soliloquies let me forget what was happening to me."

Katja leaned forward. She could see the rush of memories rising in Teresa, could see the pain they brought with them. She wanted to reach out and hold her in a comforting embrace—the same kind of embrace she'd needed so often but rarely got.

"What happened?" she asked, her voice soft.

"I don't want to remember," Teresa said. She gave Katja an apologetic look. "It's not that I can't, it's that I don't want to."

"You don't have to talk about it if you don't want to," Katja assured her. "Just because I'm putting you up, doesn't mean you have to explain yourself to me."

There was no sunshine in the smile that touched Teresa's features now. It was more like moonlight playing on wild rose bushes, the cool light glinting on thorns. Memories could impale you just like thorns. Katja knew that all too well.

"But I can't not remember," Teresa said. "That's what so sad. For all the good things in my life, I can't stop thinking of how much I hurt before the birds came."

5

I know about pain. I know about loneliness. Talking with Teresa, I realize that these are the first real conversations I've had with someone else in years.

I don't want to make it sound as though I don't have any friends, that I never talk to anyone—but sometimes it feels like that all the same. I always seem to be standing on the outside of a friendship, of conversations, never really engaged. Even last night, before I found Teresa sleeping in the doorway. I was out with a bunch of people. I was in the middle of any number of conversations and camaraderie. But I still went home alone. I listened to what was going on around me. I smiled some, laughed some, added a sentence here, another there, but it wasn't really me that was partaking of the company. The real me was one step removed, watching it happen. Like it seems I always am.

Everybody I know seems to inhabit one landscape that they all share while I'm the only person standing in the landscape that's inside of me.

But today it's different. We're talking about weird, unlikely things, but I'm *there* with Teresa. I don't even know her, there's all sorts of people I've known for years, known way better, but not one of them seems to have looked inside me as truly as she does. This alchemy, this magic, she's offering me, is opening a door inside me. It's making me remember. It's making me want to fill my head with birds so that I can forget.

That's the saddest thing, isn't it? Wanting to forget. Desiring amnesia. I think that's the only reason some people kill themselves. I know it's the only reason I've ever seriously considered suicide.

Consider the statistics: One out of every five women will be sexually traumatized by the time they reach their twenties. They might be raped, they might be a child preyed upon by a stranger, they might be abused by the very people who are supposed to be looking out for them.

But the thing that statistic doesn't tell you is how often it can happen to that one woman out of five. How it can happen to her over and over and over again, but on the statistical sheet, she's still only listed as one woman in five. That makes it sound so random, the event one extraordinary moment of evil when set against the rest of her life, rather than something that she might have faced every day of her childhood.

I'd give anything for a head full of birds. I'd give anything for the noise and clamor of their conversation to drown out the memories when they rise up inside of me.

6

Long after noon came and went, the two women still sat across from each other at the kitchen table. If their conversation could have been seen as well as heard, the spill of words that passed between them would have flooded off the table to eddy around their ankles in ever-deepening pools. It would have made for profound, dark water that was only bearable because each of them came to understand that the other truly understood what they had gone through, and sharing the stories of their battered childhoods made the burden, if not easier to bear, at least remind them that they weren't alone in what they had undergone.

The coffee had gone cold in their mugs, but the hands across the table they held to comfort each other were warm, palm to palm. When they finally ran out of words, that contact helped maintain the bond of empathy that had grown up between them.

"I didn't have birds," Katja said after a long silence. "All I had was poetry."

"You wrote poems?"

Katja shook her head. "I became poetry. I inhabited poems. I filled them until their words were all I could hear inside my head." She tilted her head back and quoted one:

Rough wind, that moanest loud
Grief too sad for song;
Wild wind, when sullen cloud
Knells all the night long;
Sad storm, whose tears are vain,
Bare woods, whose branches strain,
Deep caves and dreary main,—
Wail, for the world's wrong!

"That's so sad. What's it called?" Teresa asked.

"'A dirge.' It's by Shelley. I always seemed to choose the sad poems, but I only ever wanted them for how I'd get so full of words I wouldn't be able to remember anything else."

"Birds and words," Teresa said. Her smile came out again from behind the dark clouds of her memories. "We rhyme."

7

We wash Teresa's dress that afternoon. It wasn't very white anymore—not after her having grubbed about in it on Gracie Street all day and then worn it as a nightgown while she slept in a doorway—but it cleans up better than I think it will. I feel like we're in a detergent commercial when we take it out of the dryer. The dress seems to glow against my skin as I hand it over to her.

Her something old is a plastic Crackerjack ring that she's had since she was a kid. Her something new are her sneakers—a little scuffed and worse for the wear this afternoon, but still passably white. Her borrowed is a white leather clasp-purse that her landlady loaned her. Her blue is a small clutch of silk flowers: forget-me-nots tied up with a white ribbon that she plans to wear as a corsage.

All she needs is that missing word.

I don't have one for her, but I know someone who might. Jilly always likes to talk about things not quite of this world—things seen from the corner of the eye, or brought over from a dream. And whenever she talks about dreams, Sophie Etoile's name comes up because Jilly insists Sophie's part faerie and therefore a true dreamer. I don't know Sophie all that well, certainly not well enough to guess at her genealogy, improbable or not as the case may be. But she does have an otherworldly, Pre-Raphaelite air about her that makes Jilly's claims seem possible—at least they seem possible considering my present state of mind.

And there's no one else I can turn to, no one I can think of. I can't explain this desperation I feel towards Teresa, a kind of mothering/big sister complex. I just have to help her. And while I know that I may not be able to make myself forget, I think I can do it for her. Or at least I want to try.

So that's how we find ourselves knocking at the door of Sophie's studio later that afternoon. When Sophie answers the door, her curly brown hair tied back from her face and her painting smock as spotless as Jilly says it always is, I don't have to go into a long explanation as to what we're doing there or why we need this word. I just have to mention that Jilly's told me that she's a true dreamer and Sophie gets this smile on her face, like you do when you're thinking about a mischievous child who's too endearing to get angry at, and she thinks for a moment, then says a word that at least I've never heard before. I turn to Teresa to ask her if it's what she needs, but she's already got this beatific look on her face.

"Mmm," is all she can manage.

I thank Sophie, who's giving the pair of us a kind of puzzled smile and lead Teresa back down the narrow stairs of Sophie's building and out onto the street. I wonder what I'm going to do with Teresa. She looks for all the world as though she's tripping. But just when I decide to take her home again, her eyes get a little more focused and she takes my hand.

"I have to…readjust to all of this," she says. "But I don't want to have us just walk out of each other's lives. Can I come and visit you tomorrow?"

"Sure," I tell her. I hesitate a moment, then have to ask, "Can you really hear them?"

"Listen," she says.

She draws my head close to hers until my ear is resting right up against her temple. I swear I hear a bird's chorus resonating inside her head, conducted through skin and bone, from her mind into my mind.

"I'll come by in the morning," she says, and then drifts off down the pavement.

All I can do is watch her go, that birdsong still echoing inside me.

8

Back in my own living room, I sit on the carpet. I can feel a foreign vibe in my apartment, a quivering in the air from Teresa having been there. Everything in the room carries the memory of her, the knowledge of her gaze, how she handled and examined them with her attention. My furniture, the posters and prints on my walls, my knickknacks, all seemed subtly changed, a little stiff from the awareness of her looking at them.

It takes awhile for the room to settle down into its familiar habits. The fridge muttering to itself in the kitchen. The pictures in their frames letting out their stomachs and hanging slightly askew once more.

I take down a box of family photos from the hall closet and fan them out on the carpet in front of me. I look at the happy family they depict and try to see hints of the darkness that doesn't appear in the photos. There are too many smiles—mine, my mother's, my father's. I know real life was never the way these pictures pretend it was.

I sit there remembering my father's face—the last time I saw him. We were in the courtroom, waiting for him to be sentenced. He wouldn't look at me. My mother wouldn't look at me. I sat at the table with only a lawyer for support, only a stranger for family. That memory always makes me feel ashamed because even after all he'd done to me, I didn't feel any triumph. I felt only disloyalty. I felt only that I was the one who'd been bad, that what had happened to me had been my fault. I knew back then it was wrong to feel that way—just as I know now that it is—but I can't seem to help myself.

I squeeze my eyes shut, but the moment's locked in my brain, just like all those other memories from my childhood that put a lie to the photographs fanned out on the carpet around me. Words aren't going to blot them out for me today. There aren't enough poems in the world to do that. And even if I could gather birds into my head, I don't think they would work for me. But I remember what Teresa told me about rituals and magic.

It's having a strong enough sense of self and what's around you to not only envision it being different but making it different.

I remember the echoing sound of the birds I heard gossiping in her head and I know that I can find peace, too. I just have to believe that I can. I just have to know what it is that I want and concentrate on having it, instead of what I've got. I have to find the ritual that'll make it work for me.

Instinctively, I realize it can't be too easy. Like Teresa's dream-word, the spell needs an element to complete it that requires some real effort on my part to attain it. But I know what the rest of the ritual will be—it comes into my head, full-blown, as if I've always known it but simply never stopped to access that knowledge before.

I pick up a picture of my father from the carpet and carefully tear his face into four pieces, sticking one piece in each of the front and back pockets of my jeans. I remember something I heard about salt, about it being used to cleanse, and add a handful of it to each pocket. I wrap the fingers of my left hand together with a black ribbon and tie the bow so that it lies across my knuckles. I lick my right forefinger and write my name on the bare skin of my stomach with saliva. Then I let my shirt fall back down to cover the invisible word and leave the apartment, looking for a person who, when asked to name a nineteenth-century poet, will mistakenly put together the given name of one with the surname of another.

From somewhere I hear a sound like Teresa's birds, singing their approval.

▪ HELD SAFE BY MOONLIGHT AND VINES ▪

I

Lillie's in the graveyard again, looking for ghosts. She just can't stay away.

"I'm paying my respects," she says, but it doesn't make sense.

These days All Souls Cemetery's about as forgotten as the people buried in it. The land belongs to some big company now and they're just waiting for the paperwork to go through at city hall. One day soon they'll be moving what's left of the bodies, tearing down all those old-fashioned mausoleums and crypts and putting up something shiny and new. Who's going to miss it? Nobody goes there now except for the dealers with their little packets of oblivion and junkies looking for a fix.

The only people who care about the place are from the Crowsea Heritage Society. And Lillie. Everybody else just wants to see it go. Everybody else likes the idea of making a place gone wild safe again, never mind they don't put it quite that way. But that's what they're thinking. You can see it in the back of their eyes when they talk about it.

See, there's something that scares most people about the night, something that rises out of old memories, out of the genetic soup we all carry around inside us. Monsters in closets when we were kids and further back still, a long way, all the way back to the things waiting out there where the fire's light can't reach. It's not something anybody talks about, but I know that's what they see in All Souls because I can see it, too.

It's got nothing to do with the drug deals going down. People know a piece of the night is biding in there, thinking about them, and they can't wait to see it go. Even the dealers. You see them hanging around by the gates, money moves from one hand to the other, packets of folded paper follow suit, everything smooth, moves like magic, they're fearless these guys. But they don't go any further in than they have to. Nobody does except for Lillie.

"There's been nobody buried there in fifty years," I tell her, but that just gets her back up. "All the more reason to give those old souls some respect," she says.

But that's not it. I know she's looking for ghosts. Thing is, I don't know why.

2

Alex's problem is he wants an answer for everything. All he ever does is go around asking questions. Never lets a thing lie. Always has to know what's going on and why. Can't understand that some things don't have reasons. Or that some people don't feel like explaining themselves. They just do what feels right. Get an idea in their head and follow it through and don't worry about what someone else is going to think or if anybody else understands.

In Alex's world there's only right and wrong, black and white. Me, I fall through the cracks of that world. In my head, it's all grey. In my head, it's all like walking in the twilight, a thousand shades of moonglow and dusky skies and shadow.

He thinks of me sitting here in the dark, all those old stone mausoleums standing around me, old and battered like the tenements leaning against each other on the streets where we grew up, and it spooks him. But All Souls comforts me, I don't know why. Half the trees inside are dead, the rest are dying. Most of the grass is yellow and brown and the only flowers in this place these days grow on weeds, except in one corner where a scraggly old rosebush keeps on trying, tough old bugger doesn't know enough to give up. The stone walls are crumbling down, the cast-iron gates haven't worked in years. There's a bunch of losers crowded around those gates, cutting deals, more nervous of what's here, inside, than of the man showing up and busting them. I come in over the wall and go deep, where the shadows hide me, and they never even know I'm here. Nobody does, except for Alex and he just doesn't understand.

I know what Alex sees when he looks at this place. I see it, too, at first, each time I come. But after awhile, when I'm over the wall and inside, walking the narrow lanes in between the stones and tombs, uneven cobbles underfoot, the shadows lying thick everywhere I look, it gets different. I go someplace else. I don't hear the dealers, I don't see the junkies. The cemetery's gone, the city's gone, and me, I'm gone, too.

The only thing still with me are the walls, but they're different in that other place. Not so worn down. The stones have been fit together without mortar, each one cunningly placed against the other and solid. Those walls go up ten feet and you'd have to ram them with a bulldozer before they'd come down.

Inside, it's a garden. Sort of. A wild place. A tangle of bushes and briars, trees I've got no name for and vines hanging everywhere. A riot of flowers haunt the ground cover, pale blossoms that catch the moonlight and hold it in their petals.

The moonlight. That moon is so big in this place it feels like it could swallow the world. When I stand there in the wild garden and look up at it, I feel small, like I'm no bigger than the space of time between one moment and the next, but not the same way I feel small anywhere else. Where I come from there are millions of people living everywhere and each one of them's got their own world. It's so easy to lose a part of yourself in those worlds, to just find yourself getting sucked away until there's next to nothing left of who you are. But I don't have to be careful about that here. There aren't any of those millions of people here and that moon, it doesn't swallow up who I am; its golden light fills me up, reveling in what it knows me to be. I'm small in its light, sure, but the kind of small that can hold everything there is to be held. The moon's just bigger, that's all. Not more important than me, just different.

Those junkies don't know what they're missing, never getting any further inside the gates than the first guy in a jean vest with the right price.

3

Trouble is, Lillie doesn't understand danger. She's never had to go through the hard times some of us did, never really seen what people can do to each other when they're feeling desperate or just plain mean. She grew up poor, like everybody else in our neighbourhood, but her family loved her and she didn't get knocked around the way those of us who didn't have her kind of parents did. She was safe at home; out on the streets, I always looked after her, made sure the hard cases left her alone.

I'm working as a bouncer at Chic Cheeks the night I hear she's been going to All Souls, so I head down there after my shift to check things out. It's a good thing I do. Some of the guys hanging around by the gates have gotten bored and happened to spot her, all alone in there and looking so pretty. Guess they decided they were going to have themselves a little fun. Bad move. But then they didn't expect me to come along.

I remember a teacher I had in junior high telling me one time how wood and stone make poor conductors. Well, they conduct pain pretty good, as those boys find out. I introduce one of them face-first to a tombstone and kind of make a mess of his nose, knock out a couple of teeth. His pals aren't chickenshit, I'll give them that much. I hear the *snickt* of their blades snapping open, so I drop the first guy. He makes some kind of gurgling noise when he hits the ground and rolls onto my boot. I push him away and then ignore him. He's too busy feeling his pain to cause me any immediate grief. I turn to his buddies, a little pissed off now, but we don't get into it.

"Oh Christ," one of them says, recognizing me.

"We didn't mean nothing, Al," the other one says.

They're putting their knives away, backing up.

"We knew she was one of your people, we never would've touched her. I swear it, man."

Guess I've got a bit of a rep. Nothing serious. I'm not some big shot. What it's got to do with is my old man.

Crazy Eddie is what they used to call him on the streets. Started running numbers for the bosses back when he was a kid, then moved into collections, which is where he got his name. You don't want to think it of your own flesh and blood, but the old man was a psycho. He'd do any crazed thing came to mind if you couldn't pay up. You're in for a few yards, you better cough it up, don't matter what you've got to do to get the money, because he'd as soon as cut your throat as collect the bread.

After awhile the bosses started using him for hits, the kind where they're making a statement. Messy, crazy hits. He did that for years until he got into a situation he couldn't cut his way out of. Cops took him away in a bunch of little bags.

Man, I'll never forget that day. I was doing a short stretch in the county when I found out and I near laughed myself sick. I'd hated that old bastard for the way he'd treated Ma, for what he did to my sister Juney. He used to kick the shit out of me on a regular basis, but I could deal with that. It was the things he did to them.... I knew one day I'd take him down, didn't matter he was my old man. I just hadn't got around to it yet. Hadn't figured out a way to let the bosses know it was personal, not some kind of criticism of their business.

Anyway, I'm not mean like the old man was, I'll tell you that straight-off, but I purely don't take crap from anybody. I don't have to get into it too much anymore. People take a look at me now and think, blood is blood. They see my old man's crazy eyes when they look in mine, and they find some other place to be than where I'm standing.

So I make the point with these boys that they don't want to mess with Lillie, and all it takes is a tap against a tombstone for them to get the message. I let them get their pal and take off, then I go to see what Lillie's doing.

It's the strangest thing. She's just standing there by one of those old stone mausoleums, swaying back and forth, looking off into the space between a couple of those stone crypts. I scratch my head, and take a closer look myself. She's mesmerized by something, but damned if I know what. I can hear her humming to herself, still doing that swaying thing, mostly with her upper body, back and forth, smiling that pretty smile of hers, short black hair standing up at attention the way it always does. I'm forever trying to talk her into growing it long, but she laughs at me whenever I do.

I guess I watch her for about an hour that night. I remember thinking she'd been sampling some of the dealers' wares until she suddenly snaps out of it. I fade back into the shadows at that point. Don't want her to think I've been spying on her. I'm just looking out for her, but she doesn't see it that way. She gets seriously pissed at me and I hate having Lillie mad at me.

She walks right by me, still humming to herself. I can see she's not stoned, just Lillie-strange. I watch her climb up some vines where one of the walls is broken and low, and then she's gone. I go out the front way, just to remind the boys what's what, and catch up with Lillie a few blocks away, casual-like. Don't ask her where she's been. Just say how-do, make sure she's okay without letting on I'm worried, and head back to my own place.

I don't know exactly when it is I realize she's looking for ghosts in there. It just comes to me one day, slips in sideways when I'm thinking about something else. I try talking to her about it from time to time but all she does is smile, the way only she can.

"You wouldn't understand," she says.

"Try me."

She shakes her head. "It's not something *to* understand," she says. "It's just something you do. The less you worry at it, the more it makes sense."

She's right. I don't understand.

4

There's a boy living in the garden. He reminds me a little of Alex. It's not that they look the same. This kid's all skin and bones, held together with wiry muscles. Naked and scruffy, crazy tangled hair full of burrs and twigs and stuff, peach-fuzz vying with a few actual beard hairs, dink hanging loose when he's not holding onto it—I guess you've got to do something with your hands when you don't have pockets. Alex, he's like a fridge with arms and legs. Big, strong, and loyal as all get-out. Not school-smart, but bright. You couldn't pick a couple of guys that looked less alike.

The reason they remind me of each other is that they're both a little feral. Wild things. Dangerous if you don't approach them right.

I get to the garden one night and the trees are full of grackles. They're feeding on berries and making a racket like I've never heard before. I know it's a murder of ravens and a parliament of crows, but what do you call that many grackles all together? I'm walking around, peering up at them in the branches, smiling at the noise, when I see the boy sitting up in one of the trees, looking back down at me.

Neither of us say anything for a long time. There's just the racket of the birds playing against the silence we hold between us.

"Hey there," I say finally. "Is this your garden?"

"It's my castle."

I smile. "Doesn't look much like a castle."

"Got walls," he tells me.

"I suppose."

He looks a little put out. "It's a start."

"So when are you going to start building the rest?" I ask.

He looks at me, the way a child looks at you when you've said something stupid.

"Go away," he says.

I decide I can be as much of an asshole as he's being and play the why game with him.

"Why?" I ask.

"Because I don't like you."

"Why?"

"Because you're stupid."

"Why?"

"I don't know. Guess you were born that way."

"Why?"

"Have to ask your parents that."

"Why?"

"Because I don't know."

"Why?"

He finally catches on. Pulling a twig free from the branch he's sitting on, he throws it at me. I duck and it misses. When I look back up, he's gone. The noise of the grackles sounds like laughter now.

"Guess I deserve that," I say.

I don't see the boy for a few visits after that, but the next time I do, he pops up out of the thick weeds underfoot and almost gives me a heart attack.

"I could've just snuck up on you and killed you," he tells me. "Just like that."

He leans against a tree, one hand hanging down in between his legs like he's got a piece of treasure there.

"Why would you want to do that?" I ask.

His eyes narrow. "I don't want to play the why game again."

"I'm not. I really want to know."

"It's not a thing I do or don't want to do," he tells me. "I'm just saying I could. It was a piece of information, that's all."

There's something incongruous about the way he says this—innocent and scary, all at the same time. It reminds me of when I was a little girl, how it took me the longest time to admit that I could ever like a boy, they were all such assholes. All except Alex. I wouldn't have minded so much if he'd pulled my hair or pushed me in the schoolyard, but he never did. He was always so sweet and polite to me and then after classes, he'd go out and beat up the guys that had been mean to me. I guess I was flattered, at first, but then I realized it wasn't a very nice thing to do. You have to understand, we're both still in grade school when this is going on. Things weren't the same back then the way they are for kids now. We sure never had to walk through metal detectors to get into the school.

Anyway, I asked him to stop and he did. At least so far as I know, he did. I wonder sometimes, though. Sometimes my boyfriends have the weirdest accidents—walking into doors and stuff like that.

5

This one time Lillie's going out with this college-type. Dave, his name is. Dave Taylor. Nice enough looking Joe, I suppose, but he's not exactly the most faithful guy you'd ever meet. Happened to run into him getting a little on the side one night, so I walk up to his table and tell him I have to have a word with him, would his lady friend excuse us for a moment? He doesn't want to step outside, so I suggest to his lady friend that she go powder her nose, if she understands my meaning.

"So what the hell's this all about?" Dave asks when she's gone. He's blustering, trying to make up for the face he feels he lost in front of his girlfriend.

"I'm a friend of Lillie's," I tell him.

"Yeah? So?"

"So I don't like the idea of her getting hurt."

"Hey, what she doesn't know—"

"I'm not discussing this," I say. "I'm telling you."

The guy shakes his head. "Or what? I suppose you're going to go running to her and—"

I hit him once, a quick jab to the head that rocks him back in his seat. Doesn't even break the skin on my knuckles, but I can see he's hurting.

"I don't care who you go out with, or if you cheat on them," I say, keeping my voice conversational. "I just don't want you seeing Lillie anymore."

He's holding a hand to his head where the skin's going all red. Looks a little scared like I'm going to hit him again, but I figure I've already made my point.

"Do we understand each other?" I ask him.

He gives me a quick nod. I start to leave, then pause for a moment. He gives me a worried look.

"And Dave," I say. "Let's not get stupid about this. No one's got to know we had this little talk, right?"

"What…whatever you say…."

6

I wonder about Alex—worry about him, I guess you could say. He never seems to be happy or sad. He just is. It's not like he's cold, keeps it all bottled in or anything, and he's always got a smile for me, but there doesn't seem to be a whole lot of passion in his life. He doesn't talk much, and never about himself. That's another way he and the boy in the garden differ. The boy's always excited about something or other, always ready for any sort of mad escapade. And he loves to talk.

"Old castle rock," the boy tells me one time. His eyes are gleaming with excitement. "That's what these walls are made of. They were part of this castle on the other side and now they're here. There's going to be more of the castle coming, I just know there is. Towers and turrets and stables and stuff."

"When's the rest of it going to come?" I ask.

He shrugs his bony shoulders. "Dunno. Could be a long time. But I can wait."

"Where's it coming from?" I ask then.

"I told you. From the other side."

"The other side of what?"

He gives me that look again, the one that says don't you know *anything*?

"The other side of the walls," he says.

I've never looked over the walls—not from the garden. That's the first thing Alex would have done. He may not have passion in his life, but he's sure got purpose. He's always in the middle of something, always knows what's going on. Never finished high school, but he's smarter than most people I meet because he's never satisfied until he's got everything figured out. He's in the public library all the time, reading, studying stuff. Never does anything with what he knows, but he sure knows a lot.

I walk over to the nearest of those tall stone walls and the boy trails along behind me, joins me when I start to go up. It's an easier climb than you might think, plenty of finger- and toe-holds, and we scale it like a couple of monkeys, grinning at each other when we reach the top. It's flat up there, with lots of room on the rough stone to sit and look out, only there's nothing to see. Just fog, thick, the way it rolls into the city from the lake sometimes. It's like the world ends on the other side of these walls.

"It's always like this," the boy says.

I turn to look at him. My first impression was that he'd come in over the walls himself and I never learned anything different to contradict it, but now I'm not so sure anymore. I mean, I knew this garden was some place else, some place magical that you could only reach the way you get to Neverneverland—you have to really want to get there. You might stumble in the first time, but after that you have to be really determined to get back in. But I also thought the real world was still out there, on the other side of the garden's magic, held back only by the walls.

"Where did you come from?" I ask him.

He gives me this look that manages to be fierce and sad, all at the same time.

"Same place as you," he says and touches a closed fist to his heart. "From the hurting world. This is the only place I can go where they can't get to me, where no one can hurt me."

I shake my head. "I didn't come here looking for sanctuary. I'm not running from anything."

"Then why are you here?"

I think of Alex and the way he's always talking about ghosts, but it's not that either. I never really think about it, I just come. Alex is the one with the need to have answers to every question. Not me. For me the experience has been enough of and by itself. But now that I think about it, now that I realize I want an answer, I find I don't have one.

"I don't know," I say.

"I thought you were like me," the boy says.

He sounds disappointed. Like I've disappointed him. He sounds angry, too. I want to say something to mollify him, but I can't find those words either. I reach out a hand, but he jerks away. He stands up, looks at me like I've turned into the enemy. I guess, in his eyes, I have. If I'm not with him, then I'm against him.

"I would never hurt you," I finally say. "I've never hurt anybody."

"That's what you think," he says.

Then he dives off the top of the wall, dives into the fog. I grab for him, but I'm not fast enough. I hold my breath, waiting to hear him hit the ground, but there's no sound. The fog swallows him and I'm alone on the top of the wall. I feel like I've missed something, something important. I feel like it was right there in front of me, all along, but now it's gone, dove off the wall with the boy and I've lost my chance to understand it.

The next time I come to the garden, everything's the same, but different. The boy's not here. I've come other times, lots of times, and he hasn't been here, but this time I feel he won't be back, won't ever be back, and I miss him. I don't know why. It's not like we had a whole lot in common. It's not like we had long, meaningful conversations, or were in love with each other or anything. I mean, he was just a kid, like a little brother, not a lover. But I miss him the way I've missed a lover when the relationship ends.

I feel guilty, too. Maybe this place isn't a sanctuary for me, but it was for him. A walled, wild garden, held safe by moonlight and vines. His castle. What if I've driven him away forever? Driven him back to what he called the hurting world.

I hate that idea the most, the idea that I've stolen the one good thing he had in a life that didn't have anything else. But I don't know what to do about it, how to call him back. I'd trade my coming here for his in a moment, only how can I tell him that? I don't even know his name.

7

Lillie doesn't leave the graveyard this night. I watch her sitting there on the steps of one of those old mausoleums, sitting there all hunched up, sitting there all night. Finally, dawn breaks in the east, swallows the graveyard's spookiness. It's just an old forgotten place now, fallen in on itself and waiting for the wreckers' ball. The night's gone and taken the promise of danger away with it. I go over to where Lillie is and sit down beside her on the steps. I touch her arm.

"Lillie?" I say. "Are you okay?"

She turns to look at me. I'm expecting her to be mad at me for being here. She's got to know I've been following her around again. But all she does is give me a sad look.

"Did you ever lose something you never knew you had?" she asks.

"I only ever wanted one thing," I tell her, "but I never had it to lose."

"I don't even know what it is that I've lost," she says. "I just know something's gone. I had a chance to have it, to hold it and cherish it, but I let it go."

The early morning sunlight's warm on my skin, but a shiver runs through me all the same. I think maybe she's talking about ghosts. Maybe there really are ghosts here. I get the crazy idea that maybe we're ghosts, that we died and don't remember it. Or maybe only one of us did.

"What was the one thing you wanted that you never got?" she asks.

It's something I would never tell her. I promised myself a long time ago that I'd never tell her because I knew she deserved better. But that crazy idea won't let go, that we're dead, or one of us is, and it makes me tell her.

"It's you," I say.

8

Did you ever have someone tell you something you always knew but it never really registered until they put it into words? That's what happens to me when Alex tells me he loves me, that he's always loved me.

His voice trails off and I look at him, really look at him. He almost flinches under my gaze. I can tell he doesn't want to be here, that he wishes he'd never spoken, that he feels a hurt swelling up inside him that he would never have to experience if he'd kept his feelings to himself. He reminds me of the boy, the way the boy looked before he dove off the wall into the fog, not the anger, but the sadness.

"Why did you never say anything before this?" I finally ask.

"I couldn't," he says. "And anyway. Look at us, you and me. We grew up in the same neighbourhood, sure, but...." He shrugs. "You deserve better than me."

I have to smile. This is so Alex. "Oh right. And who decided that?"

Alex chooses not to answer me. "You were always different," he says instead. "You were always the first on the block with a new sound or a new look, but you weren't following trends. It's like they followed you. And you never lost that. Anyone looks at you and they can tell there's nothing holding you back. You can do anything, go anywhere. The future's wide open for you, always was, you know what I'm saying? The streets never took their toll on you."

Then why am I still living in Foxville? I want to ask him. How come my star didn't take me to some nice uptown digs? But I know what he's talking about. It's not really about where I can go so much as where I've been.

"I was lucky," I say. "My folks treated me decently."

"And you deserved it."

"Everybody deserves to be treated decently," I tell him.

"Well, sure."

We grew up in the same building before my parents could afford a larger apartment down the block. My mom used to feel sorry for Alex's mother and we'd go over to visit when Crazy Eddie wasn't home. I'd play with Alex and his little sister, our moms would pretend our lives were normal, that none of us were dirt poor, everybody dreaming of moving to the 'burbs. Some of our neighbours did, but most of us couldn't afford it and still can't. Of course the way things are going now, you're not any safer or happier in the 'burbs than you are in the inner city. And living here, at least we've got some history.

But we never thought about that kind of thing at the time because we were just kids. Older times, simpler times. I smile, remembering how Alex always treated me so nice, right from the first.

"And then, of course, I had you looking out for me, too," I say.

"You still do."

I hadn't really got around to thinking what he was doing here in All Souls at this time of the morning, but now it makes sense. I don't know how many times I've had to ask him not to follow me around. It gives some people the creeps, but I know Alex isn't some crazed stalker, fixated on me. He means well. He really is just looking out for me. But it's a weird feeling all the same. I honestly thought I'd gotten him to stop.

"You really don't have to be doing this," I tell him. "I mean, it was kind of sweet when we were kids and you kept me from being bullied in the playground, but it's not the same now."

"You know the reason the dealers leave you alone?" he asks.

I glance towards the iron gates at the other end of the graveyard, but there's no one there at the moment. The drug market's closed up for the morning.

"They never knew I was here," I say.

Alex shakes his head and that's enough. He doesn't have to explain. I know the reputation he has in the neighbourhood. I feel a chill and I don't know if it's from the close call I had or the fact that I live in the kind of world where a woman can't go out by herself. Probably both.

"It's still not right," I say. "I appreciate your looking out for me, really I do, but it's not right, your following me around the way you do. You've got to get a life, Alex."

He hangs his head and I feel like I've just reprimanded a puppy dog for doing something it thought was really good.

"I know," he mumbles. He won't look at me. "I...I'm sorry, Lillie."

He gets up and starts to walk away. I look at his broad back and suddenly I'm thinking of the boy from the garden again. I'm seeing his sadness and anger, the way he dove off the wall into the fog and out of my life. I'm remembering what I said to him, that I would never hurt him, that I've never hurt anyone. And I remember what he said to me, just before he jumped.

That's what you think.

I'm not stupid. I know I'm not responsible for someone falling in love with me. I can't help it if they get hurt because maybe I don't love them back. But this isn't anyone. This is Alex. I've known him longer than maybe anybody I know. And if he's looked out for me, I've looked out for him, too. I stood up for him when people put him down. I visited him in the county jail when no one else did. I took him to the hospital that time the Creevy brothers left him for dead on the steps of his apartment building.

I know that for all his fierceness, he's a sweet guy. Dangerous, sure, but underneath that toughness there's no monster like his old man was. Given a different set of circumstances, a different neighbourhood to grow up in, maybe, a different father, definitely, he could have made something of himself. But he didn't. And now I'm wondering if looking out for me was maybe part of what held him back. If I'd gotten myself out of the neighbourhood, maybe he would have, too. Maybe we could both have been somebody.

But none of that's important right now. So maybe I'm not in love with Alex. So what? He's still my friend. He opened his heart to me and it's like I didn't even hear him.

"Alex!" I call after him.

He pauses and turns. There's nothing hopeful in the way he looks, there's not even curiosity. I get up from where I've been sitting and go to where he's standing.

"I've got to let this all sink in," I tell him. "You caught me off guard. I mean, I never even guessed you felt the way you do."

"I understand," he says.

"No, you don't. You're the best friend I ever had. I just never thought of us as a couple. Doesn't mean all of a sudden I hate you or something."

He shrugs. "I never should have said anything," he says.

I shake my head. "No. What you should have done is said something a lot sooner. The way I see it, your big problem is you keep everything all bottled up inside. You've got to let people know what you're thinking."

"That wouldn't change anything."

"How do you know? When I was a kid I had the hugest crush on you. And later, I kept expecting you to ask me out, but you never did. Got so's I just never thought of you in terms of boyfriend material."

"So what're you saying?"

I smile. "I don't know. You could ask me to go to a movie or something."

"Do you want to go to a movie?"

"Maybe. Let me buy you breakfast and we'll talk about it."

9

So I'm trying to do like Lillie says, talk about stuff that means something to me, or at least I do it with her. She asks me once what I'd like to do with my life, because she can't see much future in my being a bouncer for a strip joint for the rest of my life. I tell her I've always wanted to paint and instead of laughing, she goes out and buys me a little tin of watercolours and a pad of paper. I give it a go and she tells me I'm terrible, like I don't know it, but takes the first piece I do and hangs it on her fridge.

Another time I tell her about this castle I used to dream about when I was a kid, the most useless castle you could imagine, just these walls and a garden in them that's gone all wild, but when I was there, nobody could hurt me, nobody at all.

She gives me an odd look and says, "With old castle rock for the walls."

10

So I guess Alex was right. I must have been looking for ghosts in All Souls—or at least I found one. Except it wasn't the ghost of someone who'd died and been buried in there. It was the ghost of a kid, a kid that was still living somewhere in an enclosed wild garden, secreted deep in his grown-up mind, a kid fooling around in trees full of grackles, hidden from the hurting world, held safe by moonlight and vines.

But you know, hiding's not always the answer. Because the more Alex talks to me, the more he opens up, the more I see him the way I did when I was a little girl, when I'd daydream about how he and I were going to spend the rest of our lives together.

I guess we were both carrying around ghosts.

IN THE PINES

Lifc ain't all a dance.
—attributed to Dolly Parton

I

It's celebrity night at the Standish and we have us some lineup. There are two Elvises—a young one, with the swiveling hips and a perfect sneer, and a white-suited one, circa the Vegas years. A Buddy Holly who sounds right but could've lost fifty pounds if he really wanted to look the part. A Marilyn Monroe who has her boyfriend with her; he'd be wearing a JFK mask for her finale, when she sings "Happy Birthday" to him in a breathless voice. Lonesome George Clark has come out of semi-retirement to reprise his old Hank Williams show and then there's me, doing my Dolly Parton tribute for the first time in the three years since I gave it up and tried to make it on my own.

I don't really mind doing it. I've kind of missed Dolly, to tell you the truth, and it's all for a good cause—a benefit to raise money for the Crowsea Home for Battered Women—which is how they convinced me to do that old act of mine one more time.

I do a pretty good version of Dolly. I'm not as pretty as her, and I don't have her hair—hey, who does?—but I've got the figure, while the wig, makeup and rhinestone dress take care of the rest. I can mimic her singing, though my natural voice is lower, and I sure as hell play the guitar better—I don't know who she's kidding with those fingernails of hers.

But in the end, the looks never mattered. It was always the songs. The first time I heard her sing them, I just plain fell in love. "Jolene." "Coat of Many Colors." "My Blue Tears." I planned to do a half hour of those old hits with a couple of mountain songs thrown in for good measure. The only one from my old act that I was dropping was "I Will Always Love You." Thanks to the success Whitney Houston had with it, people weren't going to be thinking Tennessee cabins and Dolly anymore when they heard it.

I'm slated to follow the fat Elvis—maybe they wanted to stick all the rhinestones together in one part of the show?—with Lonesome George finishing up after me. Since Lonesome George and I are sharing the same backup band, we're going to close the show with a duet on "Muleskinner Blues." The thought of it makes me smile and not just because I'll get to do a little bit of yodeling. With everything Dolly's done over the years, even she never got to sing with Hank Williams—senior, of course. Junior parties a little too hearty for my tastes.

So I'm standing there in the wings of the Standish, watching Marilyn slink and grind her way through a song—the girl is good—when I get this feeling that something was going to happen.

I'm kind of partial to premonitions. The last time I felt one this strong was the night John Narraway died. We were working late on my first album at Tommy Norton's High Lonesome Sounds and had finally called it quits some time after midnight when the feeling hit me. It starts with a hum or a buzz, like I've got a fly or a bee caught in my ear, and then everything seems...oh, I don't know. Clearer somehow. Precise. Like I could look at Johnny's fiddle bow that night and see every one of those horse hairs, separate and on its own.

The trouble with these feelings is that while I know something's going to happen, I don't know what. I get a big feeling or a little one, but after that I'm on my own. Truth is, I never figure out what it's all about until after the fact, which doesn't make it exactly the most useful talent a girl can have. I don't even know if it's something good or something bad that's coming, just that it's coming. Real helpful, right?

So I'm standing there and Marilyn's brought her boyfriend out for the big finish to her act and I know something's going to happen, but I don't know what. I get real twitchy all through the fat Elvis's act and then it's time for me to go up and the buzzing's just swelling up so big inside me that I feel like I'm fit to burst with anticipation.

We open with "My Tennessee Mountain Home." It goes over pretty well and we kick straight into "Jolene" before the applause dies off. The third song we do is the first song I ever learned, that old mountain song, "In the Pines." I don't play it the same as most people I've heard do—I learned it from my Aunt Hickory, with this lonesome barred F# minor chord coming right in after the D that opens every line. I remember cursing for weeks before I could finally get my fingers around that damn chord and make it sound like it was supposed to.

So we're into the chorus now—

In the pines, in the pines,
Where the sun never shines
And the shiverin' cold winds blow.

—and I'm looking out into the crowd and I can't see much, what with the spotlights in my eyes and all, but damned if I don't see her sitting there in the third row, my Aunt Hickory, big as life, grinning right back up at me, except she's dead, she's been dead fifteen years now, and it's all I can do to get through the chorus and let the band take an instrumental break.

2

The Aunt—that's what everybody in those parts called her, 'cept me, I guess. I don't know if it was because they didn't know her name, or because she made them feel uneasy, but nobody used the name that had been scratched onto her rusty mailbox, down on Dirt Creek Road. That just said Hickory Jones.

I loved the sound of her name. It had a ring to it like it was pulled straight out of one of those old mountain songs. Like Shady Groves. Or Tom Dooley.

She lived by her own self in a one-room log cabin, up the hill behind the Piney Woods Trailer Park, a tall, big-boned woman with angular features and her chestnut hair cropped close to her head. Half the boys in the park had hair longer than hers, slicked back and shiny. She dressed like a man in blue jeans and a flannel shirt, barefoot in the summer, big old workboots on those callused feet when the weather turned mean and the snows came.

She really was my aunt. She and Mama shared the same mother except Hickory had Kickaha blood, you could see it in the deep coppery colour of her skin. Mama's father was white trash, same as mine, though that's an opinion I never shared out loud with anyone, not even Hickory. My Daddy never needed much of a reason to give us kids a licking. Lord knows what he'd have done if we'd given him a real excuse.

I never could figure out what it was about Hickory that made people feel so damn twitchy around her. Mama said it was because of the way Hickory dressed.

"I know she's my sister," Mama would say, "but she looks like some no account hobo, tramping the rail lines. It's just ain't right. Man looks at her, he can't even tell she's got herself a pair of titties under that shirt."

Breasts were a big topic of conversation in Piney Woods when I was growing up and I remember wishing I had a big old shirt like Hickory's when my own chest began to swell and it seemed like it was never gonna stop. Mama acted like it was a real blessing, but I hated them. "You can't have too much of a good thing," she told me when she heard me complaining. "You just pray they keep growing awhile longer, Darlene, 'cause if they do, you mark my words. You're gonna have your pick of a man."

Yeah, but what kind of a man? I wanted to know. It wasn't just the boys looking at me, or what they'd say; it was the men, too. Everybody staring down at my chest when they were talking to me, 'stead of looking me in the face. I could see them just itching to grab themselves a handful.

"You just shut your mouth, girl," Mama would say if I didn't let it go.

Hickory never told me to shut my mouth. But then I guess she didn't have to put up with me twenty-four hours a day, neither. She just stayed up by her cabin, growing her greens and potatoes in a little plot out back, running trap lines or taking to the hills with her squirrel gun for meat. Maybe once a month she'd head into town to pick up some coffee or flour, whatever the land couldn't provide for her. She'd walk the five miles in, then walk the whole way back, didn't matter how heavy that pack of hers might be or what the weather was like.

I guess that's really what people didn't like about her—just living the way she did, she showed she didn't need nobody, she could do it all on her own, and back then that was frowned upon for a woman. They thought she was queer—and I don't just mean tetched in the head, though they thought that, too. No, they told stories about how she'd sleep with other women, how she could raise the dead and was friends with the devil and just about any other kind of foolish idea they could come up with.

'Course I wasn't supposed to go up to her cabin—none of us kids were, especially the girls—but I went anyways. Hickory played the five-string banjo and I'd go up and listen to her sing those old lonesome songs that nobody wanted to hear anymore. There was no polish to Hickory's singing, not like they put on music today, but she could hold a note long and true and she could play that banjo so sweet that it made you want to cry or laugh, depending on the mood of the tune.

See, Hickory's where I got started in music. First I'd go up just to listen and maybe sing along a little, though back then I had less polish in my voice than Hickory did. After a time I got an itching to play an instrument too and that's when Hickory took down this little old 1919 Martin guitar from where it hung on the rafters and when I'd sneak up to her cabin after that I'd play that guitar until my fingers ached and I'd be crying from how much they hurt, but I never gave up. Didn't get me nowhere, but I can say this much: whatever else's happened to me in this life, I never gave up the music. Not for anything, not for anyone.

And the pain went away.

"That's the thing," Hickory told me. "Doesn't matter how bad it gets, the pain goes away. Sometimes you got to die to stop hurting, but the hurting stops."

I guess the real reason nobody bothered her is that they were scared of her, scared of the big dark-skinned cousins who'd come down from the rez to visit her sometimes, scared of the simples and charms she could make, scared of what they saw in her eyes when she gave them that hard look of hers. Because Hickory didn't back down, not never, not for nobody.

3

I fully expect Hickory to be no more than an apparition. I'd look away, then back, and she'd be gone. I mean what else could happen? She was long dead and I might believe in a lot of things, but ghosts aren't one of them.

But by the time the boys finish their break and it's time for me to step back up to the mike for another verse, there she is, still sitting in the third row, still grinning up at me. I'll tell you, I near' choke right about then, all the words I ever knew to any song just up and fly away. There's a couple of ragged bars in the music where I don't know if I'll be finishing the song or not and I can feel the concern of the boys playing there on stage behind me. But Hickory she just gives me a look with those dark brown eyes of hers, that look she used to give me all those years ago when I'd run up so hard against the wall of a new chord or a particularly tricky line of melody that I just wanted to throw the guitar down and give it all up.

That look had always shamed me into going on and it does the same for me tonight. I shoot the boys an apologetic look, and lean right into the last verse like it never went away on me.

The longest train that I ever saw
Was nineteen coaches long,

And the only girl I ever loved
She's on that train and gone.

I don't know what anyone else is thinking when I sing those words, but looking at Hickory I know that, just like me, she isn't thinking of trains or girlfriends. Those old songs have a way of connecting you to something deeper than what they seem to be talking about, and that's what's happening for the two of us here. We're thinking of old losses and regrets, of all the things that might have been, but never were. We're thinking of the night lying thick in the pines around her cabin, lying thick under those heavy boughs even in the middle of the day, because just like the night hides in the day's shadows, there's lots of things that never go away. Things you don't ever want to go away. Sometimes when that wind blows through the pines, you shiver, but it's not from the cold.

4

I was fifteen when I left home. I showed up on Hickory's doorstep with a cardboard suitcase in one hand and that guitar she'd given me in the other, not heading for Nashville like I always thought I would, but planning to take the bus to Newford instead. A man who'd heard me sing at the roadhouse just down a-ways from Piney Woods had offered me a job in a honkytonk he owned in the city. I'm pretty sure he knew I was lying about my age, but he didn't seem to care anymore than I did.

Hickory was rolling herself a cigarette when I arrived. She finished the job and lit a match on her thumbnail, looking at me in that considering way of hers as she got the cigarette going.

"That time already," she said finally, blowing out a blue-grey wreath of smoke on the heel of her words.

I nodded.

"Didn't think it'd come so soon," she told me. "Thought we had us another couple of years together, easy."

"I can't wait, Aunt Hickory. I got me a singing job in the city—a real singing job, in a honkytonk."

"Uh-huh."

Hickory wasn't agreeing or disagreeing with me, just letting me know that she was listening but that she hadn't heard anything worthwhile hearing yet.

"I'll be making forty dollars a week, plus room and board."

"Where you gonna live?" Hickory asked, taking a drag from her cigarette. "In your boss's house?"

I shook my head. "No, ma'am. I'm going to have my own room, right upstairs of the honkytonk."

"He know how old you are?"

"Sure," I said with a grin. "Eighteen."

"Give or take a few years."

I shrugged. "He's got no trouble with it."

"Well, what about your schooling?" Hickory asked. "You've been doing so well. I always thought you'd be the first one in the family to finish high school. I was looking forward to that—you know, to bragging about you and all."

I had to smile. Who was she going to brag to?

"Were you going to come to the graduation ceremony?" I asked instead.

"Was thinking on it."

"I'm going to be a singer, Aunt Hickory. All the schooling I'm ever going to need I learned from you."

Hickory sighed. She took a final drag from her cigarette then stubbed it out on the edge of her stair, storing the butt in her pocket.

"Tell me something," she said. "Are you running from something or running to something?"

"What difference does it make?"

"A big difference. Running away's only a partial solution. Sooner or later, whatever you're running from is going to catch up to you again. Comes a time you're going to have to face it, so it might as well be now. But running to something...well."

"Well, what?" I wanted to know when she didn't go on right away.

She fixed that dark gaze of hers on me. "I guess all I wanted to tell you, Darlene, is if you believe in what you're doing, then go at it and be willing to pay the price you have to pay."

I knew what she was trying to tell me. Playing a honkytonk in Newford was a big deal for a girl from the hills like me, but it wasn't what I was aiming for. It was just the first step and the rest of the road could be long and hard. I never knew just how long and hard. I was young and full of confidence, back then at the beginning of the sixties; invulnerable, like we all think we are when we're just on the other side of still being kids.

"But I want you to promise me one thing," Hickory added. "Don't you never do something that'll make you feel ashamed when you look back on it later."

"Why do you think I'm leaving now?" I asked her.

Hickory's eyes went hard. "I'm going to kill that Daddy of yours."

"He's never tried to touch me again," I told her. "Not like he tried that one time, not like that. Just to give me a licking."

"Seems to me a man who likes to give out lickings so much ought to have the taste of one himself."

I don't know if Hickory was meaning to do it her own self, or if she was planning to put one of her cousins from the rez up to it, but I knew it'd cause her more trouble than it was worth.

"Leave 'im be," I told her. "I don't want Mama getting any more upset."

Hickory looked like she had words for Mama as well, but she bit them back. "You'll do better shut of the lot of them," was what she finally said. "But don't you forget your Aunt Hickory."

"I could never forget you."

"Yeah, that's what they all say. But then the time always comes when they get up and go and the next you know you never do hear from them again."

"I'll write."

"I'm gonna hold you to that, Darlene Johnston."

"I'm changing my name," I told her. "I'm gonna call myself Darlene Flatt."

I figured she'd like that, seeing how Flatt & Scruggs were pretty well her favourite pickers from the radio, but she just gave my chest a considering look and laughed.

"You hang onto that sense of humour," she told me. "Lord knows you're gonna need it in the city."

I hadn't thought about my new name like that, but I guess it shows you just how stubborn I can be, because I stuck with it.

5

I don't know how I make it through the rest of the set. Greg Timmins who's playing dobro for me that night says except for that one glitch coming into the last verse of "In the Pines," he'd never heard me sing so well, but I don't remember it like that. I don't remember much about it at all except that I change my mind about not doing "I Will Always Love You" and use it to finish off the set.

I sing the choruses to my Aunt Hickory, sitting there in the third row of the Standish, fifteen years after she up and died.

I can't leave, because I still have my duet with Lonesome George coming up, and besides, I can't very well go busting down into the theatre itself, chasing after a ghost. So I slip into the washroom and soak some paper towels in cold water before holding them against the back of my neck. After awhile I start to feel...if not better, at least more like myself. I go back to stand in the wings, watching Lonesome George and the boys play, checking the seats in the third row, one by one, but of course she's not there. There's some skinny old guy in a rumpled suit sitting where I saw her.

But the buzz is still there, humming away between my ears, sounding like a hundred flies chasing each other up and down a windowpane, and I wonder what's coming up next?

6

I never did get out of Newford, though it wasn't from want of trying. I just went from playing with housebands in the honkytonks to other kinds of bands, sometimes fronting them with my Dolly show, sometimes being myself, playing guitar and singing backup. I didn't go back to Piney Woods to see my family, but I wrote Aunt Hickory faithfully, every two weeks, until the last letter came back marked, "Occupant deceased."

I went home then, but I was too late. The funeral was long over. I asked the pastor about it and he said there was just him and some folks from the rez at the service. I had a lot more I wanted to ask, but I soon figured out that the pastor didn't have the answers I was looking for, and they weren't to be found staring at the fresh-turned sod of the churchyard, so I thanked the pastor for his time and drove my rented car down Dirt Creek Road.

Nothing looked the same, but nothing seemed to have changed either. I guess the change was in me, at least that's how it felt until I got to the cabin. Hickory had been squatting on government land, so I suppose I shouldn't have been surprised to find the cabin in the state it was, the door kicked in, the windows all broke, anything that could be carried away long gone, everything else vandalized.

I stood in there on the those old worn pine floorboards for a long time, looking for some trace of Hickory I could maybe take away with me, waiting for some sign, but nothing happened. There was nothing left of her, not even that long-necked old Gibson banjo of hers. Her ghost didn't come walking up to me out of the pine woods. I guess it was about then that it sunk in she was really gone and I was never going to see her again, never going to get another one of those cranky letters of hers, never going to hear her sing another one of those old mountain songs or listen to her pick "Cotton-Eyed Joe" on the banjo.

I went outside and sat down on the step and I cried, not caring if my makeup ran, not caring who could hear or see me. But nobody was there anyway and nobody came. I looked out at those lonesome pines after awhile, then I got into my rented car again and drove back to the city, pulling off to the side of the road every once in awhile because my eyes got blurry and it was hard to stay on my own side of the dividing line.

7

After I finish my duet with Lonesome George, I just grab my bag and my guitar and I leave the theatre. I don't even bother to change out of my stage gear, so it's Dolly stepping out into the snowy alley behind the Standish, Dolly turning up the collar of her coat and feeling the sting of the wind-driven snow on her rouged cheeks, Dolly fighting that winter storm to get back to her little one-bedroom apartment that she shares with a cat named Earle and a goldfish named Maybelle.

I get to my building and unlock the front door. The warm air makes the chill I got walking home feel worse and a shiver goes right up my spine. All I'm thinking is to get upstairs, have myself a shot of Jack Daniels, then crawl into my bed and hope that by the time I wake up the buzzing in my head'll be gone and things'll be back to normal.

I don't lead an exciting life, but I'm partial to a lack of excitement. Gets to a point where excitement's more trouble than it's worth and that includes men. Maybe especially men. I never had any luck with them. Oh they come buzzing around, quick and fast as the bees I got humming in my head right now, but they just want a taste of the honey and then they're gone. I think it's better when they go. The ones that stay make for the kind of excitement that'll eventually have you wearing long sleeves and high collars and pants instead of skirts because you want to hide the bruises.

There's a light out on the stairs going up to my apartment but I can't even find the energy to curse the landlord about it. I just feel my way to the next landing and head on up the last flight of stairs and there's the door to my apartment. I set my guitar down long enough to work the three locks on this door, then shove the case in with my knee and close the door behind me. Home again.

I wait for Earle to come running up and complain that I left him alone all night—that's the nice thing about Maybelle; she just goes round and round in her bowl and doesn't make a sound, doesn't try to make me feel guilty. Only reason she comes to the side of the glass is to see if I'm going to drop some food into the water.

"Hey, Earle," I call. "You all playing hidey-cat on me?"

Oh that buzz in my head's rattling around something fierce now. I shuck my coat and let it fall on top of the guitar case and pull off my cowboy boots, one after the other, using my toes for a bootjack. I leave everything in the hall and walk into my living room, reaching behind me for the zipper of my rhinestone dress so that I can shuck it, too.

I guess I shouldn't be surprised to see Hickory sitting there on my sofa. What does surprise me is that she's got Earle up on her lap, lying there content as can be, purring up a storm as she scratches his ears. But Hickory always did have a way with animals; dying didn't seem to have changed that much. I let my hand fall back to my side, zipper still done up.

"That really you, Aunt Hickory?" I say after a long moment of only being able to stand there and stare at her.

"Pretty much," she says. "At least what's left of me." She gives me that considering look of hers, eyes as dark as ever. "You don't seem much surprised to see me."

"I think I wore out being surprised 'round about now," I say.

It's true. You could've blown me over with a sneeze, back there in the Standish when I first saw her, but I find I'm adjusting to it real well. And the buzz is finally upped and gone. I think I'm feeling more relieved about that than anything else.

"You're looking a bit strollopy," she says.

Strollops. That's what they used to call the trashy women back around Piney Woods, strumpets and trollops. I haven't heard that word in years.

"And you're looking pretty healthy for a woman dead fifteen years."

Maybe the surprise of seeing her is gone, but I find I still need to sit me down because my legs are trembling something fierce right about now.

"What're you doing here, Aunt Hickory?" I ask from the other end of the sofa where I've sat me down.

Hickory, she shrugs. "Don't rightly know. I can't seem to move on. I guess I've been waiting for you to settle down first."

"I'm about as settled down as I'm ever going to be."

"Maybe so." She gives Earle some attention, buying time, I figure, because when she finally looks back at me it's to ask, "You remember what I told you back when you first left the hills—about never doing something you'd be ashamed to look back on?"

"Sure I do. And I haven't never done anything like that neither."

"Well, maybe I put it wrong," Hickory says. "Maybe what I should have said was, make sure that you can be proud of what you've done when you look back."

I don't get it and I tell her so.

"Now don't you get me wrong, Darlene. I know you're doing the best you can. But there comes a point, I'm thinking, when you got to take stock of how far your dreams can take you. I'm not saying you made a mistake, doing what you do, but lord, girl, you've been at this singing for twenty years now and where's it got you?"

It was like she was my conscience, coming round and talking like this, because that's something I've had to ask myself a whole pile of times and way too often since I first got here to the city.

"Not too damn far," I say.

"There's nothing wrong with admitting you made a mistake and moving on."

"You think I made a mistake, Aunt Hickory?"

She hesitates. "Not at first. But now...well, I don't rightly know. Seems to me you've put so much into this dream of yours that if it's not payback time yet, then maybe it is time to move on."

"And do what?"

"I don't know. Something."

"I don't know anything else—'cept maybe waiting tables and the like."

"I see that could be a problem," Hickory says.

I look at her for a long time. Those dark eyes look back, but she can't hold my gaze for long and she finally turns away. I'm thinking to myself, this looks like my Aunt Hickory, and the voice sounds like my Aunt Hickory, but the words I'm hearing aren't what the Hickory I know would be saying. That Hickory, she'd never back down, not for nobody, never call it quits on somebody else's say-so, and she'd never expect anybody else to be any different.

"I guess the one thing I never asked you," I say, "is why did you live up in that old cabin all on your ownsome for so many years?"

"I loved those pine woods."

"I know you did. But you didn't always live in 'em. You went away a time, didn't you?"

She nods. "That was before you was born."

"Where'd you go?"

"Nowhere special. I was just travelling. I...." She looks up and there's something in those dark eyes of hers that I've never seen before. "I had the same dream you did, Darlene. I wanted to be a singer so bad. I wanted to hear my voice coming back at me from the radio. I wanted to be up on that big stage at the Opry and see the crowd looking back at me, calling my name and loving me. But it never happened. I never got no further than playing the jukejoints and the honkytonks and the road bars where the people are more interested in getting drunk and sticking their hands up your dress than they are in listening to you sing."

She sighed. "I got all used up, Darlene. I got to where I'd be playing on those dinky little stages and *I* didn't even care what I was singing about anymore. So finally I just took myself home. I was only thirty years old, but I was all used up. I didn't tell nobody where I'd been or what I'd done or how I'd failed. I didn't want to talk to any of them about any of that, didn't want to talk to them at all because I'd look at those Piney Woods people and I'd see the same damn faces that looked up at me when I was playing out my heart in the honkytonks and they didn't care any more now than they did then.

"So I moved me up into the hills. Built that cabin of mine. Listened to the wind in the pines until I could finally start to sing and play and love the music again."

"You never told me any of this," I say.

"No, I didn't. Why should I? Was it going to make any difference to your dreams?"

I shook my head. "I guess not."

"When you took to that old guitar of mine the way you did, my heart near' broke. I was so happy for you, but I was scared—oh, I was scared bad. But then I thought, maybe it'll be different for her. Maybe when she leaves the hills and starts singing, people are gonna listen. I wanted to spare you the hurt, I'll tell you that, Darlene, but I didn't want to risk stealing your chance at joy neither. But now...."

Her voice trails off.

"But now," I say, finishing what she left unsaid, "here I am anyway and I don't even have those pines to keep my company."

Hickory nods. "It ain't fair. I hear the music they play on the radio now and they don't have half the heart of the old mountain songs you and me sing. Why don't people want to hear them anymore?"

"Well, you know what Dolly says: 'Life ain't all a dance.'"

"Isn't that the sorry truth."

"But there's still people who want to hear the old songs," I say. "There's just not so many of them. I get worn out some days, trying like I've done all these years, but then I'll play a gig somewhere and the people are really listening and I think maybe it's not so important to be really big and popular and all. Maybe there's something to be said for pleasing just a few folks, if it means you get to stay true to what you want to do. I don't mean a body should stop aiming high, but maybe we shouldn't feel so bad when things don't work out the way we want 'em to. Maybe we should be grateful for what we got, for what we had."

"Like all those afternoons we spent playing music with only the pines to hear us."

I smile. "Those were the best times I ever had. I wouldn't change 'em for anything."

"Me, neither."

"And you know," I say. "There's people with a whole lot less. I'd like to be doing better than I am, but hell, at least I'm still making a living. Got me an album and I'm working on another, even if I do have to pay for it all myself."

Hickory gives me a long look and then just shakes her head. "You're really something, aren't you just?"

"Nothing you didn't teach me to be."

"I been a damn fool," Hickory says. She sets Earle aside and stands up. "I can see that now."

"What're you doing?" I ask. But I know and I'm already standing myself.

"Come give your old aunt a hug," Hickory says.

There's a moment when I can feel her in my arms, solid as one of those pines growing up in the hills where she first taught me to sing and play. I can smell woodsmoke and cigarette smoke on her, something like apple blossoms and the scent of those pines.

"You do me proud, girl," she whispers in my ear.

And then I'm holding only air. Standing there alone, all strolloped up in my wig and rhinestone dress, holding nothing but air.

8

I know I won't be able to sleep and there's no point in trying. I'm feeling so damn restless and sorry—not for myself, but for all the broken dreams that wear people down until there's nothing left of 'em but ashes and smoke. I'm not going to let that happen to me.

I end up sitting back on the sofa with my guitar on my lap—the same small-bodied Martin guitar my Aunt Hickory gave a dreamy-eyed girl all those years ago. I start to pick a few old tunes. "Over the Waterfall." "The Arkansas Traveler." Then the music drifts into something I never heard before and I realize I'm making up a melody. About as soon as I realize that, the words start slipping and sliding through my head and before I know it, I've got me a new song.

I look out the window of my little apartment. The wind's died down, but the snow's still coming, laying a soft blanket that takes the sharp edge off everything I can see. It's so quiet. Late night quiet. Drifting snow quiet. I get a pencil from the kitchen and I write out the words to that new song, write the chords in. I reread the last lines of the chorus:

But my Aunt Hickory loved me,
and nothing else mattered
nothing else mattered at all.

There's room on the album for one more song. First thing in the morning I'm going to give Tommy Norton a call and book some time at High Lonesome Sounds. That's the nice thing about doing things your own way—you answer to yourself and no one else. If I want to hold off on pressing the CDs for my new album to add another song, I can. I can do any damn thing I want, so long as I keep true to myself and the music.

Maybe I'm never going to be the big star the little girl with the cardboard suitcase and guitar thought she'd be when she left the pine hills all those years ago and came looking for fame and fortune here in the big city. But maybe it doesn't matter. Maybe there's other rewards, smaller ones, but more lasting. Like knowing my Aunt Hickory loves me and she told me I do her proud.

PIXEL PIXIES

Only when Mistress Holly had retired to her apartment above the store would Dick Bobbins peep out from behind the furnace where he'd spent the day dreaming and drowsing and reading the books he borrowed from the shelves upstairs. He would carefully check the basement for unexpected visitors and listen for a telltale floorboard to creak from above. Only when he was very very sure that the mistress, and especially her little dog, had both, indeed, gone upstairs, would he creep all the way out of his hidden hobhole.

Every night, he followed the same routine.

Standing on the cement floor, he brushed the sleeves of his drab little jacket and combed his curly brown hair with his fingers. Rubbing his palms briskly together, he plucked last night's borrowed book from his hidey-hole and made his way up the steep basement steps to the store. Standing only two feet high, this might have been an arduous process all on its own, but he was quick and agile, as a hob should be, and in no time at all he'd be standing in amongst the books, considering where to begin the night's work.

There was dusting and sweeping to do, books to be put away. Lovely books. It didn't matter to Dick if they were serious leather-bound tomes or paperbacks with garish covers. He loved them all, for they were filled with words, and words were magic to this hob. Wise and clever humans had used some marvelous spell to imbue each book with every kind of story and character you could imagine, and many you couldn't. If you knew the key to unlock the words, you could experience them all.

Sometimes Dick would remember a time when he hadn't been able to read. All he could do then was riffle the pages and try to smell the stories out of them. But now, oh now, he was a magician, too, for he could unearth the hidden enchantment in the books any time he wanted to. They were his nourishment and his joy, weren't they just.

So first he worked, earning his keep. Then he would choose a new book from those that had come into the store while he was in his hobhole, drowsing away the day. Sitting on top of one of the bookcases, he'd read until it got light outside and it was time to return to his hiding place behind the furnace, the book under his arm in case he woke early and wanted to finish the story while he waited for the mistress to go to bed once more.

I hate computers.

Not when they do what they're supposed to. Not even when I'm the one who's made some stupid mistake, like deleting a file I didn't intend to, or exiting one without saving it. I've still got a few of those old war-horse programs on my machine that doesn't pop up a reminder asking if I want to save the file I was working on.

No, it's when they seem to have a mind of their own. The keyboard freezing for no apparent reason. Getting an error message that you're out of disc space when you know you've got at least a couple of gigs free. Passwords becoming temporarily, and certainly arbitrarily, obsolete. Those and a hundred other, usually minor, but always annoying, irritations.

Sometimes it's enough to make you want to pick up the nearest component of the machine and fling it against the wall.

For all the effort they save, the little tasks that they automate and their wonderful storage capacity, at times like this—when everything's going as wrong as it can go—their benefits can't come close to outweighing their annoyances.

My present situation was partly my own fault. I'd been updating my inventory all afternoon and before saving the file and backing it up, I'd decided to go on the Internet to check some of my competitors' prices. The used book business, which is what I'm in, has probably the most arbitrary pricing in the world. Though I suppose that can be expanded to include any business specializing in collectibles.

I logged on without any trouble and went merrily browsing through listings on the various book search pages, making notes on the particularly interesting items, a few of which I actually had in stock. It wasn't until I tried to exit my browser that the trouble started. My browser wouldn't close and I couldn't switch to another window. Nor could I log off the Internet.

Deciding it had something to do with the page I was on—I know that doesn't make much sense, but I make no pretence to being more than vaguely competent when it comes to knowing how the software actually interfaces with the hardware—I called up the drop-down menu of "My Favourites" and clicked on my own home page. What I got was a fan shrine to pro wrestling star Steve Austin.

I tried again and ended up at a commercial software site.

The third time I was taken to the site of someone named Cindy Margolis—the most downloaded woman on the Internet, according to the *Guinness Book of World Records*. Not on this computer, my dear.

I made another attempt to get off-line, then tried to access my home page again. Each time I found myself in some new outlandish and unrelated site.

Finally I tried one of the links on the last page I'd reached. It was supposed to bring me to Netscape's home page. Instead I found myself on the web site of a real estate company in Santa Fe, looking at a cluster of pictures of the vaguely Spanish-styled houses that they were selling.

I sighed, tried to break my Internet connection for what felt like the hundredth time, but the "Connect To" window still wouldn't come up.

I could have rebooted, of course. That would have gotten me off-line. But it would also mean that I'd lose the whole afternoon's work because, being the stupid woman I was, I hadn't had the foresight to save the stupid file before I went gadding about on the stupid Internet.

"Oh, you stupid machine," I muttered.

From the front window display where she was napping, I heard Snippet, my Jack Russell terrier, stir. I turned to reassure her that, yes, she was still my perfect little dog. When I swiveled my chair to face the computer again, I realized that there was a woman standing on the other side of the counter.

I'd seen her come into the store earlier, but I'd lost track of everything in my one-sided battle of wits with the computer—it having the wits, of course. She was a very striking woman, her dark brown hair falling in Pre-Raphaelite curls that were streaked with green, her eyes both warm and distant, like an odd mix of a perfect summer's day and the mystery you can feel swell up inside you when you look up into the stars on a crisp, clear autumn night. There was something familiar about her, but I couldn't quite place it. She wasn't one of my regulars.

She gave me a sympathetic smile.

"I suppose it was only a matter of time before they got into the computers," she said.

I blinked. "What?"

"Try putting your sweater on inside out."

My face had to be registering the confusion I was feeling, but she simply continued to smile.

"I know it sounds silly," she said. "But humour me. Give it a try."

Anyone in retail knows, you get all kinds. And the secondhand market gets more than its fair share, trust me on that. If there's a loopy person anywhere within a hundred blocks of my store, you can bet they'll eventually find their way inside. The woman standing on the other side of my counter looked harmless enough, if somewhat exotic, but you just never know anymore, do you?

"What have you got to lose?" she asked.

I was about to lose an afternoon's work as things stood, so what was a little pride on top of that.

I stood up and took my sweater off, turned it inside out, and put it back on again.

"Now give it a try," the woman said.

I called up the "Connected to" window and this time it came up. When I put the cursor on the "Disconnect" button and clicked, I was logged off. I quickly shut down my browser and saved the file I'd been working on all afternoon.

"You're a lifesaver," I told the woman. "How did you know that would work?" I paused, thought about what I'd just said, what had just happened. "*Why* would that work?"

"I've had some experience with pixies and their like," she said.

"Pixies," I repeated. "You think there are pixies in my computer?"

"Hopefully, not. If you're lucky, they're still on the Internet and didn't follow you home."

I gave her a curious look. "You're serious, aren't you?"

"At times," she said, smiling again. "And this is one of them."

I thought about one of my friends, an electronic pen pal in Arizona, who has this theory that the first atom bomb detonation forever changed the way that magic would appear in the world. According to him, the spirits live in the wires now instead of the trees. They travel through phone and modem lines, take up residence in computers and appliances where they live on electricity and lord knows what else.

It looked like Richard wasn't alone in his theories, not that I pooh-poohed them myself. I'm part of a collective that originated this electronic database called the Wordwood. Ever since it took on a life of its own, I pretty much keep an open mind about things that most people would consider preposterous.

"I'd like to buy this," the woman went on.

She held up a trade paperback copy of *The Beggars' Shore* by Zak Mucha.

"Good choice," I said.

It never surprises me how many truly excellent books end up in the secondary market. Not that I'm complaining—it's what keeps me in business.

"Please take it as thanks for your advice," I added.

"You're sure?"

I looked down at my computer where my afternoon's work was now saved in its file.

"Oh, yes," I told her.

"Thank you," she said. Reaching into her pocket, she took out a business card and gave it to me. "Call me if you ever need any other advice along the same lines."

The business card simply said "The Kelledys" in a large script. Under it were the names "Meran and Cerin" and a phone number. Now I knew why, earlier, she'd seemed familiar. It had just been seeing her here in the store, out of context, that had thrown me.

"I love your music," I told her. "I've seen you and your husband play several times."

She gave me another of those kind smiles of hers.

"You can probably turn your sweater around again now," she said as she left.

Snippet and I watched her walk by the window. I took off my sweater and put it back on properly.

"Time for your walk," I told Snippet. "But first let me back up this file to a zip disk."

That night, after the mistress and her little dog had gone upstairs, Dick Bobbins crept out of his hobhole and made his nightly journey up to the store. He replaced the copy of *The Woods Colt* that he'd been reading, putting it neatly back on the fiction shelf under "W" for Williamson, fetched the duster, and started his work. He finished the "History" and "Local Interest" sections, dusting and straightening the books, and was climbing up onto the "Poetry" shelves near the back of the store when he paused, hearing something from the front of the store.

Reflected in the front window, he could see the glow of the computer's monitor and realized that the machine had turned on by itself. That couldn't be good. A faint giggle spilled out of the computer's speakers, quickly followed by a chorus of other voices, tittering and snickering. That was even less good.

A male face appeared on the screen, looking for all the world as though it could see out of the machine. Behind him other faces appeared, a whole gaggle of little men in green clothes, good-naturedly pushing and shoving each other, whispering and giggling. They were red-haired like the mistress, but there the resemblance ended. Where she was pretty, they were ugly, with short faces, turned-up noses, squinting eyes and pointed ears.

This wasn't good at all, Dick thought, recognizing the pixies for what they were. Everybody knew how you spelled "trouble." It was "P-I-X-Y."

And then they started to clamber out of the screen, which shouldn't have been possible at all, but Dick was a hob and he understood that just because something shouldn't be able to happen, didn't mean it couldn't. Or wouldn't.

"Oh, this is bad," he said mournfully. "Bad bad bad."

He gave a quick look up to the ceiling. He had to warn the mistress. But it was already too late. Between one thought and the next, a dozen or more pixies had climbed out of the computer onto her desk, not the one of them taller than his own waist. They began rifling through her papers, using her pens and ruler as swords to poke at each other. Two of them started a pushing match that resulted in a small stack of books falling off the side of the desk. They landed with a bang on the floor.

The sound was so loud that Dick was sure the mistress would come down to investigate, her and her fierce little dog. The pixies all stood like little statues until first one, then another, started to giggle again. When they began to all shove at a bigger stack of books, Dick couldn't wait any longer.

Quick as a monkey, he scurried down to the floor.

"Stop!" he shouted as he ran to the front of the store.

And, "Here, you!"

And, "Don't!"

The pixies turned at the sound of his voice and Dick skidded to a stop.

"Oh, oh," he said.

The little men were still giggling and elbowing each other, but there was a wicked light in their eyes now, and they were all looking at him with those dark, considering gazes. Poor Dick realized that he hadn't thought any of this through in the least bit properly, for now that he had their attention, he had no idea what to do with it. They might only be a third his size, individually, but there were at least twenty of them and everybody knew just how mean a pixy could be, did he set his mind to it.

"Well, will you look at that," one of the pixies said. "It's a little hobberdy man." He looked at his companions. "What shall we do with him?"

"Smash him!"

"Whack him!"

"Find a puddle and drown him!"

Dick turned and fled, back the way he'd come. The pixies streamed from the top of Mistress Holly's desk, laughing wickedly and shouting threats as they chased him. Up the "Poetry" shelves Dick went, all the way to the very top. When he looked back down, he saw that the pixies weren't following the route he'd taken.

He allowed himself a moment's relief. Perhaps he was safe. Perhaps they couldn't climb. Perhaps they were afraid of heights.

Or, he realized with dismay, perhaps they meant to bring the whole bookcase crashing down, and him with it.

For the little men had gathered at the bottom of the bookcase and were putting their shoulders to its base. They might be small, but they were strong, and soon the tall stand of shelves was tottering unsteadily, swaying back and forth. A loose book fell out. Then another.

"No, no! You mustn't!" Dick cried down to them.

But he was too late.

With cries of "Hooray!" from the little men below, the bookcase came tumbling down, spraying books all around it. It smashed into its neighbour, bringing that stand of shelves down as well. By the time Dick hit the floor, hundreds of books were scattered all over the carpet and he was sitting on top of a tall, unsteady mountain of poetry, clutching his head, awaiting the worst.

The pixies came clambering up its slopes, the wicked lights in their eyes shining fierce and bright. He was, Dick realized, about to become an ex-hob. Except then he heard the door to Mistress Holly's apartment open at the top of the back stairs.

Rescued, he thought. And not a moment too soon. She would chase them off.

All the little men froze and Dick looked for a place to hide from the mistress's gaze.

But the pixies seemed unconcerned. Another soft round of giggles arose from them as, one by one, they transformed into soft, glittering lights no bigger than the mouth of a shot glass. The lights rose up from the floor where they'd been standing and went sailing towards the front of the store. When the mistress appeared at the foot of the stairs, her dog at her heels, she didn't even look at the fallen bookshelves. She saw only the lights, her eyes widening with happy delight.

Oh, no, Dick thought. They're pixy-leading her.

The little dog began to growl and bark and tug at the hem of her long flannel nightgown, but she paid no attention to it. Smiling a dreamy smile, she lifted her arms above her head like a ballerina and began to follow the dancing lights to the front of the store. Dick watched as pixy magic made the door pop open and a gust of chilly air burst in. Goosebumps popped up on the mistress's forearms but she never seemed to notice the cold. Her gaze was locked on the lights as they swooped, around and around in a gallitrap circle, then went shimmering out onto the street beyond. In moments she would follow them, out into the night and who knew what terrible danger.

Her little dog let go of her hem and ran ahead, barking at the lights. But it was no use. The pixies weren't frightened and the mistress wasn't roused.

It was up to him, Dick realized.

He ran up behind her and grabbed her ankle, bracing himself. Like the pixies, he was much stronger than his size might give him to appear. He held firm as the mistress tried to raise her foot. She lost her balance and down she went, down and down, toppling like some enormous tree. Dick jumped back, hands to his mouth, appalled at what he'd had to do. She banged her shoulder against a display at the front of the store, sending yet another mass of books cascading onto the floor.

Landing heavily on her arms, she stayed bent over for a long time before she finally looked up. She shook her head as though to clear it. The pixy lights had returned to the store, buzzing angrily about, but it was no use. The spell had been broken. One by one, they zoomed out of the store, down the street and were quickly lost from sight. The mistress's little dog ran back out onto the sidewalk and continued to bark at them, long after they were gone.

"Please let me be dreaming...." the mistress said.

Dick stooped quickly out of sight as she looked about at the sudden ruin of the store. He peeked at her from his hiding place, watched her rub at her face, then slowly stand up and massage her shoulder where it had hit the display. She called the dog back in, but stood in the doorway herself for a long time, staring out at the street, before she finally shut and locked the door behind her.

Oh, it was all such a horrible, terrible, awful mess.

"I'm sorry, I'm sorry, I'm sorry," Dick murmured, his voice barely a whisper, tears blurring his eyes.

The mistress couldn't hear him. She gave the store another survey, then shook her head.

"Come on, Snippet," she said to the dog. "We're going back to bed. Because this is just a dream."

She picked her way through the fallen books and shelves as she spoke.

"And when we wake up tomorrow everything will be back to normal."

But it wouldn't be. Dick knew. This was more of a mess than even the most industrious of hobs could clear up in just one night. But he did what he could until the morning came, one eye on the task at hand, the other on the windows in case the horrible pixies decided to return. Though what he'd do if they did, probably only the moon knew, and she wasn't telling.

Did you ever wake up from the weirdest, most unpleasant dream, only to find that it wasn't a dream at all?

When I came down to the store that morning, I literally had to lean against the wall at the foot of the stairs and catch my breath. I felt all faint and woozy. Snippet walked daintily ahead of me, sniffing the fallen books and whining softly.

An earthquake, I told myself. That's what it had been. I must have woken up right after the main shock, come down half-asleep and seen the mess, and just gone right back to bed again, thinking I was dreaming.

Except there'd been those dancing lights. Like a dozen or more Tinkerbells. Or fireflies. Calling me to follow, follow, follow, out into the night, until I'd tripped and fallen....

I shook my head slowly, trying to clear it. My shoulder was still sore and I massaged it as I took in the damage.

Actually, the mess wasn't as bad as it had looked at first. Many of the books appeared to have toppled from the shelves and landed in relatively alphabetical order.

Snippet whined again, but this time it was her "I really have to go" whine, so I grabbed her leash and a plastic bag from behind the desk and out we went for her morning constitutional.

It was brisk outside, but warm for early December, and there still wasn't any snow. At first glance, the damage from the quake appeared to be fairly marginal, considering it had managed to topple a couple of the bookcases in my store. The worst I could see were that all garbage canisters on the block had been overturned, the wind picking up the paper litter and carrying it in eddying pools up and down the street. Other than that, everything seemed pretty much normal. At least it did until I stopped into Café Joe's down the street to get my morning latte.

Joe Lapegna had originally operated a sandwich bar at the same location, but with the coming of Starbucks to town, he'd quickly seen which way the wind was blowing and renovated his place into a café. He'd done a good job with the décor. His café was every bit as contemporary and urban as any of the other high-end coffee bars in the city, the only real difference being that, instead of young college kids with rings through their noses, you got Joe serving the lattes and espressos. Joe with his broad shoulders and meaty, tattooed forearms, a fat caterpillar of a black moustache perched on his upper lip.

Before I could mention the quake, Joe started to tell me how he'd opened up this morning to find every porcelain mug in the store broken. None of the other breakables, not the plates or coffee makers. Nothing else was even out of place.

"What a weird quake it was," I said.

"Quake?" Joe said. "What quake?"

I waved a hand at the broken china he was sweeping up.

"This was vandals," he said. "Some little bastards broke in and had themselves a laugh."

So I told him about the bookcases in my shop, but he only shook his head.

"You hear anything about a quake on the radio?" he asked.

"I wasn't listening to it."

"I was. There was nothing. And what kind of a quake only breaks mugs and knocks over a couple of bookcases?"

Now that I thought of it, it was odd that there hadn't been any other disruption in my own store. If those bookcases had come down, why hadn't the front window display? I'd noticed a few books had fallen off my desk, but that was about it.

"It's so weird," I repeated.

Joe shook his head. "Nothing weird about it. Just some punks out having their idea of fun."

By the time I got back to my own store, I didn't know what to think. Snippet and I stopped in at a few other places along the strip and while everyone had damage to report, none of it was what could be put down to a quake. In the bakery, all the pies had been thrown against the front windows. In the hardware store, each and every electrical bulb was smashed—though they looked as though they'd simply exploded. All the rolls of paper towels and toilet paper from the grocery store had been tossed up into the trees behind their shipping and receiving bays, turning the bare-branched oaks and elms into bizarre mummy-like versions of themselves. And on it went.

The police arrived not long after I returned to the store. I felt like such a fool when one of the detectives came by to interview me. Yes, I'd heard the crash and come down to investigate. No, I hadn't seen anything.

I couldn't bring myself to mention the dancing lights.

No, I hadn't thought to phone it in.

"I thought I was dreaming," I told him. "I was half-asleep when I came downstairs and didn't think it had really happened. It wasn't until I came back down in the morning...."

The detective was of the opinion that it had been gang-related, kids out on the prowl, egging each other on until it had gotten out of control.

I thought about it when he left and knew he had to be right. The damage we'd sustained was all on the level of pranks—mean-spirited, to be sure, but pranks nonetheless. I didn't like the idea of our little area being the sudden target of vandals, but there really wasn't any other logical explanation. At least none occurred to me until I stepped back into the store and glanced at my computer. That's when I remembered Meran Kelledy, how she'd gotten me to turn my sweater inside out and the odd things she'd been saying about pixies on the web.

If you're lucky, they're still on the Internet and didn't follow you home.

Of course that wasn't even remotely logical. But it made me think. After all, if the Wordwood database could take on a life of its own, who was to say that pixies on the Internet was any more improbable? As my friend Richard likes to point out, everyone has odd problems with their computers that could as easily be attributed to mischievous spirits as to software glitches. At least they could be if your mind was inclined to think along those lines, and mine certainly was.

I stood for a long moment, staring at the screen of my computer. I don't know exactly at what point I realized that the machine was on. I'd turned it off last night before Snippet and I went up to the apartment. And I hadn't stopped to turn it on this morning before we'd gone out. So either I was getting monumentally forgetful, or I'd turned it on while sleepwalking last night, or....

I glanced over at Snippet who was once again sniffing everything as though she'd never been in the store before. Or as if someone or something interesting and strange *had*.

"This is silly," I said.

But I dug out Meran's card and called the number on it all the same, staring at the computer screen as I did. I just hoped nobody had been tinkering with my files.

Bookstore hobs are a relatively recent phenomenon, dating back only a couple of hundred years. Dick knew hobs back home in the old country who'd lived in the same household for three times that length of time. He'd been a farm hob himself, once, living on a Devon steading for two-hundred-and-twelve-years until a new family moved in and began to take his services for granted. When one year they actually dared to complain about how poorly the harvest had been put away, he'd thrown every bit of it down into a nearby ravine and set off to find new habitation.

A cousin who lived in a shop had suggested to Dick that he try the same, but there were fewer commercial establishments in those days and they all had their own hob by the time he went looking, first up into Somerset, then back down through Devon, finally moving west to Cornwall. In the end, he made his home in a small cubbyhole of a bookstore he found in Penzance. He lived there for years until the place went out of business, the owner setting sail for North America with plans to open another shop in the new land once he arrived.

Dick had followed, taking up residence in the new store when it was established. That was where he'd taught himself to read.

But he soon discovered that stores didn't have the longevity of a farm. They opened and closed up business seemingly on nothing more than a whim, which made it a hard life for a hob, always looking for a new place to live. By the latter part of this century, he had moved twelve times in the space of five years before finally settling into the place he now called home, the bookstore of his present mistress with its simple sign out front:

HOLLY RUE—USED BOOKS.

He'd discovered that a quality used bookstore was always the best. Libraries were good, too, but they were usually home to displaced gargoyles and the ghosts of writers and had no room for a hob as well. He'd tried new bookstores, but the smaller ones couldn't keep him busy enough and the large ones were too bright, their hours of business too long. And he loved the wide and eclectic range of old and new books to be explored in a shop such as Mistress Holly's, titles that wandered far from the beaten path, or worthy books no longer in print, but nonetheless inspired. The stories he found in them sustained him in a way that nothing else could, for they fed the heart and the spirit.

But this morning, sitting behind the furnace, he only felt old and tired. There'd been no time to read at all last night, and he hadn't thought to bring a book down with him when he finally had to leave the store.

"I hate pixies," he said, his voice soft and lonely in the darkness. "I really really do."

Faerie and pixies had never gotten along, especially not since the last pitched battle between them in the old country when the faeries had been driven back across the River Parrett, leaving everything west of the Parrett as pixyland. For years, hobs such as Dick had lived a clandestine existence in their little steadings, avoiding the attention of pixies whenever they could.

Dick hadn't needed last night's experience to tell him why.

After awhile he heard the mistress and her dog leave the store so he crept out from behind the furnace to stand guard in case the pixies returned while the pair of them were gone. Though what he would do if the pixies did come back, he had no idea. He was an absolute failure when it came to protecting anything, that had been made all too clear last night.

Luckily the question never arose. Mistress Holly and the dog returned and he slipped back behind the furnace, morosely clutching his knees and rocking back and forth, waiting for the night to come. He could hear life go on upstairs. Someone came by to help the mistress right the fallen bookcases. Customers arrived and left with much discussion of the vandalism on the street. Most of the time he could hear only the mistress, replacing the books on their shelves.

"I should be doing that," Dick said. "That's my job."

But he was only an incompetent hob, concealed in his hidey-hole, of no use to anyone until they all went to bed and he could go about his business. And even then, any ruffian could come along and bully him and what could he do to stop them?

Dick's mood went from bad to worse, from sad to sadder still. It might have lasted all the day, growing unhappier with each passing hour, except at midmorning he suddenly sat up, ears and nose quivering. A presence had come into the store above. A piece of an old mystery, walking about as plain as could be.

He realized that he'd sensed it yesterday as well, while he was dozing. Then he'd put it down to the dream he was wandering in, forgetting all about it when he woke. But today, wide awake, he couldn't ignore it. There was an oak king's daughter upstairs, an old and powerful spirit walking far from her woods. He began to shiver. Important faerie such as she wouldn't be out and about unless the need was great. His shiver deepened. Perhaps she'd come to reprimand him for the job so poorly done. She might turn him into a stick or a mouse.

Oh, this was very bad. First pixies, now this.

Whatever was he going to do? However could he even begin to explain that he'd meant to chase the pixies away, truly he had, but he simply wasn't big enough, nor strong enough. Perhaps not even brave enough.

He rocked back and forth, harder now, his face burrowed against his knees.

After I'd made my call to Meran, Samuel, who works at the deli down the street, came by and helped me stand the bookcases upright once more. The deli hadn't been spared a visit from the vandals either. He told me that they'd taken all the sausages out of the freezer and used them to spell out rude words on the floor.

"Remember when all we had to worry about was some graffiti on the walls outside?" he asked when he was leaving.

I was still replacing books on the shelves when Meran arrived. She looked around the store while I expanded on what I'd told her over the phone. Her brow furrowed thoughtfully and I was wondering if she was going to tell me to put my sweater on backwards again.

"You must have a hob in here," she said.

"A what?"

It was the last thing I expected her to say.

"A hobgoblin," she said. "A brownie. A little faerie man who dusts and tidies and keeps things neat."

"I just thought it didn't get all that dirty," I said, realizing as I spoke how ridiculous that sounded.

Because, when I thought about it, a helpful brownie living in the store explained a lot. While I certainly ran the vacuum cleaner over the carpets every other morning or so, and dusted when I could, the place never seemed to need much cleaning. My apartment upstairs required more and it didn't get a fraction of the traffic.

And it wasn't just the cleaning. The store, for all its clutter, was organized, though half the time I didn't know how. But I always seemed to be able to lay my hand on whatever I needed to find without having to root about too much. Books often got put away without my remembering I'd done it. Others mysteriously vanished, then reappeared a day or so later, properly filed in their appropriate section—even if they had originally disappeared from the top of my desk. I rarely needed to alphabetize my sections while my colleagues in other stores were constantly complaining of the mess their customers left behind.

"But aren't you supposed to leave cakes and cream out for them?" I found myself asking.

"You never leave a specific gift," Meran said. "Not unless you want him to leave. It's better to simply 'forget' a cake or a sweet treat on one of the shelves when you leave for the night."

"I haven't even done that. What could he be living on?"

Meran smiled as she looked around the store. "Maybe the books nourish him. Stranger things have been known to happen in Faerie."

"Faerie," I repeated slowly.

Bad enough I'd helped create a database on the Internet that had taken on a life of its own. Now my store was in Faerie. Or at least straddling the border, I supposed. Maybe the one had come about because of the other.

"Your hob will know what happened here last night," Meran said.

"But how would we even go about asking him?"

It seemed a logical question, since I'd never known I had one living with me in the first place. But Meran only smiled.

"Oh, I can usually get their attention," she told me.

She called out something in a foreign language, a handful of words that rang with great strength and appeared to linger and echo longer than they should. The poor little man who came sidling up from the basement in response looked absolutely terrified. He was all curly hair and raggedy clothes with a broad face that, I assumed from the laugh lines, normally didn't look so miserable. He was carrying a battered little leather carpetbag and held a brown cloth cap in his hand. He couldn't have been more than two feet tall.

All I could do was stare at him, though I did have the foresight to pick up Snippet before she could lunge in his direction. I could feel the growl rumbling in her chest more than hear it. I think she was as surprised as me to find that he'd been living in our basement all this time.

Meran sat on her haunches, bringing her head down to the general level of the hob's. To put him at ease, I supposed, so I did the same myself. The little man didn't appear to lose any of his nervousness. I could see his knees knocking against each other, his cheek twitching.

"B-begging your pardon, your ladyship," he said to Meran. His gaze slid to me and I gave him a quick smile. He blinked, swallowed hard, and returned his attention to my companion. "Dick Bobbins," he added, giving a quick nod of his head. "At your service, as it were. I'll just be on my way, then, no harm done."

"Why are you so frightened of me?" Meran asked.

He looked at the floor. "Well, you're a king's daughter, aren't you just, and I'm only me."

A king's daughter? I thought.

Meran smiled. "We're all only who we are, no one of more importance than the other."

"Easy for you to say," he began. Then his eyes grew wide and he put a hand to his mouth. "Oh, that was a bad thing to say to such a great and wise lady such as yourself."

Meran glanced at me. "They think we're like movie stars," she explained. "Just because we were born in a court instead of a hobhole."

I was getting a bit of a case of the celebrity nerves myself. Court? King's daughter? Who exactly *was* this woman?

"But you know," she went on, returning her attention to the little man, "my father's court was only a glade, our palace no more than a tree."

He nodded quickly, giving her a thin smile that never reached his eyes.

"Well, wonderful to meet you," he said. "Must be on my way now."

He picked up his carpetbag and started to sidle towards the other aisle that wasn't blocked by what he must see as two great big hulking women and a dog.

"But we need your help," Meran told him.

Whereupon he burst into tears.

The mothering instinct that makes me such a sap for Snippet kicked into gear and I wanted to hold him in my arms and comfort him. But I had Snippet to consider, straining in my grip, the growl in her chest quite audible now. And I wasn't sure how the little man would have taken my sympathies. After all, he might be child-sized, but for all his tears, he was obviously an adult, not a child. And if the stories were anything to go by, he was probably older than me—by a few hundred years.

Meran had no such compunction. She slipped up to him and put her arms around him, cradling his face against the crook of her shoulder.

It took awhile before we coaxed the story out of him. I locked the front door and we went upstairs to my kitchen where I made tea for us all. Sitting at the table, raised up to the proper height by a stack of books, Dick told us about the pixies coming out of the computer screen, how they'd knocked down the bookcases and finally disappeared into the night. The small mug I'd given him looked enormous in his hands. He fell silent when he was done and stared glumly down at the steam rising from his tea.

"But none of what they did was your fault," I told him.

"Kind of you to say," he managed. He had to stop and sniff, wipe his nose on his sleeve. "But if I'd b-been braver—"

"They *would* have drowned you in a puddle," Meran said. "And I think you were brave, shouting at them the way you did and then rescuing your mistress from being pixy-led."

I remembered those dancing lights and shivered. I knew those stories as well. There weren't any swamps or marshes to be led into around here, but there were eighteen-wheelers out on the highway only a few blocks away. Entranced as I'd been, the pixies could easily have walked me right out in front of any one of them. I was lucky to only have a sore shoulder.

"Do you...really think so?" he asked, sitting up a little straighter.

We both nodded.

Snippet was lying under my chair, her curiosity having been satisfied that Dick was only one more visitor and therefore out-of-bounds in terms of biting and barking at. There'd been a nervous moment while she'd sniffed at his trembling hand and he'd looked as though he was ready to scurry up one of the bookcases, but they quickly made their peace. Now Snippet was only bored and had fallen asleep.

"Well," Meran said. "It's time we put our heads together and considered how we can put our unwanted visitors back where they came from and keep them there."

"Back onto the Internet?" I asked. "Do you really think we should?"

"Well, we could try to kill them...."

I shook my head. That seemed too extreme. I started to protest, only to see that she'd been teasing me.

"We could take a thousand of them out of the web," Meran said, "and still not have them all. Once tricksy folk like pixies have their foot in a place, you can't ever be completely rid of them." She smiled. "But if we can get them to go back in, there are measures we can take to stop them from troubling you again."

"And what about everybody else on-line?" I asked.

Meran shrugged. "They'll have to take their chances—just like they do when they go for a walk in the woods. The little people are everywhere."

I glanced across my kitchen table to where the hob was sitting and thought, no kidding.

"The trick, if you'll pardon my speaking out of turn," Dick said, "is to play on their curiosity."

Meran gave him an encouraging smile. "We want your help," she said. "Go on."

The little man sat up straighter still and put his shoulders back.

"We could use a book that's never been read," he said. "We could put it in the middle of the road, in front of the store. That would certainly make me curious."

"An excellent idea," Meran told him.

"And then we could use the old spell of bell, book and candle. The churchmen stole that one from us."

Even I'd heard of it. Bell, book and candle had once been another way of saying excommunication in the Catholic church. After pronouncing the sentence, the officiating cleric would close his book, extinguish the candle, and toll the bell as if for someone who had died. The book symbolized the book of life, the candle a man's soul, removed from the sight of God as the candle had been from the sight of men.

But I didn't get the unread book bit.

"Do you mean a brand new book?" I asked. "A particular copy that nobody might have opened yet, or one that's so bad that no one's actually made their way all the way through it?"

"Though someone would have had to," Dick said, "for it to have been published in the first place. I meant the way books were made in the old days, with the pages still sealed. You had to cut them apart as you read them."

"Oh, I remember those," Meran said.

Like she was there. I took another look at her and sighed. Maybe she had been.

"Do you have any like that?" she asked.

"Yes," I said slowly, unable to hide my reluctance.

I didn't particularly like the idea of putting a collector's item like that out in thc middle of the road.

But in the end, that's what we did.

The only book I had that passed Dick's inspection was *The Trembling of the Veil* by William Butler Yeats, number seventy-one of a thousand-copy edition privately printed by T. Werner Laurie, Ltd. in 1922. All the pages were still sealed at the top. It was currently listing on the Internet in the $450 to $500 range and I kept it safely stowed away in the glass-doored bookcase that held my first editions.

The other two items were easier to deal with. I had a lovely brass bell that my friend Tatiana had given me for Christmas last year and a whole box of fat white candles just because I liked to burn them. But it broke my heart to go out onto the street around two A.M., and place the Yeats on the pavement.

We left the front door to the store ajar, the computer on. I wasn't entirely sure how we were supposed to lure the pixies back into the store and then onto the Internet once more, but Meran took a flute out of her bag and fit the wooden pieces of it together. She spoke of a calling-on music and Dick nodded sagely, so I simply went along with their better experience. Mind you, I also wasn't all that sure that my Yeats would actually draw the pixies back in the first place, but what did I know?

We all hid in the alleyway running between my store and the futon shop, except for Snippet, who was locked up in my apartment. She hadn't been very pleased by that. After an hour of crouching in the cold in the alley, I wasn't feeling very pleased myself. What if the pixies didn't come? What if they did, but they approached from the fields behind the store and came traipsing up this very alleyway?

By three-thirty we all had a terrible chill. Looking up at my apartment, I could see Snippet lying in the window of the dining room, looking down at us. She didn't appear to have forgiven me yet and I would happily have changed places with her.

"Maybe we should just—"

I didn't get to finish with "call it a night." Meran put a finger to her lips and hugged the wall. I looked past her to the street.

At first I didn't see anything. There was just my Yeats, lying there on the pavement, waiting for a car to come and run over it. But then I saw the little man, not even half the size of Dick, come creeping up from the sewer grating. He was followed by two more. Another pair came down the brick wall of the temporary office help building across the street. Small dancing lights that I remembered too clearly from last night, dipped and wove their way from the other end of the block, descending to the pavement and becoming more of the little men when they drew near to the book. One of them poked at it with his foot and I had visions of them tearing it apart.

Meran glanced at Dick and he nodded, mouthing the words, "That's the lot of them."

She nodded back and took her flute out from under her coat where she'd been keeping it warm.

At this point I wasn't really thinking of how the calling music would work. I'm sure my mouth hung agape as I stared at the pixies. I felt light-headed, a big grin tugging at my lips. Yes, they were pranksters, and mean-spirited ones at that. But they were also magical. The way they'd changed from little lights to little men...I'd never seen anything like it before. The hob who lived in my bookstore was magical, too, of course, but somehow it wasn't the same thing. He was already familiar, so down-to-earth. Sitting around during the afternoon and evening while we waited, I'd had a delightful time talking books with him, as though he were an old friend. I'd completely forgotten that he was a little magic man himself.

The pixies were truly puzzled by the book. I suppose it would be odd from any perspective, a book that old, never once having been opened or read. It defeated the whole purpose of why it had been made.

I'm not sure when Meran began to play her flute. The soft breathy sound of it seemed to come from nowhere and everywhere, all at once, a resonant wave of slow, stately notes, one falling after the other, rolling into a melody that was at once hauntingly strange and heartachingly familiar.

The pixies lifted their heads at the sound. I wasn't sure what I'd expected, but when they began to dance, I almost clapped my hands. They were so funny. Their bodies kept perfect time to the music, but their little eyes glared at Meran as she stepped out of the alley and Pied Pipered them into the store.

Dick fetched the Yeats and then he and I followed after, arriving in time to see the music make the little men dance up onto my chair, onto the desk, until they began to vanish, one by one, into the screen of my monitor, a fat candle sitting on top of it, its flame flickering with their movement. Dick opened the book and I took the bell out of my pocket.

Meran took the flute from her lips.

"Now," she said.

Dick slapped the book closed, she leaned forward and blew out the candle while I began to chime the bell, the clear brass notes ringing in the silence left behind by the flute. We saw a horde of little faces staring out at us from the screen, eyes glaring. One of the little men actually popped back through, but Dick caught him by the leg and tossed him back into the screen.

Meran laid her flute down on the desk and brought out a garland she'd made earlier of rowan twigs, green leaves and red berry sprigs still attached in places. When she laid it on top of the monitor, we heard the modem dial up my Internet service. When the connection was made, the little men vanished from the screen. The last turned his bum towards us and let out a loud fart before he, too, was gone.

The three of us couldn't help it. We all broke up.

"That went rather well," Meran said when we finally caught our breath. "My husband Cerin is usually the one to handle this sort of thing, but it's nice to know I haven't forgotten how to deal with such rascals myself. And it's probably best he didn't come along this evening. He can seem rather fierce and I don't doubt poor Dick here would have thought him far too menacing."

I looked around the store.

"Where *is* Dick?" I asked.

But the little man was gone. I couldn't believe it. Surely he hadn't just up and left us like in the stories.

"Hobs and brownies," Meran said when I asked, her voice gentle, "they tend to take their leave rather abruptly when the tale is done."

"I thought you had to leave them a suit of clothes or something."

Meran shrugged. "Sometimes simply being identified is enough to make them go."

"Why does it have to be like that?"

"I'm not really sure. I suppose it's a rule or something, or a geas—a thing that has to happen. Or perhaps it's no more than a simple habit they've handed down from one generation to the next."

"But I *loved* the idea of him living here," I said. "I thought it would be so much fun. With all the work he's been doing, I'd have been happy to make him a partner."

Meran smiled. "Faerie and commerce don't usually go hand in hand."

"But you and your husband play music for money."

Her smile grew wider, her eyes enigmatic, but also amused.

"What makes you think we're faerie?" she asked.

"Well, you…that is…."

"I'll tell you a secret," she said, relenting. "We're something else again, but what exactly that might be, even we have no idea anymore. Mostly we're the same as you. Where we differ is that Cerin and I always live with half a foot in the otherworld that you've only visited these past few days."

"And only the borders of it, I'm sure."

She shrugged. "Faerie is everywhere. It just *seems* closer at certain times, in certain places."

She began to take her flute apart and stow the wooden pieces away in the instrument's carrying case.

"Your hob will be fine," she said. "The kindly ones such as he always find a good household to live in."

"I hope so," I said. "But all the same, I was really looking forward to getting to know him better."

Dick Bobbins got an odd feeling listening to the two of them talk, his mistress and the oak king's daughter. Neither were quite what he'd expected. Mistress Holly was far kinder and not at all the brusque, rather self-centered human that figured in so many old hob fireside tales. And her ladyship…well, who would have thought that one of the highborn would treat a simple hob as though they stood on equal footing? It was all very unexpected.

But it was time for him to go. He could feel it in his blood and in his bones.

He waited while they said their goodbyes. Waited while Mistress Holly took the dog out for a last quick pee before the pair of them retired to their apartment. Then he had the store completely to himself, with no chance of unexpected company. He fetched his little leather carpetbag from his hobhole behind the furnace and came back upstairs to say goodbye to the books, to the store, to his home.

Finally all there was left to do was to spell the door open, step outside and go. He hesitated on the welcoming carpet, thinking of what Mistress Holly had asked, what her ladyship had answered. Was the leaving song that ran in his blood and rumbled in his bones truly a geas, or only habit? How was a poor hob to know? If it was a rule, then who had made it and what would happen if he broke it?

He took a step away from the door, back into the store and paused, waiting for he didn't know what. Some force to propel him out the door. A flash of light to burn down from the sky and strike him where he stood. Instead all he felt was the heaviness in his heart and the funny tingling warmth he'd known when he'd heard the mistress say how she'd been looking forward to getting to know him. That she wanted him to be a partner in her store. Him. Dick Bobbins, of all things.

He looked at the stairs leading up to her apartment.

Just as an experiment, he made his way over to them, then up the risers, one by one, until he stood at her door.

Oh, did he dare, did he dare?

He took a deep breath and squared his shoulders. Then setting down his carpetbag, he twisted his cloth cap in his hands for a long moment before he finally lifted an arm and rapped a knuckle against the wood panel of Mistress Holly's door.

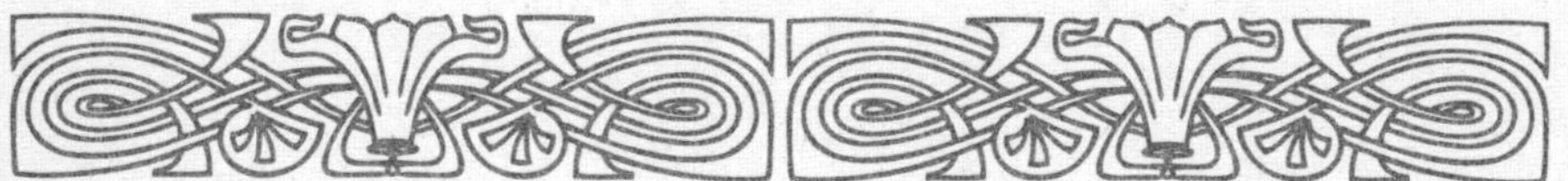

MANY WORLDS ARE BORN TONIGHT

I WENT DOWN to the Beanery that night, you know, that café down in the old factory district by the canal that's more like a warehouse than a coffee bar. Big enough for a rave, but the wildest the music gets is Chet Baker or Morcheeba. Very hip place, at least this week. Non-smoking, of course, but everything is these days. Open concept with lots of woodwork: pine floors, rustic rafters and support beams. No real general lighting, only pockets, low-hanging overhead lights illuminating tables with groups of people in earnest conversation, drinking low-fat lattés and decaf espressos, go figure. Kind of like a singles bar without the action, but I like it for that. For the anonymity it allows me. So I'm surprised when I catch a name I haven't heard in years.

"Hey, Spyboy."

It takes me back to New Orleans, Mardi Gras. Spyboys are part of the Big Chiefs' entourages during the annual parade, the Mardi Gras "Indians" who scout ahead for the other tribes on the march and just generally make a lot of mischief. I did my bit in the parades back in those days, but the name stuck because of another job I held before I retired: digging up dirt for the Couteau family. I'm good at secrets—keeping my own, uncovering those that belong to others. I guess I'd still be there, but I took exception to the use of my expertise. I don't mind tracking down deadbeats and the like, but it turned out that people died because of information I dug up. When I found out how the Couteaus were using me, I couldn't live with it, but you don't say goodbye to people like this.

See, I grew up wanting to be one of the good guys. Call me naïve. When I realized that wasn't happening, when I understood exactly what I'd fallen into, I had no choice but to disappear. That entailed getting out of town and staying out. Maintaining a low profile once I was gone and, most important, keeping my mouth shut.

So when I hear that name, one part of me wants to keep walking, but curiosity's always been a serious weakness. I turn to see what part of my past has finally caught up to me.

I don't recognize him right away. The lighting's bad where he's sitting, alone at a table, nursing a chai tea latté. Nondescript—your basic average joe, medium height, brown hair, brown eyes, no distinguishing features. The kind of man your gaze just slides over because there's nothing there to hold it. He's wearing a dark jacket and turtleneck.

"I heard you were dead," he says.

It's the voice I remember. That rasp, like it's working its way through a hundred years of abusing cigarettes and whiskey. Sammy Hale. Used to run numbers for the Couteaus until he got caught dipping his hand where it shouldn't. Not once, but twice. I check out his right hand where the fingers are cut off at the knuckles. It's Sammy all right.

I give him a shrug.

"I could say the same thing about you," I tell him.

"I got better," he says. Smiles.

It's enough to hook me, pull the line taut, then reel me in. He knows my weakness. I take one of the empty chairs at his table.

"Sounds like a story," I say.

"Maybe. You still in the information business?"

I shake my head, then touch a finger to my temple. "This is where it stays now. Can't sell anything anymore because that's like saying, 'Here I am.' But you know me."

He nods. "Yeah, you always had to know."

"So how'd you survive?" I ask.

Again that smile. "I didn't."

I hear a lot of stories, mostly from street people these days, and they'll tell you any damn thing. What intrigues me right now is that I remember Sammy from the old days. The one thing he never had was much imagination. Why do you think he got caught ripping off the Couteaus, not once, but twice?

I'm good at waiting. You learn more if you don't ask questions. But I can tell that's not how Sammy wants to play this out.

"So what happened?" I ask.

"I guess you could say I wandered out of the world."

"You know I'm not following you here," I say.

That smile of his plays out into a grin and then he tells me a story that even the skells hanging around outside the detox centre would be embarrassed to own up to.

"Come with me," he says when he's done.

"I can't," I tell him and I walk away.

Or maybe I didn't walk away.

Maybe I hear him out and that old curiosity of mine has me follow him out of the Beanery into the night. We trade the sounds of quiet conversation and the Bill Evans Trio playing on the café's sound system for the noise of the streets, the rich smell of brewing coffee for car exhaust and the faint odor of rotting garbage. Tomorrow's pick-up day downtown and all the bins are standing in a row along the curb.

Sammy keeps talking, adding details. I walk along beside him, nodding to show that I'm taking it all in.

Not that I believe him for a second.

Carnies have always been easy fall guys for mystery and trouble. People think of them with the same uneasy mix of intolerance and envy as they do Gypsies. What a life, but they'll rob you blind. Lock the doors when the tractor-trailers pull into town and the midway goes up. But what a life. Every day a different town, a whole new crowd of rubes to take advantage of. But keep your hand on your wallet and lock up your daughters.

And haunted carnivals are nothing new, either. Hell, they've got their own little category in folklore and literature, too, from Ray Bradbury to Dean Koontz. But this Ferris wheel he's talking up, it's a new one for me. It's a mechanism that doesn't make sense in the world we all inhabit, like opening a door in your house and finding it leads into a room you've never seen before. I'm haunted by the idea of his carnival ride, existing sideways to the world, a big Ferris wheel with this odd sign hanging over the entrance to the ride, "Crowded After Hours." A creaking, ancient behemoth of midway entertainment that only exists when the fair's closed down, the booths are all dark, and the carnies have closed the doors of their trailers against the night. A midnight ride where each rider is some costumed figure from nightmare or story or dream, an uneasy crowd of gargoyles and clowns and stranger beings still, like a Mardi Gras parade on a slow-spinning wheel.

There's room for Spyboy there, he tells me.

"See, you're safe on the wheel," Sammy says. "Safe from the world. Safe forever."

Maybe, I'm thinking. But are you safe from the wheel itself? Because, never mind the implausibility of it, there's something not right about this idea of chaos married to order, all these mad troubled souls doing time in the confines of their seats, the big wheel turning slowly, creaking in the mist.

"Just have a look," he says, seeing my doubt.

And I guess I will. I do. Curiosity pulling me along as we head up to the roof of the old Sovereign Building on Flood Street, just north of Kelly, in through a back door and up a stairwell until the rooftop gravel's crunching underfoot and we're standing at the edge of the roof, looking out. Sammy's eyes are shining, aglow.

"I don't see anything," I tell him.

"You have to have faith," he says. "You have to believe."

I squint and think I see something, some monstrous shape looming out of the night, clouded with mists, a wheel turning, the seats rocking slowly back and forth and all these...these beings on them, staring off into unimaginable distances.

"How often do we get a chance like this?" Sammy asks me.

I turn to look at him, still snared by his sincerity.

"Think about it," he says. "Every time we make a decision, we make another world. We do one thing, and we're in the world that decision called up, but at the same time, we didn't do it, so we're in that other world, too. It goes on forever, all these worlds."

"You know, you're not making a whole lot of sense," I say.

He smiles. "Just think of a world where you're not looking over your shoulder every couple of minutes, wondering if the Couteaus have finally tracked you down and sent one of their boys to deal with you."

"Eternity on a Ferris wheel doesn't really sound all that much better," I say.

"You're thinking of the outside," he tells me. "Concentrate on all the journeys you can take inside."

I shake my head. "I don't get it, Sammy. I like the world. I like being in it."

"You just don't know any different." He gives me that smile again, the kind you see on the statues of saints in a church. "In some world you've already stepped over. You're already riding the wheel and you can't imagine how you'd ever have hesitated."

"Why me?" I ask him. "Why'd you come to me?"

"We're linked," he says. "By bad blood. The Couteaus want both of us dead."

You're already dead, I'm thinking, but we've already covered that and it didn't get me any closer to understanding what he's talking about.

But I can see that ghostly wheel now, half here, so close we can almost reach out and grab one of the joints of its frame, half lost in a steaming mist.

"And besides," he says. "We're already there."

He points to a seat shared by a harlequin and something truly weird: a man with the head of a quarter moon, a blue moon, like something out of a kid's book. A man in the moon with Sammy's features. And I can make out my own features, too, under the harlequin's white makeup.

"What's with the moon head?" I ask him.

"You know," he says. "Once in a. I always wanted to be lucky. Different. The guy who comes and you don't know what to expect, maybe good, maybe bad, but it'll shake up your world and make some new ones because whether you like it or not, there's a big change coming. I don't want to be what I am, some loser you can't remember as soon as I walk out the door."

"I never wanted to be a harlequin," I say.

He smiles, it's like a child's smile this time, so simple and all encompassing, the whole world smiling with you.

"Spyboy was a kind of clown," he says.

"So what does that say about me?"

"That you like to see people happy. Same as me. Look at us." He points at the pair again. "Don't we make you smile?"

I'm feeling a little disoriented, dizzy almost, which is strange, though not the strangest thing to happen to me tonight. Still, I've always been good with heights, so this flicker of vertigo disturbs me, more than the wheel and Sammy's story, go figure.

"Come on," he says.

I don't know why I do it, but I jump with him, off the roof, grab hold of the wheel's frame, climb down towards where we're already sitting, Spyboy and the Blue Moon.

Only maybe I don't jump. Maybe I stand there and watch him fall, and then I go home. But I can't get it out of my head, what he told me, the way he just jumped, the height of the building, how I never heard him land on the pavement below. I wonder if someone can die twice, except there's no body this time, waiting for me when I step out of the door and into the alleyway. Maybe there wasn't when the Couteaus had him shot either.

The next day I go to work, walk in the back door of the restaurant, same as always. Raul looks up when I come in. He waits until I take off my jacket, put on an apron, start in to work on the small mountain of pots and dishes that've accumulated since I was last standing here at the sink.

"There was a guy looking for you after you left yesterday," he says.

Sammy, I think. I want to forget all about what maybe happened last night, but the thoughts keep coming back like bad pennies.

"Did he say what he wanted?" I ask, curious as to what Sammy might have said, still looking for a clue, trying to figure him out, where he went when he jumped off that roof.

Raul shakes his head. "Didn't say much of anything. He was a big guy, mean looking. Talked a little like François, only not so much. Same accent, you know?"

I go cold at that little piece of news.

I'll tell you the truth, I never thought the Couteaus would bother to track me down. Where was the percentage? I didn't rip them off like Sammy, I've kept my mouth shut all along, stayed low, working shit jobs, minded my own business. But I guess just walking away was insult enough for them.

"He say anything about coming back?" I ask.

Raul shrugged. "I didn't like the look of him," he says, "so I told him you quit."

"You didn't lie," I tell him, already removing the apron.

"What's this guy got on you?" Raul asks.

"Nothing. He just works for some freaks who don't like to hear the word 'no.' He comes back, you tell him you never saw me again."

Raul shrugs. "I can do that, but—"

"I'm not saying this for me," I tell him. "I'm saying it for you."

I guess he sees something in my face, a piece of how serious this is, because he swallows hard and nods. Then I'm out the door, walking fast, pulse working overtime. There's a sick feeling in my gut and the skin between my shoulderblades is prickling like someone's got a rifle site aimed at my back.

Except the kind of boys the Couteaus hire like to work close, like to see the pain. I'm almost at the end of the alley, thinking I'm home free, except suddenly he's there in front of me, like he stepped out of nowhere, knife in hand. I have long enough to register his fish cold eyes, the freak's grin that splits his face, then the knife punches into my stomach. He pulls it up, tearing through my chest, and I go down. It happens so fast that the pain follows afterwards, like thunder trailing a lightning bolt.

And everything goes black.

Only maybe I didn't go out the back door, where I knew he could be waiting.

Maybe I grabbed my jacket and bolted through the restaurant, out the front, and lost myself in the lunchtime crowd. But I know he's out there, looking for me, and I don't have anywhere to go. I never had much of a stake and what I did have is long gone. Why do you think I'm washing dishes for a living?

So I go to ground with the skells, trade my clean jacket for some wino's smelly coat, a couple of bucks buys me a tuque, I don't want to know where it's been. I rub dirt on my face and hands and I hide there in plain sight, same block as the restaurant, sprawled on the pavement, begging for spare change, waiting for the night to come so I can go looking for this wheel of Sammy's.

The afternoon takes a long slow stroll through what's left of the day, but I'm not impatient. Why should I be? I'm just some harmless drunk, got an early start on the day's inebriation. Time doesn't mean anything to me anymore, except for how much of it stretches between bottles. Play this kind of thing right and you start to believe it yourself.

I'm into my role, so much so that when I see the guy, I stay calm. He's got to be the shooter the Couteaus sent, tall, sharp dresser, whistling a Doc Cheatham tune and walking loose, but the dead eyes give him away. He's looking everywhere but at me. That's the thing about the homeless. They're either invisible, or a nuisance you have to ignore. I ask him for some spare change, but I don't even register for him, his gaze slides right on by.

I watch him make a slow pass by the restaurant, hands in his pockets. He stops, turns back to read the menu, goes in. I start to worry then. Not for me, but for Raul. I'm long past letting anyone else get hurt because of me. But the shooter's back out a moment later. He takes a casual look down my side of the street, then ambles off the other way and I let out a breath I didn't realize I was holding. So much for staying in character.

It takes me a little longer to settle back into my role, but it's an effort well-spent, for here he comes walking by again. Lee Street's not exactly the French

Quarter—even in the middle of the day Bourbon Street's a lively place—but there's enough going on that he doesn't seem out of place, wandering here and there, window shopping, stopping to buy a cappuccino from a cart at the end of the block, a soft pretzel from another. He finishes them slowly on a bench near the restaurant, one of those iron and wood improvements that the merchants' association put in a few years ago.

He doesn't give up his watch until it gets dark, the stores start to close down, the restaurants are in the middle of their dinner trade. I stay where I am when he leaves. It's a long time until midnight and I might as well wait here as wander the streets. I give it until eleven-thirty before I shuffle off, heading across town to Flood Street. By the time I reach the alley behind the Sovereign Building, it's a little past midnight.

I'm not sure I even expected it to be there again. Maybe, if I'm to believe Sammy, in some other world I come here and find nothing. But as I step around the corner into the alley, everything shifts and sways. I walk into a thick mist that opens up a little after a few paces, but never quite clears. The Ferris wheel's here, but it's further away than I expected.

I'm standing in a field of corn stubble, the sky immense above me, the sound of crickets filling the air, a full moon hanging up at the top of the sky. A long way across the cornfield I can see a darkened carnival, the midway closed, all the rides shut down. The Ferris wheel rears above it, a black shadow that blocks the stars with its shape. I pause for a long time, taking it all in, not sure any of this is real, unable to deny that it's here in front of me all the same. Finally I start walking once more, across the field, past the darkened booths, dry dirt scuffling underfoot. It's quiet here, hushed like a graveyard, the way it feels in your mind when you're stepping in between the gravestones.

It takes me a long time to reach the wheel. The sign's still there above the entrance, "Crowded After Hours," but the seats are all empty. The spokes of the wheel and the immense frame holding it seem to be made of enormous bones, the remains of behemoths and monsters. The crosspieces are carved with roses, the paint flaked and peeling where it isn't faded. Vines grow up and around the entire structure and its massive wooden base appears to be half-covered with a clutter of fallen leaves.

No, I realize. Not leaves, but masks. Hundreds of them, some half-buried in the dirt, or covered by the vines that grow everywhere like kudzu, their painted features flaked and faded like the roses. But others seem to be almost brand new, so new the paint looks like it'd be tacky to the touch. Old or new, they run the gamut of human expression. Smiling, laughing, weeping, angry....

I start to move a little closer to have a better look at them, when a man suddenly leans out of the ticket booth. My pulse jumps into overtime.

"Ticket, please," he says.

I blink, looking at him, an old black man in a top hat, teeth gleaming in the moonlight.

"I don't have a ticket," I tell him.

"You need a ticket," he says.

"Where can I buy one?"

He laughs. "Not that kind of ticket, Spyboy."

Before I can ask him what he means, how he knows my name, the mists come flowing back, thick and impenetrable for a long moment. When they clear once more, I'm back in the alleyway. Or maybe I never left. The whole experience sits inside my head like a dream.

I look up to the roof of the Sovereign Building, remembering how it was last night. The door Sammy led me through is right here in front of me. I don't even hesitate, but open it up and start climbing the stairs. When I get out onto the roof, I walk across the gravel once more to where Sammy and I stood last night. The mists are back and I can see the wheel again through them, turning slowly, all the seats filled. I watch for a long time until the harlequin and the man with the blue moon for a head come into sight. The blue moon looks at me and lifts a hand.

There's something in that hand, a small slip of paper or cardboard. I step closer to the edge of the roof and see it's a ticket. I'm so caught up in the presence of the wheel and what the blue moon's holding, that the footsteps on the gravel behind me don't really register until someone calls my name.

"Spyboy."

I don't need to hear the French accent to know who it is. I turn to find the shooter standing there. He either doesn't see the wheel, or he's only got eyes for me.

"I have a message for you," he says. "From Madame Couteau."

I see the pistol in his hand, hanging by his side. As he starts to lift it, I turn and jump, launching myself towards the seat where the blue moon Sammy is holding my ticket.

And all those possibilities open up into new worlds.

Maybe I just hit the pavement below.

Maybe I take a bullet, still hit the pavement, but I'm dead before the impact.

Maybe I reached the wheel, hands slipping on the bone joints, my scrabbling feet finding purchase, allowing me to climb up into my seat, my face falling off like a mask to reveal another face underneath, made up like a harlequin. A carnival Spyboy.

Or maybe I never went to the Beanery that night, didn't meet Sammy, turned in early and went to work the next day.

They're all possible. Maybe somewhere, they're all true.

I sit there in the gently swaying seat and look out over a darkened carnival, out past the fields of corn stubble, into the mists where anything can happen, everything is true. I remember what Sammy told me last night, though it seems like an eternity ago.

You're thinking of the outside, he told me. *Concentrate on all the journeys you can take inside.*

I have, I had, a thousand thousand lives out there. Past, present, future, they're all happening at the same time in my head. This world, all the other worlds that are born every time I made a choice, all these lives that I can journey through inside my head.

I guess what I can't figure out is, which one is really mine. Either I'm living one of those lives and dreaming this, or I'm here and those lives belong to someone else, someone I once was, someone I could have been.

I sit there beside the blue moon Sammy, the ticket he gave me held in my hand, and I think about it as the wheel takes our seat up, all the way to where the stars are whispering and the Ferris wheel kisses the sky.

::SISTERS::

One: Appoline

I

It's not like on that TV show, you know where the cute blonde cheerleader type stakes all these vampires and they blow away into dust? For one thing, they don't disappear into dust, which would be way more convenient. Outside of life in televisionland, when you stake one, you've got this great big dead corpse to deal with, which is not fun. Beheading works, too, but that's just way too gross for me and you've still got to find some place to stash both a head and a body.

The trick is to not turn your victim in the first place—you know, drain all their blood so that they rise again. When that happens, you have to clean up after yourself, because a vamp is forever, and do you really want these losers you've been feeding on hanging around until the end of time? I don't think so.

The show gets a lot of other things wrong, too, but then most of the movies and books do. Vamps don't have a problem with mirrors (unless they're ugly and don't want to look at themselves, I suppose), crosses (unless they've got issues with Christianity), or garlic (except who likes to smell it on anybody's breath?). They don't have demons riding around inside them (unless they've got some kind of satanic inner child), they can't turn into bats or rats or wolves or mist (I mean, just look at the physics involved, right?) and sunlight doesn't bother them. No spontaneous combustion—they just run the same risk of skin cancer as anybody else.

I figure if the people writing the books and making the movies actually do have any firsthand experience with vampires, they're sugarcoating the information so that people don't freak out. If you're going to accept that they exist in the first place, it's much more comforting to believe that you're safe in the daylight, or that a cross or a fistful of garlic will keep them at bay.

About the only thing they do get right is that it takes a vamp to make a vamp. You do have to die from the bite and then rise again three days later. It's as easy as that. It's also the best time to kill a vamp—they're kind of like ragdolls, all loose and muddy-brained, for the first few hours.

Oh, and you do have to invite us into your house. If it's a public place, we can go in the same as anyone else.

What's that? No, that wasn't a slip of the tongue. I'm one, too. So while I like the TV show as much as the next person, and I know it's fiction, blonde cheerleader types still make me twitch a little.

2

Appoline Smith was raking yellow maple leaves into a pile on the front lawn when the old four-door sedan came to a stop at the curb. She looked up to find the driver staring at her. She didn't recognize him. He was just some old guy in his thirties who'd been watching way too many old *Miami Vice* reruns. His look—the dark hair slicked back, silk shirt opened to show off a big gold chain, fancy shades—was so been there it was prehistoric. The pair of dusty red-and-white velour dice hanging from the mirror did nothing to enhance his image.

"Why don't you just take a picture?" she asked him.

"Nobody likes a lippy kid," he said.

"Yeah, nobody likes a pervert either."

"I'm not some perv'."

"Oh really? What do you call a guy cruising a nice neighbourhood like this with his tongue hanging out whenever he sees some teenage girl?"

"I'm looking for A. Smith."

"Well, you found one."

"I mean, the initial 'A,' then 'Smith.'"

"You found that, too. So why don't you check it off on your life list and keep on driving."

The birder reference went right over his head. All things considered, she supposed most things would go over his head.

"I got something for you," he said.

He reached over to the passenger's side of the car's bench seat, then turned back to her and offered her an envelope. She supposed it had been white once. Looking at the dirt and a couple of greasy fingerprints smeared on it, she made no move to take it. The guy looked at her for a long moment, then shrugged and tossed it onto the lawn.

"Don't call the cops," he said and drove away.

As if they didn't have better things to do than chase after some guy in a car making pathetic attempts to flirt with girls he happened to spy as he drove around. He was one of just too many guys she'd met, thinking he was Lothario when he was just a loser.

She waited until he'd driven down the block and turned the corner before she stepped closer to look at the envelope he'd left on the lawn.

Okay, she thought, when she saw that it actually had "A. Smith" and the name of her street written on it. So maybe it wasn't random. Maybe he was only stalking her.

She picked up the envelope, holding it distastefully between two fingers.

"Who was in the car?"

She turned to see her little sister limping down the driveway towards her and quickly stuck the envelope in her jacket pocket.

"Just some guy," she told Cassie. "How're you doing?"

Cassie'd had a bad asthma attack this morning and was still lying down in the rec room watching videos when Apples had come out to rake leaves.

"I'm okay," Cassie told her. "And besides, I've got my buddy," she added, holding up her bronchodilator. "Can I help?"

"Sure. But only if you promise to take it easy."

It wasn't until a couple of hours later that Apples was able to open the envelope. She took it into the bathroom and slit the seal, pulling out a grimy sheet of paper with handwriting on it that read:

> I no yer secret. Meet me tonite at midnite at the cow castle, or they'll be trouble. I no you got a little sister.
>
> Don't call the cops. Don't tell nobody.

Okay, Apples thought, getting angry as she reread the note. The loser in the car just went from annoying pervert to a sick freak who needed to be dealt with.

Nobody threatened her little sister.

By "cow castle" she assumed he meant the Aberdeen Pavilion at Lansdowne Park, commonly known as the Cattle Castle because the cupola on its roof gave it a castle-like appearance. And though it was obviously a trap of some sort, she'd be there all the same. She couldn't begin to guess what he wanted from her, what he hoped to accomplish. It didn't matter. By threatening Cassie, he'd just gone to the head of her "deal with this" list.

3

Okay, here's the thing. I didn't ask to get turned, but it's not like we sat down and talked out how I felt about it. By the time it's over, I've been three days dead, I rise, and here I am, vamp girl, and I don't mean sexy, though I can play that card if I have to. Anybody can do it. It just needs the right clothes and makeup, with one secret ingredient: attitude.

It's funny. I didn't have too many friends before I got turned. I don't have so many now either, mind you, but now it's by choice. Getting turned gave me this boost of self-confidence, I guess, and that's really what people find attractive. Everybody's intrigued by someone comfortable in their own skin because most of us aren't.

The parents freaked, of course. Not because I'm a vamp—they still don't know that—but because so far as they know, I just did the big disappearing act the night I got turned. Went to a concert and came back home four days later. Trust me, that did not go over well. I was canned for a solid month, which made feeding a real pain—having to sneak out through a window between two A.M., when Dad finally goes to bed, and dawn to find what I can at that time of the night. I never much cared for booze or drugs when I was human and that's carried over to what I am now. I still hate the taste of it in someone's blood.

Yeah, I drink blood. But it's not as gross as it sounds. And it's not as messy as it is in some of the movies.

4

The Aberdeen Pavilion was a wonderfully eccentric building in the middle of Lansdowne Park where the Central Canadian Exhibition, the oldest agricultural fair in Canada, was held every year. The pavilion was the largest of the exhibition buildings that dotted the park, an enormous barn-like structure surrounded by parking lots, with an angled roof curved like a half-moon and topped with a cupola. For a city kid like Apples, going inside during the Ex had always been a wonderful experience. The air was redolent of farm smells—cattle, sheep, horses, hogs—and she'd loved to walk along the stalls to look at the livestock, or sit with Cassie on the wooden seats in the huge arena and watch the animals vying for first place ribbons.

Though she still took Cassie to the midway every August, she hadn't gone inside the pavilion for a couple of years now.

As she walked across a parking lot towards the Cattle Castle, Apples wondered if this was part of the freak's plan, if he knew that this was where she'd gotten turned. It had been right here, between the Cattle Castle and the Coliseum when she'd come to see a Bryan Adams concert a few years ago.

She didn't have to close her eyes to be able to visualize the woman, that first sight of her coming out from between the parked cars. Tall and svelte, with a loose walk that lay somewhere between the grace of a panther and a runway model. Golden blonde hair fountained over her shoulders and down her back in a spill of ringlets and she was dressed all in black: short velvet skirt, low-cut T-shirt and high-heeled ankle boots. Apples remembered two conflicting sensations: that this woman was so unbelievably gorgeous, and that no one else seemed to notice her.

"Come with me a moment," the woman said and without a word to her friends, Apples had left them to follow the stranger into a darker part of the parking lot.

And nothing was the same for Apples, not ever again.

I no your secret.

Maybe he did.

The area around the Cattle Castle appeared to be deserted, though there were a handful of cars in the parking lot. Apples recognized the sedan that had come by her house earlier in the day and walked in its direction. There was no one seated in it, but Apples could smell the driver. She assumed her semiliterate pervert was lying across the seat, waiting until she'd walked by so that he could jump out and take her by surprise.

That was okay. She had a surprise of her own. But first she wanted to know how he'd gotten her name and address. With her luck, somebody had put up a directory of known vamps Web site on the Internet and every would-be Van Helsing and Buffy was looking for her now.

She walked by the car and pretended to be shocked when he opened the door and confronted her, a gun in hand.

I hope you've got wooden bullets for that thing, she wanted to tell him, but she kept silent.

"Get in the car," he told her, waving the gun. "Not there," he added as she started to walk around to the passenger's side. "Behind the wheel. You can drive, right?"

To some remote location, Apples supposed. Where he'd have his nasty way with her. Or kill her. Probably, he planned to do both, hopefully in that order. Though technically, any physical relationship with her had to be classified as necrophilia. Ehew.

This whole business was so clichéd that she could only sigh. Still, a remote location would work for her, too.

She came back around to the driver's side and got in.

"Where to, gun boy?" she asked.

His face reddened and she watched the veins lift on his brow.

"This isn't some joke," he told her, waving the barrel of the gun in her face. "You're in way over your head now, kid."

Apples looked at him for a long beat.

"You still haven't said where to."

He frowned. "Just drive. I'll tell you where."

"Okay. You're the boss."

She started the car and put it in drive.

"Turn right after the gate," he told her.

She did as he told her, pulling out of the parking lot and turning right onto the Queen Elizabeth Driveway.

"So what's your deal?" she asked as they went under the Lansdowne Bridge at Bank Street and continued west.

"Shut up."

"Why? Are you going to shoot me? I'm driving the car, moron."

"Just shut up."

"Where'd you get my name and address?"

"I told you, just—"

"Shut up. Yeah, yeah. Except I'm not going to. So why don't you stop sounding like a skipping CD and tell me what your problem is."

"You're the problem," he said. "End of story."

"Maybe. Except where does it begin?"

They'd driven under the bridge at Bronson now and the Rideau Canal on their right became Dows Lake. She noticed that they'd started draining the water in the canal in preparation for winter.

"Take a right at the lights," he said, "and then a left on Carling."

"Not unless you start talking, I won't."

"I've got two words for you: Randall Gage."

"Those aren't words, they're a name. And they don't mean anything to me."

"You killed him."

Apples made the right onto Preston Street and stopped at the red light waiting for them at Carling Avenue. She turned to look at her captor.

"I'm not saying I did," she told him, "but how would you know anyway?"

She was always careful. There were never any witnesses.

"He told me you would."

"It's still not ringing any bells," she said.

The light went to green and she made the left turn onto Carling. She could smell the first telltale hint of nervousness coming from her captor, could almost read his mind:

Why's she so calm? Why isn't she scared?

Because I'm already dead, moron.

"Well?" Apples asked.

"Randall was about five-eight, a hundred-and-sixty pounds. Blonde, good looking guy. He used to come into the coffee shop where you work."

A face rose up in Apples's mind, sharp and sudden. She remembered Randall Gage now, remembered him all too well, though she hadn't known his name. After the first time he'd seen her at the Second Cup where she worked, he seemed to come in every time she had a shift. "A. Smith," he'd always read from her nametag, fishing for the first name, which she never gave him. Then he'd made the mistake of grabbing her after a late shift and forcing her into the back of his van. He'd bragged to her about other girls he'd snatched, how the last one hadn't survived, so if she wanted to live, she'd better just lie back and enjoy it, but no problem there, sweetcakes, because this he guaranteed, she was going to enjoy it.

Rather than find out, she'd drained him.

And then not been able to get back to where she'd stashed his body when his three days were up and he rose from the dead. She'd had to track him for most of the night before she finally found him trying to hide from the dawn in somebody's garden shed, the idiot. Like the sun was going to burn him.

"You still haven't explained how you got my address," she said.

"Legwork," her captor said.

"Or what you plan to do to me."

"Same as you did to Randall. Take the Queensway on-ramp," he added as they passed Kirkwood Avenue.

Apples felt like driving the car into the nearest lamppost, but then she reminded herself that whatever remote location he was directing her to would benefit her as well.

"He raped and killed a twelve-year-old girl," she said, her voice gone hard and cold.

Her captor shook his head. "He was never connected to anything."

"He *told* me he did, you moron."

"Don't matter. You still had no right to kill him."

"I never said I did."

"He told me you were coming for him—called me up, told me your name, where you worked, what you looked like."

Apples supposed that Gage hadn't bothered to explain that he was already dead by that point.

"So what's it to you?" she asked.

"He was my brother."

Now, that, Apples could understand.

5

Who turned me? I never learned her name. She just said she liked the look of me—the inside look of me. She drained me, took me away and watched over me for the three days until I rose as a vamp. Then she cut me loose.

Yeah, of course we talked before I went home to face the music. She filled me in on the rules and regs. I don't mean there's vamp police, running around handing out tickets if you do something wrong. There's just things you can do and things you can't and she straightened me out on them. Gave me the low-down on all the mythology. Useful stuff. She never did get into why she turned me besides what I've already told you, so your guess is as good as mine.

No, I never saw her again.

6

"How did I kill him?"

"What?"

"Your brother. How am I supposed to have killed him?"

They were on the Queensway now, the multiple lane divided highway that bisected the city running east to west. Apples kept to the speed limit—100 kilometers—but they were already passing Bayshore Shopping Centre and about to leave the city. The last few kilometers they'd ridden in silence. The surviving Gage sibling rested his gun on his thigh and stared out the front windshield. He turned to Apples.

"That's one of the things I need to know."

"Have you ever killed anybody?" she asked.

He shrugged. "A couple of guys. Once was in the middle of a holdup, the other time in jail. I never got connected to either one."

"How did it feel?"

"What the hell kind of a question is that?"

Apples shot him a glance. "Did it feel good? Did it feel righteous? Did you feel sad? Did it give you a hard-on?"

"How did it feel for you?"

"Like a waste."

"So you did kill Randall."

"I never said that."

"Anybody looks at you, they see this sweet little kid—what are you, sixteen?"

I was when I died, she thought. And she hadn't aged a day since. That wasn't causing problems yet, but it would soon. Still, she only had to wait one more year. That was when Cassie turned sixteen and she planned to turn her. The thing about vamps is, they don't get sick. And if you've got something wrong with you, it's gone once you're turned. Goodbye leg brace and asthma. Cassie didn't know it, but Apples planned for them to be sixteen together. Forever.

"I'm nineteen," she told Gage.

He nodded. "But everybody looks at you and just sees this sweet little kid. Nobody knows the monster hiding under your skin."

Apples shot him another look. That was about as good a way to put it as any. How much did he know? And how many people, if any, had he told?

"I guess you'd know all about monsters," she said. "Seeing how your little brother grew up to be one and you're not exactly an angel yourself."

Anger flickered in his eyes and the gun rose to point at her.

"You shoot me now," she reminded him, "and you're killing yourself as well."

"Just shut up and drive."
"I think we've already played that song."

7

So what are my weaknesses? You mean, beyond getting staked or beheaded? Hey, how stupid do I look? Figure it out for yourself.

Just kidding.

Apparently, the way it works is that whatever meant the most to you when you were alive, becomes anathema to you when you're dead. Not people, but things and ideas. So I guess if you did worship the sun, then it could fry you as a vamp. Same if you loved eating Italian, with all that garlic in the sauces. Or maybe you were way serious about church.

Here's a funny fact: pretty much any vampire turned in the past few decades can be warded off with chocolate. And if not chocolate, then some kind of junk food, not to mention cigarettes, coffee or beer. Junkies are probably the biggest problem for normal people since you can only ward them off with needles and drugs. There's not much by way of sacred icons anymore.

8

Apples kept following her captor's directions. Eventually they exited the Queensway and drove down increasingly small backroads in the rural area west of the city. When they finally reached a bumpy track that was only two ruts on the ground with branches raking the sides of the car, he had her stop.

"Get out," he said.

She did, stretching her back muscles and looking around her with interest. She didn't get out of the city much, but ever since she'd been turned, she'd had this real yearning to just run in the woods.

Gage slid across the bench seat and joined her on her side of the car, the gun leveled at her once more.

"So you killed Randall because he told you some B.S. story about boffing some twelve-year-old."

"Not to mention killing her."

"So how was that your business?"

"Well, call me crazy, but I take offence to misogynist morons hurting kids."

"So you're just some do-gooder."

"Not to mention his intention to do the same to me."

Gage gave a slow nod. "But I still don't get how you killed him. You're just some—"

"Slip of a girl. I know."

"With a big mouth."

He frowned at her. His nervousness was a stronger scent now, some animal part of his brain already registering what the rest of him hadn't worked out yet.

"I just don't get it," he said.

"And that's where you made your mistake," she told him. "That's the question you should have asked yourself before you ever came by my house with your little party invitation and threatening my little sister."

The gun rose, muzzle pointing at her head.

"You're way out of your league, kid."

"I don't know." She grinned, showing him a pair of fangs. "See, I'm faster than you."

Her hand moved in a blur of motion, plucking the gun from his hand and flinging it a half-dozen feet away.

"I'm stronger than you."

She grabbed his hand and twisted it, bending it up around his back, exerting pressure so that he couldn't move.

"And I'm hungry."

She bit his neck and the hollowed fangs sank deep. He began to jerk as she drew the blood up from his veins, but it was no use.

It never was.

Afterwards, she sat down by his body and began to talk, conversing with the corpse as though it was asking her questions. She took her time in responding. After all, they had three days to wait.

Normally she would have simply stashed the body and come back when it was time for it to rise, but considering the problems she'd already had with his brother, she didn't feel like tempting fate a second time with one of these Gage boys. She called home on her cell phone and luckily got the answering machine, which let her leave a message without having to explain too much. Her parents would still be mad when she got home, but hey, she was nineteen now, no matter how young she might look.

When she stashed the phone back in the pocket of her jacket, she went and found a good-sized branch that she could carve into a stake while she talked and waited.

9

Do I have any regrets? Sure. I can't have babies, for one thing. Well, yeah, I can still have sex. I just can't have a baby and that sucks. I always figured when I got old—you know, like in my twenties—I'd get married and have kids.

I miss eating, too. I mean, I can eat and drink the same as you, but I can't process it, so afterwards I have to go throw it up like some bulimic. It's so gross. Annalee—she works at the coffee shop with me—caught me doing it one time and it was really awkward. She's all, "Don't do this to yourself. Trust me, you're not fat. You need help to deal with it. It's nothing to be ashamed of."

"It's not what you think," I tell her. "I've just got a touch of stomach flu."

"Every time you eat you throw up," she says, and I'm thinking, what? Are you keeping tabs on me? How weird is that? But I know she just means well.

I guess the other thing I'm going to miss is growing old. I'll always look sixteen, but inside I age the same as you. What happens when I'm all old and ancient? The only guys that'll be my age—you know, in their thirties and forties—interested in being with me then are going to be these pedophile freaks. And who wants to hang out with sixteen-year-old boys forever?

But I didn't choose it and I'm not the kind to get all weepy and do myself in. I figure, if this is what I am, then I might as well make myself useful getting rid of losers like you and your brother. I guess I read too many superhero comics when I was a kid or something.

And I really want this chance to give Cassie a shot at a better life. Well, a different one, anyway. She deserves to see what it's like to walk around without her leg brace and bronchodilator.

Maybe she'll join me in this little crusade of mine, but it'll have to be her choice. Just like getting turned has to be her choice. I'll give her the skinny, the bad and the good, and she can decide. And it's not like we *have* to kill anybody. I only do it when losers like you don't leave me any choice. Most times, I just feed on someone until they get so weak they just can't hurt anybody for a long time. I check up on them from time to time—a girl gets hungry, after all—and if they've gone back to their evil ways, I turn them into these anemics again. They usually figure it out. When they don't...well, that's what stakes are for, right?

My weakness? I guess I can tell you that. It's anything to do with Easter. I used to be an Easter maniac—I loved every bit of it. I guess because it's like Halloween, a serious candy holiday, but without the costumes. I was never one for dressing up and scary stuff never turned me on. Good thing, the way things worked out. Imagine if the very thought of vamps and ghouls was my nemesis. I'd be long gone by now. But Easter's tough. I have to avoid the stores—which is not easy, but better than trying to avoid Christmas—and play sick on the day itself.

10

Apples saw Gage's eyes move under his lids. She didn't get up from where she was kneeling on the ground beside his shoulder, just reached over for her now-sharpened stake and lifted it. Gage's eyes opened.

"How…how do you live with yourself…?" he asked.

Apples shivered. She'd never stopped to think that he could actually hear everything she'd been saying. She'd only talked to pass the time. Because there was no one else she could talk to about it.

"The only other choice is where you're going," she said.

"I welcome it."

When he said that, forgotten memories returned to her. The nightmare she'd had to undergo through her own three days of change from dead human to what she was now. It was like swimming through mud, trying to escape the clinging knowledge of the worst that people were capable of doing to each other, but drowning in it at the same time. Not for three days, but for what felt like an eternity. It had been such a horrifying experience that the only way she'd managed to deal with it was by simply blocking it away.

How had she forgotten?

Better yet, how could she forget it again? The sooner the better.

"That's because you're a loser," she said.

"And you're going to do this to your sister."

"You don't know anything about me or my sister!"

She brought the stake down harder than necessary. Long after he was dead, she was still leaning over him, pressing the stake down.

Finally, she let it go and rocked back onto her ankles. She got up and dragged his body back into the car, wiped the vehicle down for any fingerprints she might have left in it. She soaked a rag in gas, stuck it in the gas tank, and lit it.

She was out of sight of the car and walking fast when the explosion came. She didn't turn to look, but only kept walking. Her mind was in that dark place Gage had called back into existence.

How could she put Cassie through that?

But how could she go on, forever, alone?

For the first time since she'd been turned, she didn't know what to do.

Two: Cassandra

Apples has a secret and I know what it is.

Her real name's Appoline, but everybody calls her Apples, just like they call me Cassie instead of Cassandra, except for Mom. She always calls us by our given names. But that's not the secret. It's way bigger than having some weird name.

My sister is so cool—not like I could ever be.

I was born with a congenital birth defect that left me with one leg shorter than the other so I have to wear this Frankenstein monster leg brace all the time. At least that's what the kids call it. "Here comes the bride of Frankenstein," they used to say when I came out for recess—I was always last to get outside. I'm glad Apples doesn't know, because she'd beat the crap out of them and you can't do that just 'cause people call you names.

I've also got asthma real bad, so I always have to carry my puffer around with me. Even if I didn't have the leg brace and could run, the asthma wouldn't let me. I get short of breath whenever I try to do anything too strenuous, but I'm lucky 'cause I've only had to go to the hospital a few times when an attack got too severe.

I know you shouldn't judge people by their physical attributes, but we all do, don't we? And if you just aren't capable of simple things like walking or breathing properly, you're not even in the running so far as most people are concerned. People see any kind of a disability and they immediately think your brain's disabled as well. They talk to me slower and never really listen to what I'm saying.

Oh, I'm not feeling sorry for myself. Honest. I'm just being pragmatic. I'm always going to be this dorky kid with the bum leg who can't breathe. I could live to be eighty years old, with a whole life behind me, but inside, that's who I'll always be.

But Apples has never seen or treated me that way, not even when we have a fight, which isn't that often anyway. I know that sounds odd, because siblings are just naturally supposed to argue and fight, but we don't. We get along and share pretty much everything. Or at least we did up until the night of that Bryan Adams concert. She went with a bunch of friends and then didn't come back from it until four days later. Boy, were Mom and Dad mad. I was just really worried, and then I guess I felt hurt because she wouldn't tell me where she'd been.

"It's not that I won't," she'd tell me. "It's that I can't. That chunk of time is just like this big black hole in my head."

But I know she remembers something from it. She just doesn't think I can handle whatever it was.

And that was when she changed. Not slowly, over time, like everybody does, you get older, you stop playing with Barbies, start listening to real music. But bang, all of a sudden. She was always fun, but after that four-day-long night out, she became this breezy, confident person that I still adored, but felt I had to get to know all over again.

That wouldn't be a problem, but she also got all *X-Files*, too. All mysterious about simple things. Like I'll never forget her face when I announced just before dinner one day that I was now a vegetarian. I simply couldn't condone the slaughter of innocent animals just so that I could live. "You are what you eat," I told them, not understanding Apples's anguished expression until much later.

And Easter was particularly weird when it came around the following year. Used to be her favourite holiday, bar none, but that year she claimed she'd developed a phobia towards it and wouldn't have anything to do with any of it. When Dad asked why, she said with more exasperation than usual, "That's why they call it a phobia, Dad. It's an *unreasonable* fear."

Okay, maybe those aren't the best examples, but when you add everything together. Like there was this period when I thought she was bulimic, but although she was throwing up a lot after meals, she didn't have any of the other symptoms. She never seems overly concerned about her weight, she doesn't lose weight. In fact, she just seems to keep getting stronger and healthier all the time. So I couldn't figure out what and where she was eating.

She also stopped having a period. I caught her throwing out unused tampons one day around the time she was usually menstruating, so I watched out for it the next month, but she threw them out then, too, like she didn't want anyone to know that she wasn't still using them. It seemed unlikely that she was pregnant—and as the months went by, it was obvious she wasn't—and she sure couldn't be hitting menopause.

By now you're thinking I'm this creepy kid, always spying on my sister, but it's not like that. I came across all these things by accident. The only reason I looked further into them was that I was worried. Wouldn't you have been, if it was happening to your sister? And the worst was I had no one to talk to about it. I couldn't bring it up with my parents, I sure wasn't going to talk about it to anyone outside of the family, and I couldn't begin to think of a way to ask Apples herself. I couldn't follow her around either, not with my leg brace and having to catch my breath all the time. So while I know she snuck out at night, I could never follow to see where she was going, what she was doing.

I got to thinking, maybe I should write one of those anonymous letters to an advice columnist. The only reason I thought of that is that I'm just this help column junkie—Dear Abby, Ann Landers, the "Sex & Body" and "Hard Questions" columns in *Seventeen.* My favourite is Dan Savage's "Savage Love" which runs in *XPress,* our local alternative weekly, though Mom and Dad'd probably kill me if they knew I was reading it. I mean, it's all about sex and gay stuff and I know I'm never going to have a boyfriend—who wants the Frankenstein monster on their arm?—but I still figure it's stuff I should know.

Imagine writing in to one of them with my problem. I'd try Dan first.

> Dear Dan,
>
> My sister doesn't eat or menstruate anymore, but she's not losing weight, nor is she pregnant. She has a phobia about Easter and sneaks out of the house late at night, going I don't know where.
>
> I'm not trying to butt into her life, but I'm really worried. What do you think is wrong with her? What can I do?
>
> Confused in Ottawa

What's wrong with her? I started to think that the answer lay in one of those cheesy old sci-fi or horror movies that they run late at night. That she'd become a pod person or a secret monster of some kind. Except not in a bad way. She's not mean to me, or anyone else that I can see. She's just...weird.

And then on my sixteenth birthday, I find out. It's after the big dinner and presents and everything. I'm lying on my bed, looking up at the ceiling and trying to figure out why I don't feel different—I mean, turning sixteen's supposed to be a big deal, right?—when Apples comes in and closes the door behind her. I scoot up so that I'm leaning against a pillow propped up at my headboard. She props the other pillow up and lies down beside me. We've done this a thousand times, but tonight it feels different.

"I've got something to tell you," she says and my head fills up with worry and questions that only gets worse when she goes on to add, "I'm a vampire."

I turn to look at her.

"Oh, please."

"No, really," she says.

As she starts to explain how it all began after that concert when she did her four-day mystery jaunt, all the oddities and weirdnesses of the past few years start to make sense—or at least they make sense if I'm willing to accept the basic premise that my sister's turned into a teenage Draculetta.

"Why didn't you ever tell me before?" I ask.

"I wanted to wait until you were the same age as I was when I...got turned."

"But *why*?"

"Because I want to turn you."

She's sitting cross-legged on the bed now, facing me, her face so earnest.

"If you get changed," she goes on, "you can get rid of both your leg brace and your puffer."

"Really?"

I can't imagine life without them. The chance to be normal. Then I catch myself. Normal, but dead.

But Apples is nodding, a big grin stretching her lips. She holds out her right hand, pointer finger extended.

"Remember when I lost my nail in volleyball practice?" she asks. "The whole thing came right off."

I nod. It was so gross.

"Well, look," she says, still waving her finger in front of my face. "It's all healed."

"Apples," I say. "That was four years ago. Of *course* it's healed."

"I mean it healed when I changed. I had no fingernail the night I went to the concert, but there it was when I came back four days later. The...woman who changed me, she said the change heals anything."

"So you're just going to bite me or something and I become like you?"

She nods. "But we have to work this out just right. It takes three days before you're changed, so we'll have to figure out how and where we can do that so that no one gets suspicious. But don't worry. I'll be there for you the whole time, watching over you."

"And then we'll live forever?"

"Forever sixteen."

"What about Mom and Dad?"

"We can't tell them," she says. "How could we even begin to explain this to them?"

"You're explaining it to me."

But she shakes her head. "They wouldn't understand—how could they?"

"The same way you think I can."

"It's not the same."

"So we live forever, but Mom and Dad just get old and die?"

She gets this look on her face that tells me she never thought it out that far.

"We can't change everybody," she says after a long moment.

"Why not?"

"Because then there'd be no one left for us to...."

"What?" I ask when her voice trails off.

She doesn't say anything for a long moment, won't meet my gaze.

"To feed on," she says finally. I guess I pull a face, because she quickly adds, "It's not as bad as it sounds."

She's already told me a whole lot of things about the differences between real vamps and the ones in the books and movies, but drinking blood's still part of the deal and I'm sorry, but it still sounds gross.

Apples get up from the bed. She looks—I don't know. Embarrassed. Sad. Confused.

"I guess you need some time to process all of this stuff I've been telling you," she says.

I give her a slow nod. I'd say something, but I don't know what. I feel kind of overloaded.

"Okay, then," she says and she leaves me in my bedroom.

I slouch back down on the bed and stare at the ceiling again, thinking about everything she's told me.

My sister's a vampire. How weird is that?

Does she still have a soul?

I guess that's a bizarre question in some ways. I mean, do any of us have souls? It's like asking, Who is God? I guess. The best answer I've heard to that is when Deepak Chopra says, "Who is asking?" It makes sense that God would be different to different people, but also different to you, depending on who you are at the time you're asking.

I guess I believe we have souls. And when we die, they go on. But what that means for Apples, I don't know. She's dead, but she's still here.

She's different now—but she's still the big sister I knew growing up. There's just *more* to her now. Maybe it's like asking "Who is God?" She's who she is depending on who I am when I'm wondering about her.

Sometimes I think it's only kids that wonder about existential stuff like this. Grown-ups always seem to be worried about money, or politics, or just stuff that has physical presence. It's like somewhere along the way they lost the ability to think about what's inside them.

Here's a story I like: One day Ramakrishna, this big-time spiritual leader back in the nineteenth century, is praying, when he suddenly has this flash that what he's doing is meaningless. He's looking for God, but already everything is God—the rituals he's using, the idols, the floor under him, the walls, *everything.* Wherever he looks, he sees God. And he's just so blown away by this, he can't find the words to express it. All he can do is dance, like, for hours. This joyful Snoopy whirling and dervishing and spinning.

I just love the image of that—some old wise man in flowing robes, just getting up and dancing.

I'd love to be able to dance. I love music. I love the way I can feel it in every pore of my body. When your body's moving to the music, it's like you're part of the music. You're not just dancing to it anymore, you're somehow helping to create it at the same time.

But the most I can do is sort of shuffle around until I get all out of breath and I never let anyone see me trying to do it. Not even Apples.

Boy, can she dance. Every movement she makes is just so liquid and smooth. She's graceful just getting up from a chair or crossing a room. And I don't say this because of the contrast between us.

But none of this helps with what she's told me. All I can do is feel the weight of the door that she closed behind her and stare at the ceiling, my head full of a bewildering confusion.

Normally when I have something I can't work out, Apples is the one who helps me deal. But now she's the problem....

Did you ever play the game of if you could only have one wish, what would you wish for? It's so hard to decide, isn't it? But I know what I would do. I would wish that all my wishes come true.

But real life isn't like that. And too often you find that the things you think you really, really want, are the last things in the world that you should get.

I've always wanted to be able to walk without my leg brace, to run and jump and dance and just be normal. And breathing. Everybody takes it for granted. Well, I wish I could. And here's my chance. Except it comes with a price, just like in all those old fairy tales I used to read as a kid.

I have to choose. Go on like I am, a defect, a loser—at least in other people's eyes. Or be like Apples, full of life and vigor, and live forever. Except to do that I've got to drink other people's blood and everybody else I care about will eventually get old and die.

What kind of a choice is that?

This is the hardest thing I've ever had to try to work out.

I get Mom to drive me to the mall the next day. I know she worries about me being out on my own, but she's good about it. She reminds me not to overexert myself and we arrange what door she'll meet me at in a couple of hours, and then I'm on my own.

I don't want to go shopping. I just want to sit someplace on my own and there's no better place to do that than in the middle of a bunch of strangers like in the concourse of this mall.

I watch the people go by and find myself staring at their throats. I can't imagine drinking their blood. And then there's this whole business that Apples explained about how she only feeds on bad people. That just makes me feel sicker. When she told me that, all I could think about was that time at dinner when I announced I was becoming a vegetarian and the look on her face when I told them why.

You are what you eat.

I don't want the blood of some *freak serial killer nourishing me. I don't even want the blood of a jaywalker in me.*

After awhile I make myself stop thinking. I do the people-watching thing, enjoying the way all these people are hurrying by my little island bench seat.

But of course, as soon as I start to relax a little, some middle-aged freak in a trenchcoat has to sit down beside me, putting his lame moves on me. He walks by, once, twice, checks out the leg brace, sees I'm alone, and then he's on the bench and it's "That's such a beautiful blouse—what kind of material is it made of?" and he's reaching over and rubbing the sleeve between his fingers....

If I was Apples, with this vamp strength she was telling me about, I could probably knock him on his ass before he even knew what was happening. Or I could at least run away. But all I can do is shrink away from him, feeling scared, until I see one of the mall's rent-a-cops coming.

"Officer!" I yell. They're all wanna-be-cops and love it when you act like they're real policemen.

The pervert beside me jumps up from the bench and bolts down the hall before the security guard even looks in my direction. But that's okay. I don't want a scene. I just want to be left alone.

"Was he bothering you?" the guard asks.

I see him take it in. The leg brace. Me, so obviously helpless—and damn it, it's true. And he's all solicitous and pretty nice, actually. He asks if I'm on my own and when I tell him I'm meeting my mom later, offers to walk me to the door where I'm supposed to meet her.

I take him up on it, but I'm thinking, it doesn't have to be this way. If I let Apples change me, nobody will ever bother me again. It'd be like my own private human genome project. Only maybe I'm not supposed to be healthy. I keep thinking that maybe my asthma and bad leg are compensating for some other talent that just hasn't shown up yet.

I think of people throughout history who've overcome their handicaps to give us things that no one but they could have. Stephen Hawking. Vincent Van Gogh with his depressions. Terry Fox. Teddy Roosevelt. Stevie Wonder. Helen Keller.

I'm not saying that they had to be handicapped to share their gifts with us, but if they hadn't been handicapped, maybe they would have gone on to be other people and not become the inspirations or creative people they came to be.

And I'm not saying I'm super smart or talented, or that I'm going to grow up and change the world. But it doesn't seem right to just become something else. I won't have earned it. It's just too...too easy, I guess.

"There's a reason why I am the way I am," I tell Apples later.

We're sitting in the rec room, the TV turned to MuchMusic, but neither of us are really watching the Christina Aguilera video that's playing. Dad's in the kitchen, making dinner. Mom's out in the garden, planting tulip and crocus bulbs.

"You mean like it's all part of God's plan?" Apples asks.

"No. I don't know that I believe in God. But I believe everything has a purpose."

Apples shakes her head. "You can't tell me you believe your asthma and your leg are a good thing."

"It might seem like they weaken me, but they actually make me strong. Maybe not physically, but in my heart and spirit."

Apples sighs and pulls me close to her. "You always were a space case," she says into my hair. "But I guess that's part of the reason I love you as much as I do."

I pull back so that we can look at each other.

"I don't want you to change me," I say.

Apples has always been good at hiding what she's feeling, but she can't hide the disappointment from me.

"I'm sorry," I tell her.

"Don't be," she says. "You need to do what's right for you."

"I feel like I'm letting you down."

"Cassie," she says. "You could never let me down."

But she moved out of the house the next day.

Three: Appoline

Life sucks.

Or maybe I should say, death sucks, since I'm not really alive—but everybody thinks death sucks because for them it's the big end. So that doesn't work either.

Okay. How about this: undeath sucks.

Or at least mine does.

I had to move out of the house. After four years of waiting to be able to change Cassie, I just couldn't live there anymore once she turned me down. I can't believe how much I miss her. I miss the parents, too, but it's not the same. I've never been as close to them as Cassie is. But I adore her and talking on the phone and seeing her a couple of times a week just isn't enough.

Trouble is, when I do see her or talk to her, that hurts, too. Everything just seems to hurt these days.

I've been thinking a lot about Sandy Browning, my best friend in grade school. We were inseparable until we got into junior high. That's when she starting getting into these black moods. Half the time you couldn't see them coming. It was like these black clouds would drift in from nowhere and just envelop her. When I discovered she was cutting herself—her arms and stomach were criss-crossed with dozens of little scars—I couldn't deal with it and we sort of drifted apart.

There's two reasons people become cutters, she told me once, trying to explain. There's those that can't feel anything—the cutting makes them feels alive. And then there are the ones like her, who have this great weight of darkness and despair inside them. The cutting lets it out.

I couldn't really get it at the time—I couldn't imagine having that kind of a bleak shadow swelling inside me—but I understand her now. Ever since Cassie turned me down, I've got this pressure inside me that won't ease and I feel like the only way I can release it is to open a hole to let it out. But it doesn't work for me. The one time I ran a razor blade along the inside of my forearm, it hardly bled at all and the cut immediately started to seal up. Within half an hour, there wasn't a mark on my skin.

Sandy had been completely addicted to it. Her family moved away the year before I became a vamp and I don't know what ever happened to her. I wish I'd been a better friend. I wish a lot of things these days.

I wish I'd never talked to Cassie about my wanting to turn her.

Sometimes I wonder: did I want to do it for her, so that she could finally put aside the limitations of her physical ailments, or did I do it for me, so I wouldn't have to be alone?

I guess it doesn't matter.

I'm sure alone now.

I live in a tiny apartment above the Herb and Spice Natural Foods shop on Bank Street. I like the area. During the day, it's like a normal neighbourhood with shops along Bank Street—video store, comic book shop, gay bookstore, restaurants—and mostly residential buildings in behind on the side streets. But come the night, the blocks up north around the clubs like Barrymore's become prime hunting grounds for someone like me. All the would-be toughs, the scavengers and the hunters, come out of the woodwork, hoping to prey on the people who come to check out the bands and the scene.

And I prey on them.

But even stopping them from having their wicked way doesn't really mean all that much anymore. I'm too lonely. It's not that I can't make friends. Ever since I got turned, that's the least of my problems. It's that I don't have a foundation of normalcy to return to anymore. I don't have a home and family. I just have my apartment. My job at the coffee shop. My hunting. I can't seem to get close to anyone because as soon as I do, I remember that I'm going to be like I am forever, while they age and die. Sometimes I imagine I can see them aging, that I can see the cells dying. It's even worse when I'm back home, seeing it happen to Cassie and my parents, so it's not like I can move back there again either.

That's when I decide it's time to track down the woman who turned me.

It's harder than I think. I don't really know where to start. Because she found me outside a concert at the Civic Centre, I spend most of December and January going to the clubs and concerts, thinking it's my best chance. Zaphod Beeblebrox 2 closes down at the end of November, but Barrymore's is still just up the street from where I live, so I drop in there almost every night, sliding past the doorman like I'm not even there. I can almost be invisible if I don't want to be noticed—don't ask me how that works. That's probably why I can't find the woman, but I don't give up trying.

I frequent the Market area, checking out the Rainbow and the Mercury Lounge, the original Zaphod's and places like that. Cool places where I think she might hang out. I go to the National Arts Centre for classical recitals and the Anti-Land Mines concert in early December. To Centrepoint Theatre in Nepean. Further west to the Corel Centre. I even catch a ride up to Wakefield, to the Black Sheep Inn, for a few concerts.

This calls for more serious cash than I can get from my salary at the coffee shop and the meager tips we share there, so I take to lifting the wallets of my victims, leaving them with less cash as well as less blood. My self-esteem's taking a nosedive, what with already being depressed, making no headway on finding the woman, and having become this petty criminal as well as the occasional murderer—I ended up having to kill another guy when I discovered he was raping his little sister and I got so mad, I just drained him.

It's weird. I exude confidence—I know I do from other people's reactions to me, and it's not like I'm unaware of how well I can take care of myself. But my internal life's such a mess that sometimes I can't figure out how I make it through the day with my mind still in one piece. I feel like such a loser.

I have this to look forward to forever?

Cassie's the only one who picks up on it.

"What's the matter?" she asks when I stop by for a visit during her Christmas holidays.

"Nothing," I tell her.

"Right. That's why you're so mopey whenever I see you." She doesn't look at me for a moment. When she does look back, she has this little wrinkle between her eyes. "It's because of me, isn't it? Because I didn't want to become a…to be like…."

"Me," I say, filling in for her. "A monster."

"You're not a monster."

"So what am I? Nothing anybody else'd ever choose to be."

"You didn't choose to be it either," she says.

"No kidding. And I don't blame you. Who'd ever *want* to be like this?"

She doesn't have an answer and neither do I.

Then one frosty January evening I'm walking home from the coffee shop and I see her sitting at a window table of the Royal Oak. I stop and look at her through the glass, struck again by how gorgeous she is, how no one else seems to be aware of it, of her. I go inside when she beckons to me. Today she's casual chic: jeans, a black cotton sweater, cowboy boots. Like me, she probably doesn't feel the cold anymore, but she has a winter coat draped over the back of her chair. There's a pint glass in front of her, half full of amber beer.

"Have a seat," she says, indicating the empty chair across from her.

I do. I don't know what to do with my hands. I don't know where to look. I want to stare at her. I want to pretend I'm cool, that this is no big deal. But it is.

"I've been looking for you," I finally say.

"Have you now."

I nod. Ignoring the hint of amusement in her eyes, I start to ask, "I need to know—"

"No, don't tell me," she says, interrupting. "Let me guess. First you tried to turn…oh, your best friend, or maybe a brother or a sister, and they turned you down and made you feel like a monster even though you only feed on the wicked. But somehow, even that doesn't feel right anymore. So now you want to end it all. Or at least get an explanation as to why I turned you."

I find myself nodding.

"We all go through this," she says. "But sooner or later—if we survive—we learn to leave all the old ties behind: friends, family, ideas of right and wrong. We become what we are meant to be. Predators."

I think of how I wanted to turn Cassie and start to feel a little sick. Up until this moment, her refusing to be turned had seemed such a personal blow. Now I'm just grateful that of the two of us, she, at least, had some common sense. Bad enough that one of us is a monster.

"What if I don't want to be a predator?" I ask.

The woman shrugs. "Then you die."

"I thought we couldn't die."

"To all intents and purposes," she says. "But we're not invincible. Yes, we heal fast, but it's genetic healing. We can deal with illnesses and broken bones, torn tissues and birth defects. But if a car hits us, if we take a bullet or a stake in the heart or head, if we're hurt in such a way that our accelerated healing faculties don't have the chance to help us, we can still die. We don't need Van Helsings or chipper cheerleaders in short skirts to do us in. Crossing the street at the wrong time can be just as effective."

"Why did you turn me?"

"Why not?"

All I can do is stare at her.

"Oh, don't take it so dramatically," she says. "I know you'd like a better reason than that—how I saw something special in you, how you have some destiny. But the truth is, it was for my own amusement."

"So it was just a…whim."

"You need to stop being so serious about everything," she tells me. "We're a different species. The old rules don't apply to us."

"So you just do whatever you want?"

She smiles, a predatory smile. "If I can get away with it."

"I'm not going to be like that."

"Of course you won't," she says. "You're different. You're special."

I shake my head. "No, I'm just stronger. I'm going to hold onto my ideals."

"Tell me that again in a hundred years," she says. "Tell me how strong you feel when anything you ever cared about, when everybody you love is long dead and gone."

I get up to leave, to walk out on her, but she beats me to it. She stands over me, and touches my hair with her long cool fingers. For a moment I imagine I see a kind of tenderness in her eyes, but then the mockery is back.

"You'll see," she says.

I stay at the table and watch her step outside. Watch her back as she walks on up Bank Street. Watch until she's long gone and there are only strangers passing by the windows of the Royal Oak.

The thing that scares me the most is that maybe she's right.

I realize leaving home wasn't the answer. I'm still too close to the people I love. I have to go a lot farther than I have so far. I have to keep moving and not make friends. Forget I have family. If I don't have to watch the people I love age and die, then maybe I won't become as cynical and bitter as the woman who made me what I am.

But the more I think of it, the more I feel that I'd be a lot better off just dying for real.

Four: Cassandra

In the end, I did it for Apples, though she doesn't know that. I don't think I can ever tell her that. She thinks I did it to be able to run and breathe and be as normal as an undead person can be. But I could see how being what she is and all alone was tearing her apart and I started to think, who do I love the best in the world? Who's always been there for me? Who stayed in with her weak kid sister when she could have been out having fun? Who never complained about taking me anywhere? Who always, *genuinely* enjoyed the time she spent with me?

She never said anything to me about what she was going through, but I could see the loneliness tearing at her and I couldn't let her be on her own anymore. I started to get scared that she might take off for good, or do something to herself, and how could I live with that?

Besides, maybe this *is* my destiny. Maybe with our enhanced abilities we can be some kind of dynamic duo superhero team, out rescuing the world, or at least little human pieces of the world.

The funny thing is, when I told her I wanted her to turn me, she was the one who argued against it. But I wouldn't take no and she finally gave in.

And it's not so bad. Even the blood-sucking's not so bad, though I do miss eating and drinking. I guess the worst part was those three days I was dead.

You're aware, but not aware, floating in some kind of goopy muck that feels like it's made up of all the bad things people have ever done or thought.

But you get over it.

What's my fear? Fuzzy animal slippers. I used to adore them, back when I was alive. Even at sixteen years old, I was still wearing them around the house. Now I break into a cold sweat just thinking about them.

Pretty lame, huh? But I guess it's a better weakness than some you can have. Because, really. How often do you unexpectedly run into someone wearing fuzzy animal slippers?

I still have this idea that we should turn Mom and Dad, too, but I'm going to wait awhile before I bring it up again. I think I understand Apples's nervousness better after she told me what she learned the last time she saw the woman who turned her. I don't think it's that she doesn't love our parents. She's just nervous that they won't make the transition well. That they'll be more like the woman than us.

"Let's give it a year or two," she said, "till we see how we do ourselves."

Mom and Dad sure weren't happy about me moving out and into Apples's apartment. I wish I could at least tell them that I'm not sick anymore, but I'm kind of stuck having a secret identity whenever we go back home for a visit. I have to carry around my puffer and pretend to use it. I have to put the leg brace on again, though we had to adjust it since my leg's all healed.

What's going to happen to us? I don't know. I just know that we'll be together. Always. And I guess, for now, that's enough.

::PAL O' MINE::

1

GINA ALWAYS BELIEVED there was magic in the world. "But it doesn't work the way it does in fairy tales," she told me. "It doesn't save us. We have to save ourselves."

2

One of the things I keep coming back to when I think of Gina is walking down Yoors Street on a cold, snowy Christmas Eve during our last year of high school. We were out Christmas shopping. I'd been finished and had my presents all wrapped during the first week of December, but Gina had waited for the last minute as usual, which was why we were out braving the storm that afternoon.

I was wrapped in as many layers of clothes as I could fit under my overcoat and looked about twice my size, but Gina was just scuffling along beside me in her usual cowboy boots and jeans, a floppy felt hat pressing down her dark curls and her hands thrust deep into the pockets of her pea jacket. She simply didn't pay any attention to the cold. Gina was good at that: ignoring inconveniences, or things she wasn't particularly interested in dealing with, much the way—I was eventually forced to admit—that I'd taught myself to ignore the dark current that was always present, running just under the surface of her exuberantly good moods.

"You know what I like best about the city?" she asked as we waited for the light to change where Yoors crosses Bunnett.

I shook my head.

"Looking up. There's a whole other world living up there."

I followed her gaze and at first I didn't know what she was going on about. I looked through breaks in the gusts of snow that billowed around us, but couldn't detect anything out of the ordinary. I saw only rooftops and chimneys, multi-coloured Christmas decorations and the black strands of cable that ran in sagging geometric lines from the power poles to the buildings.

"What're you talking about?" I asked.

"The 'goyles," Gina said.

I gave her a blank look, no closer to understanding what she was talking about than I'd been before.

"The gargoyles, Sue," she repeated patiently. "Almost every building in this part of the city has got them, perched up there by the rooflines, looking down on us."

Once she'd pointed them out to me, I found it hard to believe that I'd never noticed them before. On that corner alone there were at least a half-dozen grotesque examples. I saw one in the archway keystone of the Annaheim Building directly across the street—a leering monstrous face, part lion, part bat, part man. Higher up, and all around, other nightmare faces peered down at us, from the corners of buildings, hidden in the frieze and cornice designs, cunningly nestled in corner brackets and the stone roof cresting. Every building had them. *Every* building.

Their presence shocked me. It's not that I was unaware of their existence—after all, I was planning on architecture as a major in college; it's just that if someone had mentioned gargoyles to me before that day, I would have automatically thought of the cathedrals and castles of Europe—not ordinary office buildings in Newford.

"I can't believe I never noticed them before," I told her.

"There are people who live their whole lives here and never see them," Gina said.

"How's that possible?"

Gina smiled. "It's because of where they are—looking down at us from just above our normal sightline. People in the city hardly ever look up."

"But still. . . ."

"I know. It's something, isn't it? It really is a whole different world. Imagine being able to live your entire life in the middle of the city and never be noticed by anybody."

"Like a baglady," I said.

Gina nodded. "Sort of. Except people wouldn't ignore you because you're some pathetic street person that they want to avoid. They'd ignore you because they simply couldn't *see* you."

That thought gave me a creepy feeling and I couldn't suppress a shiver, but I could tell that Gina was intrigued with the idea. She was staring at that one gargoyle, above the entrance to the Annaheim Building.

"You really like those things, don't you?" I said.

Gina turned to look at me, an expression I couldn't read sitting in the back of her eyes.

"I wish I lived in their world," she told me.

She held my gaze with that strange look in her eyes for a long heartbeat. Then the light changed and she laughed, breaking the mood. Slipping her arm in mine, she started us off across the street to finish her Christmas shopping.

When we stood on the pavement in front of the Annaheim Building, she stopped and looked up at the gargoyle. I craned my neck and tried to give it a good look myself, but it was hard to see because of all the blowing snow.

Gina laughed suddenly. "It knows we were talking about it."

"What do you mean?"

"It just winked at us."

I hadn't seen anything, but then I always seemed to be looking exactly the wrong way, or perhaps *in* the wrong way, whenever Gina tried to point out some magical thing to me. She was so serious about it.

"Did you see?" Gina asked.

"I'm not sure," I told her. "I think I saw something...."

Falling snow. The side of a building. And stone statuary that was pretty amazing in and of itself without the need to be animated as well. I looked up at the gargoyle again, trying to see what Gina had seen.

I wish I lived in their world.

It wasn't until years later that I finally understood what she'd meant by that.

3

Christmas wasn't the same for me as for most people—not even when I was a kid: my dad was born on Christmas day; Granny Ashworth, his mother, died on Christmas day when I was nine; and my own birthday is December twenty-seventh. It made for a strange brew come the holiday season, part celebration, part mourning, liberally mixed with all the paraphernalia that means Christmas: eggnog and glittering lights, caroling, ornaments and, of course, presents.

Christmas wasn't centered around presents for me. Easy to say, I suppose, seeing how I grew up in the Beaches, wanting for nothing, but it's true. What enamoured me the most about the season, once I got beyond the confusion of birthdays and mourning, was the idea of what it was supposed to be: peace and goodwill to all. The traditions. The idea of the miracle birth the way it was told in *the Bible* and more secular legends like the one about how for one hour after midnight on Christmas Eve, animals were given human voices so that they could praise the baby Jesus.

I remember staying up late the year I turned eleven, sitting up in bed with my cat on my lap and watching the clock, determined to hear Chelsea speak, except I fell asleep sometime after eleven and never did find out if she could or not. By the time Christmas came around the next year I was too old to believe in that sort of thing anymore.

Gina never got too old. I remember years later when she got her dog Fritzie, she told me, "You know what I like the best about him? The stories he tells me."

"Your dog tells you stories," I said slowly.

"Everything's got a voice," Gina told me. "You just have to learn how to hear it."

4

The best present I ever got was the Christmas that Gina decided to be my friend. I'd been going to a private school and hated it. Everything about it was so stiff and proper. Even though we were only children, it was still all about money and social standing and it drove me mad. I'd see the public school kids and they seemed so free compared to all the boundaries I perceived to be compartmentalizing my own life.

I pestered my mother for the entire summer I was nine until she finally relented and let me take the public transport into Ferryside where I attended Cairnmount Public School. By noon of my first day, I realized that I hated public school more.

There's nothing worse than being the new kid—especially when you were busing in from the Beaches. Nobody wanted anything to do with the slumming rich kid and her airs. I didn't have airs; I was just too scared. But first impressions are everything and I ended up feeling more left out and alone than I'd ever been at my old school. I couldn't even talk about it at home—my pride wouldn't let me. After the way I'd carried on about it all summer, I couldn't find the courage to admit that I'd been wrong.

So I did the best I could. At recess, I'd stand miserably on the sidelines, trying to look as though I was a part of the linked fence, or whatever I was standing beside at the time, because I soon learned it was better to be ignored, than to be noticed and ridiculed. I stuck it out until just before Christmas break. I don't know if I would have been able to force myself to return after the holidays, but that day a bunch of boys were teasing me and my eyes were already welling with tears when Gina walked up out of nowhere and chased them off.

"Why don't you ever play with anybody?" she asked me.

"Nobody wants me to play with them," I said.

"Well, I do," she said and then she smiled at me, a smile so bright that it dried up all my tears.

After that, we were best friends forever.

5

Gina was the most outrageous, talented, wonderful person I had ever met. I was the sort of child who usually reacted to stimuli; Gina created them. She made up games, she made up stories, she made up songs. It was impossible to be bored in her company and we became inseparable, in school and out.

I don't think a day went by that we didn't spend some part of it together. We had sleepovers. We took art and music and dance classes together and if she won the prizes, I didn't mind, because she was my friend and I could only be proud of her. There was no limit to her imagination, but that was fine by me, too. I was happy to have been welcomed into her world and I was more than willing to take up whatever enterprise she might propose.

I remember one afternoon we sat up in her room and made little people out of found objects: acorn heads, seed eyes, twig bodies. We made clothes for them and furniture and concocted long extravagant family histories so that we ended up knowing more about them than we did our classmates.

"They're real now," I remember her telling me. "We've given them lives, so they'll always be real."

"What kind of real?" I asked, feeling a little confused because I was at that age when I was starting to understand the difference between what was make-believe and what was real.

"There's only one kind of real," Gina told me. "The trouble is, not everybody can see it and they make fun of those who can."

Though I couldn't know the world through the same perspective as Gina had, there was one thing I did know. "I would never make fun of you," I said.

"I know, Sue. That's why we're friends."

I still have the little twig people I made, wrapped up in tissue and stored away in a box of childhood treasures; I don't know what ever happened to Gina's.

We had five years together, but then her parents moved out of town—not impossibly far, but far enough to make our getting together a major effort and we rarely saw each other more than a few times a year after that. It was mainly Gina's doing that we didn't entirely lose touch with each other. She wrote me two or three times a week, long chatty letters about what she'd been reading, films she'd seen, people she'd met, her hopes of becoming a professional musician after she finished high school. The letters were decorated with fanciful illustrations of their contents and sometimes included miniature envelopes in which I would find letters from her twig people to mine.

Although I tried to keep up my side, I wasn't much of a correspondent. Usually I'd phone her, but my calls grew further and further apart as the months went by. I never stopped considering her as a friend—the occasions when we did get together were among my best memories of being a teenager—but my own life had changed and I didn't have as much time for her anymore. It was hard to maintain a long-distance relationship when there was so much going on around me at home. I was no longer the new kid at school and I'd made other friends. I worked on the school paper and then I got a boyfriend.

Gina never wanted to talk about him. I suppose she thought of it as a kind of betrayal; she never again had a friend that she was as close to as she'd been with me.

I remember her mother calling me once, worried because Gina seemed to be sinking into a reclusive depression. I did my best to be there for her. I called her almost every night for a month and went out to visit her on the weekends, but somehow I just couldn't relate to her pain. Gina had always seemed so self-contained, so perfect, that it was hard to imagine her being as withdrawn and unhappy as her mother seemed to think she was. She put on such a good face to me that eventually the worries I'd had faded and the demands of my own life pulled me away again.

6

Gina never liked Christmas.

The year she introduced me to Newford's gargoyles we saw each other twice over the holidays: once so that she could do her Christmas shopping and then again between Christmas and New Year's when I came over to her place and stayed the night. She introduced me to her dog—Fritzie, a gangly, wire-haired, long-legged mutt that she'd found abandoned on one of the country roads near her parents' place—and played some of her new songs for me, accompanying herself on guitar.

The music had a dronal quality that seemed at odds with her clear high voice and the strange Middle Eastern decorations she used. The lyrics were strange and dark, leaving me with a sensation that was not so much unpleasant as uncomfortable, and I could understand why she'd been having so much trouble getting gigs. It wasn't just that she was so young and since most clubs served alcohol, their owners couldn't hire an underage performer; Gina's music simply wasn't what most people would think of as entertainment. Her songs went beyond introspection. They took the listener to that dark place that sits inside each and every one of us, that place we don't want to visit, that we don't even want to admit is there.

But the songs aside, there didn't seem to be any trace of the depression that had worried her mother so much the previous autumn. She appeared to be her old self, the Gina I remembered: opinionated and witty, full of life and laughter even while explaining to me what bothered her so much about the holiday season.

"I love the *idea* of Christmas," she said. "It's the hypocrisy of the season that I dislike. One time out of the year, people do what they can for the homeless, help stock the food banks, contribute to snowsuit funds and give toys to poor children. But where are they the rest of the year when their help is just as necessary? It makes me a little sick to think of all the money that gets spent on Christmas lights and parties and presents that people don't even really want in the first place. If we took all that money and gave it to the people who need it simply to survive, instead of throwing it away on ourselves, we could probably solve most of the problems of poverty and homelessness over one Christmas season."

"I suppose," I said. "But at least Christmas brings people closer together. I guess what we have to do is build on that."

Gina gave me a sad smile. "Who does it bring closer together?"

"Well...families, friends...."

"But what about those who don't have either? They look at all this closeness you're talking about and it just makes their own situation seem all the more desperate. It's hardly surprising that the holiday season has the highest suicide rate of any time of the year."

"But what can we do?" I said. "We can't just turn our backs and pretend there's no such thing as Christmas."

Gina shrugged, then gave me a sudden grin. "We could become Christmas commandos. You know," she added at my blank look. "We'd strike from within. First we'd convince our own families to give it up and then...."

With that she launched into a plan of action that would be as improbable in its execution as it was entertaining in its explanation. She never did get her family to give up Christmas, and I have to admit I didn't try very hard with mine, but the next year I did go visit the residents of places like St. Vincent's Home for the Aged and I worked in the Grasso Street soup kitchen with Gina on Christmas day. I came away with a better experience of what Christmas was all about than I'd ever had at home.

But I just couldn't maintain that commitment all year round. I kept going to St. Vincent's when I could, but the sheer despair of the soup kitchens and food banks was more than I could bear.

7

Gina dropped out of college during her second year to concentrate on her music. She sent me a copy of the demo tape she was shopping around to the record companies in hopes of getting a contract. I didn't like it at first. Neither her guitar-playing nor her vocal style had changed much and the inner landscape the songs revealed was too bleak, the shadows it painted upon the listener seemed too unrelentingly dark, but out of loyalty I played it a few times more and subsequent listenings changed that first impression.

Her songs were still bleak, but I realized that they helped create a healing process in the listener. If I let them take me into the heart of their darkness, they took me out again as well. It was the kind of music that while it appeared to wallow in despair, in actuality it left its audience stronger, more able to face the pain and heartache that awaited them beyond the music.

She was playing at a club near the campus one weekend and I went to see her. Sitting in front were a handful of hard-core fans, all pale-faced and dressed in black, but most of the audience didn't understand what she was offering them anymore than I had the first time I sat through the demo tape. Obviously her music was an acquired taste—which didn't bode well for her career in a world where, more and more, most information was conveyed in thirty-second sound bites and audiences in the entertainment industry demanded instant gratification, rather than taking the time to explore the deeper resonances of a work.

She had Fritzie waiting for her in the claustrophobic dressing room behind the stage, so the three of us went walking in between her sets. That was the night she first told me about her bouts with depression.

"I don't know what it is that brings them on," she said. "I know I find it frustrating that I keep running into a wall with my music, but I also know that's not the cause of them either. As long as I can remember I've carried this feeling of alienation around with me; I wake up in the morning, in the middle of the night, and I'm paralyzed with all this emotional pain. The only people that have ever really helped to keep it at bay were first you, and now Fritzie."

It was such a shock to hear that her only lifelines were a friend who was hardly ever there for her and a dog. The guilt that lodged inside me then has never really gone away. I wanted to ask what had happened to that brashly confident girl who had turned my whole life around as much by the example of her own strength and resourcefulness as by her friendship, but then I realized that the answer lay in her music, in her songs that spoke of masks and what lay behind them, of puddles on muddy roads that sometimes hid deep, bottomless wells.

"I feel so…so stupid," she said.

This time I was the one who took charge. I steered her towards the closest bus stop and we sat down on its bench. I put my arm around her shoulders and Fritzie laid his mournful head upon her knee and looked up into her face.

"Don't feel stupid," I said. "You can't help the bad feelings."

"But why do I have to have them? Nobody else does."

"Everybody has them."

She toyed with the wiry fur between Fritzie's ears and leaned against me.

"Not like mine," she said.

"No," I agreed. "Everybody's got their own."

That got me a small smile. We sat there for a while, watching the traffic go past until it was time for her last set of the night.

"What do you think of the show?" she asked as we returned to the club.

"I like it," I told her, "but I think it's the kind of music that people have to take their time to appreciate."

Gina nodded glumly. "And who's got the time?"

"I do."

"Well, I wish you ran one of the record companies," she said. "I get the same answer from all of them. They like my voice, they like my playing, but they want me to sexy up my image and write songs that are more upbeat."

She paused. We'd reached the back door of the club by then. She put her back against the brick wall of the alley and looked up. Fritzie was pressed up against the side of her leg as though he was glued there.

"I tried, you know," Gina said. "I really tried to give them what they wanted, but it just wasn't there. I just don't have that kind of song inside me."

She disappeared inside then to retune her guitar before she went back on stage. I stayed for a moment longer, my gaze drawn up as hers had been while she'd been talking to me. There was a gargoyle there, spout-mouth open wide, a rather benevolent look about its grotesque features. I looked at it for a long time, wondering for a moment if I would see it blink or move the way Gina probably had, but it was just a stone sculpture, set high up in the wall. Finally I went back inside and found my seat.

8

I was in the middle of studying for exams the following week, but I made a point of it to call Gina at least every day. I tried getting her to let me take her out for dinner on the weekend, but she and Fritzie were pretty much inseparable and she didn't want to leave him tied up outside the restaurant while we sat inside to eat. So I ended up having them over to the little apartment I was renting in Crowsea instead. She told me that night that she was going out west to try to shop her tape around to the big companies in L.A. and I didn't see her again for three months.

I'd been worried about her going off on her own, feeling as she was. I even offered to go with her, if she'd just wait until the semester was finished, but she assured me she'd be fine and a series of cheerful cards and short letters—signed by either her or just a big paw print—arrived in my letterbox to prove the point. When she finally did get back, she called me up and we got together for a picnic lunch in Fitzhenry Park.

Going out to the west coast seemed to have done her good. She came back looking radiant and tanned, full of amusing stories concerning the ups and downs of her and Fritzie's adventures out there. She'd even gotten some fairly serious interest from an independent record label, but they were still making up their minds when her money ran out. Instead of trying to make do in a place where she felt even more like a stranger than she did in Newford, she decided to come home to wait for their response, driving back across the country in her old station wagon, Fritzie sitting up on the passenger seat beside her, her guitar in its battered case lying across the backseat.

"By the time we rolled into Newford," she said, "the car was just running on fumes. But we made it."

"If you need some money, or a place to stay...." I offered.

"I can just see the three of us squeezed into that tiny place of yours."

"We'd make do."

Gina smiled. "It's okay. My dad fronted me some money until the advance from the record company comes through. But thanks all the same. Fritzie and I appreciate the offer."

I was really happy for her. Her spirits were so high now that things had finally turned around and she could see that she was going somewhere with her music. She knew there was a lot of hard work still to come, but it was the sort of work she thrived on.

"I feel like I've lived my whole life on the edge of an abyss," she told me, "just waiting for the moment when it'd finally drag me down for good, but now everything's changed. It's like I finally figured out a way to live someplace else—away from the edge. *Far* away."

I was going on to my third year at Butler U. in the fall, but we made plans to drive back to L.A. together in July, once she got the okay from the record company. We'd spend the summer together in La La Land, taking in the sights while Gina worked on her album. It's something I knew we were both looking forward to.

9

Gina was looking after the cottage of a friend of her parents when she fell back into the abyss. She never told me how she was feeling, probably because she knew I'd have gone to any length to stop her from hurting herself. All she'd told me before she went was that she needed the solitude to work on some new songs and I'd believed her. I had no reason to worry about her. In the two weeks she was living out there I must have gotten a half-dozen cheerful cards, telling me what to add to my packing list for our trip out west and what to leave off.

Her mother told me that she'd gotten a letter from the record company, turning down her demo. She said Gina had seemed to take the rejection well when she called to give her daughter the bad news. They'd ended their conversation with Gina already making plans to start the rounds of the record companies again with the new material she'd been working on. Then she'd burned her guitar and all of her music and poetry in a firepit down by the shore, and simply walked out into the lake. Her body was found after a neighbour was drawn to the lot by Fritzie's howling. The poor dog was shivering and wet, matted with mud from having tried to rescue her. They know it wasn't an accident because of the note she left behind in the cottage.

I never read the note. I couldn't.

I miss her terribly, but most of all I'm angry. Not at Gina, but at this society of ours that tries to make everybody fit into the same mold. Gina was unique, but she didn't want to be. All she wanted to do was fit in, but her spirit and her muse wouldn't let her. That dichotomy between who she was and who she thought she should be was what really killed her.

All that survives of her music is that demo tape. When I listen to it, I can't understand how she could create a healing process for others through that dark music, but she couldn't use it to heal herself.

10

Tomorrow is Christmas day and I'm going down to the soup kitchen to help serve the Christmas dinners. It'll be my first Christmas without Gina. My parents wanted me to come home, but I put them off until tomorrow night. I just want to sit here tonight with Fritzie and remember. He lives with me because Gina asked me to take care of him, but he's not the same dog he was when Gina was alive. He misses her too much.

I'm sitting by the window, watching the snow fall. On the table in front of me I've spread out the contents of a box of memories: The casing for Gina's demo tape. My twig people and the other things we made. All those letters and cards that Gina sent me over the years. I haven't been able to reread them yet, but I've looked at the drawings and I've held them in my hands, turning them over and over, one by one. The demo tape is playing softly on my stereo. It's the first time I've been able to listen to it since Gina died.

Through the snow I can see the gargoyle on the building across the street. I know now what Gina meant about wanting to live in their world and be invisible. When you're invisible, no one can see that you're different.

Thinking about Gina hurts so much, but there's good things to remember, too. I don't know what would have become of me if she hadn't rescued me in that playground all those years ago and welcomed me into her life. It's so sad that the uniqueness about her that made me love her so much was what caused her so much pain.

The bells of St. Paul's Cathedral strike midnight. They remind me of the child I was, trying to stay up late enough to hear my cat talk. I guess that's what Gina meant to me. While everybody else grew up, Gina retained all the best things about childhood: goodness and innocence and an endless wonder. But she carried the downside of being a child inside her as well. She always lived in the present moment, the way we do when we're young, and that must be why her despair was so overwhelming for her.

"I tried to save her," a voice says in the room behind me as the last echo of St. Paul's bells fades away. "But she wouldn't let me. She was too strong for me."

I don't move. I don't dare move at all. On the demo tape, Gina's guitar starts to strum the intro to another song. Against the drone of the guitar's strings, the voice goes on.

"I know she'll always live on so long as we keep her memory alive," it says, "but sometimes that's just not enough. Sometimes I miss her so much I don't think *I* can go on."

I turn slowly then, but there's only me in the room. Me and Fritzie, and one small Christmas miracle to remind me that everything magic didn't die when Gina walked into the lake.

"Me, too," I tell Fritzie.

I get up from my chair and cross the room to where he's sitting up, looking at me with those sad eyes of his. I put my arms around his neck. I bury my face in his rough fur and we stay there like that for a long time, listening to Gina sing.

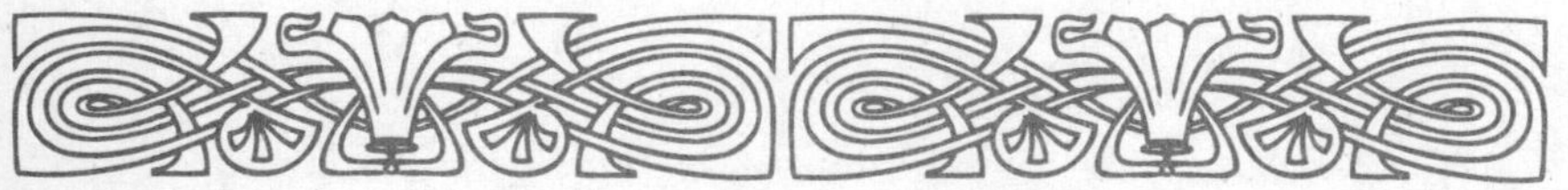

⁂THAT WAS RADIO CLASH⁂

December 23, 2002

"Why so down?" the bartender asked the girl with the dark blue hair.

She looked up, surprised, maybe, that anyone had even noticed.

At night, the Rhatigan was one of the last decent live jazz clubs in town. The kind of place where you didn't necessarily know the players, but one thing the music always did was swing. There was none of your smooth jazz or other ambient crap here.

But during the day, it was like any other low-end bar, a third full of serious drinkers and no one that looked like her.

"Joe Strummer died yesterday," she said.

Alphonse is a good guy. He used to play the keys until an unpaid debt resulted in some serious damage to his melody hand. He can still play, but where he used to soar, now he just walks along on the everyday side of genius with the rest of us. And while maybe he can't express the way things feel with his music anymore, the heart that made him one of the most generous players you could sit in with is still beating inside that barrel chest of his.

"I'm sorry," he said. "Was he a friend of yours?"

The hint of a smile tugged at the corner of her mouth, but the sadness in her eyes didn't change.

"Hardly," she said. "It's just that he was the heart and soul of the only band that matters and his dying reminds me of how everything that's good eventually fades away."

"The only band that matters," Alphonse repeated, obviously not getting the reference. In his head he was probably running through various Monk or Davis lineups.

"That's what they used to call the Clash."

"Oh, I remember them. What was that hit of theirs?" It took him a moment, but then he half-sang the chorus and title of "Should I Stay or Should I Go."

She nodded. "Except that was more Mick Jones's. Joe's lyrics were the ones with a political agenda."

"I don't much care for politics," Alphonse said.

"Yeah, most people don't. And that's why the world's as fucked up as it is."

Alphonse shrugged and went to serve a customer at the other end of the bar. The blue-haired girl returned her attention to her beer, staring down into the amber liquid.

"Did you ever meet him?" I asked.

She looked up to where I was sitting a couple of barstools away. Her eyes were as blue as her hair, such a vibrant colour that I figured they must be contacts. She had a pierced eyebrow—the left—and pale skin, but by the middle of winter, most people have pretty much lost their summer colour. She was dressed like she was auditioning for a black and white movie: black jersey, cargos and boots, a grey sweater. The only colour was in her hair. And those amazing eyes.

"No," she said. "But I saw them play at the Standish in '84."

I smiled. "And you were what? Five years old?"

"Now you're just sucking up."

And unspoken, but implied in those few words was, You don't have a chance with me.

But I never thought I did. I mean, look at me. A has-been trumpet player who lost his lip. Never touched the glory Alphonse did when he played—not on my own—but I sat in with musicians who did.

But that's not what she'd be seeing. She'd be seeing one more lost soul with haunted eyes, trying to drown old sorrows in a pint of draught. If she was in her teens when she caught the Clash at the Standish, she'd still only be in her mid- to late-thirties now, ten years my junior. But time passes differently for people like her and people like me. I looked half again my age, and shabby. And I knew it.

No, all I was doing here was enjoying the opportunity for a little piece of conversation with someone who wasn't a drunk, or what she thought me to be: on the prowl.

"I knew him in London," I said. "Back in the seventies when we were all living in squats in Camden Town."

"Yeah, right."

I shrugged and went on as though she hadn't spoken. "I remember their energy the most. They'd play these crap gigs with speakers made out of crates and broomstick mike stands. Very punk—lots of noise and big choppy chords." I smiled. "And not a hell of a lot of chords, either. But they already had a conscience—not like the Pistols who were only ever in it for the money. Right from the start they were giving voice to a whole generation that the system had let down."

She studied me for a moment.

"Well, at least you know your stuff," she said. "Are you a musician?"

I nodded. "I used to play the trumpet, but I don't have the lip for it anymore."

"Did you ever play with him?"

"No, I was in an R&B cover band in the seventies, but times were hard and I ended up living in the squats for awhile, same as him. The closest I got to playing the punk scene was when I was in a ska band, and later doing some Two-Tone. But the music I loved to play the most was always jazz."

"What's your name?"

"Eddie Ramone."

"You're kidding."

I smiled. "No, and before you ask, I got my name honestly—from my dad."

"I'm Sarah Blue."

I glanced at her hair. "So which came first?"

"The name. Like you, it came with the family."

"I guess people who knew you could really say they knew the Blues."

"Ha ha."

"Sorry."

"'sokay."

I waited a moment, then asked, "So is there more to your melancholy than the loss of an old favourite musician?"

She shrugged. "It just brought it all home to me, how that night at the Standish was, like, one of those pivotal moments in my life, only I didn't recognize it. Or maybe it's just that that's when I started making a lot of bad choices." She touched her hair. "It's funny, but the first thing I did when I heard he'd died was put the eyebrow piercing back in and dye my hair blue like it was in those days—by way of mourning. But I think I'm mourning the me I lost as much as his passing."

"We can change our lives."

"Well, sure. But we can't change the past. See that night I hooked up with Brian. I thought he was into all the things I was. I wanted to change the world and make a difference. Through music, but also through activism."

"So you played?"

"Yeah. Guitar—*electric* guitar—and I sang. I wrote songs, too."

"What happened?"

"I pissed it all away. Brian had no ambition except to party hearty and that whole way of life slipped into mine like a virus. I never even saw the years slide away."

"And Brian?"

"I dumped him after a couple of years, but by then I'd just lost my momentum."

"You could still regain it."

She shook her head. "Music's a young person's game. I do what I can in terms of being an environmental and social activist, but the music was the soul of it for me. It was everything. Whatever I do now, I just feel like I'm going through the motions."

"You don't have to be young to make music."

"Maybe not. But whatever muse I had back in those days pissed off and left me a long time ago. Believe me, I've tried. I used to get home from work and pick up my guitar almost every day, but the spark was just never there. I don't even try anymore."

"I hear you," I said. "I never had the genius—I just saw it in others. And when you know what you *could* be doing, when the music in your head's so far beyond what you can pull out of your instrument...."

"Why bother."

I gave a slow nod, then studied her for a moment. "So if you could go back and change something, is that what it would be? You'd go to that night and go your own way instead of hooking up with this Brian guy?"

She laughed. "I guess. Though I'd have to *apply* myself as well."

"I can send you back."

"Yeah, right."

I didn't take my gaze from those blue eyes of hers. I just repeated what I'd said. "I can send you back."

She let me hold her gaze for a couple of heartbeats, then shook her head.

"You almost had me going there," she said.

"I can send you back," I said a third time.

Third time's the charm and she looked uneasy.

"Send me back in time."

I nodded.

"To warn myself."

"No. *You'd* go back, with all you know now. And it's not really back. Time doesn't run in a straight line, it all happens at the same time. Past, present, future. It's like this is you now." I touched my left shoulder. "And this is you then." I touched the end of a finger on my left hand. "If I hold my arm straight, it seems linear, right?"

She gave me a dubious nod.

"But really—" I crooked my left arm so that my finger was touching my shoulder, "—the two times are right beside each other. It's not such a big jump."

"And you can send me there?"

I nodded. "On one condition."

"What's that?"

"You come back here on this exact same day and ask for me."

"Why?"

"Because that's how it works."

She shook her head. "This is nuts."

"Nothing to lose, everything to gain."

"I guess...."

I knew I almost had her, so I smiled and said, "Should you stay or should you go?"

Her blue gaze held mine again, then she shrugged. Picking up her beer, she chugged the last third down, then set the empty glass on the table.

"What the hell," she said. "How does it work?"

I slipped off my stool and closed the few steps between us.

"You think about that night," I said. "Think about it hard. Then I put two fingers on each of your temples—like this. And then I kiss your third eye."

I leaned forward and pressed my lips against her brow, halfway between my fingers. Held my lips there for a heartbeat. Another. Then I stepped away.

She looked at me for a long moment, before standing up. She didn't say a word, but they never do. She just laid a couple of bills on the bar to pay for her drink and walked out the door.

DECEMBER 23, 2002

"I feel like I should know you," the bartender said when the girl with the dark blue hair walked into the bar and pulled up a stool.

"My name's Sarah Blue. What's yours?"

"Alphonse," he said and grinned. "And you're really Sarah Blue?" He glanced towards the doorway. "I thought you big stars only travelled with an entourage."

"All I've got is a cab waiting outside. And I'm not such a big star."

"Yeah, right. Like 'Take It to the Streets' wasn't the big hit of—when was it? Summer of '89."

"You've got a good memory."

"It was a good song."

"Yeah, it was. I never get tired of playing it. But my hit days were a long time ago. These days I'm just playing theatres and clubs again."

"Nothing wrong with that. So what can I get you?"

"Actually, I was expecting to meet a guy in here today. Do you know an Eddie Ramone?"

"Sure, I do." He shook his head. "I should have remembered."

"Remembered what?"

"Hang on."

He went to a drawer near the cash and pulled out a stack of envelopes held together with a rubber band. Flipping through them, he returned to where she was sitting and laid one out on the bar in front of her. In an unfamiliar hand was written:

SARAH BLUE
DECEMBER 23, 2002

"Do those all have names and dates on them?" she asked.

"Every one of them."

He showed her the top one. It was addressed to:

JONATHAN BLOCK
JANUARY 27, 2003

"You think he'll show?" she asked.

"You did."

She shook her head. "What's this all about?"

"Damned if I know. People just drop these off from time to time and sooner or later someone shows up to collect it."

"It's not just Eddie?"

"No. But most of the time it's Eddie."

"And he's not here?"

"Not today. Maybe he tells you why in the letter."

"The letter. Right."

"I'll leave you to it," Alphonse said.

He walked back to where he'd left the drawer open and dropped the envelopes in. When he looked up, she was still watching him.

"You want a drink?" he asked.

"Sure. Whatever's on tap that's dark."

"You've got it."

She returned her attention to the letter, staring at it until Alphonse returned with her beer. She thanked him, had a sip, then slid her finger into the top of the envelope and tore it open. There was a single sheet inside, written in the same unfamiliar script that was on the envelope. It said:

Hello Sarah,

Well, if you're reading this, I guess you're a believer now. I sure hope your life went where you wanted it to go this time.

Funny thing, that might amuse you. I was talking to Joe, back in the Camden Town days, and I asked him if he had any advice for a big fan who'd be devastated when he finally went to the big gig in the sky.

The first thing he said was, "Get bent."

The second was, "You really think we're ever going to make it?"

When I nodded, he thought for a moment, then said, "You tell him or her—it's a her?—tell her it's never about the player, is it? It's always about the music. And the music never dies."

And if she wanted to be a musician? I asked him.

"Tell her that whatever she takes on, stay in for the duration. Maybe you can just bang out a tune or a lyric, maybe it takes you forever. It doesn't matter how you put it together. All that matters is that it means something to you, and you play it like it means something to you. Anything else is just bollocks."

I'm thinking, if you got your life straight this time, you'd probably agree with him.

But now to business. First off, the reason I'm not here to see you is that this isn't the same future I sent you back from. That one still exists, running alongside this one, but it's closed to you because you're living that other life now. And you know there's just no point in us meeting again, because we've done what needed to be done.

At least we did it for you.

If you're in the music biz now, you know there's no such thing as a free ride. What I need you to do is, pass it on. You know how to do it. All you've got to decide is who.

Eddie

Sarah read it twice before she folded the letter up, returned it to the envelope and stowed it in the pocket of her jacket. She had some more of her beer. Alphonse approached as she was setting her glass back down on the bar top.

"Did that clear it up for you?" he asked.

She shook her head.

"Well, that's Eddie for you. The original man of mystery. He ever start in on his time travel yarns with you?"

She shook her head again, but only because she wasn't ready to admit it to anyone. To do so didn't feel right, and that feeling had made her keep it to herself through all the years.

Alphonse held out his right hand. "He wanted to send me back to the day before I broke this—said I could turn my life around and live it right this time."

"And…did you?"

Alphonse laughed. "What does it look like?"

Sarah smiled. Of course, he hadn't. Not in this world. But maybe in one running parallel to it....

She thought about that night at the Standish, so long ago. The Clash playing and she was dancing, dancing, so happy, so filled with music. And she was straight, too—no drinks, no drugs that night—but high all the same. On the music. And then right in the middle of a blistering version of "Clampdown," her head just…*swelled* with this impossible lifetime that she'd never, she *couldn't* have lived.

But she knew she'd connect with a guy named Brian. And she did.

And she *knew* how it would all go downhill from there, so after the concert, when they were leaving the theatre from a side door, she blew him off. And he got pissed off and gave her a shove that knocked her down. He looked at her, sobered by what he'd done, but she waved him off. He hesitated, then walked away, and she just sat there in the alley, thinking she was going crazy. Wanting to cry.

And then someone reached a hand to her to help her up.

"You okay there?" a voice with a British accent asked.

And she was looking into Joe Strummer's face. The Joe Strummer she'd seen on stage. But superimposed over it, she saw Joe Strummers that were still to come.

The one she'd seen fronting the Pogues in...some other life.

The one she'd seen fronting the Mescaleros....

The one who'd die of a heart attack at fifty years young....

"You want me to call you a cab?" he asked.

"No. No, I'm okay. Great gig."

"Thanks."

On impulse, she gave him a kiss, then stepped back. Away. Out of his life. Into her new one.

She blinked, realizing that Alphonse was still standing by her. How long had she been spaced out?

"Well...." she said, looking for something to say. "Eddie seemed like a nice guy to me."

Alphonse nodded. "He's got a big heart—he'll give you the shirt off his back. Hasn't got much of a lip these days, but he still sits in with the band from time to time. You can't say no to a guy like that and he never tries to showboat, like he thinks he plays better than he can. He keeps it simple and puts the heart into what he's playing."

"Maybe I'll come back and catch him one night."

"Door's always open during business hours, Miss Blue."

"Sarah."

"Sarah, then. You come back any time."

He left to serve a new customer and Sarah looked around the bar. No one stood out to her—the way she assumed she had to Eddie—so she'd have to come back.

She put a couple of bills on the bar top to cover the cost of her beer and went out to look for her cab. As she got into the backseat, she found herself hoping that Eddie had made himself at least one world where he'd got his lip back.

That was the only reason she could think that he kept passing along the magic of a second chance—paying back his own attempts at getting it right.

It was either that, or he was an angel.

JANUARY 27, 2003

Alphonse smiled when she came in. When he started to draw her a draught, she shook her head.

"I'll have a coffee if you've got one," she said.

"We don't get much call for coffee, even at this time of day, so it's kind of grungy. Let me put on a fresh pot."

He busied himself at the coffee machine, throwing out the old grounds, inserting a filter full of new coffee.

"So what brings you in so early?" he asked when he turned back to her.

"I can't get those envelopes out of my head."

"The...oh, yeah. They're a bit of a puzzle all right. But I can't let you look at them."

"I'm not asking. But when you were giving me mine, I saw the date on the one on the top of the stack."

"Today's date," Alphonse guessed.

She nodded. "Do you mind if I hang around and wait?"

"Not at all. But it could be a long haul."

"'sokay. I've got the time."

She sat chatting with Alphonse for a while, then retired to one of the booths near the stage with her second cup of coffee. Pulling out her journal, she did some sketches of the bar, the empty stage, Alphonse at work. The sketches were in pictures and words. At some point they might find a melody and swell into a song. Or they might not. It didn't matter to her. Doodling in her journal was just something she always did—a way to occupy time on the road and provide touchstones for her memory.

Jonathan Block didn't show up until that evening, after she'd had a surprisingly-good Cajun stew and the band was starting to set up. He looked nothing like what she'd expected—not that she'd had any specific visual in mind. It was just that he looked like a street person. Medium height, gaunt features, a few days worth of stubble and greasy hair, shabby clothes. She'd expected someone more...successful.

She waited until he'd collected his envelope and had a chance to read it before approaching him.

"I guess your replay didn't turn out," she said.

He gave her a look that was half wary, half confused.

"What do you mean?" he asked.

She pulled out her own envelope, creased and wrinkled from living in her pocket for over a month, and showed it to him.

"Do you feel like talking?" she asked. "I'll buy you a drink."

He hesitated, then shrugged. "Sure. I'll have a ginger ale."

She got one for him from Alphonse, then led Jonathan back to her booth.

"What did you want to talk about?" he asked.

"You have to ask? I mean, this, all of this...." She laid her envelope on the Formica tabletop between them. "It's just so strange."

He gave a slow nod and laid his own down beside his drink.

"But it's real, isn't it?" he said. "The letters prove that."

"What happened to you? Why didn't it work out?"

"What makes you think it didn't?"

"I'm sorry. It's just...the way you...you know...."

"No, I should be the one apologizing. It was a fair question." He looked past her for a moment, then returned his gaze to hers. "It worked for me and it didn't. I just didn't think it through carefully enough. I should have focused on a point in time *before* I got drunk—before I even had a problem with drinking. But I didn't. So when I went back the three years, suddenly I'm in the car again, pissed out of my mind, and I know that the other car's going to come around the corner, and I know I'm going to hit it, and I know it's too late to just pull over."

He wasn't telling her much, but Sarah was able to fill in the details for herself.

"Oh, how horrible," she said.

"Yeah, it wasn't very bright on my part. But hey, who'd have ever thought that a thing like that would even work? When he kissed me on my forehead I thought he was just some freaky guy getting some weird little thrill. I was going to take a swing at him, but then I was there. Back in the car. On that night."

"What happened?"

"Well, the good thing was, even drunk as I was, I knew what was coming and whatever else I might have been, I wasn't a bad guy. Thoughtless as shit, oh yeah, but not bad. So instead of letting myself hit the car, I just drove into a lamppost in the couple of moments I had left. The twelve-year-old girl who would have died—who *did* die the first time around—was spared."

"And you?"

"Serious injuries. I didn't have any medical, so I lost everything paying for the bills. Lost my job. Got charged with drunk driving, and it wasn't the first time, but since I hadn't hurt anybody, they just took away my license. But after that it was pretty much the same slide downhill that it was the first time."

"You don't sound...." Sarah wasn't sure how to put it.

"Much broke up about it?"

"Yeah, I guess."

"It's like I told you," he said. "This time the little girl lived. I wasn't any less stupid, but this time no one else had to pay for my stupidity. I've still got a chance to put my life back together. I've been sober since that night. I just need a break, a chance to get cleaned up and back on my feet. I know I can do it."

Sarah nodded. Then she asked the question that troubled her the most.

"Did you ever try to change anything else?" she asked.

"What do you mean?"

"Some disaster where a little forewarning could save a lot of lives."

"You mean like 9/11?"

"Yeah. Or the bombing in Oklahoma."

He shook his head. "It's a funny thing. As soon as I heard about them, it all came back, that I'd been around when they happened the first time and I *remembered*. But the memory just wasn't there until it actually happened."

"Like all we're changing is our own lives."

"Pretty much. And even that's walking blind, the further you get from familiar territory."

Sarah knew exactly what he meant. It had been easy to change things at first, but once she was in a life that was so different from how it had gone the first time, there were no more touchstones and you had to do like everybody did: do what you could and hope for the best.

"I was afraid there was something wrong with me," she said. "That I was so self-centered that I just couldn't be bothered with anything that didn't personally touch my life."

"You don't really believe that."

"How would you know?"

"Well, c'mon. You're Sarah Blue. You're like a poster child for causes."

"I never told you my name."

He smiled and shook his head. "What? Suddenly you're anonymous? Maybe the charts got taken over by all these kids with their bare midriffs, but there was a time not so long ago when you were always on the cover of some magazine or other."

She shrugged, not knowing what to say.

"I don't know what your life was like the first time around," he went on, "but you've been making a difference this time out. So don't be so hard on yourself."

"I guess."

They sat quietly for a moment. Sarah looked around the bar and saw that the clientele had changed. The afternoon boozehounds had given way to a younger, hipper crowd, though she could still spot a few grey heads in the crowd. These were the people who'd come for the music, she realized.

"Will you do like it says in the letter?" she asked, turning back to her companion.

"You mean pass it on?"

She nodded.

"First chance I get."

"Me, too," she said. "And I think my go at it should be to help you."

"You haven't passed it on yet?"

She shook her head.

"I don't know if you get a third try," he said.

She shrugged. "If it doesn't work out, I can always front you some money, give you a chance to get back on your feet, and use the whatever-the-hell-it-is on someone else."

"You'd do that for me—just like that?"

"Wouldn't you?"

He gave a slow nod. "Not before. But now, yeah. In a heartbeat." He looked at her for a long moment. "How'd you know I'd be here?"

"I saw your name and the date on your envelope when I was collecting my own. I just…needed to talk to someone about it and Eddie doesn't seem to be available."

"Eddie," he said. "What do you think he is?"

"An angel."

"So you believe in God?"

"I...I'm not sure. But I believe in good and evil. I guess I just naturally think of somebody working on the side of good as being an angel."

He nodded. "It's as good a description as any."

"So let's give this a shot," she said. "Only this time—"

"Concentrate on a point in time where I can make the decision not to drink before it's too late."

She nodded.

She gave him a moment, turning her attention back to the bandstand. Looks like tonight they had a keyboard player, a guitarist, a bass player, a drummer, and a guy on saxophones. They were still tuning, adjusting the drum kit, soaking the reeds for the saxes.

She turned back to Jonathan.

"Have you got it?" she asked.

"Yeah. I think I do."

"I'm not going to try to tell you how to live your life, but I think it helps to have something bigger than yourself to believe in."

"Like God?"

She shrugged.

"Or like a cause?" he added.

She smiled. "Like a whatever. Are you ready?"

"Do it," he said. "And thanks."

She leaned over the table, put her hands on his temples and kissed him where Eddie had kissed her, on—what had he called it? Her third eye. She kept her lips pressed against his forehead for a couple of moments, then sat back in her seat.

"Don't forget to come back here on the same day," she said.

But Jonathan only gave her a puzzled look. Without speaking, he got up and left the booth. Sarah tracked him as he made his way through the growing crowd, but he never once looked back.

Weird. How was she even supposed to know if it had worked? But she guessed that in this world, she wouldn't.

Her gaze went to Jonathan's half-drunk ginger ale and she noticed that he'd left his letter behind. There was another puzzle. How did they go from world to world, future to future?

Maybe it had something to do with the Rhatigan itself. Maybe there was something about the bar that made it a crossroads for all these futures.

She thought of asking Alphonse, but got the sense that he didn't know. Or if he knew, he wouldn't be telling. But maybe if she could track down Eddie....

He appeared beside her table as though her thoughts had summoned him.

"Never thought about third chances," he said.

He slid a trumpet case onto the booth seat, then sat down beside it, smiling at her from the other side of the table.

"Is—was that against the rules?" she asked.

He shrugged. "What rules? The only thing that's important is for you to come back and get the message to pass it on."

"But what *is* it that we're passing on? Where did this thing come from?"

"Sometimes it's better to just accept that something is, instead of trying to take it apart."

"But—"

"Because when you take it apart, it might not work anymore. You wouldn't want that, would you, Sarah?"

"No. Of course not. But I've got so many questions...."

He made a motion with his hands like he was breaking something, then he held out his palms looking down at them with a sad expression.

"Okay, I get the point already," she said. "But you've got to understand my curiosity."

"Sure, I do. And all I'm doing is asking you to let it go."

"But...can you at least tell me who you are?"

"Eddie Ramone."

"And he's...?"

"Just a guy who's learned how to give a few people the tools to fix a mistake they might have made. Doesn't work on everybody, and not everybody gets it right when they do go back. But I give them another shot. Think of me as a messenger of hope."

Sarah felt as though she was going to burst with the questions that were swelling inside her.

"So'd you bring a guitar?" Eddie asked.

She blinked, then shook her head. "No. But I don't play jazz."

"Take a cue from Norah Jones. Anything can swing, even a song by Hank Williams...or Sarah Blue."

She shook her head. "These people didn't come to hear me."

"No, they came to hear music. They don't give a rat's ass who's playing it, just so long as it's real."

"Okay. Maybe." But then she had a thought. "Just answer this one thing for me."

He smiled, waiting.

"In your letter you said that this is a different time line from the one I first met you in."

"That's right, it is."

"So how come you're here and you know me in this one?"

"Something's got to be the connection," he told her.

"But—"

He opened his case and took out his trumpet. Getting up, he reached for her hand.

"C'mon. Jackie'll lend you his guitar for a couple of numbers. All you've got to do is tell us the key."

She gave up and let him lead her to where the other musicians were standing at the side of the stage.

"Oh, and don't forget," Eddie said as they were almost there. "Before you leave the bar, you need to write your own letter to Jonathan."

"I feel like I'm going crazy."

"'Crazy,'" Eddie said. "Willie Nelson. That'd make a nice start—you know, something everybody knows."

Sarah wanted to bring the conversation back to where she felt she needed it to go, but a look into his eyes gave her a sudden glimpse of a hundred thousand different futures, all banging up against each other in a complex, twisting pattern that gave her a touch of vertigo. So she took a breath instead, shook her head and just let him introduce her to the other musicians.

Jackie's Gibson semi-hollow body was a lot like one of her own guitars—it just had a different pick-up. She took a seat on the center-stage stool and adjusted the height of the microphone, then started playing the opening chords of "Tony Adams." It took her a moment to find the groove she was looking for, that hip-hop swing that Strummer and the Mescaleros had given the song. By the time she found it, the piano and bass had come in, locking them into the groove.

She glanced at Eddie. He stood on the side of the stage, holding his horn, swaying gently to the rhythm. Smiling, she turned back to the mike and started to sing the first verse.

For Joe Strummer, R.I.P.

OLD MAN CROW

OLD MAN CROW lifted his head from its pillow of moss and pine needles and sniffed the air. Something walked in the pine woods around him, invisible as the wind, and more silent than a spider's bite. But he was Old Man Crow and he could be as quiet as the movement of that spider's web in the wind. When he sat up, it was without a whisper of sound. His dark gaze searched the shadows under the trees. He tracked the flight of a blue jay cousin through the upper boughs, then studied the hollows that the granite rib-rocks had made as they pushed their way out of the forest floor, back in the long ago.

"Little sister, little sister," he said. "I know you're there. You can't fool this old crow with your sneaking about and hiding."

"Not so little and not your sister," a gruff voice said almost in his ear. "So who's the fool now?"

When he turned around, his features hid his surprise that someone could get this close to him, that they could move even more quietly than he could.

"I don't know you," he said.

The woman sitting cross-legged on the pine needles smiled. She was big—bigger than him and almost as tall. Her skin was white from her widow's peak to her smallest toe, her hair was the colour of a snowdrift in the sunlight, her eyes the dark of graveyard secrets. Her breath was apple-sweet.

"And here I was told that Old Man Crow knew everyone," she said.

"Then you've been talking to the wrong people."

She shrugged and her breasts bounced with the movement.

"Do you mind putting some clothes on?" he said.

She gave him a puzzled look. "Just what do you see when you look at me?"

"A big, handsome woman—too damn handsome to be walking around buck-naked."

"Well, I'll be," she said.

"What?"

"I don't know if I should be flattered or insulted."

Now it was Old Man Crow's turn to be puzzled.

"About what?" he asked.

"I'm no woman, Joey Creel. I live up by Spirit Lake."

Old Man Crow leaned back against the pine tree.

"Well, now," he said. "That's different. What can I do for you, cousin?"

He wasn't surprised that she knew his waking name. The spirit bears who lived up the mountain on the glacial shores of Spirit Lake were like that. They were supposed to have a way of knowing things about you without your having to say a word. Much like the cousins could when they walked about in the world of the five-fingered beings.

"I need you to see something," she said.

When she stood up, it was like watching water flow. She reached a hand to him and he let himself be pulled to his feet. She was as strong as she was quick and silent.

"What kind of some—" he began.

But then the pine forest dissolved and they stood in the middle of an intersection, with cars stopped all around them as far as the eye could see. Buildings rose, sleek and tall as the first trees must have been in the long ago. They, too, went on forever and ever, it seemed, off into the horizon in each of the four directions.

Old Man Crow couldn't hide his surprise over this. He blinked and looked around himself. All the cars were motionless, many with their doors hanging ajar. It took him a long moment to realize that this busy street was utterly still. It was as though he and the spirit bear had stepped into the middle of a photograph. And then, as he slowly settled into accepting their surroundings, he realized something else.

"Where are all the people?" he asked.

She shrugged again and he kept his gaze on her face.

"This is what it would be like," she said, "if we stepped back into the long ago."

"Except for the buildings and cars, and all the other crap."

"That's true."

She fell silent. Old Man Crow waited, but she seemed content to simply stand with him on the street, surrounded by the motionless, empty vehicles.

If there had been people in those cars, he thought, they'd have all come to a halt anyway when this glorious woman appeared in front of them.

"So why are you showing me this?" he asked.

"I thought you might find it interesting."

"I liked those pine woods better."

"And I thought maybe you could fix it."

"Fix what?"

"Whatever's going to happen here."

Joey Creel woke up in his familiar bed, in his familiar apartment, with the familiar sounds of the city coming in through the bedroom window. Traffic, people talking, dustbins clanging, a distant police siren.

He sat up, half-expecting the spirit bear to still be with him, but he was alone in the room.

Getting up, he went into the bathroom and had a long morning pee. Washing his hands, he looked at his reflection. His beard was going so grey it looked almost white against his dark skin. He gave the bristles a rub and pushed his hair back from his face.

He thought about his dream, about the task the spirit bear had set him, and he shook his head. It was a powerful dream—a power dream—and he didn't understand a bit of it.

"I guess we're finally getting old," he told his reflection.

His reflection stared silently back at him until he finally turned away.

Returning to the bedroom, he got dressed. Dark trousers, cowboy boots, an old white shirt. He took his change from the dresser and dropped it in his pocket. Grabbing his suit jacket from the back of the sofa where he'd left it last night, he went to the diner on the corner for breakfast and a coffee. He didn't bother to lock the apartment door behind him. There was nothing there to steal—not even that old guitar of his was worth any real money.

Anything he had of worth, he carried around in his head.

"I had the strangest dream last night," Ruby the waitress said when she came over to his booth.

She brought a coffee along with a plate of beans, eggs and toast and set them in front of him. He couldn't remember the last time he'd actually placed an order here. Ruby just gave him whatever she decided he wanted. So long as coffee was a part of the equation, Joey was happy to let her decide.

"Was there a big naked white woman in it?" Joey asked.

Ruby laughed. "I guess we're never too old to dream, are we?"

"Bad enough I call myself old. Don't you start doing it, too."

Ruby was a cute, curvy young thing—twentysomething and flirty, with tousled blonde hair and a tattoo of a magpie on her upper arm. When she reached for something on the top shelf behind the counter, you could just see the tip of that magpie's long tail poking out from under her sleeve.

She gave a look around the diner to make sure nobody needed her attention, then slipped into Joey's booth.

"So in this dream," she said, "Jay-Z's living in the neighbourhood, and he comes right here into the diner and wants to know if I'll be in his new video."

"I thought he'd retired and was running some record company now."

She shakes her head. "How do you know that? You always know the strangest things."

"I've been around," Joey said.

And he had. Not back to the days of the long ago, maybe, when Raven first pulled the world out of that big black pot of his, and not even back when the Indians first came wandering through these lands, but he'd been around for awhile. His name wasn't Joey Creel any more than it was Old Man Crow, though they'd both grown to be a part of his story.

That would have been a good name for this old corbae: Story Man. He collected stories—or at least what he called stories. He rarely knew how they began or ended because mostly they came to him piecemeal. Something overheard at a bus stop. Something read in a newspaper, or in a magazine at the checkout counter of the grocery store. Something a drunk might tell him in a bar. Something the squirrel cousins gossiped about with the pigeons.

There were stories everywhere, or at least pieces of them, and corbae had always been collectors. The baubles he hoarded just happened to be made of words rather than gleams and glitters.

"So what did you say to Jay-Z?" he asked Ruby.

"I told him I wasn't that kind of a girl."

"And what kind of a girl are you?"

She smiled. "A good girl with attitude."

"Works for me. And I tell you what. Come visit me in my dreams sometime. Look a little older and I'll look a little younger—who knows what could happen."

"In your dreams!"

"That's what I just said."

"I don't think so. I'm still waiting for Kyle to ask me out."

"What? Is that boy blind? I need to have a talk with him."

"Don't you dare!"

He grinned, not saying yes, not saying no.

"So what about you?" she asked. "Did you really dream about a big naked white woman last night?"

Joey nodded and grew thoughtful.

"She was actually a spirit bear in human form," he said. "Funny thing was, she didn't know she looked human. She came to give me a vision."

"A vision?"

"Yeah, she brought me from the pine woods where I was napping into the city, just like that." He snapped his fingers. "And the whole place was empty. There were no people anywhere. No sounds at all. Not even a single bird's call."

"There's days when I'd find that kind of nice."

"This was different," he said. "There were cars in the middle of the street with their doors hanging open—but no wrecks. It was like people just stopped whatever they were doing and went away."

"What did your naked woman have to say about that?"

"That I was supposed to fix it."

Ruby shook her head. "You have the weirdest dreams."

He nodded. He *could* have said, "It's something that comes to a lot of the corbae cousins—you know, crows like me. We have the gift of portent and prophecy, and mostly *we're* the ones that take people out of this world and into the other. Places like the land of dreams."

But all he said was, "I suppose I do."

A bell rang on the counter behind them to let Ruby know that an order was up. She carried the tray like the pro she was, four breakfast plates, juice and coffee, not spilling a drop. When she'd delivered the meals, she came back to Joey's booth.

"Are you free this afternoon?" she asked.

"Are you asking me on a date?"

"Yeah, right. No, I just thought maybe you can show me a new song. I've pretty much got that last one down now."

"Sure, I'd like that," he told her. "I'll be home after lunch—unless that spirit bear comes looking for me again."

Ruby touched the magpie tattoo on her arm. She often did it when their conversation turned to the cousins. He knew it was an involuntary gesture that she wasn't even aware of doing.

"Why do you always say things like that?" she asked.

"Things like what?"

"You know. Spirit bears and visions. Yesterday you were trying to tell me something you said a cat had told you."

"A bobcat cousin."

"Whatever. You know what it can sound like, don't you?"

"That I see more in the world than most people do?"

She laughed. "I guess. Or maybe that you're not all there."

She touched a finger to her temple.

"I'm never all here," he told her. "I've always got one foot in the otherworld."

"But there is no…."

She let her voice trail off instead of finishing.

"Well, here's something you can think of as real," he said. "When young handsome Kyle comes in for his lunch today, why don't *you* ask *him* out?"

"I couldn't do that."

"Why not? Where's that attitude?"

She opened her mouth, then laughed again.

Joey grinned. "You can't think of one good reason, can you?"

"No," she said. "I guess I can't."

"You need to remember," he told her, "that you don't have another life in the bank. You got to make the most of the one you're living right now."

Ruby McCaulay paused to watch Joey after he left the diner. She'd been wiping off a table in one of the window booths, and leaned on the backrest, one knee on the seat, as she watched him cross the street. He turned left, heading south on Lee. When she couldn't see him anymore, she went back to what she'd been doing.

She just liked that old man and couldn't say why. She might be having the worst day—cranky customers, crappy tips, her back and calves aching—but when he came in, his presence in the diner pushed all of that away. It was like he changed her into someone younger than her twenty-three years, like she was a kid again, full of energy, with the whole world waiting, laid out before her.

Not everybody felt that way.

"God, he just gives me the creeps," Eileen had said one morning, a couple of weeks ago.

She had just come on shift when Joey was leaving that day. Ruby'd turned to her, surprised.

"Dirty old man creeps?" she asked. "Because he's really harmless."

Eileen shook her head. "I don't think he is. I know that guys from his generation love to flirt, and I know they don't mean anything by it, but...well, that's not it."

"Then what *is* it?"

"He just...he knows too much. It's like he knows something about everything, it doesn't matter what the subject is."

"He's smart, that's all."

"And sometimes, when he looks at me, it's like he's right inside my head."

Ruby gave a slow nod. It was eerie how often he knew exactly what she was thinking without her having to say a word. She'd accused him once of being a mind reader and he'd laughed, telling her he was a people reader. That he just knew things about people from the way they carried themselves, from—and this was a weird thing to say, she'd thought at the time, and still did—how they fit in their skin.

But she kind of liked that, too—the way he'd always know the right thing to say, or how he'd call her on it when she was sugarcoating something, or trying to B.S.

"And that bothers you?" she asked when Eileen didn't go on.

"God, yes. It doesn't bother you?"

Ruby shook her head.

"No, I guess it wouldn't," Eileen said, "considering how you see him outside of work. What do you guys *do* anyway?"

"I've told you. He teaches me songs. He must know thousands of them."

"So when are you going to go out and play some of them?"

"You mean like get a gig?"

Eileen nodded.

"I'm not learning them for that," Ruby said. "I'm learning them so that when Joey's gone, someone will still remember them."

Eileen shook her head.

"You're getting as weird as him," she said, but she smiled.

"No," Ruby said. "I think Joey's got the weird all sewn up for himself."

"Says you."

Ruby smiled, remembering. She finished wiping down the table, then went and helped Anna, who was checking that all the condiment holders were filled for the lunch rush.

It was funny, she thought. If you saw Anna and her together, Anna always came off as the more subdued. She usually wore her brown hair pulled back in a tight ponytail, had glasses instead of contacts, and never used makeup at work, whereas Ruby had the funky hair and her tattoo, and the only time she made herself up was when she was working at the diner. Or if she had a date.

But of the two of them, Anna was the freer spirit, ready for anything. This year alone she'd already gone whitewater rafting in the Kickahas, had her first parachute jump, and had applied to teach English in Thailand.

Ruby was happy just to be at home playing her guitar.

Anna looked up as she approached.

"Hey," she said.

"Hey, yourself."

Ruby unscrewed the lid of a sugar dispenser and started to fill it.

"Do you ever ask guys out on a date?" she said.

Anna laughed. "Of course. How else would I get to go with a guy I *want* to go out with?" Then she cocked her head and grinned. "Why? Are you going to ask Joey out?"

"I don't think so. He's old enough to be my grandfather."

Anna nodded. "And he's nice like a grandfather."

"That, too."

"Then who do you—wait, never mind. I already know. It's that Kyle guy."

"I think he's cute."

"You and I'm sure every other girl he meets."

"But I don't think he knows it."

"Or it's a good act," Anna said.

"So, you don't think I should ask him out?"

Anna laughed. "Are you kidding? Go for it. What's the worst he can do?"

"Say no?"

"See, that's where we're different," Anna said. "You like to hold on to possibilities, while I just like to go out and grab life by the ass." Like a good comedian, she held the beat for a moment before adding, "Or some cute guy's."

She grinned and played a rim-shot on the tabletop with her hands.

"Maybe I'll surprise you," Ruby said.

"I totally hope you do," Anna told her.

Kyle Foster worked at Freewheeling, the bicycle repair shop down the street, and ate lunch at the diner every day. He always made a point to sit in Ruby's section, and had for the better part of six weeks, which was when he began working at the shop and first started coming in. He was soft-spoken and invariably polite—which Ruby hoped only meant that he was shy, not disinterested.

When he arrived at around quarter to one, she and Anna were standing behind the counter, waiting on orders. Anna gave her a nudge, but Ruby had already seen him come in.

"You are *so* going to rock his world," Anna told her.

Ruby nodded—more to indicate she'd heard than that she agreed. She got a glass of ice water, plucked a menu from the holder on the side of the counter, and walked over to his table.

She wished that she'd never said anything to Anna, because now she felt trapped into having to do it.

"Hey, Kyle," she said as she set the water and menu on the table in front of him.

Okay, that was good. Inane. Innocuous. But at least she hadn't choked yet.

He smiled up at her. "Busy morning?" he asked, then he dropped his gaze.

"No more than usual."

He put his hand on the closed menu and slid it across the tabletop in her direction.

"I know what I want," he said. "A grilled cheese and tomato sandwich and a side salad."

"Coming right up," she told him, but then she continued to stand at his table.

"Is...um...is everything okay?" he asked.

Ruby took a breath, then blurted, "Do you want to go out for dinner or something sometime?"

"I...."

"It's okay if you don't want to, or you have a girlfriend—what am I saying? Of course you must have a girlfriend."

Oh, god. She was babbling.

"I don't have a girlfriend," he said.

"Oh."

"And I'd like that."

"You would? I mean, good. That's good."

"How about tonight?" he asked.

"Tonight would be great." She picked up the menu. "I…you don't think it was weird of me…to…you know?"

He shook his head. "I've been trying to get my own nerve up for weeks."

"You were?"

He nodded. "But I was sure *you* had a boyfriend."

She smiled. "I don't. I'll go put your order in."

She was sure she floated back to the counter.

"Girl," Anna said, "with that silly grin on your face I don't even have to ask how it went."

"He wanted to ask me out. But he was too shy."

"Do you want me to come along—just to make sure you two remember you're on a date and actually talk to each other?"

Ruby stuck out her tongue and went over to the kitchen window to place Kyle's order.

Joey thought he'd have a nap before Ruby came over. He tuned up his guitar so that it would be ready and leaned it against the side of the couch. Then he stretched out and put a hand over his eyes. He never had trouble either falling asleep, or waking when he wanted to, and it was no different this afternoon.

Old Man Crow had him a thought and so, when he crossed over to the otherworld this time, he flew on black wings. He didn't go to the pine woods, but stayed in the city, right here in the otherworld where night had already fallen. Time didn't always quite match up between one world to another.

He perched on a lamppost and watched the night people go about their business. Cab drivers and clubbers, dealers and police patrols, people walking their dogs and the homeless setting up their cardboard shelters along McKennitt Street.

But then, between one moment and the next, suddenly there were no more people and everything went silent. Still, still. Deep still. This wasn't the quiet of late night, because it didn't matter how late it got, the city never slept. There was always a hum in the air—electricity in the wires, a footstep, just the sound of people breathing.

Tonight, there was nothing. There were still cars on the streets, but they were empty now, their doors ajar—just like the spirit bear had shown him last night. He'd been watching carefully, but he never saw the people abandon them.

Then finally, he heard a sound. There came a soft pad of paws on the pavement, and looking up, he saw her, walking in between the stopped cars. The spirit bear, wearing her fur skin now and walking on all fours.

He'd wondered if she would come, and if she did, what shape she'd wear to meet an old crow in his black feathers.

He fluttered down from the lamppost and landed on one of the parked cars, talons gripping the open door frame. The spirit bear stopped beside him.

"Look," she said and pointed upward with her snout.

Old Man Crow looked up and saw what she meant. The tops of the buildings weren't there anymore. Ten, fifteen stories up, they just kind of faded away.

"You need to stop it," she told him.

"Stop what? What's going on here?"

"Everything's going away. The people, the city."

"No disrespect," he said, "but since when do you care what the five-fingered beings do?"

"I don't. But you do."

"What's causing it?" he asked.

"Something up there," she said, her snout pointing up again. "And something in you."

"In me?"

"Go look."

She pointed a third time, up into the dark night sky that was swallowing the buildings.

Something wasn't right here—Old Man Crow knew that. He could feel it all the way down to the marrow of his old bones. And maybe the spirit bear wasn't so far off the mark, because what he felt in his bones was the same dark that enveloped the sky.

So he stretched those black wings of his and lifted from the car door. Up he flew, one story, three stories, and then he was in the darkness. It didn't matter which way he looked, up, down, either side. It was all dark.

His chest felt tight, and then something happened to his left wing. It went all numb and he couldn't make it work anymore. He started falling. He tried to break the fall with his right wing, but all that did was put him in a spiral, going around and around, down and down....

Joey awoke to a light so bright it blinded him, so he closed his eyes again.

"Joey?" a familiar voice asked.

He couldn't quite place it. The voice was out of context. He was out of context in whatever this place was.

Place.

He realized he was lying on something soft. It felt like a bed.

"Joey?"

He opened his eyes again, squinting so that the bright light wouldn't hurt them. Ruby's face filled his vision, then he couldn't see again, but that was because she'd bent over him to give him a hug.

"Thank god you're back," she said.

"Back...."

But then he remembered. Crossing over. The spirit bear. The darkness that had just swallowed him....

"What...happened?" he asked.

Ruby sat up and he could see where he was. In a hospital room. One of four beds. Ruby was on a chair beside his.

"I came by your apartment for my lesson," she said, "and found you just lying there, sprawled out on the floor in the middle of your living room, so I called 9-1-1."

"I was flying...."

"Yeah, well, and then I guess you must have fallen down. I told them at the nurse's station that I'm your granddaughter so that they'd let me sit with you."

"We are kin."

Ruby smiled. And he knew what she was thinking. Right, the old black man and the little punky white girl.

"How do you figure that?" she asked.

He lifted his arm and touched the sleeve that covered her tattoo.

"Magpie and crow. We're both corbae—I've told you that before."

She smiled again. "You've told me a lot of things, Joey."

"But you never believed any of them."

He could see that now and he felt like a fool. He'd thought they had a connection. That she could see their kinship. Why else would she have so much time for an old man? Why else would she want to learn the old songs?

Now he realized she'd just been feeling sorry for him. It was charity, not kinship.

The only thing he had left to hold on to was that her love of the music had been real. You couldn't hide a thing like that.

"I like your stories," she said.

"They're not just stories."

"I know they're not—for you. But it's not the same for me."

"Did you ever wonder why I keep telling them to you?" he asked.

"Because you like to."

He shook his head. "I'm trying to wake the cousin blood that's sleeping deep inside you. It still remembers, even if you don't."

"What do you mean?"

"Why'd you get that magpie tattoo?"

She looked surprised.

"Humour me," he said.

"I guess I just wanted to."

"But why a magpie?"

"I don't know. I've always liked them." She gave him a small smile, almost as though she was apologizing. "I feel connected to them. Like in that song you taught me."

She sang softly:

Magpie, magpie in a piney tree
singing, true love, won't you come to me
long black tail and snow white breast
she's the one I love the best

Joey nodded. He sighed and closed his eyes.

"Well, I did what I could," he said.

"Joey."

He kept his eyes closed. It happened, he thought. Sometimes it just didn't take. Sometimes the old blood just wanted to stay hidden. It was nobody's fault.

"Don't be like that." He felt her hand on his arm. "I didn't mean to upset you. I'm just so glad you're going to be all right."

He looked at her again.

"The doctor said he doesn't think it was a stroke, but he's still waiting for some tests to come back."

"Tests?"

"You were unconscious for *ages*, Joey."

He nodded. The darkness had taken him away. He remembered that. His wing had gone numb and he'd gone spiraling down and down.

"He thinks you might have just fainted—though at your age that's serious enough, because they don't know *why* you did."

"Cousins don't get sick—not the way the five-fingered beings do."

She gave him a puzzled look, then nodded.

"Right," she said. "Except *something* happened to you. So they're keeping you for observation."

"There's nothing to observe. Just an old man with too many stories and not enough sense."

"Oh, Joey. I didn't mean to—"

"Let's just talk about something else. Did you ask that boy out?"

That was the perfect thing to distract her.

"He said yes!" she told him. "We're going to—oh, God." She looked at her watch. "I'm supposed to meet him when he gets off work."

"Then go."

"No, I can't just leave you."

"I'm fine," he said. "I'm in a hospital. They know how to look after people here. You should go and then, if I'm still here tomorrow, you can tell me all about it."

She didn't leave readily, but he finally convinced her. She leaned over and kissed his brow before she stood up.

"You're sure," she began again.

He gave her a bright smile. "I'm sure. Go, go. I need to get some rest anyway. I've had too much excitement today as it is."

"I'll come by when my shift's done tomorrow. I'll probably be able to take you back home."

He nodded. "Bring me a coffee when you come, would you? I can just imagine what they'll have here."

"I will."

He closed his eyes when she left.

So Old Man Crow crossed over again, black wings cutting the air between the worlds. This time he didn't wait for the spirit bear to find him, but went looking for her by that hidden lake, high in the mountains, fed by a glacier. Spirit Lake.

He flew above the pine woods, heading north through the dreamlands, up and up into the mountains. He left the tree line behind as the air grew thin and he had to work hard to keep aloft up there because there weren't many winds to ride. But there wasn't that darkness, either, the enveloping black that had swallowed him in the city, so he counted himself lucky.

Finally, he sailed through a pass and came down into that long green valley where Spirit Lake dreams like a jewel in a wild bower of tamarack and pine. He let his wings rest as he glided down to it in a long spiral that let him see all parts of the shore. He settled on the branch of a dead pine tree overlooking the north part of the lake.

"I know you're here," he said, once he'd caught his breath.

"Do you now?"

He turned on his perch to see the spirit bear regarding him from the shadows under the pines.

"Yeah," he said. "At least I do now."

He caught a flicker of humour in her eyes, then she padded out over the limestone outcrop that lay between the forest and the dead pine where Old Man Crow waited for her.

"What did you do to me?" he asked. "That last time I was dreaming."

"I didn't do anything. I only came to show you."

"The darkness, yes. It swallowed me whole."

"I know. I saw."

"What is it? You said it's making everything go away and that it's inside me."

The spirit bear nodded.

"I don't understand. Why can't you tell me plain?"

She studied him for a long moment, then nodded again.

"You've become a man dreaming he's a crow," she finally said.

"What?"

"You used to be a crow, dreaming he was a man, and your old blood ran strong. But now?" She shrugged. "It's as though you never lived that long life of yours. You've become a five-fingered being, old and at the end of his years."

"How did this happen?"

Old Man Crow was asking himself as much as the spirit bear, because he could see the weight of truth in her words. He *was* more man than crow, and had been for years. Living like a man, only flying in his dreams.

"Do I need to tell you?" she asked.

He shook his head.

"It can happen to anyone," she said. "Living too long in that otherworld, walking on two legs, talking, talking, talking."

"Crows always talk."

She nodded. "To each other. Not to five-fingered beings. Not and expect to be understood."

"But some of them have the old blood running in them, thin and dreaming. All it needs is to be wakened."

"And you can teach them that without living your whole life among them."

"I see."

"I'm not your conscience or your mother," the spirit bear told him. "Your life is yours to spend as you wish."

He nodded.

"And mostly I don't concern myself with the whys and wherefores of the corbae clans."

"I understand."

But then she smiled. "Except, just as you have that inclination to wake sleeping cousins, I find myself drawn to reminding cousins of who they are—or who they once were."

"That darkness," Old Man Crow said. "That was my mortality, wasn't it?"

She nodded.

"And when you said everything was going away, you meant my perception of it was going away. That's why I woke in a hospital bed. I was dying."

She nodded again.

"Am I still dying?"

"We're all dying, Old Man Crow. Each and every day. It's the same for cousins as it is for five-fingered beings. But we're living, too. Sometimes we forget that."

They didn't talk for a while. It was quiet here, too, Old Man Crow thought, but it was a natural quiet. A breeze sighing through the pine boughs. The lap of water on the shore.

"It doesn't mean you need to stop helping people," the spirit bear said.

Old Man Crow nodded. "But I need to remember who I am, too."

"You do."

"So what now?" he asked.

She shrugged. "You could try to be a crow again and only dream of being a man."

Ruby was in a cheerful mood as she took the subway back to Lee Street. Old Joey had given her quite a scare there earlier, finding him like that, all sprawled out on the floor of his living room. But she felt better now. Before she'd left the hospital, his doctor had assured her that he wasn't on death's bed just yet.

"Your grandfather has the constitution of a horse," he'd told her.

"Then why did he collapse like that?"

"I don't know yet. I need to wait until we get the test results back. But as things stand, I'm fairly certain he can be discharged tomorrow morning."

So there was still a little something to worry about, but right now, she knew he was okay and in good hands, and she finally had a date with Kyle. She turned and checked her reflection in the window, but the glass was so dirty and smudged it was hard to tell what shape her face was in. She took out her compact and used it to reapply her lipstick and dust a little colour onto her cheeks, then it was her stop and she had to get off and hurry down the street.

Freewheeling would have closed about ten minutes ago. What if Kyle wasn't waiting? What if he thought she'd blown him off?

But then she saw Kyle waiting for her outside the shop, his face lighting up with pleasure when he saw her, and she couldn't help grinning herself. A moment later she was standing in front of him and suddenly neither of them had anything to say.

But she thought of Joey—the scare he'd given her, the advice he was always passing on to her along with his stories. How nobody ever got anything they wanted if they didn't take a chance.

She felt good, so she was just going to tell Kyle she did. She wasn't going to go all clingy and weird on him, but she wasn't going to play games, either.

"I'm so glad we're getting together like this outside of work," she said.

"Me, too. Like I said, I've…you know…been wanting to ask you out…."

She smiled. "Does this suddenly feel weird to you, too? I mean, I've been serving you lunch for weeks at the diner, but now all of a sudden, here we are, and it's a whole new ball game."

He lifted an eyebrow. "Are you a sports fan?"

"Um, not so much."

"Me, either."

He took her arm. "Let's go find a restaurant and have another waitress bring us dinner. What are you in the mood for?"

"I don't know—what do you like?"

"Everything, pretty much. Danny—one of the guys I work with—says there's a new Vietnamese soup place just south of McKennitt. We could give it a try. He's says the food's good and cheap."

"That sounds wonderful. I'm on a bit of a budget. I'm saving up for a new guitar."

"You play guitar?"

"Mmm. When I'm playing it's like the whole world's gone perfect—even when I'm flubbing my chords or forget the words or something."

"I used to play mandolin in a band," he said. "Before I moved to the city…."

And just like that, they were deep in conversation and it stayed like that all the way to the restaurant and through dinner. The food was great, and the company was better, but as they were waiting for their bill, something reminded Ruby of Joey, lying there in his hospital bed, alone. Maybe it was the old black man she saw walking by the window of the restaurant. Maybe it was because Kyle had mentioned liking her tattoo, telling her it reminded him of this old song his band used to play, which turned out to be the same song that Joey had taught her when she first started taking lessons from him. Maybe it was because, even with the doctor's reassurances, she couldn't quite shake the worry that had settled in her chest this afternoon when she'd opened the door to Joey's apartment and found him lying there, so still.

"Is everything okay?" Kyle asked.

"What? Oh, sorry. I was just thinking of Joey—one of the regulars at the diner. But he's also a friend of mine and he had a…I don't know quite what today. But I ended up having to take him to the hospital and they're keeping him overnight for observation."

"Would I know him?"

"Probably."

Kyle nodded as she started to describe Joey.

"He's got those eyes that seem to see everything."

"That's Joey, all right."

She went on to tell him about how she'd found him that afternoon, how he was teaching her all these old songs, how she just liked him because he made the day seem better whenever he came into the diner.

"What time are visiting hours over?" Kyle asked.

"Nine, I think."

He looked at his watch. "There's still time. We could stop in and see him, if you like."

"Really?"

He nodded. "It's good to take care of the people that mean something to us."

"I just checked in on him," the nurse said when they arrived at the nurse's station, "and he was still sleeping. But you could sit with him for awhile if you like. Visiting hours are over at nine."

Ruby nodded. "I know. Thank you."

She led Kyle off down the hall to Joey's room before the nurse could ask who he was. But when they got to the room, Joey's bed was empty. There were men asleep on the other three beds, but none of them were him. He hadn't changed beds. The bathroom door was open, so they could see there was no one in there.

"This is weird," Ruby said.

She went back to the nurse's station with Kyle to check that she had the right room.

"He's still in 318, dear."

Ruby started to feel panicky again—the way she had while she was waiting for the ambulance this afternoon.

"Not anymore, he's not," she said.

The nurse gave her a puzzled look. "But I was just in his room, and no one's come down the hall since."

She led the way back to 318, but Joey was still gone. When she hurried off to get help, Ruby walked over to the bed. She had the oddest feeling that while Joey wasn't dead, she wasn't going to see him again.

"What's that?" Kyle asked.

He pointed to the pillow. A long black feather lay there.

A crow's feather, Ruby thought. She touched the magpie on her arm and could almost hear Joey's voice in her head.

Magpie and crow. We're both corbae—I've told you that before.

And then there was this curious sensation in her chest, as though something was stretch*ing inside her. And she heard…she heard….*

"That's weird," Kyle said from beside her, his voice soft. "Did you hear that?"

Ruby turned to him. "What did it sound like?"

"Like wings."

Ruby nodded. That's what she'd heard, too. It had been *just* like the sound of flapping that you could sometimes hear when there was a lull in the city's general hubbub and a large bird flew overhead.

A pigeon or a gull. A crow.

Or a magpie.

She picked up the black feather and took Kyle's hand.

"What about your friend?" he asked as she pulled him towards the door.

"I think he's already gone."

"But—"

"Shh," she said. "Did you hear it again?"

Kyle nodded and looked up, as though he expected to see a bird, here in the hospital. But Ruby had felt the stirring begin in her chest once more and knew where the sound was really coming from.

"I guess all those stories he was always telling me were true," she said.

"What do you mean?"

She let go of his hand and slipped hers into the crook of his arm.

"I'll tell you on the way," she said.

"On the way to where?"

She shrugged and smiled.

"To wherever it is we find ourselves going," she said.

THE FIELDS BEYOND THE FIELDS

I just see my life better in ink.
—Jewel Kilcher, from an interview on MuchMusic, 1997

SASKIA IS SLEEPING, but I can't. I sit up at my rolltop desk, writing. It's late, closer to dawn than midnight, but I'm not tired. Writing can be good for keeping sleep at bay. It also helps me make sense of things where simply thinking about them can't. It's too easy to get distracted by a wayward digression when the ink's not holding the thoughts to paper. By focusing on the page, I can step outside myself and look at the puzzle with a clearer eye.

Earlier this evening Saskia and I were talking about magic and wonder, about how it can come and go in your life, or more particularly, how it comes and goes in my life. That's the side of me that people don't get to see when all they can access is the published page. I'm as often a skeptic as a believer. I'm not the one who experiences those oddities that appear in the stories; I'm the one who chronicles the mystery of them, trying to make sense out what they can impart about us, our world, our preconceptions of how things should be.

The trouble is, mostly life seems to be exactly what it is. I can't find the hidden card waiting to be played because it seems too apparent that the whole hand is already laid out on the table. What you see is what you get, thanks, and do come again.

I want there to be more.

Even my friends assume I'm the knowledgeable expert who writes the books. None of them knows how much of a hypocrite I really am. I listen well and I know exactly what to say to keep the narrative flowing. I can accept everything that's happened to them—the oddest and most absurd stories they tell me don't make me blink an eye—but all the while there's a small voice chanting in the back of my head.

As if, as if, as if. . . .

I wasn't always like this, but I'm good at hiding how I've changed, from those around me, as well as from myself.

But Saskia knows me too well.

"You used to live with a simple acceptance of the hidden world," she said when the conversation finally turned into a circle and there was nothing new to add. "You used to live with magic and mystery, but now you only write about it."

I didn't know how to reply.

I wanted to tell her that it's easy to believe in magic when you're young. Anything you couldn't explain was magic then. It didn't matter if it was science or a fairy tale. Electricity and elves were both infinitely mysterious and equally possible—elves probably more so. It didn't seem particularly odd to believe that actors lived inside your TV set. That there was a repertory company inside the radio, producing its chorus of voices and music. That a fat, bearded man lived at the North Pole and kept tabs on your behaviour.

I wanted to tell her that I used to believe she was born in a forest that only exists inside the nexus of a connection of computers, entangled with one another where they meet on the World Wide Web. A wordwood that appears in pixels on the screen, but has another, deeper existence somewhere out there in the mystery that exists concurrent to the Internet, the way religion exists in the gathering of like minds.

But not believing in any of it now, I wasn't sure that I ever had.

The problem is that even when you have firsthand experience with a piece of magic, it immediately begins to slip away. Whether it's a part of the enchantment, or some inexplicable defense mechanism that's been wired into us either by society or genetics, it doesn't make any difference. The magic still slips away, sliding like a melted icicle along the slick surface of our memories.

That's why some people need to talk about it—the ones who want to hold on to the marvel of what they've seen or heard or felt. And that's why I'm willing to listen, to validate their experience and help them keep it alive. But there's no one around to validate mine. They think my surname Riddell is a happy coincidence, that it means I've solved the riddles of the world instead of being as puzzled by them as they are. Everybody assumes that I'm already in that state of grace where enchantment lies thick in every waking moment, and one's dreams—by way of recompense, perhaps?—are mundane.

As if, as if, as if....

The sigh that escapes me seems self-indulgent in the quiet that holds the apartment. I pick up my pen, put it down when I hear a rustle of fabric, the creak of a spring as the sofa takes someone's weight. The voice of my shadow speaks then, a disembodied voice coming to me from the darkness beyond the spill of the desk's lamplight, but tonight I don't listen to her. Instead I take down volumes of my old journals from where they're lined up on top of my desk. I page through the entries, trying to see if I've really changed. And if so, when.

I don't know what makes sense anymore; I just seem to know what doesn't.

When I was young, I liked to walk in the hills behind our house, looking at animals. Whether they were big or small, it made no difference to me. Everything they did was absorbing. The crow's lazy flight. A red squirrel scolding me from the safety of a hemlock branch, high overhead. The motionless spider in a corner of its patient web. A quick russet glimpse of a fox before it vanishes in the high weeds. The water rat making its daily journeys across Jackson's Pond and back. A tree full of cedar waxwings, gorging on berries. The constantly shifting pattern of a gnat ballet.

I've never been able to learn what I want about animals from books or nature specials on television. I have to walk in their territories, see the world as they might see it. Walk along the edges of the stories they know.

The stories are the key, because for them, for the animals, everything that clutters our lives, they keep in their heads. History, names, culture, gossip, art. Even their winter and summer coats are only ideas, genetic imprints memorized by their DNA, coming into existence only when the seasons change.

I think their stories are what got me writing. First in journals, accounts as truthful as I could make them, then as stories where actuality is stretched and manipulated, because the lies in fiction are such an effective way to tell emotional truths. I took great comfort in how the lines of words marched from left to right and down the page, building up into a meaningful structure like rows of knitting. Sweater stories. Mitten poems. Long, rambling journal entries like the scarves we used to have when we were kids, scarves that seemed to go on forever.

I never could hold the stories in my head, though in those days I could absorb them for hours, stretched out in a field, my gaze lost in the expanse of forever sky above. I existed in a timeless place then, probably as close to Zen as I'll ever get again. Every sense alert, all existence focused on the present moment. The closest I can come to recapturing that feeling now is when I set pen to paper. For those brief moments when the words flow unimpeded, everything I am is simultaneously focused into one perfect detail and expanded to encompass everything that is. I own the stories in those moments, I am the stories, though, of course, none of them really belong to me. I only get to borrow them. I hold them for awhile, set them down on paper, and then let them go.

I can own them again, when I reread them, but then so can anyone.

According to Jung, at around the age of six or seven we separate and then hide away the parts of ourselves that don't seem acceptable, that don't fit in the world around us. Those unacceptable parts that we secret away become our shadow.

I remember reading somewhere that it can be a useful exercise to visualize the person our shadow would be if it could step out into the light. So I tried it. It didn't work immediately. For a long time, I was simply talking to myself. Then, when I did get a response, it was only a spirit voice I heard in my head. It could just as easily have been my own. But over time, my shadow took on more physical attributes, in the way that a story grows clearer and more pertinent as you add and take away words, molding its final shape.

Not surprisingly, my shadow proved to be the opposite of who I am in so many ways. Bolder, wiser, with a better memory and a penchant for dressing up with costumes, masks, or simply formal wear. A cocktail dress in a raspberry patch. A green man mask in a winter field. She's short, where I'm tall. Dark-skinned, where I'm light. Red-haired, where mine's dark. A girl to my boy, and now a woman as I'm a man.

If she has a name, she's never told me it. If she has an existence outside the times we're together, she has yet to divulge it either. Naturally I'm curious about where she goes, but she doesn't like being asked questions and I've learned not to press her because when I do, she simply goes away.

Sometimes I worry about her existence. I get anxieties about schizophrenia and carefully study myself for other symptoms. But if she's a delusion, it's singular, and otherwise I seem to be as normal as anyone else, which is to say, confused by the barrage of input and stimuli with which the modern world besets us, and trying to make do. Who was it that said she's always trying to understand the big picture, but the trouble is, the picture just keeps getting bigger? Ani DiFranco, I think.

Mostly I don't get too analytical about it—something I picked up from her, I suppose, since left to my own devices, I can worry the smallest detail to death.

We have long conversations, usually late at night, when the badgering clouds swallow the stars and the darkness is most profound. Most of the time

I can't see her, but I can hear her voice. I like to think we're friends; even if we don't agree about details, we can usually find common ground on how we'd like things to be.

There are animals in the city, but I can't read their stories the same as I did the ones that lived in the wild. In the forested hills of my childhood.

I don't know when exactly it was that I got so interested in the supernatural, you know, fairy tales and all. I mean, I was always interested in them, the way kids are, but I didn't let them go. I collected unusual and odd facts, read the Brothers Grimm, Lady Gregory, Katharine Briggs, but *Famous Monsters* and ghost stories, too. They gave me something the animals couldn't—or didn't—but I needed it all the same.

Animal stories connected me to the landscape we inhabited—to their world, to my world, to all the wonder that can exist around us. They grounded me, but were no relief from unhappiness and strife. But fairy tales let me escape. Not away from something, but *to* something. To hope. To a world beyond this world where other ways of seeing were possible. Where other ways of treating each other were possible.

An Irish writer, Lord Dunsany, coined the phrase "Beyond the Fields We Know" to describe fairyland, and that's always appealed to me. First there's the comfort of the fields we do know, the idea that it's familiar and friendly. Home. Then there's the otherness of what lies beyond them that so aptly describes what I imagine the alien topography of fairyland to be. The grass is always greener in the next field over, the old saying goes. More appealing, more vibrant. But perhaps it's more dangerous as well. No reason not to explore it, but it's worthwhile to keep in mind that one should perhaps take care.

If I'd thought that I had any aptitude as an artist, I don't think I'd ever have become a writer. All I ever wanted to capture was moments. The trouble is, most people want narrative, so I tuck those moments away in the pages of a story. If I could draw or paint the way I see those moments in my head, I wouldn't have to write about them.

It's scarcely an original thought, but a good painting really can hold all the narrative and emotional impact of a novel—the viewer simply has to work a little harder than a reader does with a book. There are fewer clues. Less taking the viewer by the hand and leading him or her through all the possible events that had to occur to create this visualized moment before them.

I remember something Jilly once said about how everyone should learn to draw competently at an early age, because drawing, she maintains, is one of the first intuitive gestures we make to satisfy our appetites for beauty and communication. If we could acknowledge those hungers, and do so from an early age, our culture would be very different from the way it is today. We would understand how images are used to compel us, in the same way that most of us understand the subtleties of language.

Because, think of it. As children, we come into the world with a natural desire to both speak and draw. Society makes sure that we learn language properly, right from the beginning, but art is treated as a gift of innate genius, something we either have or don't. Most children are given far too much praise for their early drawings, so much so that they rarely learn the ability to refine their first crude efforts the way their early attempts at language are corrected.

How hard would it be to ask a child what they see in their head? How big should the house be in comparison to the family standing in front of it? What is it about the anatomy of the people that doesn't look right? Then let them try it again. Teach them to learn how to see and ask questions. You don't have to be Michelangelo to teach basic art, just as you don't have to be Shakespeare to be able to teach the correct use of language.

Not to be dogmatic about it, because you wouldn't want any creative process to lose its sense of fun and adventure. But that doesn't mean you can't take it seriously as well.

Because children know when they're being patronized. I remember, so clearly I can remember, having the picture in my head and it didn't look at all like what I managed to scribble down on paper. When I was given no direction, in the same way that my grammar and sentence structure and the like were corrected, I lost interest and gave up. Now it seems too late.

I had a desk I made as a teenager—a wide board laid across a couple of wooden fruit crates. I'd set out my pens and ink, my paper, sit cross-legged on a pillow in front of it and write for hours. I carried that board around with me for years, from rooming house to apartments. I still have it, only now it serves as a shelf that holds plants underneath a window in the dining room. Saskia finds it odd, that I remain so attached to it, but I can't let it go. It's too big a piece of my past—one of the tools that helped free me from a reality that had no room for the magic I needed the world to hold, but could only make real with words.

I didn't just like to look at animals. I'd pretend to be them, too. I'd scrabble around all day on my hands and knees through the bush to get an understanding of that alternate viewpoint. Or I'd run for miles, the horse in me effortlessly carrying me through fields, over fences, across streams. Remember when you'd never walk, when you could run? It never made any *sense* to go so slow.

And even at home, or at school, or when we'd go into town, the animals would stay with me. I'd carry them secreted in my chest. That horse, a mole, an owl, a wolf. Nobody knew they were there, but I did. Their secret presence both comforted and thrilled me.

I write differently depending on the pen I use. Ballpoints are only good for business scribbles, or for making shopping lists, and even then, I'll often use a fountain pen. When I first wrote, I did so with a dip pen and ink. Coloured inks, sometimes—sepia, gold, and a forest green were the most popular choices—but usually India ink. I used a mapping nib, writing on cream-coloured paper with deckled edges and more tooth than might be recommended for that sort of nib. The dip pen made me take my time, think about every word before I committed to it.

But fountain pens grew to be my writing implement of choice. A fat, thick-nibbed, deep-green Cross from which the ink flowed as though sliding across ice, or a black Waterman with a fine point that made tiny, bird track-like marks across the page.

When I began marketing my work, I typed it up—now I use a computer—but the life of my first drafts depends on the smooth flow of a fountain pen. I can, and did, and do, write anywhere with them. All I need is the pen and my notebook. I've written standing up, leaning my notebook on the cast-iron balustrade of the Kelly Street Bridge, watching the dark water flow beneath me, my page lit by the light cast from a streetlamp. I've written in moonlight and in cafés. In the corner of a pub and sitting at a bus stop.

I can use other implements, but those pens are best. Pencil smears, pen and ink gets too complicated to carry about, Rapidographs and rollerballs don't have enough character, and ballpoints have no soul. My fountain pens have plenty of both. Their nibs are worn down to the style of my hand, the shafts fit into my fingers with the comfort of the voice of a longtime friend, met unexpectedly on a street corner, but no less happily for the surprise of the meeting.

Time passes oddly. Though I know the actual contrast is vast, I don't feel much different now from when I was fifteen. I still feel as clumsy and awkward and insecure about interacting with others, about how the world sees me, though intellectually, I understand that others don't perceive me in the same way at all. I'm middle-aged, not a boy. I'm at that age when the boy I was thought that life would pretty much be over, yet now I insist it's only begun. I have to. To think otherwise is to give up, to actually *be* old.

That's disconcerting enough. But when a year seems to pass in what was only a season for the boy, a dreamy summer that would never end, the long cold days of winter when simply stepping outside made you feel completely alive, you begin to fear the ever-increasing momentum of time's passage. Does it simply accelerate forever, or is there a point when it begins to slow down once again? Is that the real meaning of "over the hill"? You start up slow, then speed up to make the incline. Reach the top and gravity has you speeding once more. But eventually your momentum decreases, as even a rolling stone eventually runs out of steam.

I don't know. What I do know is that the antidote for me is to immerse myself in something like my writing, though simply puttering around the apartment can be as effective. There's something about familiar tasks that keeps at bay the unsettling sense of everything being out of my control. Engaging in the mundane, whether it be watching the light change in the sky at dusk, playing with my neighbour's cat, enjoying the smell of freshly brewed coffee, serves to alter time. It doesn't so much stop the express, as allow you to forget it for awhile. To recoup, catch your breath.

But writing is best, especially the kind that pulls you out of yourself, off the page, and takes you into a moment of clarity, an instant of happy wonder, so perfect that words, stumbling through the human mind, are inadequate to express.

The writer's impossible task is to illuminate such moments, yes, but also the routines, the things we do or feel or simply appreciate, that happen so regularly that they fade away into the background the way street noise and traffic become inaudible when you've lived in the city long enough. It's the writer's job to illuminate such moments as well, to bring them back into awareness, to acknowledge the gift of their existence and share that acknowledgment with others.

By doing this, we are showing deference to the small joys of our lives, giving them meaning. Not simply for ourselves, but for others as well, to remind them of the significance to be found in their lives. And what we all discover, is that nothing is really ordinary or familiar after all. Our small worlds are more surprising and interesting than we perceive them to be.

But we still need enchantment in our lives. We still need mystery. Something to connect us to what lies beyond the obvious, to what, perhaps, *is* the obvious, only seen from another, or better-informed, perspective.

Mystery.

I love that word. I love how, phonetically, it seems to hold both "myth" and "history." The Kickaha use it to refer to God, the Great Mystery. But they also ascribe to animism, paying respect to small, mischievous spirits that didn't create the world, but rather, are *of* the world. They call them mysteries, too. *Manitou*. The little mysteries.

We call them faerie.

We don't believe in them.

Our loss.

Saskia is still sleeping. I look in on her, then slowly close the bedroom door. I put on my boots and jacket and go downstairs, out onto the pre-dawn streets. It's my favourite time of day. It's so quiet, but everything seems filled with potential. The whole world appears to hold its breath, waiting for the first streak of light to lift out of the waking eastern skies.

After a few blocks, I hear footsteps and my shadow falls in beside me.

"Still soul searching?" she asks.

I nod, expecting a lecture on how worrying about "what if" only makes you miss out on "what is," but she doesn't say anything. We walk up Lee Street to Kelly, past the pub and up onto the bridge. Halfway across, I lean my forearms on the balustrade and look out across the water. She puts her back to the rail. I can feel her gaze on me. There's no traffic. Give it another few hours and the bridge will be choked with commuters.

"Why can't I believe in magic?" I finally say.

When there's no immediate response, I look over to find her smiling.

"What do you think I am?" she asks.

"I don't know," I tell her honestly. "A piece of me. Pieces of me. But you must be more than that now, because you've had experiences I haven't shared since you...left."

"As have you."

"I suppose." I turn my attention back to the water flowing under us. "Unless I'm delusional."

She laughs. "Yes, there's always the risk of that, isn't there?"

"So which is it?"

She shrugs.

"At least tell me your name," I say.

Her only response is another one of those enigmatic smiles of hers that would have done Leonardo proud. I sigh, and try one more time.

"Then tell me this," I say. "Where do you go when you're not with me?"

She surprises me with an answer.

"To the fields beyond the fields," she says.

"Can you take me with you some time?" I ask, keeping my voice casual. I feel like Wendy, waiting at the windowsill for Peter Pan.

"But you already know the way."

I give her a blank look.

"It's all around you," she says. "It's here." She touches her eyes, her ears. "And here." She moves her hand to her temple. "And here." She lays a hand upon her breast.

I look away. The sun's rising now and all the skyscrapers of midtown have a haloing glow, an aura of morning promise. A pair of crows lift from the roof of the pub and their blue-black wings have more colour in them than I ever imagined would be possible. I watch them glide over the river, dip down, out of the sunlight, and become shadow shapes once more.

I feel something shift inside me. A lifting of...I'm not sure what. An unaccountable easing of tension—not in my neck, or shoulders, but in my spirit. As though I've just received what Colin Wilson calls "absurd good news."

When I turn back, my companion is gone. But I understand. The place where mystery lives doesn't necessarily have to make sense. It's not that it's nonsense, so much, as beyond sense.

My shadow is the parts of me I'd hidden away—some because they didn't fit who I thought I was supposed to be, some that I just didn't understand.

Her name is Mystery.

St. John of the Cross wrote, "If a man wants to be sure of his road he must close his eyes and walk in the dark."

Into his shadow.

Into mystery.

I think I can do that.

Or at least I can try.

I pause there a moment longer, breathing deep the morning air, drawing the sun's light down into my skin, then I turn, and head for home and Saskia. I think I have an answer for her now. She'll still be sleeping, but even asleep, I know she's waiting for me. Waiting for who I was to catch up with who I'll be. Waiting for me to remember who I am and all I've seen.

I think I'll take the plants off that board in the dining room and reclaim the desk it was.

I think I'll buy a sketchbook when the stores open and take one of those courses that Jilly teaches at the Newford School of Art. Maybe it's not too late.

I think I'll reacquaint myself with the animals that used to live in my chest.

I think I'll stop listening to that voice whispering "as if," and hold onto what I experience, no matter how far it strays from what's supposed to be.

I'm going to live here, in the Fields We Know, fully, but I'm not going to let myself forget how to visit the fields beyond these fields. I'll go there with words on the page, but without them, too. Because it's long past time to stop letting pen and ink be the experience, instead of merely recording it.

BOOKS BY CHARLES DE LINT

Muse and Reverie
The Mystery of Grace
Dingo
Promises to Keep
Little (Grrl) Lost
Widdershins
Triskell Tales: 2
The Blue Girl
Medicine Road
Spirits in the Wires
A Circle of Cats
Tapping the Dream Tree
Waifs and Strays
Seven Wild Sisters
The Onion Girl
The Road to Lisdoonvarna
Triskell Tales
Forests of the Heart
Moonlight and Vines
Someplace to be Flying
Trader
Jack of Kinrowan

The Ivory and the Horn
Memory and Dream
The Wild Wood
I'll Be Watching You
Into the Green
Dreams Underfoot
From a Whisper to a Scream
Spiritwalk
The Little Country
The Dreaming Place
Angel of Darkness
Ghostwood
The Hidden City
The Valley of Thunder
Svaha
Wolf Moon
Greenmantle
Yarrow
Mulengro
The Harp of the Grey Rose
Moonheart
The Riddle of the Wren